Acclaim for

The Vexing Heirloom

"What makes *The Vexing Heirloom* such a remarkable debut—and T. G. Monahan such a formidable writer—is the combination of a rich Cuban history with elements of magic realism overlain, delivered with page-turning and crackling tension. This is polished prose, a solid story, and a unique voice. This is a writer to watch."

—Les Edgerton, author of *Hooked, Bomb!,* and others

"With the spirit of poets, T. G. Monahan delivers Cuba—myth, legend and history, in an epic journey of ever-unfolding mystery. With lucid descriptions, heartfelt characters and a pace that draws you in like treasure to the jungle, *The Vexing Heirloom* screams *Cuba Libre!*"

—Liam Sweeny, author of *Welcome Back, Jack!*

"Monahan has crafted a gorgeous novel, artfully balancing action and adventure with obsession and intrigue, and delivers it near perfectly, through beautifully crafted prose."

—Maegan Beaumont, award-winning author of *Blood of Saints*

"*The Vexing Heirloom* is a lyrical, mystical journey through a Cuba the world has never seen before, but definitely should. Rich with mythology and magic, it's an experience readers will not soon forget."

—Leah Rhyne, author of *Heartless*

"Monahan's intricate and timely debut is told in stunning prose tying together history, fantasy, and suspense with an ending that lingers."

—Carol White, playwright and author of *A Divided Duty*

THE VEXING HEIRLOOM

F. G. Moratan

THE VEXING HEIRLOOM

a Novel

T.G. MONAHAN

Editing by Jaime Cox
Spanish editing by Mario B. Martin Pedroso
Interior design by Penelope Love
Cover design by Rolf Busch
Map illustration by T.G. Monahan

Library of Congress Cataloging-in-Publication Data

Monahan, T.G.
The Vexing Heirloom

p. cm.
Paperback ISBN: 978-0-9975470-2-3
Ebook ISBN: 978-0-9975470-3-0
Library of Congress Control Number: 2016956435

10 9 8 7 6 5 4 3 2 1
First Edition, May 2017

CITRINE PUBLISHING

Boca Raton, Florida, U.S.A.
561.299.1150
Publisher@CitrinePublishing.com
www.CitrinePublishing.com

"And the LORD said unto Moses, I have surely seen the affliction of my people which are in Egypt, and have heard their cry by reason of their taskmasters; for I know their sorrows; and I am come down to deliver them out of the hand of the Egyptians, and to bring them up out of that land unto a good land and a large..."

Exodus 3:7-8

CUBA

OCCIDENTAL

~1896~

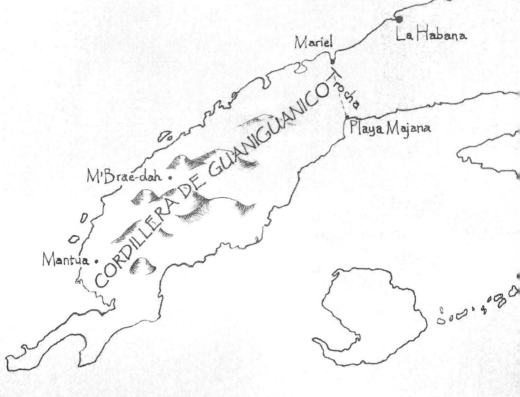

Mariel

La Habana

Trocha

Playa Majana

M'Brae-dah

CORDILLERA DE GUANIGUANICO

Mantua

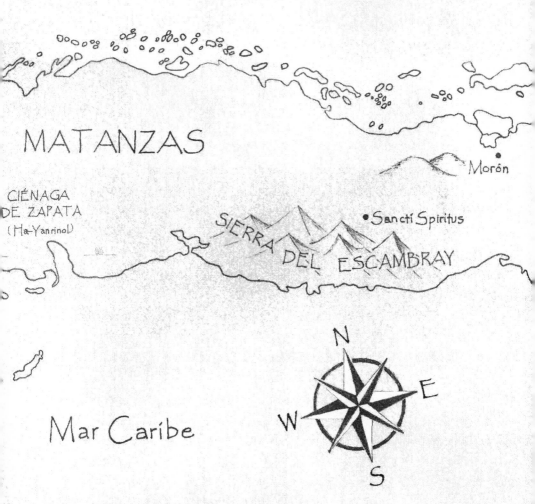

Estrecho de la Florida

MATANZAS

CIÉNAGA
DE ZAPATA
(Ha-Yanrinol)

SIERRA DEL ESCAMBRAY

Morón

• Sancti Spiritus

Mar Caribe

N
E
S
W

PREFACE

The *Vexing Heirloom* begins in the summer of 1896, near Pinar del Río, Cuba. The Cuban War of Independence (1895-98) has raged for one and one-half years, and moved from its cradle in eastern Cuba, or Oriente, into the bountiful western provinces, or Occidente. The Cuban revolutionary army, or Mambíses, led by the Bronze Titan, Antonio Maceo Grajales, and fresh off their victory at Cacarajícara, has occupied the highlands around Viñales and Pinar del Río. In a bid to crush the Mambíses, the Spanish imperial army, led by the ruthless Butcher, Valeriano Weyler, devises an ambitious scheme: trap the Mambíses in the west by building a fortified trench line, called a Trocha, across the island's narrowest neck from Mariel in the north to Playa Majana in the south, then attack the Mambíses with relentless force. Atrocities abound on both sides. Mambíses and Spanish jaegers alike put torch to farms and villages, to deny their enemy resources and claim for themselves the spoils of war. And as the people of western Cuba flee to the relative safety of the cities and coast, another, even more sinister, threat awaits them in the highlands...

i.

Hilaríon wrenched the woman's neck and drew his machete under her throat. She sank to her knees. Through her mat of coal-black hair, against her olive skin he could see it, shimmering like a moonlit sea. The medallion. He drew shallow breath. He'd done plunder before but never like this. It was a king's ransom—priceless, even. He'd be prophet, priest, and savior in the Towns before night even fell. He'd be free of the eyes at last.

"Old wines and young whores," Montez said. "Make way for the Devils Three!"

Hilaríon grinned. The Devils Three. He'd waited long to hear it.

The setting sun splashed fire across the western sky, helming the hills with golden crowns. The canopy throbbed with the ready thrum of owls, anoles, and eleuths, minstrels at play in the red Cuban sunset, and prelude to a gaudy night. Their latest catch of captives, refugees bound for Pinar del Río or the emigrant boats at Santa Lucia, sniveled face-down in the dirt. Hilaríon snaked the blade through the twine and drew the treasure from the woman's shirt. She jerked aside. He pressed the machete back to her throat and snapped the braiding. "Many thanks—"

"Not so fast," Grijalva, their leader, said. "This time, I want to see it."

"See what?" Hilaríon said. But he knew.

"You've walked with us long enough. We don't suffer snakes, boy. Show me some spine. Make me believe." Grijalva leered at the woman's bare neck. "Do it."

Montez stepped towards the trees. "Never mind all that," he said to Hilaríon. "Time's wasting. Bring the spoils."

"He can have it," Grijalva said. "Both our shares. Fuck the spoils. I want to know he's one of us."

"There are three that bear record, and these three are one," Montez said. "Take it, boy, and let's be off."

A pang shook Hilarión's gut. He'd seen the hilldevils kill before, but never a woman or in cold blood. It was all for sport, for sure. To lighten the mood he quipped, "The pink's getting cold in the Towns—"

"Do it," Grijalva repeated. It was no game.

The shadows of the forest spread. Twilight was falling fast. "You were a Mambí, weren't you?" Grijalva said, "One of the Bronze Titan's own. What would he do?"

Hilarión bit his tongue. He could thank the Bronze Titan for the eyes. He knew what that exalted brute would have done. Even Grijalva would have been sickened.

"Take it and let's go," Montez said, "before any Mambí patrols catch wind."

Grijalva leaned into Hilarión's ear, speaking through his rancid breath, "All the spoils just for you and you'll be a man. Don't make me wait any longer."

Hilarión steadied the blade. Who was this woman, anyhow? All she was was in his way, an obstacle to be removed. His palms moistened. The medallion squirmed inside his grasp. She lowered her head, baring her neck, and let her arms drop to her sides. She was braver than he would have been. His grip slackened. They could still walk away. He said, "Isn't this enough?"

"Do it," Grijalva said, "*or I'll kill you both.*"

He swallowed in a stone-dry throat. Grijalva meant what he'd said. He'd slit him lengthwise, like a shad. But he could still save himself. A thrust, a slice, and he'd be in the Towns, regaling the others with song, fucking the cleanest whore he could buy. It would be legend. It was his for the taking.

He pressed the blade deeper. The woman turned and faced him. She whispered, "*Cuba Libre.*" She opened her piercing, gunwale-gray eyes.

The eyes! Those eyes burned fast to his quick. He'd carried that private hell with him, ever since Cacarajícara. He could still see every

2

last one of them, watching. How could he kill her? How could he add more eyes to his hell?

The blade trembled in his hand. The woman held perfectly still. Her lips curled into the slightest of smiles. He couldn't pull himself from her stare. He couldn't take this final step into the wilderness of sin. "She's not worth—"

"Look out!" Montez cried.

Crack! A rock, hidden in the woman's fist, slammed into Hilarion's skull. His world burst into a motley swirl. Montez and Grijalva lunged at the woman. She nonchalantly stepped aside. The hilldevils tumbled to the ground. The captives leapt to their feet and scattered. Montez and Grijalva raced after them, cursing in their bluest tongues.

The woman loomed above Hilarion. She grabbed the medallion, and his blade. From somewhere in the ether, her grainy voice rang out. "Many thanks," she said, "to *you*." She tore off into the shadows.

His head swam. His stomach churned. Always, it was the eyes.

The captives' voices faded, helter-skelter through the woods. Montez and Grijalva hadn't bothered to chase. In the twilight, unco-ordinated, their chance of catching anyone, let alone someone with something worth taking, was next to nil. And the cause of their ire was still in the glade.

Hilarion staggered to his knees. Grijalva leapt and threw him down. "Coward and weakling," the hilldevil said.

"Three nights in the hills, for what?" Montez said. He stomped on Hilarion's chest. "The wind."

The pain burst deep in Hilarion's gut. He gasped for air as the hilldevils kicked him, again and again, roaring with rage. He fumbled about for something, *anything*—

"What did I tell you?" Grijalva said. "We don't suffer snakes."

The hilldevils drew their machetes.

ii.

Hilaríon's fingers closed on a rock, the same rock that had felled him. Montez whipped his blade back and said, "So much for the Devils Three—"

Hilaríon cracked the rock on his shin. The hilldevil roared as he fell to the ground. "Filthy turncoat Judas! I'll gut you like a bonefish!"

Grijalva drove his heavy blade down at Hilaríon's face. Hilaríon swiftly rolled aside. But a clean pain burst in his upper arm. He'd been nicked by the blade.

He scrambled to his feet. Grijalva's blade had lodged in the earth where it'd grazed Hilaríon's arm. The hilldevil struggled to yank it free. Hilaríon clubbed Grijalva's jaw and tore the machete out of the dirt. Grijalva lunged at Hilaríon's legs. Hilaríon raised the blade, to chop at the hilldevil's shoulders—

Ugh! A withering pain sang through his arm, all strength seeping out of his fingers and wrist. Grijalva reared up, laughing, "Weakling boy, can't kill a bitch, or wield a baby's blade."

He couldn't hope to stand his ground. Even to try was lunacy. Hilaríon wheeled off into the woods. The hilldevils' voices echoed behind. "Judas!" Montez cried, "We'll find you! You can run to the ends of the earth."

"He won't get far," Grijalva said, "not with *that* bite."

Beneath his shirt-sleeve, blood was swelling. This was no nick: he'd been gashed to the bare, white bone. But there was nothing he could do. He gritted his teeth and charged ahead.

"By and by!" Montez called out. The hilldevils' voices faded behind, drowned by the gloaming's euphony.

Hilaríon rushed through the shadows. The land billowed skyward in forested slopes: the mighty Cordillera de Guaniguanico, gateway to the east. Below, in the distance, the thatch rooftops of the Towns seemed like toadstools sprung from a patchwork valley. He could never set foot there again. Montez and Grijalva would look for him there. The Townsmen would know what he'd done. Any friends he had were gone.

He looked down. Twilight limned trampled seedlings, broken bramble, then gracile tracks, leading into the highlands.

The woman.

He clenched his fists. Shamed and bloodied, torn from the brink of his hard-won glory, all in the blink of an eye. A few seconds more and he'd have killed her. Now, he'd make her pay. He'd been a tracker all his life, having learned the least forgiving way. He still remembered his aunt's every lesson, and even more so the monthly ordeals where she'd leave him for dead in some forsaken place, alone, to find his way back. He'd spent the bulk of his youth in the woods, and most of that time at night. The forest, by darkness, might well have been home, and the woman couldn't be more than moments ahead. He tore a swatch from his cloak, bound his wound, and charged off into the tangle of hills. He'd have that medallion yet.

The ridges steepened, the gorges plunged. He fixed his eyes on the ground. She'd hidden nothing. Her boot prints burst from the hillside mud. Her stride was steady, long, and deep. She'd run at an even pace, not the gait of someone in flight. She didn't know he was coming.

He ran harder. The woods grew thicker, pulling him right, then pushing him left, and binding his knees with brush. The shadows grew longer, the western sky darker. He'd overtake her any minute. Wouldn't he? She could only have gotten so far.

His arm throbbed. The blood-soaked poultice squished at his side. He stopped and tied a new one. But the blood dripped just as red. He flung it from his fingers. Whore! He'd make her just as bloody. He'd cut off her nose, just like the jaegers at—

He retched in his throat. Cacarajícara was the past. The medallion was the future, his key to golden days. He'd go to La Habana. There he'd taste the sweets, the wines, the dark-eyed girls adorned with gold, forbidden fruits the Towns' barren womb could never yield. There, the past would hold no sway. He could be anyone for as long as he wanted, or nothing, or no one, at all. He'd have all the time he'd ever need. And the eyes would vanish, gone.

He pressed on. The hillside bared its craggy bones. He clambered over a rocky ledge, keeping to her trail: smeared mud, broken lichens, crushed moss, shredded cloth. To track across rock was an uncommon skill, his unyielding aunt's hardest lesson. He'd made a life on it; Mambíses and hilldevils, alike, had prized him for it. But he, alone, would profit now.

He dropped to his knees. The mud she'd left on the rock was moist but crumbled in his fingers. She'd made better time than he'd thought. She'd turned a few moments' start into nearly half an hour's lead. Some of her tracks pointed west. He looked out over the hillside, as she, by the look of her tracks, must have done. Though evening was falling, the woods below were bright. He had to assume she'd seen him approaching.

He raced up the mountainside. Twilight turned a regal dusk. The western sky bled purple. Her trail would be harder to find now, even for his well-honed eye. Her pace had quickened, her stride had lengthened. She'd taken fewer steps, treading where ground was hardest or bramble softest. She was masking her trail: she *had* seen him coming. A well-hidden print could cost precious minutes.

The stars took flame, peeking gray through the treetops. Hilarión kept to the chase. Her tracks led into a woodland stream and up the opposite bank. He looked closer. The trail looped back on itself, then disappeared into the water. She'd taken the stream, but which way? The stones midstream were wet in places, dry in others. The current was weak, not enough to have wet them itself. She'd splashed the stones to throw him off track. By the looks of the drying patterns, she'd gained some time since the overlook. He was falling behind.

He cleared his head. She'd struck him with the rock in her left hand. She might be inclined to go left. But the stream flowed rightwards. Its currents would have muffled her noise. But she'd likely wager that he'd know that.

He closed his eyes, and listened. The woods began to sing: nightjars, katydids, bulldog bats, and always the chorus of highland frogs, all in silken harmony. When all else lied, the earth never did. To the right the frogs sang from the water. To the left they hid on the banks in silence. Something had scared them from the left branch.

He raced to the left along the stream, to where the frogs resumed their chorus. On the opposite bank the rushes were splintered. He crossed the stream on stepping stones. The duckweed near the stones had been stirred. He pushed the rushes aside. In the mud, clear as day, was the print of a boot. "Too easy," he said. He chugged a handful of water. It was putrid, but no matter. Soon there'd only be Havanese wines. He tore off after her trail.

The murky highlands swallowed him whole, its stems made whips in the darkness. He leaned into the hillside. His arm throbbed all the more. Her boot prints pocked the mud again. She was taunting him, or sure he hadn't followed. But her tracks were the freshest he'd seen so far. He was gaining ground.

From the trees and bramble came unearthly sounds. His skin turned gooseflesh. Was it woodland beasts in the shadows? Or had the sounds been made by *them*?

He'd heard stories told in whisper and hush: the wicked people of the mountain, the M'Brae. They kept to themselves, at the tops of the hills, in the forests and the grimy caves where no one else dared tread. Their kind had perished long ago, in some unspoken calamity. But now their bodies breathed, and walked, through the will of darkness. Ghoulish half-breeds, hard of voice, they suffered no strangers to their lands. Like attercops they'd drink the blood of all unlucky trespassers. But those were just old stories, weren't they, to frighten young children to bed? He shook his bleary head and pressed on.

The forest heaved in piney hillocks. The trees, like troops, closed ranks. Her trail stopped dead at a stand of pines. He stared at the ground. She'd wanted him to think she'd climbed into the pines, hopping tree to tree. But dry straw covered the ground. If she'd climbed, the ground would be smattered with green. He peered into her tracks. In the broken moonlight, he could see the heels were deeper than the toes. She'd backtracked in her boot prints. Her real trail was somewhere behind.

He followed her prints until they shallowed. He searched the brush on either side. The rough hid any sign of her passing. The bramble around the felled pines was broken. The scent of the pines masked any whiff of her clothes. She could have gone in any direction.

He let his eyes adjust to the darkness, then cocked his head to the side. To look straight ahead in the dark was useless. The corners of his eyes told more. He panned his head across the rough. Not five paces into the thicket, the forest floor teemed with motion: ants, streaming from a toppled mound. Something had knocked it over.

He stepped past the ants. In the bramble was a pointed imprint. Crushed inside was dry pine straw, the same as under the trees. She'd leapt from her tracks into the bramble. She'd toppled the mound when she landed.

Fending off nausea, he stared at the track. His focus drifted in and out. His fingertips tingled, his upper arm burned. He needed medicines, if he could get them, and he needed help. But there was nowhere to go, and no turning back.

He crashed ahead through the underbrush. Her pace had grown frantic, her tracks now even harder to see. She'd kept to the rocks and logs and other places her prints wouldn't show. In places she'd backtracked, in others she'd wiped her tracks with brush. She knew he was gaining ground on her.

The stars glowed brighter, the moon took flight. Her tracks led into an open glade, stretching wide across the hilltop. He stopped. He knew better than to rush through the open. She could be watching him across the way, or lying in ambush in the tall grass. Even if time was wasting, recklessness would risk life and limb.

He dropped to his back and slithered low. His arm grew number with each passing moment. The pain roared through his shoulder like a kiss from white-hot steel. He crawled as the wind blew and rustled the grass to mask the sounds of his movement. Then, at length, he raised his head. He'd reached the opposite tree line.

He staggered off along the trail. His arm fell limp against his side, fingers turning white. Her tracks were wild, helter-skelter. She'd bounced like a game quail down the gullies, and into and out of the thicket. But she'd wasted time doing it. He was hard on her heels.

In the fast-thinning air, he willed himself on. He smacked head-long against the trees. The pain sang up and down his arm. But the anguish would be fleeting. La Habana would be worth the pain. He could almost hear the festival—

The woman's tracks stopped dead. The trail looped around and doubled back, then vanished altogether.

Hilarión shivered, alone in the night. She'd known he'd keep the chase. She'd known he'd only push harder. She'd lured him deeper, onto familiar turf, no doubt. He'd solved the riddles but the last laugh was hers. She'd been hunting *him*. He laughed in surrender. Maybe he wasn't so clever.

"Get back," a voice whispered. Hilarión froze. Someone in the thicket behind him said, "Not there. They'll see you."

The crunching of footsteps shattered the silence. Upwards, through the trees downhill, a phalanx of soldiers was stalking his way.

iii.

He squinted. They were nearly upon him, bejeweled shadows in close formation. Their sabers were bright and their blouses drawn smart. In the moonlight their buttons flashed golden, like cats' eyes. The plumes of their shakos danced in the breeze. They were carrying Mauser rifles. They were Castilian jaegers, fiercest of the fierce. To earn their stripes they'd been made to kill a next of kin, or so he'd been told.

A stranger pulled him into the thicket, saying, "Cuba Libre." A second man crouched nearby. Hilarión sighed: the men were Mambíses, rebels in the Bronze Titan's army. The jaegers sidled through the growth and vanished past the shadows. Hilarión took a step—

"Wait," the Mambí said. A final jaeger was passing.

Hilarión's blood ran cold. This last one seemed more wraith than man. His flesh was bluish-pale, like the embers of a dying flame. His coat was faded dappled gray and fraying at the seams. Some of his buttons were broken or missing. His boots bore the scars of shrapnel, belched hot from incoming shells. He craned his neck from side to side, as if searching for tracks in the dark. Across his eye and nose to his mouth, a blood-red snake of a scar slashed his face. Hilarión bit his lower lip. With ocelot stealth the fiend slunk away. His twin sabers gleamed in the moonlight, like ice. "The Gray Jaeger," the Mambí said. "The man the Devil fears." The enemy footsteps faded until only the sounds of the woods remained.

The Mambíses crept from the thicket. The crouching man was clad in fatigues, threadbare and smeared with dirt. The one who'd grabbed Hilarión, just a boy, wore spit-and-polish garb. "Brother," the boy said, "share your name."

"Hil—" In his fugue, he'd almost forgotten. If the Mambíses

found out who he was, he might as well fall on his blade. But to run would alarm them even more. "Guamá."

The boy raised an eyebrow. "Hilguamá?"

"Just Guamá."

The boy said, "I am Brother Concepcíon. This is my sector, and this is Brother Elídio." He pointed towards the other man.

Hilaríon started to roll his eyes but quickly thought the better. He'd known young upstarts like this before. He'd *been* one. He had to extract himself gently. "Strength to you both."

"I've seen you before," Elídio said, "I'd swear. Were you at——?"

"Oriente," Hilaríon said, "all this time." As a lie this was his old reliable. "I was there when the Poet fell. *¡Joven, a la carga!* he'd said. So I did." He took a step between them.

Concepcíon smiled. "Hero."

Elídio peered closer. "No, I know I've seen you, and not long ago."

"We all look alike, once we've been bloodied." The pain ran up his arm. He could never explain such a wound. If the Mambíses discovered who he was, they'd finish what Grijalva had started. He had to find that woman's trail. "Strength to you, brothers," he said. "My orders said to make haste. Cuba Libre! And strength to the Bronze Titan."

"Where do you think you're going?" Concepcíon took his arm. "We're dug in up and down this hillside. You'll be cut to shreds without us. We can take you——"

The boy jerked away, hands dappled with blood. "Guamá, you've been stabbed."

"A love scratch from the Butcher. It's nothing. Now I really have to——"

"Guamá," Elídio said. "Where are you going to, *Guamá*, if that is really your name? If you came from Oriente, why are you climbing the west-facing slope?"

His tongue was digging his grave. But all he needed was space to run. "I came... by way of Mantua."

"Mantua?" Elídio said. "The Bronze Titan has abandoned Mantua. How could you have come from there?"

"Brother, enough," Concepcíon said. "He fought with the Poet. That should be good for us."

"He wouldn't be the first to claim that, boy."

"Boy?"

Elídio scowled. "Lugarteniente."

"That's better," Concepcíon said. "For now, come this way. There'll be aid in our camp." He smiled eagerly. "And then you can tell me about the Poet."

Hilaríon bristled. No doubt, someone in their camp would recognize him. His arm was exsanguinating, fast. And somewhere in the highlands were the woman and medallion. When the moment was right he'd have to run.

"Guamá," Elídio said, "we've met before, I know it. And I won't rest until I'm sure where."

Anywhere else, Hilaríon would have made short work of this obnoxious zealot. He smiled over his shoulder. "Then sleepless nights—"

"That face!" Elídio said. "*You* were at Cacarajícara, head of the Faceless Legion."

Like a venomous curse, the word chewed his brain. "Cacarajícara?"

"That's right," Elídio said. "My wife was with them, Lux León."

A cold sweat broke at his temples. So *this* was Lux's husband, Elídio. Hilaríon had plucked her from his ranks. She'd been good hip-pocket sport in garrison. He could still feel her sweet and silky charms. But he'd watched as the enemy laid her low. It was the last thing he'd seen before he ran. "Who's Lux León?"

"It *is* him," Concepcíon said, "in the flesh and in my sector." The masquerade was over.

Hilaríon lurched aside. Concepcíon grabbed his wrist and kicked his legs from under him. He fell to the ground. The boy laid his blade on Hilaríon's neck. "The Coward of the Faceless Legion. How long have I waited for something like this? The Bronze Titan will mint me a capitán now."

"He's mine," Elídio said. "It's my right." He pushed Concepcíon away and kicked Hilaríon into the mud.

Blood trickled from his wound. But for the tracker, honed to details, weaknesses were easy to spot. "Wait!" Hilaríon gasped. "I remember Lux… and what she told me."

Elídio lowered his blade. "What?"

"Don't listen to him," Concepcíon said.

"Shut your mouth, boy. Why should I believe you?"

"In the benediction, before the charge on Bernal's brigade," he said. "Red hair twisting in the breeze, no truer Valkyrie ever was. She said she had a message, for her husband."

"He's lying," Concepcíon said. "Don't you see?"

"Shut up," Elídio said. "Get on with it, coward."

He'd go to hell for doing this. But he was probably going there anyway. "She said that… that… and this was important. She wanted you to know the truth. She wanted me to get it right. She told me… Oh, what was it? That's right. She said that if she happened to fall, that you should…" He paused. "That you should…"

"What?"

"That you should… On second thought, bring me to your capitáns."

"Tell me!"

"No," he said. "I've done wrong, I know. But I've done some good for the cause. I should get to beg for my life."

"You can beg from me," Concepcíon said.

Elídio said, "The coward is right. He has to confess to the capitáns."

"He has to die," Concepcíon said. "He's lying and you're a fool. Your dead wife told him nothing. He doesn't tell us what to do."

"Neither do you, child."

"Lugarteniente!" Concepcíon said. Hilaríon clasped a handful of dirt.

"He's my captive," Concepcíon said. "I'll decide what happens. Now stand aside, before I take *two* heads." He lowered his blade to Hilaríon's neck. "The capitáns will welcome your head, spitted on my—"

"No!" Elídio hacked at Concepcíon's arm. The boy's blade fell in a splatter of blood. Elídio leapt at Hilaríon. Hilaríon threw dirt in Elídio's eyes. Elídio staggered, clutching his face. Hilaríon pulled back his fist—

"*¡Dispara!*"

Mausers crackled all around. Balls whizzed through the trees. The jaegers had circled back downhill. The Mambíses crumpled in gurgling heaps. Elídio stared blankly. "Lux," he muttered. "Damn you, coward." He keeled onto his side, dead.

Hilaríon raced up the hillside. A reptilian hiss sliced the clamor. "Alto al fuego."

Hilaríon glanced back downhill as the Gray Jaeger stepped from the ranks. Concepcíon spread his arms in surrender. The Jaeger plunged his sabers through the boy's hands, spitting him to the mud, as if in crucifixion. Then he looked Hilaríon's way. "*Cerca,*" the Jaeger said, "*Cerca... o lejos?*"

Towards? Or away?

Hilaríon ran. The jaegers gave chase. His head was faint, arm gushing red. But all he could do was keep running.

"¡Por aquí! ¡Por aquí! ¡Se fue por aquí!" they cried.

He crested the hilltop, through crumbling ruins, tall and round like overripe melons. A faint light shimmered from the ground. The soil was littered with wreckage: shattered lanterns, broken tools, drinking gourds covered in moss. He gasped. Among the wreckage were human bones: he'd crossed into M'Brae lands. If the jaegers didn't catch him, those ghouls surely would. Whore! This was her fault. When he found her, he'd—

But he wouldn't. She was gone, so too the medallion. His lifeblood was draining. He couldn't run, or even walk. He withered to the ground. The eyes! Now there were two pairs more, Elídio and Concepcíon. They were smiling. He deserved it. Maybe now they'd all find rest—

"Where Seven Angels dance on high," a lilting voice whispered in his ear. "Show me where the way begins."

His mind was playing tricks. "Seven Angels?"

Sinewy arms embraced him. His body went limp. The voice spoke again, "Only you can find it. Our Vexing Heirloom."

"Vexing... what?" he said.

"¡El Mambí pasó por aquí!" The enemy was closing in.

Soft hands took his wrists. He felt himself dragged across the forest floor.

"¡Anda cerca!"

The hands pulled him over a crumbling wall and inside a ruined foundation. "Where Seven Angels dance on high," the voice said. "That's where we'll be together." A pair of lips pressed against his. His blood ran hot. He opened his eyes.

"¡Mátalo!"

Through the shadows of the forest, a graceful figure slipped away. It seemed to float above the brush, making no sound as it vanished. In the moonlight, it looked like the woman.

"¡Mátalo!"

The jaegers were upon him. He shut his eyes, and prayed it would be over soon.

iv.

A blinding pain, like hellfire, burst across Hilaríon's arm. "Lay still, Mambí," a burly voice said. Hilaríon heaved upright. He was in a straw pile, inside a stone courtyard. Beside him was an enormous man. But this was no jaeger, or Mambí.

The big man spread the wound. "This is deep," he said. "I've a moiling sew ahead of me." He dabbed a blood-soaked rag on a bottle and pressed it to Hilaríon's arm. "I'll get you back in the fight, Mambí. The attack could come any moment."

"Attack?"

"Best you don't struggle," the big man said.

Hilaríon's head rolled sideways. Slowly it all came back, shred by terrible shred: the wound, the highlands and the chase, the Mambíses and the Gray Jaeger, the medallion and the voice. "That woman," he said. "Where is she?"

"Never chase a woman, Mambí. Stand for something. Stand very tall. Then they'll chase after *you*." He winked.

"No, she was there. I heard her. *Where Seven Angels dance on high.*" He pushed from the ground.

The big man yanked him back. "Gently," he said, "you've lost a lot of blood." He threaded catgut through a needle. "If I hadn't found you when I did... you're lucky you fell inside the ruins. The phéa-sjant don't go there. They think they're haunted."

"Phéa... what?"

"Crown soldiers—those jaegers. They passed you over. Now, if they'd circled back—"

"But the woman. Where did she go?"

"I already told you. No women here."

He looked around. Tunnels ran from a courtyard, each ending in stairs that led to ramparts. Its guardhouses had collapsed in heaps and its cannon mounts were draped with vines. But the walls were patched with fresh stone, and the doors of its keep bound with struts. The ground was strewn with tools and supplies. Beside him was a fire pit, tinder crackling beneath a flame. "Where's here?"

The big man said, "Golgaj, west gate of M'Brae-dah. Get used to these defiant walls. It's here we'll make our stand—"

"*M'Brae-dah*?" He recoiled. He was inside the attercops' lair, being prepared for some blood-splattered rite. He reached for his blade. His scabbard was empty.

"Sorry," the big man said. He pointed across the redoubt. Hilaríon's machete leaned against a wall. "Everyone disarms for now. Don't take anything by it. My name is Phellhe. What can I call you?"

He had to get back to the ruins and try to pick up the woman's trail. He had to escape from this monstrous wildman. Hilaríon lurched from the straw. "Call me gone!"

Phellhe held him. "You're not going anywhere, *Gone*, not with a wound like that."

"My blade."

"You can have your blade when I'm finished. You won't get far unless I do."

He stretched towards the blade. Phellhe held his wrist. "How long do you think you'll last out there, Mambí? The highlands swarm with hilldevils. If they found you, wounded and alone, you might not be as lucky. And don't forget, you came looking for *me*, remember?"

He slackened. "I what?"

"To the meeting place. I've been begging your brothers for months. Just send me an envoy, I told them. Just let me meet with your capitáns. They finally came to their senses, I see."

"Meeting place? What are you talking about?"

"Truly, Mambí, you don't have to fear me. No need to keep pretending. My people are alive because of Mambíses, in the first rebellion—but you know that. And thanks to you, we'll survive the next war. There's no time to waste now. I'll finish more quickly if you don't resist."

Timely or not, he needed help. Phellhe was the only one offering.

Hilaríon sat down, warily. The big man spread the wound again and drew the needle through his flesh. "Now," he said, "what is your name?"

This wasn't at all how he'd pictured an M'Brae: burlier and less ghoulish, not so different from the Townsmen, save for his size and graying mane pulled into a knotty braid. He settled to the straw. There was no use running, yet. "Guamá."

"It's all happening again, Guamá. The dogs of war are coming, fast."

"In the ruins where you found me, did you see someone else?"

"My village's days are numbered." He drew a stitch.

"Maybe trampled bramble, or a trail?"

"Except it will be different this time. The M'Brae will be ready. No foolish quests for riches. No swindlers to lead us astray."

"Or maybe something left behind?"

Phellhe laughed warmly. "You've a single mind, Guamá. That's a precious gift. I'm glad it'll be you at my side." He drew another stitch.

"I don't know what you think I am. But in those ruins—"

"The attack could come any time now. The Butcher sends a diversion west. But in secret he marches down from the sea. The main attack comes from the north."

"Then get to the south," Hilaríon said. "And get me to the ruins."

Phellhe grabbed a clump of kindling straw. He broke it into two small piles and set a pebble between them. "M'Brae-dah straddles the only north-south pass for miles in either direction," he said. "To his plan, the pass is essential. The Butcher will raze M'Brae-dah. He'll kill everything inside of ten miles." He flicked the pebble into the fire. "Neither of our forces can stop him. Combined, we won't have enough men. But the Mambíses can still prevail. And the M'Brae can still survive."

"Yes, you can flee, like everyone else."

Phellhe stopped stitching. "That's the worst that could happen."

"You'd live," Hilaríon said. "Now, if you could point the way to the ruins..."

"What would that matter, just to live? What kind of Mambí wants only to run? M'Brae-dah is our only home. We've always lived in the shadow of death. We've weathered every storm, whether plague or hunger or foreign devils come to kill us. But we can't stand alone this time. We need your help again."

Hilaríon clasped the bridge of his nose. Phellhe was as boneheaded as he was strong. With each wasted moment, woman and medallion sped farther away. "You don't need my help," he said. "I'm not—"

"A leader. A warrior, bold and true."

"None of those," he said. He wanted to add, "Not anymore."

"I'm not so sure," Phellhe said. "A true leader's never his own herald."

"Whatever you think I am, I'm not. All I am is tracking that woman. She took something from me."

Phellhe seemed doubtful. "What did she take?"

"A treasure."

Phellhe's lips curled. "Treasure?" The needle tumbled from his hand. He burst from the fireside onto his feet. "*Treasure!*"

He winced. "Wait—!"

Phellhe grabbed Hilaríon by the throat and pressed him to the wall. "Leeches and looters, picking our bones. I'll show you what happens to hilldevil swine." Phellhe pulled back his fist. "Make your peace!"

"Wait, wait!" Hilaríon said. Now, there was no way out. There was only deeper in. "Cuba Libre! *Cuba Libre!*"

Phellhe lowered his fist. Hilaríon said, "They warned me that might happen."

"They?"

"My Mambí brothers."

"*Now* you're a Mambí?"

"I always have been. Ducasse's Raiders, the heroes of Cacarajícara. I lived through that butchery. To think I'd die like this."

Phellhe fidgeted. "I'm sorry, I thought you were..."

"Like I said, they warned me. Hotheaded as he's strong. Still bitter after all these years. But I had to be sure it was you, like you had to be sure about me. Mention treasure, they said. You'll know if it's him."

"I despise that word," Phellhe said. "The hilldevils still think the ground under M'Brae-dah flows with rivers of treasure."

Hilaríon's earlobes tingled. "What?"

"Don't tell me you've never heard."

Rivers of treasure. It echoed in Hilaríon's ears like an august hymn of praise. "No."

"Rumor and myth," Phellhe said. "There's no way in or out of those caves." He motioned Hilaríon back to the fire and picked up the dangling needle.

Hilaríon scanned Phellhe's eyes. Tracking meant getting inside your quarry's head. Phellhe knew more than he had let on. He said, "But no treasure?"

Phellhe drew a stitch, then several more. Moments passed in silence. The moon climbed higher in the west. Somewhere in the shadowy hills, his medallion was waiting. Or was it?

Rivers of treasure. Phellhe hadn't actually denied it. Hilaríon's imagination whirled. He could only bask in its hypnotic glow. "Suppose there was a way in."

"There isn't."

"Say someone stumbled—"

"It's just a legend, Guamá." He dabbed the rag against the wound. "The Vexing Heirloom is a myth."

"Vexing Heirloom? That's what the woman—"

"*What?*" Phellhe shot to his feet.

"Um, nothing. What I meant to say was… one of my sisters dropped those words. An old timer. Said she fought here years ago. But I never caught her name."

"Loose lips," Phellhe grumbled, sitting. He drew another stitch.

Golden thoughts tossed in Hilaríon's mind. "About the heirloom…"

"That story's forbidden. I've already said too much."

"But if I knew the rumors, I could better help you stamp them out. When we join forces, that is."

Phellhe drew another stitch. "No."

"They said I needed to hear it."

"It needs to die," Phellhe said. "It's brought only pain."

Fortunately for Hilaríon, Phellhe's weakness, like Elídio's, was plain. "Just as well," Hilaríon said. "They warned me about that, too."

"About what?"

"The Mambíses warned me. Strong, hardheaded, and maybe just a little bit, slightly... well, I don't want to repeat it."

"Tell me."

"Two-faced," he said, "if you really must know. It's too bad."

"They ought to know me better." Phellhe's staunch expression flaked to fear. "We fought together years ago. Who told you that?"

"I'm not giving names. My orders were clear. Bring him back to the meeting place, if I think he deserves our trust. If not..." He nodded towards the stairwell.

Phellhe said, "I can't believe I'm doing this. I swore I'd never again. It's a blight on all we've built. But if I need to gain your trust." He heaved despondent breath.

"The legend's as old as M'Brae-dah itself. Ages ago, the story goes, my race possessed a priceless treasure. It made them powerful beyond compare. They sailed the oceans of the world. They solved the riddles of the earth. But in time their greatness waned. They dwindled in strength, and wisdom, and numbers. Some of them came to these very shores, with what was left of the treasure. But by then they were a broken race, far beyond saving. Rather than squander it, or try to use what they knew they could not, they hid the treasure. They left it for their children to find. But their children had to be worthy. So with their last remaining wit and strength, they raised a lethal gauntlet. The M'Brae would have to prove themselves. That gauntlet, if you believe in such, we call our Vexing Heirloom."

Hilaríon's every sinew tensed. "And the treasure is?"

"Riches, I suppose," Phellhe said. "Diamonds, rubies, gold. No one knows for sure. But some say a piece of it—no, I shouldn't." He drew another silent stitch.

Hilaríon glanced at his blade, then the stairwell, and let Phellhe see him do it. "Some say a piece of it, what?"

"May my sires forgive me," Phellhe said. "Some say a piece was left behind. A silver medallion." In rich baritone he sang,

"A ruthless path through living earth
A Steeled Elect whose will is true.

"Who holds the medallion, alone, solves the heirloom. The Steeled Elect, he's called. And that, I swear, is all I know. Don't ask me anymore."

Hilaríon's pulse raced. The woman had asked him where *it* began. She'd pressed the medallion into his palm, and said only he could find it. But better to keep that to himself.

Phellhe drew the needle through the wound. "This is going to hurt," he said. He untied the catgut, wrapped the loose end on his finger, and twirled. The stitches tightened. Hilaríon winced. Phellhe tied off the stitches. "Make a fist."

Hilaríon crunched his fingers closed. He could feel his arm regaining strength. "So if somebody found the medallion—"

"Guamá, it's just a legend. You and I are real." He raised his arms triumphantly and stood before the iron doors. "This fortress is coming back to life. The keep is finished... secured, stocked, and ready for the others. We will lead every last one of my people here. Your brothers will fight from the ramparts. You'll strike the marauding enemy's flanks, then melt into the shadows. This is a new day, Guamá, the dawn of a new M'Brae-dah. This time we won't be tricked by swindlers."

"*You won't?*" A terrible voice rang through the redoubt. "Isn't that too bad."

Hilaríon knew that voice too well. He looked up. Leering down from the ramparts was Montez. The hilldevil said, "Folks need a good tricking, now and then."

Phellhe reached for his weapon. Montez leapt. He tackled the big man to the ground. "Judas," he said to Hilaríon, "we tracked you by your blood, like you taught us. Now bring your forty pieces here."

Phellhe glared at Hilaríon, and gasped, "Hilldevil—?"

Montez struck Phellhe's head with the butt of his blade. The big man fell, out cold. Like a heathen cleric, Montez lifted his blade over Phellhe. "Oh, ram in a bush..."

Hilaríon kicked the kindling logs. The flaming cinders showered Montez. The hilldevil yowled and dropped to the ground, patting the sparks from his cloak. Hilaríon raced up the ramparts. Montez lumbered along behind, singing in throaty strains, "Who is this coming up from the wilderness, like a column of smoke..."

Hilaríon clambered over the redoubt and into the unforgiving woods. The piney tangles ripped his face. He staggered towards the higher ground, but Montez seemed only to gain, singing, "King Solomon made for himself the carriage; he made it of wood from Lebanon—"

Grijalva sprung from the shadows. He smothered Hilaríon to the dirt. "Still running, as ever, I see."

Montez sauntered up beside them and handed Grijalva back his machete. "The sweet wayward lamb," Montez said. "Never again shall you wander, my child."

Hilaríon fumbled along the ground. Whatever he grabbed turned sludge in his hands. "No stone this time," Montez said.

Hilaríon said, "I can explain— wait!" Something in the dirt caught his glance.

Grijalva stepped on Hilaríon's knee. "You can die with a blade through your lily-white spleen." The hilldevils raised their machetes.

"Wait! Just wait!" Hilaríon railed. He could hardly believe his eyes. In the ground below was the woman's trail.

v.

Hilarión scanned the bramble. Her tracks led up the ridge. "I can get the medallion," he said.

"Fuck the medallion," Grijalva said. "Blood's all I need from you."

"Hold on," Montez said. "I like how Judas thinks."

"He's one of *them*," Grijalva said. "He let that bitch knock him cold. He took an oath." He pulled Hilarión's sleeve up his arm, revealing a brand of molten flesh. He rolled his own sleeve, revealing a similar mark. "*We* took an oath."

"But no vow of poverty," Montez said. "Let's wring one last triumph. He's never been wrong before."

"You've forgotten what they did to us." Grijalva pressed his wrists together, as if they were bound by shackles.

"Spoils make me forget," Montez said. "They'd do the same for you." He wrenched Hilarión's head by his hair. "Lead on, Judas. Bring me those forty pieces. Maybe we'll only kill half of you."

Hilarión tore through the bramble. The woman's trail looped every which way. It doubled and tripled back on itself. It brought them back near where they'd begun. The brush was dark and nigh impenetrable, a nightmare made of leaves. There was no use trying to escape. At the smallest sign he meant to run, they'd skewer him through his back.

"The Devils Three," Montez said, mockingly wistful. "Oh, what could have been?"

Hilarión said, "It still can be."

"It never was," Grijalva said. "You think you know what loss is, boy?" He pulled a yellowed scrap from his pocket and thrust it in Hilarión's face. In the moonlight, he could just make out a daguerreotype of man, woman, and child. The man, smiling proudly, was Grijalva. Grijalva shoved it back in his pocket. "You'll always be one of them."

The thicket thinned, the bramble retreated. The ridge gave way to a moss-capped hilltop. In the center was a crumbling shrine: five fish-faced giants in a ring, standing hand-in-fluke with five smaller, human figures. The stone was ancient, covered in lichens. Most of their limbs had broken away. Past the ruins dropped a cliff. His heart sank as he scanned the hilltop. There was no sign of the woman.

"So much for spoils," Grijalva said. "Let that be a lesson."

Montez shook his head. "Stopped at the eye of the needle, again."

Hilarión ripped at the earth. There had to be *something*: a hair, a thread, a pebble out of place. He said, "I can find her."

"I don't care," Grijalva said. "Treasure won't set you free, boy." He whipped back his blade. "That's why there's no Devils Three—!"

Hilarión lunged up the hilltop. Grijalva swung behind him. The hilldevil's blade whined past his feet. Hilarión dove through a stone giant's legs and into the crumbling shrine.

The hilldevils ambled nearer, grinning diabolically. "M'Brae witchcraft won't save you, Judas," Montez said. "What happens when we get inside?"

The ring was tight, easy to defend. A stone arm lay below. Hilarión raised it over his head. "Then... *this*—!"

It cracked in half, leaving a stump. Grijalva feinted low then swung, chopping at Hilarión between two giants. Montez crawled between giant-legs. Hilarión parried the strike with the stump, then swiped at Montez's head. The hilldevils pulled away. The arm-stump brushed a statue giant. Pebbles fell from its thigh. The statue-stone was barely solid.

"Not as smart as you think you are, Judas." Montez kicked the statue's leg. The giant toppled inward.

Hilarión threw himself aside. The statue crashed behind him. He tumbled towards the tree line. Grijalva cut him off. He raced back up the hilltop. They let him run: there was only the cliff. There was nowhere else to go.

The hilldevils closed in, snarling like distempered dogs. "Now," Montez said, "it's over. *You're* over. You'll be over straight away."

Hilarión chopped his backwards steps and glanced over his

shoulder. The cliff beetled violently over a slope, disappearing in rocky ravines far below. His feet slipped on the mossy stones. He waved the stump in the hilldevils' faces. But they just laughed all the harder. "To the ninth with you, Judas," Montez said. "One epic fall for another—"

"Leave some for me," a grainy voice said. "He's worth his weight in hidden gold."

He turned. It was the woman.

She leaned against the crumbled shrine. She looked them over coolly, as a queen surveys her vassals. Something in the way she stood made him think of Leónese nobility, her figure lithe, her features sharp. He hadn't realized how striking she was, even at a distance: not beautiful as beauty went, but gripping just the same.

"Her first," Grijalva said.

She raised her blade in a high block. The hilldevils rushed. With a stride she was against their backs. Montez swung high, Grijalva low. She parried both strikes in a lissome thrust. She dropped down, spinning, cutting across their upper calves, then rising in a flourish. The hilldevils squealed like hogs. She cleaved her blade through Montez's shoulders, then down the thick of Grijalva's flank. Blood sprayed red across the ruins. Montez and Grijalva crumpled, dead.

She drew their eyes closed. Silver flashed beneath her neck.

It was the medallion. It was *his.*

Hilaríon grabbed a blade and sprang. She swung to block him. Their machetes kissed in a shower of sparks. "Guamá," she said, "I know who you are. Better than you know yourself."

He hacked at her face. She slipped to his back. He spun around, swinging. Wherever he turned she also turned. She said, "*Where Seven Angels dance on high.* Tell me where it starts."

He swung behind. "So it *was* you."

She dropped. "I saved your life. You're welcome." She smacked his calves with the broad of her blade.

He steadied himself. "I saved yours first."

"Not killing me isn't saving me." She rolled and jumped upright.

He caught his breath. "Be glad you're still alive, for now." He feinted high and swung at her legs. She hollowed away. He whiffed through the air. She swept his legs. He collapsed to his back, breath knocked from his lungs.

"Glad to be alive," she said.

He gathered his wits. "You can thank me right." He pointed to the medallion.

"It's not mine to give."

"I'll take it off your corpse then, whore." He thrust at her heart. She side-stepped his strike and flicked her blade against his neck. He tumbled to his back again.

"Look," she said, calmly, "it's just not mine to give." She drove her knee between his legs and slunk to a straddle across his chest. "And you have what I need."

He leered. "I'll bet I do." He arched his back and flipped her, then clambered onto her hips. "We'll see to that later." He rubbed her thigh.

"It's a date," she said. "As for now…" She clapped her palms against his head. A horrible ringing split his eardrums. She leapt to her feet and threw him down, and ground her boot against his wrist. His hand released the machete. She pulled the medallion from her shirt. "This won't help you when you're dead. And then you can't help us."

"You think I'm someone else."

"I don't," she said. "And I can't do it alone."

He wrenched her leg and shoved her away, and said, "Then you can't do it."

He grabbed the blade and rushed at her. She back-pedaled as she fell, gaining her footing, carving the air in front of her to keep him at arm's length. He barreled down upon her. She came to a standstill, holding her ground. He sliced and slashed in every which way, with every trick he'd ever learned, but she turned every one of his strikes. He fell back. She hadn't moved an inch.

"Before this ends badly," she said. "*Where Seven Angels dance on high.* Where is it?"

"I don't know about angels. And you don't know about me." He pointed to the medallion and said, "That prize is my golden days."

Her nostrils flared. She growled, "Prize?" Hilarión lunged.

She spun through the air, a whirlwind made flesh, swinging at his head. He staggered backwards. She kicked him down. She chopped the blade from his grip and flipped it into her empty hand. She crossed the blades beneath his throat. Her rage congealed back into calm. "I was wrong," she said. "You're not who I thought. Too bad for me. Worse for you."

His body went limp. She hoisted him between the blades, a lever at his neck. "I'll keep this clean, if anyone comes looking." She nodded towards Montez and Grijalva. "At least you won't look like them."

But he deserved to look like them, or worse. They were just bandits. He'd been a coward and turncoat, to boot. He'd never thought it'd end this way. He'd seen himself falling in battle, a tattered standard in his hand. But that man was gone, or had never been. At least he'd be rid of the eyes. "I'm sorry, Hilarión," she said. "Yes, I know your real name."

She drew his head skywards between the blades. The stars shone brilliant white and blue against an inky night. He loved them, and always had. They'd never changed and never would. No matter what else, he could always count on—

It couldn't be. The stars. *Those* stars.

She crunched the blades closed. They groaned like a vise. "Goodbye—"

"Stop!" The force of his cry shook the blades from his neck. "Seven Angels! *Where Seven Angels dance on high*." He fell to his hands and pointed. "There!"

The faintest glimmer of golden dawn was breaking across the haystack hills. The range spread wide before them, sprawling and endless, lyrical towers mounting the sky like scattered dragon's-teeth. Apart from the others, standing alone, loomed two identical hillocks. Their silhouettes blotted the stars behind them. And between and just above their peaks, burning white through the vastness of space, they hung in rapt repose.

The Pleiades. Seven Angels.

She lifted him to his feet. She was stronger, even, than Phellhe. She ran her hand across his face. "It *is* you," she said.

28

"So I can have the medallion?"

Her hands drifted downwards, nearing his waist. "Better," she said, "and much, much more."

She grabbed his face between both hands and pulled his mouth to hers. Her flushed cheeks burned against his own. He'd never been kissed so mordantly. What did this mad wildling want? Did she know something he didn't? Did *he* know something he didn't?

"I am Ypriána," she said. "And you, Hilaríon, are my—"

"*¡Adelante!*" Distant shouting rent the calm. Below and all around them, the forest burst to life. "*¡Ahora! ¡Adelante!*"

From the heights above and hollows beneath, through the woods on every side they swarmed: legions of jaegers, banners held high, Mausers glinting in the dawn. The invasion of M'Brae-dah had begun, just as Phellhe had said.

She thrust the machete back into his hand. "Come with me," she said.

vi.

Necío split the earth with his shovel and threw the spoil of silt aside. A ruddy dawn stained the river beside him, its calm broken only by chattering herons. It'd been years since he'd stepped openly into M'Brae-dah. Phellhe had banished him unto the fringes. His mother's warning, her dying words, echoed in his ears. *Don't bother trying. That quest's for better men than you.* Had she dared him to try? Or was it just more scorn? He wiped his face. He'd show her.

He glanced towards the village. Time was running out. If Phellhe found out, it'd be their necks. "Faster," he told the other diggers. "Sunrise in minutes." They groaned and thrust their shovels deeper into the ruined foundation.

Three maudlin months since his great mother's death had led him to this place. She'd spent the better of thirty years searching. She'd found the trailhead but without the key, they'd never find their way inside, or so she'd concluded. He'd assembled all the clues she'd gathered, connected all the drifting dots. He'd enlisted a handful of helpers: orphans, delinquents, fellow outcasts. The answer would lie in these ruins—it *had* to. Their lives and his family's name were at stake. He'd find that medallion if it killed him.

"Necío," twiggish Aryei said. "Tell us what we're doing."

He threw another shovelful. "No."

"It's been five hours, ten minutes, and twenty-seven seconds."

"Less counting, more digging."

"I can't help counting, remember? It's just the way my mind works. Why won't you tell us?"

He'd begged and cajoled them; some he'd bribed. Since nightfall they'd been shoveling faithfully. "No questions. That was our deal."

"That wasn't *our* deal," Chropher said. He pitched his spade into the ground. "What are you hiding?"

The others stopped digging. Sunovín, Unish, Fenn, and Chay: crooks and slippery ragamuffins. "The less you know, the better."

"That's what Phellhe says," Chropher said. "I'm sure he'd like *not* to know about this. Maybe I'll ask him."

"Stop," Necío said. Chropher was a weasel, but Phellhe could never know. He gathered them closer. "Swear to keep this to yourselves." They nodded weakly. "These ruins were once somebody's home. It belonged to the dar Se family—Mellín and Leisha, their sons Blaish and Rontu, and their daughter Ypriána. They'd lived here generations, but always kept to themselves. But then they disappeared, right before it happened."

Aryei said, "Before what happened?"

Necío leaned closer. He never spoke aloud of his parents' failed quest. Phellhe would have his tongue cut out. "The Days of Strife," he whispered.

"Where'd they get off to?" Aryei said.

"No one knows. But I think the answer's here."

"What does it matter?" Chropher said.

Necío said, "They may have had something valuable. When they left they took it with them. I need to know what happened to them. If we had this thing then we might be able to find—er, we'd, have a better chance of surviving, if war ever comes."

Chropher said, "Might be able to find what?" By his smirk, he'd already guessed.

"That's all you need to know," Necío said. "Now get back to digging."

"Like treasure?"

Necío threw his hands up. "Quiet! I told you not to ask. Now it's all of your necks, and mine. If Phellhe found out—"

"I'd what?" Phellhe's tall figure burst through the trees. Necío's heart sank. "Not one shovelful more," Phellhe said. He rushed to the ruins. His face was bruised and bloodied.

Necío donned his best worried look. "Phellhe," he said, "your face."

Phellhe shoved him to the mud. "Hilldevils are in M'Brae-dah.

They struck in Golgaj. I barely survived. I came to warn you. And this is what I find?"

The diggers hid their blushing cheeks. "He swindled you into this?" Phellhe said. "You're lucky your mothers and fathers were smarter. Most of us can't say the same."

A crowd from the village gathered at the ruins. Necío felt the pangs of grief. The M'Brae looked even more hungry and sick than last he'd seen them, too weak to do much more than stare. Phellhe looked hale and hearty. The big man waved a meaty fist. The M'Brae faces tightened, then bellowed in ungodly jeers, cursing Necío and his kin.

Necío said, "My mother wanted me to—"

"Your mother wanted?" Phellhe said. "We wanted the riches she promised us, she and your pompous excuse for a father. But you know how that turned out."

A chill breeze moaned through the treetops, carrying with it the first hints of rain. It winnowed the rags on knobby legs and bony M'Brae bodies. Elders clutched their pallid arms. Beneath their matted tufts of hair, their eyes flashed angry cinders. Who they were mad at—Phellhe or himself—Necío couldn't tell. "No one said it was riches," he said.

"This is how it begins," Phellhe said, "with questions best un-asked. The order melts away. We turn to prey for swindlers." He pointed to the diggers. "Half of you I ought to kill, the others banish. Leave the legends be."

The boys dropped their shovels and ran into the crowd. Necío stared at the dirt, alone. Somewhere beneath the ruined foundation lay the answer his mother had spent her life seeking. Or there was only worm-ridden earth. Either way, he'd dithered too long. From the misty hereafter, her scathing voice rang. *That quest's for better men than you.* Had she been right?

She hadn't.

His fingers closed around the shovel. He staggered to his feet. He pitched the shovel into the earth and flung the spoil of silt aside. Phellhe pushed him down. "What did I say?"

Necío clambered standing again and picked up the shovel. Phellhe grabbed the handle between Necío's hands. "Why do you carry this torch for her? She never cared much for your soul... *fool*."

His stomach turned. Why had his mother named him Necío? It was bad enough having a Vujóie name—why did it have to be their word for fool? Its shame never let him be.

"This is your final chance," Phellhe said. "Send them home, let myths be myths. Don't put me to the test."

Necío ripped the shovel away. "You weren't worthy. Her task falls to me."

Phellhe said, "Then you can join her."

Necío pulled as Phellhe's grip tightened. Necío heaved with all his strength, then let go the shovel. Phellhe tumbled backwards into the mud. A chorus of heckles rose from the crowd. Necío picked up another shovel. He thrust it towards the soil—

"*Rah-yuloh!*" a woman's voice cried. "They're coming!"

Necío spun. This voice he didn't recognize. It was long since he'd heard the Ancients' tongue spoken. Phellhe had forbidden that, too.

"Rah-yuloh! Rah-yuloh!" From the west, a woman burst from the trees. Behind her ran a Vujóie man, resembling a Mambí. But the woman, dressed threadbare, had to be M'Brae. How else could she know their tongue?

Phellhe pointed at the man and snarled, "*Guamá.*"

The glinting of metal caught Necío's eye. He squinted. Across the river, through the trees, were strange men carrying rifles. They halted, shifting formation. Broken sunlight gleamed off brass buttons. Epaulettes flashed against drab wood. They trained their weapons to the south.

The strange woman cried, "Crown soldiers are coming!" But she hadn't seen the riflemen yet, or that she stood in their line of fire.

Necío said, "They're already here!" He threw the strange man and woman down.

Across the river, a voice bellowed, "*¡Fuego!*"

vii.

Hilarío buried his face in the mud. Ypriána curled against him. The boy had tackled them not a second too soon. "Stay low," the boy said.

A crackle, like thunder, slammed across the riverbank. Balls screamed past his head like bees. All around him people fell, like sheaves of wheat at threshing. A grisly chorus rent the woods: the thud of bullets into flesh, the piercing shrieks of wounded men, the ghostly silence of the dead. The barrage rolled on, fizzling into a slew of commands.

"¡Listos para atacar! Prepárense..."

He raised his head. Bodies lay lifeless in the currents. Others cringed in the reeds. The air was thick with sulfur, smoke, and the battle cries of jaegers.

"¡Ataquen! ¡Ahora!"

Their voices carried through the wood, fast bearing down on the M'Brae.

"¡Mátalos a todos! ¡Elimínalos a todos!"

The jaegers swarmed across the banks. From the opposite shore, sharpshooters rained fire ahead of the charge.

"¡Por ahí!"

Ypriána waved her machete aloft. "All of you, follow me!" She led the survivors into the trees.

They stumbled through the smoky thicket. Phellhe barked orders no one obeyed. The boy who'd tackled them trailed behind, urging the others on ahead. Hard on their heels, the jaegers stomped, shouting for their quarry.

"¡No puedes huir toda la vida!"

Hilarío glanced back. The jaegers were bayoneting M'Brae necks, trampling bodies into the mud. They screamed in vain surrender. It was Cacarajícara all over again. This was no place for him. He caught up to Ypriána. "Now'd be a very good time," he said. He reached for the medallion.

"¡Ahora! ¡Adelante!" The jaegers were gaining.

She glared at him incredulously. He said, "Then I'll be on my way."

"Get ready," she said. "We're meant to do this."

"But I—"

"Awake! Awake!" she bellowed aloud as they crashed through the trees to the sleepy village. "Get moving!" she shouted, over and over, calling through windows and rapping on walls. Hilarión kept quiet. He had no business being here.

Listless faces peeked from doorways. The eyes that met them seemed carefree. "Open your ears!" Ypriána cried. "Run, or you'll roast on phéa-sjant spits!"

The woodlands shook with the clamor of war. The people broke wildly, running for cover, grasping whatever wares they could snatch. "Leave it all behind," she said. But the people went on gathering.

She called to mothers, barely dressed, infants clutched to their breasts. She shouted to farmers, shoes unlaced, picking through baseboards for eggs. She splashed across a shallow creek, warning anglers, scaring fish. Those who were ready she pushed ahead, those who were speedy she sent for the sluggish, those who resisted she pulled from their doorways, and those who hid she found. Hilarión lurked a step behind: she was a wildling with a death wish. One errant Mauser ball and the medallion was his. She said to him, "Do something."

"Give me what you promised."

She grunted scornfully and charged. The medallion jingled inside her collar. If he could only get to her back when she wasn't looking—

"¡Adelante!"

The jaegers railed, the highlands groaned: grinding engines, braying beasts, the squealing wheels of cannon being hauled to key terrain. The battlefield was taking shape, the enemy advancing.

"¡Ahora!"

From every corner M'Brae streamed, saddled with rations and tools, tramping in haste like stampeding cattle, in defiance of their elders' pleas for orderly withdrawal. Through the hills rang martial voices, the strains of a deathly duet: jaegers from the north and east, Mambíses to the west, jealous masters and defiant rebels, daring each the other to strike. Above the clamor, Phellhe's voice cried, "This way to Golgaj!" He pointed west.

"Not that way," Ypriána said. "East, between the hillocks."

' The people scampered helter-skelter, some with Phellhe and some with her. Phellhe had foreseen everything. *The Butcher will raze M'Brae-dah,* he'd said. *He'll kill everything inside of ten miles.* To linger would be suicide.

Hilaríon peered across the village. To the south, the downs rolled wide and empty. He could cut across them, turn the enemy's flank before they even stepped from the woods. Then he'd make for the Eastbound Road, and La Habana—and freedom. But he wasn't leaving empty-handed.

Ypriána kept on shouting. She crossed through the village square, then slowed. Hilaríon drew his blade. Ypriána dropped to lift a child. He drove the handle towards her head. She coolly leaned aside—

"¡Disparen!"

Gunners bellowed, highlands roared: a monstrous demon, belching flame. Fire, like Judgment, rained from the north. Cannon exhaled their lethal barrage, shaking the bedrock, scattering shot, and razing the courtyards and rooftops to cinders. The earth beneath Hilaríon heaved, the village collapsing, falling to ash. Above the flames rose M'Brae voices: warning, wailing, begging, then... silence. No two were alike, but their ends had been the same.

Then it stopped. He opened his eyes. The streets were strewn with scattered limbs. The living and dying screamed in anguish, fathers for daughters, sons for mothers, friends for friends and lovers.

"¡Ahora! ¡Avanza... ahora!"

From the northern slopes and southern woods, the jaegers streamed onto the downs. From the hills to the west the Mambí guns answered, firing into the enemy's flanks.

Ypriána glowered down at him. "If what you still want's a prize, Guamá, our time together won't be long."

"But I told you. I'm not—"

"Choose your words well, thief. You're balls-deep already. You're either priceless or worthless to me." She waved her blade eastward. "Now there's no other way. To the place between the hillocks, now!" She vanished past the smoke.

Hilarión fumed. The way to the south was blocked by the jaegers. The fire from the western slopes would thresh them if they made for Golgaj. The vise was grinding closed. There was only one way out. Moments more and there'd be no escape. But better alive with her than dead on the way to the Eastbound Road—

"Help," came a faint voice. "Help me."

Hilarión looked down. From beneath the rubble, a grisly assortment of arms reached out. He retched in his throat. The last time so many had reached for him, at Cacarajícara, he'd—

"Get up!" he cried, "Follow me!" He drew an old man to his feet and grabbed each reaching hand in turn, pulling them from the wreckage. "This way!" They charged eastwards through swirling ash, pushing and pulling survivors along.

From the west came the crackle of Mambí rifles. Balls broke the sooty air in sheets. At his feet more M'Brae fell, ripped by the breath of indifferent metal. The jaegers laughed, not far behind, prodding the dead and the dying. Their voices grew louder, their threats bloodier.

"¡Tasajéenlos! ¡Destrípenlos como conejos!"

Hilarión hurried the people onward, out of the smoldering ruins.

A murky fog embalmed the downs, masking the stirrings of battle: jaegers to the north and south, readying ranks, emplacing Maxim guns, loading rifles, sharpening bayonets. He looked at the quivering M'Brae: elders, children, one mother with child. They would chance the downs now or die in the crossfire.

Above the fog, the twin hillocks loomed. "It isn't far," Hilarión said. He took the nearest M'Brae hands. They whimpered and grabbed for their loved ones. "Stay together," he said, "and don't stop." He lowered his head and lurched through the fog.

They ran ahead with arms entwined. The mist obscured the way. The din of jaegers echoed around them. Children toppled, mothers stumbled, and fathers slowed to catch their breath. But Hilaríon hurried them on, "Keep going."

The elders fell back. He raced to the rear. Ahead, the hilltops rose higher. "Almost there," he said, and pushed the stragglers forward.

The mists began to lift away, burned in the morning sun. He could see them now: Mambíses dug into the western slopes, jaegers massing for a charge. Their guidons skewered the morning sky, their war-cries split the air.

"¡Los caballos! ¡Adelante!"

A wave of horsemen charged from the south. The thunder of hoof-beats rattled his bones. From the heights came the grinding of Mambí guns, spitting fire into enemy lines. Balls whistled past his ears. They'd be trampled if they ran too slowly, shot to pieces if they stopped.

"Run to the hillocks!" Hilaríon shouted. The M'Brae raced past him. The sky grew black with dust.

"¡Adelante!"

From the south the thunder swelled: warhorses snorting, gnashing their bits, their heavy stench thick on the driving wind.

"¡Adelante!"

The M'Brae scrambled from the field. The horsemen drew their swords. The bestial torrent broke all around: horses roaring, riders cursing, taut legs of chargers whirring like scythes. He spun around, then back; then back the other way and fell. The jaegers swung above his head. Hoof-beats pounded the ground by his hands. He'd be trampled to death where he lay—

"Hilaríon!" Ypriána winched him away from the hooves and hurried him into the trees.

The people charged uphill. Ypriána raced ahead. He ran behind them, guarding their rear. The twin hillocks soared above, like tidal waves of limestone. The trees grew close together. Even in the dappled morning the woods loomed dark and ominous, like the bones of a ruined cathedral.

"¡Tiren!"

The roaring of cannons rang from the north. The trees beside them burst in flames. The rocky ledges high above blew wide in stony showers. The pungent smoke stung his eyes. "Keep going," Ypriána said.

The earth swelled upwards into a mound. Cut into the mound was a cave. Its mouth was cemented by boulders. She looked at Hilaríon and said, "Now what?"

"We need to reach Golgaj," Phellhe said. "We wait for nightfall, then cut through the woods."

She said, "We need to get inside the cave."

"There *is* no way inside," Phellhe said. "That's just an old legend. There's nothing here. Golgaj is the only way."

"He's wrong," the boy said.

"Shut your mouth, Necío," Phellhe said.

"We both know what's there."

"All you know are your mother's lies."

Necío said, "You know it's the—"

"Don't!"

"—hell's-jaws!" Necío said.

Ypriána said, "The way to the caverns?"

"Yes," the boy said. He ran into the thicket and ripped up a blanket of moss. "Phellhe knows what's there. He's the one who walled it up. But he didn't know about *this*." A hatch yawned from the forest floor. "The side door. My mother called it hell's nostril." He smirked.

The thumping of cannon intensified. The shells screamed towards them, bursting like thunder. The pine straw underfoot took flame. "Get inside," Ypriána said.

A figure leapt from the thicket. "*No más allá,*" he hissed, brandishing twin sabers. Hilaríon's heart slammed into his throat.

It was the Gray Jaeger.

viii.

The people quailed. Hilaríon stood transfixed, turned to stone in the Jaeger's glare. Ypriána raised her blade and said, "Get inside."

The Jaeger lunged. She swung to meet his strike. He somersaulted past her and sliced behind him as he rolled. His blades grazed her legs. She jerked herself forward. The medallion popped outside her shirt. It caught the light of the swelling flames, and shimmered bluish-gold. The Jaeger's spell on Hilaríon shattered, replaced by the medallion's.

She chopped at the Jaeger's back. He sprang backwards and parried the strike. He smacked her blade broadside, into her temple, then rolled it through her legs.

"Inside," Necío said. He hurried the M'Brae into the thicket and down into the hatch. Hilaríon took a tepid step backwards. If the battling titans killed each other, the medallion would be his.

The Jaeger pressed the blade to her crotch. "Puta," he leered, "puedes coger a esta."

She let go her blade and pummeled his ribs. She re-grabbed the blade and hollowed away. The Jaeger hissed. She thrust at his face. He sliced the machete out of her hand. She stumbled backwards, to the ground. The Jaeger crouched above her.

Hilaríon rocked on the balls of his feet. Ypriána was as good as dead, but the prize could still be his. He'd snatch it off her corpse and run. In the highlands and the fog of war, not even the Jaeger could track him.

The Jaeger raised his saber. Ypriána opened her eyes. He plunged his blade toward her gut. She rolled and kicked the backs of his knees. The Jaeger fell to his face.

She leapt to her feet. The Jaeger gave chase. She backed towards the thicket, blade held ready, Hilaríon safely behind her.

Wind stoked the ire of the flaming pine straw. A mad inferno burst around, engulfing the woods on every side. The fire enveloped the Jaeger's body. The whine of incoming metal ripped through the crackling canopy.

She stuffed Hilaríon into the hatch. They dropped through a shaft to a tunnel. A shell burst far overhead. The earthen walls rattled. Flames filled the tunnel, then shriveled to embers, blocking the hatch. All was still. Hilaríon said, "The Jaeger's not dead."

"No thanks to you. If you won't make a stand, at least make a torch." She threw him a branch. He wrapped it in cloth and touched it to the embers. A delicate flame shimmied up from the gloom. She shoved him down the tunnel.

The sweltering heat of burning wood gave way to the cool of the earth. The thrum of chanting rose from the darkness. It wafted in whispers and honeyed hums, then turned into a wan madrigal. "What is that music?" Hilaríon asked.

"Don't talk," she said. "Let him finish."

He rounded a corner. The M'Brae lined the tunnel walls. Their clothing was singed, cheeks smeared with soot, gasping in exhausted panic. He counted nearly twenty heads. His eyes adjusted to the dark. Necío leaned on bended knee, singing,

> "Our sires' yawning chasm spreads
> Parched our glories, myths untold
> And doubt devours my wasted heart
> Prayers unanswered, blood turned cold
> We'll be one in Ahr.
>
> "Envoys of a better land
> In benthic depths, our sires' cry
> Leads me, weary wand'rer, on
> Roused my wonder, by and by
> We'll be one in Ahr."

The song was beautiful, oppressively so, and eerie just the same. It made him think of chances missed. He felt like his soul had sprouted wings, a gossamer shearwater out to sea, bound for golden days—

"Enough!" Phellhe strode from the tunnel and shoved Necío down. "Not while I'm Oíc."

Necío said, "But there's one more verse."

"That blasphemy's forbidden."

"They'll toss upon the Wailing Vale."

"That witchcraft's brought enough pain. M'Brae do not sing." Phellhe shook his fists. "Let me hear one of you sing, just once. Your life would be forfeit, as we decided."

Necío said, "*You* decided."

"All the same. Sunovín, Bolivar, Lanyan, get out of sight." Phellhe pointed up the tunnel. "You too, fool." The boys hung their heads.

Ypriána stopped them. "Stay."

Phellhe said, "They lost the right to be called M'Brae."

"That'll be first to change."

"They broke laws, contribute nothing. I won't live or die beside them. And as for you..." He swiped at Hilaríon. Ypriána shoved Phellhe against the wall as if he was a child. "I saved his life," Phellhe said. "I can take it back."

She said, "He's important."

"He's a thief."

"You're a tyrant. What's more useful where we're going? I only keep things that are useful." She let go his throat and turned to the others. "Divvy what you have... food, rope, water skins. It has to last at least two days." She handed Hilaríon flint and steel. "Keep the torches going." She unfastened a drawstring bag from her waist. She dumped its contents into her palm, cornmeal and dried fishes. She motioned the children to take the food.

Phellhe pushed them away. "Where do you think you're taking us, woman?"

"Seems we have one choice."

Phellhe said, "I have this in hand. We're going to join with the Mambíses, battle from the ramparts like our fathers."

"You'll be overrun in minutes."

"Spoken like a Vujoíe bitch. You left this land and never looked back. I remember you, Ypriána."

Necío gasped, "Ypriána dar Se?" She nodded in acknowledgment.

"Don't think we've forgotten," Phellhe said. "The Ancients' blood is in this soil."

"Yet only one of you speaks their language," she said.

"We don't turn our backs on our home," Phellhe said. "We'll hide in this tunnel until we have a clear escape. We'll make for Golgaj by dark. We'll slip behind their lines to the south, then come up from the east. We'll find our way to safety yet."

"You'll die like rats in a hole," she said. "The village is burned, jaegers hold the highlands. What's to go back to?" She pointed down the tunnel. "This is the only way."

"You'd never get out alive," Phellhe said. "You'd go mad trying. The way was lost."

"No longer." She drew the medallion off her neck. Even in the musty gloom, its contours shimmered gracefully, like starlight off a summer's mist. "Our Vexing Heirloom begins here."

The M'Brae muttered softly. Necío whispered, "My mother was right."

"That story's a lie," Phellhe said. "There is no M'Brae treasure."

"You're wrong," she said, "and this proves it. The treasure belongs to all of us, and so will the trials to claim it."

Necío held out his hand. "May I?" She placed it into his palm. Hilaríon peered closely. It looked as if it had been sliced in two, more like half of a medallion. Along its lower edge was a hole, oval in shape, like the seat for a missing shaft. Its flip side, which he hadn't seen, was carved with writhing serpents. Grotesque or not, it would still fetch a fortune. Necío said, "There's writing, in the Ancients' tongue." He read aloud,

"Where Seven Angels dance on high
Ere pilgrims' path confound their sight
Their birth thus writ in flood and stone
Your Vexing Heirloom called to light."

He handed it back. "What's it mean?"

She answered, "I don't know."

Phellhe scoffed, "You don't know? How can you think we'd follow you?"

"I said *I* don't know. But luckily, one of us does." She looked at Hilaríon. "I take it you've all met Guamá?"

ix.

Hilaríon scanned their faces. The M'Brae were staring with searching eyes. "Me?"

"Who solved the Seven Angels?" she said.

"That was a lucky—" He bit off the word *guess*. He was only alive as long as he was useful.

"The treasure might not be far," she said. "It might be around the next bend. But not just anyone can find it. What were you saying... a lucky what?"

He remembered her blades crossed under his throat. "It was, um... lucky I remembered in time," he said. "The Seven Angels, of course. But as for the rest of it—"

"He's a hilldevil," Phellhe said. "He was tracking you, to steal our medallion."

"*Your* medallion?"

"Better ours than his," Phellhe said. "He'd have killed you and now you vouch for him?"

"I vouch for what he knows," she said, "and what he's going to do. I have it on good counsel. Only he can find the way. If you trust me—"

"We don't. And I'll never trust a hilldevil. The phéa-sjant can't stay forever. We'll wait until they leave. Then we'll go back."

"They won't leave," she said. "You'll wait 'til kingdom come. Make your choices now. Grisly deaths on jaeger spikes, or follow me to safety. The caverns are the only way out. Treasure or none, whatever's on the other side, it will be better than rotting in Golgaj."

"Not for all the world," Phellhe said. He started up the tunnel. Chropher and Unish followed Phellhe. The others stood fast. He looked them over, growling, "*Not for all the world.*"

The cavern fell silent, save for the dribbling of water on stone.

The people fixed their eyes on the ground. No one moved an inch. Ypriána seemed as self-assured as ever.

Necío stepped from the wall. "Not even my mother found the medallion."

"To hell with your lying mother, fool," Phellhe said. "If she'd cared about M'Brae-dah, she'd have drowned herself before you were born. She'd have given you a decent name."

Necío looked like he wanted to cry. He pointed towards the hell's-jaws. "You all know where that way leads. You all know where it ends." He stepped to Hilaríon's side. Aryei quivered and followed along.

The silence intensified. A mouse scurried between their feet, then disappeared into the darkness. An adult woman and tiny girl each took tentative steps from the wall. "Hetta and Mabba?" Necío said.

Hetta looked at Phellhe and said, "There's nothing for us here." She stepped beside Hilaríon, pulling little Mabba along.

A freckled, chestnut-maned woman and a well-built man followed. "Jacinda and Hrama," Necío said. "Good."

Unish stepped away from Phellhe and stood beside Jacinda. The rest of the people looked at Ypriána. Then they looked at Hilaríon. Some of them grumbled and some of them whispered. At length, they looked at Phellhe. Then they all fell silent again. And then they raised their heads. One by one they stepped from the wall. They gathered behind Hilaríon. Chropher dropped his eyes to the ground and scurried to the others' side.

Phellhe said, "What will it take to make you see? Still, this might be for the best. I'll let you learn for yourselves." He fell in.

"Keep in pairs, or threes," Ypriána said. "No one walks alone. No outcasts anymore." She stepped behind Hilaríon and gave his back a hearty shove. "On to golden days."

Hilaríon stumbled when she pushed. What in the world was he doing? But there was no use arguing now. He'd done this to himself. He stepped off down the passage. The people followed close behind.

The torchlight flickered in the gloom. Its flames cast spindly shadows about, dancing like imps in perdition. His eyes darted back and forth, from the path to the people and back again, deeper and deeper into the earth. The walls bore crumbling slivers of paint, relics of some masterwork, long forgotten down the years. The stillness of the stolid air was broken only by scuttling roaches or wayward bats above their heads. They stopped to make more torches, but the thin air grew only colder.

Time leached away like stagnant rain into sodden earth. Ypriána guarded the rear, pacing backwards, blade aloft. The children kept to the center. Phellhe walked with the elders, watching Hilaríon with hawkish glare. Necío straggled along on the flanks, plucking fish from cockpit pools or poking drowsy bats from eaves.

The ground began to slope down ahead, giving a sensation of falling. The tunnel tapered, then dropped away. The air grew warmer, laced with mist. Droplets pooled on the torches. At the incline's end the tunnel gaped high into a soaring chamber. Necío said, "Where are we?"

Hilaríon raised his torch. The chamber was wide and perfectly round. The walls were smooth, like glass. The ceiling—if there was a ceiling—soared so high into darkness above he couldn't even see it. There were no other tunnels or doorways. "Now what, thief?" Phellhe said.

"We'll rest," Ypriána said. "Douse all but one of the lights."

Phellhe grumbled and led the people into camp. Unish put out the torches. An eerie glow, like a hunter's moon, spread across the chamber. The M'Brae sprawled along the stone. In no time they were snoring.

Hilaríon yawned. He'd forgotten how tired he was. He hadn't slept in days. He let his head fall to his chest. Then something poked him. "Get up."

He opened a heavy eye. "Huh?"

Ypriána nudged him. "Up."

"I'm tired."

"I'm more tired."

He groaned, "It can wait." She yanked him to his feet. He shoved her. "What do you want?"

"Every minute we're sitting," she said, "they get closer to siding with Phellhe. Men turn on you out of fear. They'll turn faster out of boredom." She pushed him towards the far wall. "Get us out of here."

"Sure, I'll just chew through this rock."

"Bon appétit."

"Woman! I don't know the way."

"You'll find it, or you're not who I think."

"I already told you I'm not. I'm—" He bit his tongue. He'd lied his way into this bind. The truth would only waste his breath.

She held the medallion in front of his face. "*Where Seven Angels dance on high, Ere pilgrims' path confound their sight, Their birth thus writ in flood and stone—*"

"*Your Vexing Heirloom called to light.* I listened."

"Splendid. Thirty minutes." She lay down with the others. In moments she was sleeping.

He walked to the far side of the chamber. He ran his hands along the stones. A disguised doorway? A false wall? Some hidden mechanism to show the way on? He paced around the chamber once, then back around again. There was nothing. They were trapped in a cell of rock.

In the center was an outcropping. He climbed atop to sit. He ran his fingers through his hair. It was still caked thick with ashes, the scatter of M'Brae-dah. Why hadn't he slit her throat when he could? He should have been in the Towns, sprawled among the plushest whores, sleeping off the best night of his life. For one thrilling, brilliant moment, the Devils Three had been real. He almost missed Montez and Grijalva. How did it slip away? "How did this all begin?" he said.

A timid voice behind him said, "It all began with the sea."

He turned. Necío stood there, blushing. Hilaríon said, "The what?"

"The sea," Necío said. "You asked how it all began. In the beginning, there was only the sea—the raging tempest, swirling gales. And the sea swelled, and spread, and filled the timeless void."

"Huh?"

Necío drew closer. "But then the sea gave form to its thoughts, and from its depths came life—the towering trees of the forest and beetling bugs of the ground, the soaring terns astride the winds and the scuttling skinks of the underbrush. And they thrived, and grew, and the world was born.

"But when the first man clambered from the churning tides, he was the same as any other—"

"That's plenty." He had no time for treacly creation myths. "Skip to the part where they get through the tunnels, preferably with the gold."

"No one said the treasure is gold. And only you know the way."

"And if I can't remember?"

Necío's smile faded. "You wouldn't be the first. No one knows the truth anymore. We were a great people once, long ago. My mother taught me all she knew. But even she didn't know everything."

"I'm not one of you," he said. An awkward hush descended. Necío stared at him blankly. Phellhe slouched against the far wall, snoring. Hilaríon pointed and said, "He doesn't like us much, does he?"

Necío said, "He's afraid. This isn't the first time someone's gone for the treasure. It isn't even the first time for Phellhe."

"Could have fooled me."

"It happened twenty-five years ago. The Mambíses and phéasjant had gone to war. The fighting started in the east, but surely in time the fires crept westward. The M'Brae had to choose. Would we stay and fight, or seek refuge to someday return? Or would we scatter to the winds? For days on end they talked, and debated, and compromised, and argued, but in the end they couldn't decide."

"Imagine that," Hilaríon said. He had less time for history than myth. Myth, at least, was good for drinking.

Necío said, "It isn't a joke. You really ought to listen."

Hilaríon leaned back. There was nothing to do *but* listen.

Necío went on, "Fear fell upon us as never before. The strong attacked the weak. The weak ganged up against the strong. Neighbors turned against neighbors, stealing and killing for any advantage.

It seemed as if M'Brae-dah would destroy itself long before the phéa-sjant could.

"Out of this chaos two leaders arose. The first was Bollísh, our greatest fighter. The second was Gnath, our greatest bard." He drew a forlorn breath. "Bollísh and Gnath were my father and mother. And their right-hand man was Phellhe.

"Bollísh and Gnath promised better days, what the people longed to hear. They swore they could find the Ancients' treasure. They tore M'Brae-dah to its roots, searching. All the while, the phéa-sjant marched, closer and closer each day. The people began to doubt Gnath and Bollísh. Maybe they started to doubt themselves.

"So Bollísh and Gnath turned against each another. My mother was certain the treasure lay beneath M'Brae-dah. My father was certain it lay somewhere else… beside a white lake, I'd been told. M'Brae-dah splintered in three groups—Bollísh's, Gnath's, and those who held with neither. Gnath and Phellhe searched inside M'Brae-dah. Bollísh and his faithful struck out to the north. I was just a baby. I've never seen my father since.

"But that was not the end. The phéa-sjant came to M'Brae-dah as feared, burning whatever stood in their way. That's when Phellhe disavowed Gnath and forged an alliance with the Mambíses. With their help he saved many M'Brae lives, but not his father or brothers. They all fell to phéa-sjant guns. Weak and unprepared, our suffering was abysmal. Between starvation, torment and torture…" His eyes welled. "There was nothing anyone could have done. The soul of M'Brae-dah was cut from its body. I have to live with that shame." His eyes brightened. "But now, thanks to you, those wounds might be healed."

Necío was guileless. Hilaríon said, "Don't count on it."

"She has the medallion. You both saved our lives. We never lost hope this day would come. I trust you, Guamá. You got us this far."

"That's Hilaríon. My name."

"Call me Necío. Just don't call me—"

"Fool?"

He scowled. "We'll see about that." He trudged off towards the others.

Hilaríon sat alone. He ground his teeth and wrung his hands. He had no business on this death march. The rivers of treasure were only a myth. He wasn't who Ypriána thought. The Seven Angels had been a good guess, but he didn't know the way on. In her heart, he knew, she knew he didn't, either. The medallion was the only way. He tried to picture the life it would furnish, in some far-flung corner of the globe, where M'Brae-dah, Phellhe, and Ypriána would fade in time to memories. That world was so close he could taste its nectar, feel its caress on his cheek. His path shined brutally clear. He had only to take the medallion.

He crept towards Ypriána. The prize lay just inside her shirt. He'd snatch it like the thief he was. He'd head through the hell's-jaws, out of the hillocks, and past the jaegers' lines to the east. He drew his blade: he meant it this time. He'd been soft for long enough.

The medallion shimmered. In the torchlight it looked like the serpents were squirming. His fingers closed around it and squeezed. He was off to golden days—

"What?" His boots sloshed in liquid. He pulled away. Water was pooling around his feet.

Ypriána opened her eyes. "Well?" she said and looked at her arms. They were dripping wet.

One by one the M'Brae rose. Their clothes were soaked with water. Above their groans, he could hear something whispering, like the breath of a giant serpent.

He looked at the cavern walls. Lithe cascades were trickling down them, gathering speed. The chamber was filling with mist. It was almost as if they'd fallen, to the bottom of a—

"Necío," Hilaríon said. "That story you started to tell me. What did the people do first?"

Necío was groggy. "Do... first?"

He shook the boy. "Where did the first people come from?"

Necío said, "From the ocean. They clambered from the churning tides. That's how the M'Brae race came to be."

Hilaríon's mind raced. Necío's story. The cryptic inscription, *Their birth thus writ in flood and stone.* It'd been jargon just minutes ago. Now it all made sense.

He turned to Ypriána. "I know how to pass the tunnels," he said.

The stone trembled. The cavern walls groaned. The churning tides were coming.

x.

"Take cover," Phellhe said. "In the tunnel."

"No," Hilaríon said. "Get to the center and hold your breath."

"We'll drown."

"We'll drown in the tunnel." He pointed up. "We're at the bottom of a well."

The hiss of the oncoming rush grew louder. The people took hold of each other's hands. They fumbled towards the outcropping. Phellhe grabbed Hilaríon's cloak at his neck. "I won't warn you again, thief. Send them—"

"Up is the only way out." A foamy jet spewed from the tunnel. It knocked the people against the wall. A thunderous deluge spilled from the ceiling. With a roar it swamped the outcropping, and scattered the people into the flood. "We have to swim," he shouted. "We have to clamber from the churning tides!"

The waves broke over Hilaríon's back. They knocked him from Phellhe's grasp. They spun Phellhe about and carried him off.

The flood filled the cavern and swirled as it rose. It lashed against Hilaríon's face. The M'Brae shrieked and flailed their arms. He grabbed at whomever he brushed against. But the current only scattered them more.

Hilaríon wiped the foam from his eyes. The stone of the well-walls flickered red. Unish had managed to salvage a torch and held it high, ablaze. The current throttled the people upwards. Hilaríon threw his head back. They'd be smashed against the ceiling, unless—

"Raise your torch!" he said. "At the walls!" The light revealed a hidden ledge, above, just out of reach. He pointed. "There!" His throat filled with froth. The currents sucked him down. He felt himself trundling into the depths. He pumped his arms against his sides, then thrust his head to the surface again.

Ypriána had already climbed the ledge. She winched Phellhe up behind her. The people took their outstretched hands. The able-bodied hoisted themselves, then turned to help the others. Hilaríon treaded the whirling currents. He couldn't fight the flood much longer. He reached for Ypriána's hand. "Help them," she said, "behind you."

He turned. Chay and Fenn were drowning.

He swam to the men. Their eyes were rolling into their heads, mouths frothing over with foam as they floundered. He wrapped his arms around their chests. The currents swirled faster. The ceiling was close enough to touch. He flung the men towards Ypriána. The currents twisted them back to him.

He reached a second time. The men thrashed in the smothering tide. Hilaríon's thighs and forearms burned. The water clogged his nose. His grip went slack, his fingers loosened. The bodies drifted out of his grasp. Chay and Fenn were past saving. He had already risked enough.

A wall of water rose behind him. The two men vanished inside it. Hilaríon reached for Ypriána's arm. She dived past him into the flood.

The water slammed across the ledge and crashed across his body. It cracked his head against the stone. For a moment the world went silent, save for ringing in his ears. Then he heard Ypriána say, "Guamá, on your feet."

He concentrated on her voice. It sounded soothing, as it had in the ruins. Two sets of arms helped him onto his feet, then dragged him down a passage. One was Ypriána's, the other Chay's. Hilaríon felt a nibble of guilt. He'd left Chay for dead.

Ahead, the M'Brae scrambled fast, a shrieking mass of bodies. The water barreled close behind. It sent stones spinning towards their faces and snapping at their heels. The tunnel pitched, then leveled, then climbed. The M'Brae staggered up the slope. Hilaríon threw his body down and hacked the water from his lungs. The floodwaters roared, then leveled off, then hissed their final breath.

Hilaríon raised his head. They were all inside another chamber, barely tall enough for them to stand. Phellhe crouched in the opposite corner. Necío tended a sobbing Mabba. Past the people the chamber widened and disappeared in darkness. From the tunnels, the rumble of draining tides echoed. There was no sign of Fenn. Hilaríon leaned in Ypriána's ear and said, "And the other man?"

She shook her head, then said for all to hear, "You were brave to go back for him, Guamá. It's to your credit, but we have to keep moving."

The nibble of guilt turned into a sting.

"This has gone far enough," Phellhe said. "A man's drowned."

Necío said, "We'd all be drowned if not for Guamá—er, Hilaríon."

"We'd all be alive if we'd done what I said. It's madness to go any further. We'll wait until the passage is safe, then go back the way we came."

"There *is* no back," Hilaríon said. "You want to chance those waters again?" No one spoke a single word, but all eyes turned to him. Their gazes bore assurance he'd know what to do. "I didn't think so," he said.

Deep within the inky dark, something glittered violet. Hilaríon took the torch from Unish and crept off towards the dancing light. The people parted. The shadows spread. The torchlight, even, seemed to fade. The echoes of his footsteps jumped, then bounced into the distance. The people followed close behind. Something big loomed up ahead. He raised the torch above his head.

A metallic glow broke all around. The people gasped. He staggered back. Before them soared a silver wall. Bored through it were three gold-rimmed portals, each as wide as two men stood tall. Through each portal, a geode-encrusted tunnel led off into the distant dark: one left, one right, and one straight ahead. The tunnels glittered warm, rich purple, like royal corridors. Necío squealed, "The treasure!" He climbed into a portal—

"Wait." Hilaríon grabbed him. Something felt wrong. He rubbed his hand along the wall. Silver flaked off on his palm. It was only painted rock. "Not treasure."

Necío was crestfallen. "What, then?"

He looked the tunnels over. Each seemed as good a path as the others. But he'd been a tracker long enough. There was always a right way, and a wrong. "A choice."

"Which one?" Phellhe said.

He scanned them left to right, then back. *"Ere pilgrims' path confound their sight... Necío, what happened after the churning tides?"*

"We were the same as any creature," Necío said. "Our eyes were filled with vile dust, our mouths were filled with lies, our bitter days turned endless night. We crawled as beasts along the ground. Or so the story goes."

Hilaríon lowered the torch underfoot. Below the center portal spread a crevice in the floor. He knelt for a better look. The crevice was shaped like a crooked half-moon. It was just wide enough for a man to fit. "This is the way," Hilaríon said.

Necío peered inside. "Are you sure?"

"No."

Ypriána turned her head. Her eyes caught the torchlight and threw it back into his. "I'm sure," he said, "we crawl from here."

Phellhe said, "I'll chance the portals."

"The portals are not the way."

"And you know that how, hilldevil?" Hilaríon bit his tongue. Phellhe pulled himself into the center portal. "Serves you well, Guamá, worm that you are. You can squirm in there for days. We'll be waiting on the other—"

Ypriána yanked him back. She tossed a stone through the portal. It skipped along the corridor, echoing fainter. Its skittering shadow disappeared. Then it stopped altogether.

A furious groan, like tree trunks splitting, cracked across the chamber. A blast of dust burst in their faces. The corridor crumbled in a shower of geodes, scattering into an abyss. Where it had been was now but a shaft of air. "Hear that?" Ypriána said. "That's the sound of an old world dying, and a new one being born. Leaders listen, leaders serve. And if they have to, leaders crawl. We go as one or not at all."

Phellhe looked away, then stepped towards the crevice. She

stopped him. "We don't know how narrow it gets. I don't want you clogging it. I'll go first." She slipped head-first inside. The M'Brae clustered at its mouth, watching her sidle out of sight.

Hilarión looked the people over. He'd been trapped in rock before. He'd tracked runaway slaves through caves with his aunt. He remembered the maddening torment. This would be torture for most of the M'Brae. The going would be slow and painful. For all they knew, it was a blind alley. But no one was making them do it.

Moments passed in silence. Then Ypriána's voice came, "Send them on."

Hilarión pushed the others aside, then dropped inside. "Good luck—"

He stopped. He could tell by their vacant stares, not one of them knew what to do. He said, "Like this," and demonstrated. "Hands and knees, look straight ahead." They stared, flummoxed. He sighed, "Alright." He hoisted himself out. He broke sticks off the torch and passed them out. "Tear a swatch off your clothes to burn. Wrap it on the stick."

Necío touched his stick to the flame, then dropped inside the crevice. Chropher and Aryei followed suit. Their legs, then feet, disappeared. Their grunts echoed through the stone.

He counted a minute between each departure: two children, Mabba and Revaj, one elder named Wresh, then the healthy youths and adults. He helped them into their crouches, then lit each of their miniscule torches. He patted the tops of their heads as they crawled. Only high spirits would carry them through—the sooner to flee from these miserable caves and on to La Habana.

A flush-faced woman tottered his way. By the look of her heaving belly, she was about seven months pregnant. "What if I can't fit?"

"Stay behind, I guess," he said.

"Her father," she stammered, clutching her belly. "I can't lose them both." She crouched—

"Wait." He stopped her. He'd helped his share of pregnant Mambíses. They needed a gentler hand and a less acrid mouth. "Tell me your name."

She sobbed, "Maith."

"Take this, Maith." He took off his cloak and wrung it of water, and wrapped it around her body. "That'll keep her safe. Slide on your back so you don't scrape your belly." He lowered her into the crevice. She shined a grateful smile.

The people squeezed ahead. The torch burned down to half its size. The chamber emptied. Then there was only one M'Brae left.

Phellhe.

In the ghostly light he seemed even bigger, a mythical giant sprung from stone. "Now, what would happen," Phellhe said, "if you didn't make it through?"

Hilaríon threw him a flame stick. "You'd never see daylight again."

Phellhe laughed, "Already, it's beginning. You may be the quickest yet." He snuffed the flame against his palm.

"Bet on it," Hilaríon said. He was always the quickest, at everything.

"Quickest to succumb," Phellhe said. "To think you're more than you are. We've all had to dance with that devilry once. The treasure casts a spell. It chokes you with hubris, the closer you *think* you're getting. Most learn quickly it's only a myth. Others take longer. Some never learn."

"Which were you?"

"I was full of that bile, once. It had to be smoked from me, whole." He drew up his shirt. His flesh was melted in rubbery knots.

He'd underestimated Phellhe. He wasn't the foolhardy oaf he'd seemed. He handed him another stick. "I just want to get to the other side."

"Whether or not you believe me," Phellhe said, "I want that for you, too. In here, you'd die a prophet. They'd always wonder what could have been. But out there, starving and treasure-less, all you'd ever be is a thief." Phellhe dropped inside and crawled away.

The torch crackled in the musty air. He could still escape. He could wait for the water to come again, then ride it down the well. Then he'd run. And run. And run. And yet...

Rivers of treasure. He stared at the geodes and gold-rimmed

portals. They looked like treasure should have looked, even if they were doorways to death. Someone had gone to very great lengths to build a cunning gauntlet, or it was his imagination. Either way, Ypriána had the medallion. That would be treasure enough.

He squirmed head-first into the crevice. The rock clamped hard around him. He dragged himself ahead by his elbows, pushing along with the tips of his toes. His every lurch loosed a spatter of dust.

The passage banked right, then left, then twisted backwards under itself. He cradled what was left of the torch, then rolled onto his back. To hold it beneath him further risked burns, or accidentally snuffing it out. He drove his heels against the walls and guided his body along with his shoulders. The passage flattened. He held the flame closer. Ashes scattered along his neck—

"*What?*" Through tinkling pebbles, he could swear he'd heard something close behind: a hollow rasp, like a serpent slithering through dead leaves. "Hello?" He held his breath.

Silence.

He was exhausted and delirious. It had to have been ringing in his ears, or at worst an echo.

He heaved onward. The torchlight wavered. The passage narrowed further. Its fangs nibbled the crown of his skull. For Phellhe, the passage must have been nothing short of perdition. He sneered silently to himself, "Serves that oaf right—"

A bony hand wrapped round his foot. A telltale voice sliced from the dark. "*Cerca,*" the foul voice hissed, "*Cerca... o lejos?*"

The Gray Jaeger was upon him.

xi.

The passage clenched him in its jaws. He couldn't move or breathe. He fumbled the dying torch in his hands. It fell to his chest in cinders, momentarily bathing the passage in light. From the gloom, the Jaeger leered. His scar, like a worm, seemed to writhe in the glow of the embers before they died.

The passage fell black again. Hilarion lurched—

No! He stopped himself. The Jaeger would be counting on that. To open up space was the worst he could do. He'd be giving his enemy room to strike.

The Jaeger slithered closer. Hilarion could hear his breath. His hand crept up Hilarion's leg and curled around his knee. His other hand clutched Hilarion's ankle. His viperine panting grew louder and louder. The sound of metal scraping stone came from near the Jaeger's hips. Hilarion felt a surge of hope. The Jaeger hadn't drawn his blade. He'd entered the fissure with it sheathed and was waiting for his quarry to flee. For Hilarion, there was still a way out. The Jaeger would never foresee such boldness.

He cinched himself rigid, then held his breath, waiting. The Jaeger's grip tightened. He dug his thumb into the soft beneath Hilarion's knee. Hilarion made no sound. The Jaeger adjusted his weakening grip. His movements felt rushed, his fumblings panicked. He'd expected—and needed—Hilarion to move. Hilarion clenched his lip in his teeth. Any second—

The Jaeger let go. Hilarion whipped his legs apart and hurled himself into the Jaeger. His legs slid past the Jaeger's arms. He grabbed the Jaeger's wrists with his hands. He locked his ankles together. He closed his calves like a vise around the Jaeger's neck.

The Jaeger struggled backwards. He sank his teeth in Hilarion's thigh. The pain welled deep but Hilarion only clamped his knees closer, and dug his thumbs in the Jaeger's wrists. His hands and thighs burned with fatigue. But he'd break the bastard's neck if he had to, or he'd die where he lay. At least his corpse would block the passage, and save the other M'Brae.

The Jaeger gasped, releasing his jaws. He tried to roll to his side. His blade ground against rock. He heaved a shoulder into Hilaríon's crotch. Dust fell into Hilaríon's face. He tucked his chin into his shoulders, and rolled his head to the side. The crags of the passage bit through his flesh and ripped his sodden clothing. But his body slid ahead. The Jaeger was driving him out.

The passage banked upwards. The Jaeger drove his legs all the harder. They trundled forward, faster. The passage widened, then leveled off. He threw his head back. A faint light was shining ahead of him. The others had to be nearby.

The Jaeger stopped. Hilaríon tensed. The Jaeger had to have seen the light, too. It was coming from a fissure above them, only a few feet away. He could break his hold and try to flee. But the passage had widened. The Jaeger could unsheath his blade and still have room to strike.

"*Cerca,*" the Jaeger hissed, "*Cerca... o lejos?*"

The words bit deep, to places unspoken, same as they'd done when first he'd been asked. "*Días dorados,*" Hilaríon said.

"No habrá fortuna que te salve," the Jaeger replied. "No te librarás de mí—"

"*But I will,*" rang Ypriána's voice. Her hands reached through the fissure above and grabbed Hilaríon's shoulders. He slackened his legs. His body went limp. She yanked him out of the passage.

Open air swirled. She pulled him standing inside a cavern, wide and tapering into a tunnel. Necío ushered them aside. Phellhe, helped by the M'Brae men, strained against a ponderous boulder, scraping along the cavern floor. With a final roar, they heaved the boulder into the fissure, sealing the Jaeger inside. "Too bad you're not still in there, Guamá," Phellhe said.

"Last one through," Hilaríon said. "Perils of leadership—"

"Quiet!" Necío said. Faint tapping came from inside the passage. The Jaeger had started to chisel the stone.

The M'Brae fretted and whimpered, then streamed into the tunnel. Ypriána, Phellhe, and Hilarión stood. They waited for the others to flee, then broke and ran themselves.

The ground sloped downwards. The sound of rushing water rose. The tunnel walls dampened. Ahead, the fleeing people shrieked. Hilarión tumbled into a chute. It felt like polished stone, or glass. It plunged down into darkness.

Water gushed from cracks in the walls. Hilarión flopped onto his back. A veil of mist engulfed his body as he gathered speed. Up ahead, he could see the M'Brae clustered on top of a wedge-shaped platform, thrust into the open shaft of another massive well. A sound, like gurgling stew, rumbled on.

Necío held out his hands. "Slow down!"

Hilarión, with Ypriána and Phellhe, slid onto the platform. Like an unmoored hulk heaved off a pier, the platform lurched, then listed. Half the people plopped away into liquid below.

Hilarión looked up. Sunlight was breaking through a ceiling-hole. In the meager light he could see a stony dome arcing over their heads, a rocky trough below them. The trough, like a cauldron, squalled and bubbled. It was filled with stagnant mud. The people thrashed inside. He grabbed Necío. "What happens next?"

Necío dithered. "Happens... next?"

"The story."

"Story?"

Hilarión shook him. "The creation story!"

Necío's face lit up. "I remember! Our world was—"

The sloppy glugs of mudslides echoed. Necío's mouth moved rapidly, but Hilarión heard nothing. Black glue oozed down from the ceiling, swamping the platform whole. Then through the slurps came Necío's voice, *"Our world was plunged into chaos and filth, until—"*

The platform rolled. Phellhe tumbled off. Hilarión said, "Until what?"

"No time!" Ypriána said, and shoved them off the edge.

Hilarión plopped into the mud. It smelled like decaying fish, filling every nook of his clothes. The platform crashed in the mud behind them and set the mud spinning as it sank. The filthy people thrashed about. The center of the swirling mud plunged, the outer edges rose. The cauldron turned a gathering cyclone.

An overhang loomed above as they rose. The current surged them upwards. Hilarión reached to warn Ypriána, "Look out—!"

Bang! Her head slammed into the overhang.

The current dragged Hilarión down. He flung himself to the surface. Beside him, Ypriána bobbed. He shook her body. She didn't move. She was dead, or out cold. He couldn't tell which. Then the current pitched her back, peeling aside her shirt. Through the pall of fetid mud, it glittered.

The medallion.

He ripped it from her neck with gusto. Golden days, at last, were his. He could almost taste the pungent wines and smell the painted ladies' necks. He could feel the purple, satin robes—

"Hilarión!" Necío cried, "You have to finish this."

He fondled the medallion. "No."

The swirling intensified. The people shrieked louder. Necío floundered at the rim. "You have to lift the darkness."

"I have what I came for."

"Then everyone dies. You have to call the Light!"

Hilarión grabbed a ledge and hoisted himself from the mud. Above him, hewn into the stone, were climbing-rungs for hands. The rungs led up to the luminous ceiling-hole, his path to golden days.

The funnel trough hollowed. The people tumbled deep inside, like flotsam in a swell. Aryei groped for Necío's hand. The currents flung the boy away. Necío pointed to the ceiling and said, "Only you can—"

"I'm not who she thinks," Hilarión said.

"But you *are*. Only you can call the Light. Or else—" He sank.

The funnel belched. The M'Brae flailed. The currents spun them deeper.

The medallion caught the shaft of light. It shimmered like the mighty Nile or twisting Orinoco. La Habana sang its siren song. All he had to do was climb, then scurry through the hole. But through the mire of swirling mud flashed twenty pairs of innocent eyes. He already had enough eyes to reckon with. La Habana could wait a few moments more.

He winched himself upwards. The sunlight grew brighter. The ceiling had not one hole but many. Around a larger, central hole, five pairs of spectral eyes peered out. They belonged to giant, misshapen faces, neither man nor beast, much like the hilltop statues. Each of the faces' eyes was a hole, but there were countless more. Each hole was a different shape: some wide, some long, some narrow slats, and some shaped just like the medallion. He had to set it in one of them. But which?

Did it matter?

He fitted it to the nearest hole. The rock around it clicked. A wave of rotten-smelling mud burst across the trough. The funnel spun faster. The M'Brae shrieked louder.

He pried the medallion from the rock. His odds, at least, were better now. Another one had to be the right choice. He said, "*Where Seven Angels dance on high, ere pilgrims' path confound their sight, their birth thus writ in flood and stone, your Vexing Heirloom called to light...*"

He slammed it into the largest hole. A second gush of mud crashed down. The people railed. The cavern shook. "Hilarión!" Necío cried.

Hilarión repeated it aloud, poring over every word, "*Where Seven Angels dance on high, ere pilgrims' path confound their sight, their birth thus writ in flood and stone, your Vexing Heirloom called to light.*" What was he missing?

Necío said, "Now!"

The funnel bottomed out. "I know!" The mud raged into a furious cyclone. The M'Brae would soon be dashed to their deaths. He had just seconds to figure it out. "*Where Seven Angels dance on high, ere pilgrims' path confound their sight, their birth thus writ in flood and stone, your Vexing Heirloom—*"

He stopped. The eyes: always, it was the eyes. He'd been distracted by them. The face in the center's mouth was parsed, a slot wide enough for the medallion, edgewise. "*Called* to light," he said. He paused.

Had he been meant to do this?

He fitted the medallion. The rock around it clicked. He turned it once, then back. The rock clicked again and released the medallion. The swirling cyclone gathered speed. The cavern heaved and rumbled. The stone around him cracked. The climbing rungs shivered to dust.

He splashed into the cyclone. The ceiling crumbled away. He clutched the medallion and sank in the mud. It oozed in his nose and caked in his eyes. It clogged his gasping mouth. The world turned black, and spun. And spun. And spun...

xii.

The slurping sound of draining mud rumbled far below. The cyclone slowed. The trough leveled off. The spinning stopped altogether. The mud seeped away like sand through a sinkhole. Hilarión hurtled downwards, clasping his nose, his other hand on the medallion. His shoulders smacked bedrock. He flopped to his back. A gush of cold water crashed on his face.

M'Brae voices rose around him, sounding neither harmed nor frightened. They muttered in untrammeled wonder. "Have you ever?" they said. "Can you believe?"

A welcome heat beat on his cheeks. The cauldron of mud had broken away, revealing a golden reticulate web, inlaid with lustrous, crystalline prisms. The afternoon sunlight blazed down through them. The chamber was carved with living images: trees of every size and shape and beasts of every stripe. In the center stood a fountain, capped by statues of fish-faced giants. The words to capture the image escaped him. It was like nothing he'd ever dreamed.

"And the Light burst across our world," Necío said. "Our minds were filled with questions, and the demons shriveled like dust in a void."

Hilarión marveled at its cleverness. *Their birth thus writ in flood and stone.* The M'Brae creation myth had shown the way. The astonished people were beginning to believe. He looked at the brilliant dome again. Maybe he was, too.

His hand pressed something rough. He'd almost forgotten the medallion. And now, it was no longer half. Inserting it into the ceiling slot had joined it to its missing twin. Now it was worth twice as much.

La Habana. It was time.

A tunnel nearby led out to the sunlight. He curled against a mound of rock. The M'Brae went on exploring the chamber, eyes wide in bewilderment. They hadn't thought to look for him, yet.

He dropped to his elbows and crawled from the mound. He peeked: still, no one had seen him. The prize was his for the taking. He shot to his feet and ran for the—

"Off to golden days already?" Ypriána was standing inside the tunnel.

He stopped in place. "How's your head?"

"Lighter than yours. Still think you need a prize?"

He felt no shame. "I did what you wanted. We're through the caverns."

"That's just the beginning."

"For you." He stepped around her.

She moved aside. "I'm not going to take it. But you'll give it back."

"I'm a thief," he said. "I don't give things back."

"You *were* a thief. Now you're one of us."

The hilldevils, once, had said the same. "I'm happy just to be one," he said.

She pointed to Necío. "Boy, read the fountain."

Necío wiped the mud and read,

> "From out the rage of primal flood
> 'Neath Seven Angels' starlit veil
> Through sun-starved pits in hexen gloom
> So come you where begins the trail
> On spine of hills to stagger forth
> 'Cross greenwoods towards the rising day
> Where Lightleaf Grove looms 'midst the pines
> Its seed to reap and hide to flay
> Now nerve to steel and heart to gird
> For hither lies the priceless trove
> Your Vexing Heirloom's fruit at last
> But laced with visions fast uphove."

She beamed, childlike. Necío seemed less sanguine. "Fast uphove?" Hilaríon said, "I have all I need, twice-over now."

"But they don't," she said, "and the Ancients promised them."

"The Ancients were swindlers," Phellhe said. "It's all just vicious lies. How many more have to die so you'll see?"

The faces of M'Brae slaughtered by jaegers and gurgles of drowning Fenn rent his mind. He said, "For once, I'd listen to Phellhe."

"Look around you," she said. "Don't you wonder what comes next?"

"Oblivion comes," Phellhe said. "We're the only ones left. If we die, then what?"

Hilaríon craned his head about. Pines and palmettos, hewn in stone, soared to the heights of the chamber. Trogons and macaws filled the tree branches, while frigate birds soared on invisible updrafts. Porpoises spun through a sun-drenched sea, so lifelike they seemed as if they might burst from the walls and flop to the floor. What *did* come next? He wanted to know.

She leaned into his ear. "Jason, Sinbad... Saint Brendan, even. We would stand among them. And no one's gotten even *this* far."

The tunnel mouth gaped. She wasn't stopping him. He could sense dishonesty like a stench, but she'd meant every word. The medallion was his. He had only to walk away. "Is it worth my life if you're wrong?" he said.

"Was Cuba Libre worth your life... or theirs?" She ran her finger along his nose and around his mouth, as if angrily slashing his flesh. His slaughtered legion was with him, still. Their eyes burned bright as ever.

The M'Brae gathered behind Ypriána. Every eye turned to him. He could feel the bracing weight of their stares. He was back, again, at Cacarajícara—only he wasn't. The M'Brae eyes held sparks of trust. There was no malice, only wonder. It had been long since he'd seen anything like it.

Ypriána held out her palm. "To Lightleaf Grove?" she said.

There was no denying all that had happened. He'd found the Seven Angels. He'd gotten the people into the hell's-jaws. He'd solved churning tides and stony gauntlet, while holding the Gray Jaeger at bay. He'd brought the light from shadow and mud. *Rivers of treasure.* It *had* to be real. He'd while his days in opulence soon. La Habana would be but the start. Then the eyes would truly be gone.

And if the quest turned out to be fake, he could always just steal the medallion.

He hesitated, dithering, quite sure he'd live to regret his decision, then sighed and dropped it into her hand. His hopes congealed to a single word, which he uttered through clenched teeth, "*Yes.*"

She closed her hands around his. "The people will look to me for their lives," she said. "And I will look to you."

She was wild, insane, and full of delusions. But what did it matter? One prize or another would be his soon. "Don't worry."

"I will," she said, "for everyone. You should, too. We go as one or not at all." He looked into her eyes. She'd hold him to his word.

Phellhe said, "This isn't the end. They'll all see soon enough. And I'll be there to gather the pieces, and lead them back to M'Brae-dah."

"M'Brae-dah is wherever the M'Brae are," Ypriána said. "So M'Brae-dah comes with us."

"You can remind them that when they're starving," Phellhe said. He stepped behind the others.

The people wrung muddy filth from their clothes, laughing and joking at the days ahead. They bundled their disheveled locks into braids. They seemed like festive children, already forgetting what they'd just survived. Hilaríon laughed in spite of himself, at how surreal it all really was. How many would die without seeing treasure? The greater that number, the larger his prize. He'd let the farce play out.

They stepped into the open air. Dusk was drawing its fiery veil. To the west, past the hills, rose columns of smoke: the ashes of M'Brae-dah, still swirling on the winds. The medallion shimmered like the sea, twice as radiant as before. He could still feel its splendid weight in his hand. He wouldn't wait to take it again should things not go as planned. He said to Ypriána, "You wouldn't have let me walk off with it, would you?"

She kissed him and said, "You wouldn't have gone."

He hurried the people out of the tunnel, off the bald hilltop and into the pines. He stepped off to follow, then stopped and turned. A sound was coming from inside the cavern. "*Cerca,*" it seemed to hiss, "*Cerca... o lejos?*"

xiii.

They walked by night and rested by day. They bedded down in mossy dales, dipping hands to crystal streams, savoring drink in the heavy heat and cleansing their bodies and clothing of sweat. They shared old tales and bawdy riddles, keeping spirits high. But fear stalked their every step. They could advance neither quickly nor well, harried by age, numbers, and a path already treacherous made worse under cover of dark. But the M'Brae pressed onward, a people in motion, trudging defiantly in danger's face.

Hilarío kept himself at arm's-length. Wresh was taciturn, Graciela mute, and Phellhe couldn't stand to be near him. He kept to the front, keeping their bearings, shadowed by garrulous Necío, who had a story for every occasion. The rank-and-file moved as a mass: Hetta and Mabba with pregnant Maith; Wresh, always wearing an odd, single glove; Graciela, hiding her eyes; and then the boys Aryei, Chropher, and Revaj. The young men Bolivar, Lanyan, Sunovín, Unish, and Chay followed them. Sturdy Jacinda and Hrama held the north flank, the likely direction of danger, and even Phellhe walked the flanks time to time. At the rear like an alpha, alert for attack, ever stalked Ypriána.

The land rolled along like a following sea, heaving high to palm-laced crests, plunging hard to bambooed hollows. The highlands seemed a promised land, their white cascades and swarthy soil roiling with a thousand years of rainfall and sunlight. For fleeting moments, some of them thought, the treasure might as well have been the earth beneath their feet. But the earth was not the treasure, and the land was not their friend, and every step brought them farther from home and closer to mortal peril.

✶ ✶ ✶ ✶

Hilaríon awoke, bleary-eyed and sore, in a bower of mariposas. The sun was sinking into the west. Soon, it'd be time to step off again. They'd been staggering in the hills for weeks, and still no sign of Lightleaf Grove. All the days had seemed to meld to bland, monotonous rote. Were they ever going to find this place? Should he cut his losses and steal the medallion?

The sound of the M'Brae striking camp rustled through the trees. Then he heard another noise: gentle splashing, to the south. He peeked through the bramble. Past a vine-draped outcropping, a mountain spring flowed into a pool. Gloaming had scattered light on the leaves, and painted the limpid water with flame. And Ypriána was bathing there.

She spun through the pool with the poise of a woman at home in her defiant skin, neither graceful nor lithe but sure of herself, like a hardscrabble Nereid. The water seemed to part in homage as she stroked her arms. It trickled along her sinewy back as she slipped from the pool and under the spring. She wrung the water from her hair.

A flame smoldered inside him, and grew. She turned around and said, "Seen enough?"

"I..." He looked down. "I wasn't—"

"Hilaríon," Necío called, "Ypriána, come here."

The water ran along her breasts and pooled around her feet. She stepped into her pants and boots, then pulled on her shirt and cloak. He lied, "I didn't see anything."

She patted his face. "Pity your heart if you had."

They caught up to the others. Necío pointed eastwards. "Look."

Past the scrub and bramble, the highlands dwindled in sprawling plains. From each horizon, north to south, a massive line of trenches ran, bolstered by fortifications. From the plains rose the sounds of endless toil: spades breaking ground, hammers driving spikes, whirring wheels and grinding gears and shouts of weary workers. It looked, and sounded, as if the very war itself had been wrought into a monstrous chain and draped across their path. The Butcher was every inch the fiend the legends said he was. Hilaríon said, "So it *is* true."

Necío said, "What is it?"

"The Butcher's gambit," Hilaríon said, "an armed bulwark to split the island, and trap the Mambíses in Occidente. They call it a *Trocha*."

Necío whispered, "Trocha." He sounded as if he was praying.

"There were rumors," Phellhe said. "Travelers swore they'd seen it rising. I never believed them."

"No one believed it," Hilaríon said. "No one thought it could be done." He peered eastwards, past the Trocha. A shadowy forest rolled to the horizon. Lightleaf Grove was out there, somewhere. The treasure was on the other side.

"Day and night, they told me," Phellhe said, "the phéa-sjant toil—digging, laying tracks, stringing wire, raising towers. It's a monster. It's invincible."

"How invincible could it really be?" Hilaríon said.

"The line runs coast to coast," Phellhe said. "Even where it's least defended it's impregnable. Even birds, they say, don't dare fly above it. It's meant to keep an army from crossing. What makes you think we've a better chance?"

Every moment paused west of the line was a moment that crossing it got less likely. "Plan for an army," Hilaríon said, "a tiny band slips by. They won't be expecting us. And there are bound to be gaps."

"Gaps they'll defend," Ypriána said. She pointed to a knot of lights, where roads and railroad tracks converged. "They're too strong here." To the north, the line disappeared among hills. "Rough terrain gives us an advantage. That's where we'll get across."

"It can't be crossed anywhere," Phellhe said. "We have to turn back."

Hilaríon scanned the horizon. Time was against them: Phellhe would grow bolder, the people more timid, and the treasure would only slip farther away. They'd have to cross forthwith or, as Phellhe wished, slink back to M'Brae-dah. "That'd be leagues of open ground," he said. "Even if we could get there, it'd be a long way south again. Lightleaf Grove is just to the east. We're better crossing here."

"And I thought you were learning," she said. "You're still a work in progress, Guamá."

"Progress towards what?"

"Towards *me*." She waved the people onward. "Keep below the ridgeline."

Phellhe said, "Both of your hands get redder each day."

The M'Brae walked all night. Maith doddered, clutching her belly, trying not to lose her balance. Ypriána helped her along. Hilaríon watched the girl, admiringly. Maith was braver than she knew.

The heights gave way to rolling downs. A ruddy dawn broke in the east. They crossed from the highlands onto the plains. The carnage of war lay all around them: wandering livestock, empty carts, bloated cattle torn by dogs; tobacco hangars burned to ash, smoking in the early light. Normally, they'd have pitched camp by now, but Hilaríon could read Ypriána's eyes. Any time wasted finding a crossing, Phellhe would take advantage of.

They wended past a sugarcane field. The smell of sulfur and flesh hung thickly in the air. In the road lay bodies of a Mambí patrol. Their blood-smeared faces crawled with flies. They were still clutching their rifles. Ypriána halted the column. She said to Hilaríon, "They shouldn't see this."

"No," Phellhe said, "they *need* to see it." He called the people forward. They formed a ring around the bodies. Necío retched. Maith spun away. Phellhe lifted a bloody Mauser ball. "Filthy phéa-sjant," he said. "Don't think this can't still happen to us." He bent over a young man's body and said, "He looks like you, Guamá."

Hilaríon looked at the Mambí. It was almost a year since he'd fled their ranks. He could still feel the drumbeat, the thrill of command; the rush of impending battle. But war had quickly lost its sheen, even if the eyes never let him forget. "It almost *was* me."

Phellhe said, "It still might be."

Hilaríon stifled whatever esteem he held for the dead Mambíses. Somewhere in the distance, but not so far away, the treats of La Habana waited. He could almost smell its decadent airs. Others could die like beasts in war. He'd live for himself. He peeled off fronds from the sugarcane stalks and strewed them across the dead Mambí faces.

Old Wresh tugged him and said, "Some respect?" Wresh, for weeks, had kept to himself. But now his face gleamed indignation, staring at yet past the dead. Hilaríon knew that look. Wresh had eyes of his own. "They died for a better world."

"They died for *this*." He flung the stems.

Wresh batted them away. "Sugar?"

"Poison. Some fight for land or God. Mambíses fight so they can sell sugar."

Wresh pulled off his glove, revealing a hand with only three fingers. "Thanks to Mambíses I still have *this*. My wife and children... not so lucky."

Hilaríon said, "Nor was Hoyo Colorado—razed by Mambíses, their own people's army, because that was easier than defending it. In the end, it won't matter... Bronze Titan or Butcher, Charybdis or Scylla. Call me a lockstep iconoclast."

"Then what will you fight for?"

Hilaríon drew the men's eyes closed and answered, "Golden days."

"Lower your voices," Ypriána said. She looked around warily. "We're not safe here."

Boot prints, pooled with blood, led west from the road, vanishing into the sugarcane field. "This is fresh," Hilaríon said. "An hour?"

"Not even," she said. "We need to get off the road, then head north—"

"¡Adelante!" a voice boomed. "Hombres, ¡Adelante!"

Past the stalks rose a wide-brimmed hat, followed by another, then a squad-sized column behind. A crown patrol was headed their way.

xiv.

Maith broke into tears. Hetta pulled Mabba close to her side. Aryei jumped behind Chropher and Unish. Chropher shoved him to the ground. Wresh grabbed a rake and turned towards the soldiers. "I'll take at least two down—"

"No!" Hilarío held him back.

"I don't want to die in my bed."

Hilarío squeezed his withered hand. "You'll get your chance, warhorse." In the distance, a gabled rooftop rose from the field. Hilarío pointed. "There."

"You want to help?" Ypriána asked Wresh. "Lead them to that hacienda."

Phellhe said, "He's old and weak."

"Better than hale and cruel," she said. "Follow my lead, Hilarío. Do what I do, the opposite way. Meet at the hacienda." She shoved Wresh ahead. "Go now!"

The old man stood upright. Years seemed to melt from his spindly frame, replaced by youthful vigor. He held his head high with a warrior's bearing. He waved the M'Brae into the stalks. Their rustling footfalls faded. Ypriána slipped behind the green. Hilarío crouched, and waited.

The soldiers stepped from the sugarcane. Their khakis were stained with blood and grease. Their eyes lit up at the sight of the bodies. They gloated, "Isla de cerdos."

"Huellas," a stubby man said. "Alguien pasó por aquí."

"Mucha gente ha estado aquí," a taller man quipped.

The stubby one pointed to the bodies. "¿Por qué las caras embarradas de azúcar?"

The soldiers spread out, searching the roadside. Hilarío braced himself. Alone and unarmed, he'd make short work for them.

They drifted towards his hiding place. His hand inched towards his blade—

"*Cuba Libre,*" a soft voice cooed. The voice was Ypriána's.

The two nearest soldiers stirred but said nothing. He watched their eyes. They'd heard her. She was clever: he knew what she wanted from him. The soldiers might ignore a ghost, but they could never ignore two. He stepped backwards into the bramble and whispered, "Cuba Libre."

The soldiers turned. "¿Oiste eso?" the stubby one said.

"Cuba Libre," she said again, from farther across the field, where she'd moved.

The soldiers prodded the corpses. "¿Muerto?"

Their capitán said, "Ispada, Garcíd... está donde le toca."

"¿De qué se enteró?" Garcíd, the tall one, pleaded.

"¿Qué oí?"

The other soldiers laughed. The capitán grabbed their collars. "Avanza!"

Hilaríon drew a silent breath. He knew what words would boil their blood. They seemed to roll from his throat like rum, "¡Viva el Titán de Bronce!"

The capitán whimpered. The soldiers shrank into a ring, Mausers raised at the ready. "¿Quién anda ahí?"

The soldiers were theirs for the luring, now. Hilaríon backed away, whispering, "Cuba Libre... *Cuba Libre...*"

From far away, Ypriána answered, "¡Viva el Titán de Bronce! Viva..."

The soldiers formed a narrow wedge and moved out towards his voice. Hilaríon snaked between the ratoons. The enemy followed mere paces behind, eyes darting nervously around the field. Their capitán urged them, "Por este camino. A la izquierda... no. ¡Coge a la derecha!"

Ypriána's voice dwindled. "¡*Viva el Titán de Bronce!*" he heard one last time. Then she passed from earshot.

The hacienda vanished into the distance. The cane gave way to woodlands, thickening with every step. He crawled inside a hollow log, moments before the soldiers arrived.

"¡Fantasma!" they called, passing by, "¡Sal… fantasma!" They scanned the woods with fiery eyes, until their weapons and bearing sagged again.

"¡Basta!" the capitán said. "Basta… ¡A la Trocha!"

Hilaríon looked back towards the fields. Time was wasting, with little to spare. But wherever the soldiers were headed to might be a place the M'Brae could cross. He needed to see for himself.

The soldiers slackened. They slung their rifles and lit their cigars, and collapsed into a sloppy file. They ragged about food, and home, and festooned ladies of the night.

"Esto es miserable."

"Si. Yo no he cogido nada en un mes."

The woodlands turned to forest edge. The bramble thinned to brush. The screech of a train whistle ripped the air, loud as a banshee's war cry. Hilaríon scrambled into a ditch and squeezed his ears between his hands.

"¡Vuelvan a sus puestos!" the capitán ordered. "¡Apaguen las luces!"

They dropped their cigars and raised their rifles. They shifted to a spread echelon, then stomped off past the tree line. "¡Abajo la revolución!" they cheered

The whistle died down. Hilaríon peeked. In the distance flashed a glint of metal, then another, then hundreds more. He rose to his knees, then up to his feet. He waited for the soldiers to clear the tree line, then he crept ahead. Through the leaves, its grisly face came into view.

The Trocha.

Hilaríon marveled at what he saw. Past the trees, the land lay cleared for one quarter mile, lined by stumps and felled saplings. Sentries prowled the woodland edge, their pacing slow and deliberate: stepping, turning, scanning about, then stepping off again. Their eyes and their Mausers were ever alert. A stone's throw behind them, logs lay side-by-side in piles draped in barbed wire. The wire's teeth were stained with blood and strewn with strings of flesh. Past the logs, the land sloped upwards and hollowed away to a line of trenches, flanked by stone breastworks and Maxim-gun parapets, fixed to the west and manned by steely-eyed gunners. At the gunners' backs rose mounds of spoil, dug from the trenches, scored by barricades and strung across with heavy wire.

And those were only the outer defenses.

Behind the mounds a stone wall rose, waist-high to a man, broken in places to accommodate cannons. Past the wall, the line spread deep, dotted with guardhouses of stone and cement, their western-facing walls honeycombed with Maxim-gun turrets, their rooftops lined with sharpshooters' nests. Every few hundred paces or so, watchtowers soared above the rooftops, mounted with horns and electric floodlights, manned by lookouts gazing through field-glasses. At the nearest watchtower's base lay a rail yard, its steel tracks running to the east. Between the structures flowed an unbroken stream of humanity: gunners and scouts and engineers; men and boys and garish painted ladies; grizzled sergeants, green lieutenants, and captains decked with polished brass. It was a hellish nation unto itself, stretched thin and strung long across a beleaguered isthmus of land.

The locomotive screamed again. Hilarión peered across the line. On the eastern side, the outer defenses were the same as those on the west. His heart sank: Phellhe was right.

The Trocha was invincible.

xv.

"¡Abre!" The outer defenders stepped aside. The patrol stepped past them. "¡Cierra!" They vanished into the monster's belly. For a moment, Hilarión pitied the Mambíses, even the Bronze Titan.

He pushed off the tree he'd hidden behind and back into the ditch. Time, as ever, was racing away. To try to cross here would be suicide. But the treasure was on the other side. Wishing it closer, or the Trocha away, wouldn't change a thing. He'd have to be bold: there was always a way. It was just a matter of finding it.

He stepped off to the south, following the line. The woodlands thinned. The Trocha's grinding voice rose higher. He skirted the line from the edge of the woods, dodging the sentries' hawkish glares. The Trocha widened into a camp: the hub, it seemed, of the Crown's command. Leaving, for a moment, the tree line's safety, he peered through the slats of a wooden stockade.

Inside, the troops pulsed with a conqueror's vigor. Platoons marched in lockstep, to the beat of a drum. Stable-hands hot-walked braying chargers while squires brushed motley caparisons. Lowly troopers buffered cannons, giving smart salutes to spit-and-polish mounted officers. The smell of freshly cooked food wafted tantalizingly through the air. His stomach snarled: he hadn't eaten in over a day. And they'd even less chance of crossing here. He raced off farther south.

Past the camp the woodlands thickened, rising skyward in stocky pines. The Trocha narrowed, its bellicose elegance turning crude at this point: creaky latrines, canvas tents, and mess lines out in the open. Shallow trenches with crumbling walls gaped beside rusty guns. Lowly guard huts, fewer and farther between than before, stood wobbling in the morning winds, their roofs overhung with branches. Here, also, the ranks had thinned. Bejeweled officers gave way to harried troopers, gallant horsemen replaced with listless gunners.

His stride quickened with stirrings of hope. The Trocha was weakening. There was bound to be a gap—

"*¡Despierta!*"

He threw himself against a dirt mound. The voice was so loud it might as well have been screamed in his ear.

"¡Despierta! ¡Ya!"

From the Trocha, an angry sergeant stomped. Hilarión crouched low to the ground. Dirt crumbled into his eyes. A Maxim-gun muzzle loomed over his head. He'd rolled against an earthen breastwork, the outer edge of a fighting position.

"Ustedes puercos vagos!" the sergeant said.

He peeked past the breastwork's edge. Behind it were five fighting-holes with Maxim-gun parapets and mounted guns, arranged in a half-circle arc. At the rims of the holes bobbed soldier heads, in various states of sleep. The sergeant stomped between their prone forms, and smacked his baton on their helmets. "¡Nos van a matar a todos!"

They straightened their heads and pulled themselves smart. The sergeant walked back to the Trocha. "¡Despierta!" he added once more, for good measure.

"Cabrón," the gunners groaned. Within moments, most were sleeping again.

Hilarión held his breath. There was no use trying to run now. At least one of the gunners would see him. He had to wait for cover of dark, or until the gunners changed shifts. Ypriána would be waiting for him. Phellhe would be biding his time. A storm of possibilities flashed through his mind. He was trapped, with all the time in the world—and yet no time at all.

He huddled closer to the berm. Nearby, the gunners snored away. He peered out towards the Trocha. The trees at the woodland edge were thin. He had an unobstructed view.

The Trocha here was narrow, barely three stone's-throws across. The ground ran clear to an unfinished wall, save for mounds of spoil. Where obstacles should have been emplaced, logs lay jumbled in piles, while barbed wire rusted in clumps. Threadbare soldiers stood knee-deep in trenches, winching tree roots and shoveling dirt, their backs scarred and caked in mud. Behind the wall their officers hollered, "¡Más rápido! ¡Trabajen más duro!"

One of the soldiers, short and scrawny, seemed particularly spent. His shovel toppled out of his hands. An officer lifted a stone and yelled, "Rolón! ¡Vuelve al trabajo!" He lobbed the stone over the mound, striking the boy's back. The boy shook his head, grabbed the shovel, and jammed it back into the mud.

Hilaríon looked north up the line. Past the wall stood a guardhouse, and beside it a wooden shed. Farther up the line stood two more guardhouses, with an open latrine and barracks between them. Crooked and cracking at their bases, the guardhouses seemed crude, cobbled together by hasty greenhorns. Between the guardhouse and latrine stood the stunted base of a watchtower. From the looks of the towers he'd seen up the line, this one was only half-finished. It had the look of a project begun in earnest, then neglected for more pressing things. But for now it was useless, either as a lookout or platform for lamps. At night these woods would be plunged into darkness, except for the soldiers' fires.

The boy soldier, Rolón, wavered again. The officer cried, "¡Para la otra, te mato a golpes!" and launched another rock.

Daylight leached away, waddling clumsily towards noon. Afternoon passed with a flourish. The sun crept westward, nearer the treetops. The soldiers hammered guardhouse roofs and splattered mud on berms. Others dragged stones, stacked bricks, and pushed cannons into position. Their faces were anguished, their stomachs empty. Their gripes and grunts found but more haughty orders: "¡Trabajen duro!"

Hilaríon waited, then waited some more. Evening flew its azure flags. The Trocha here seemed a rusty machine, tired and ready to break. He'd memorized its full routine, but still he'd seen no weakness. Ypriána would be wondering where he was. She might come looking for him, but that would leave the others to the mercy of Phellhe, and Phellhe wouldn't wait very long. He'd talk them into turning back, or worse. Necío would try to stand firm, but he could only do so much. Every moment spent west of the Trocha, the treasure slipped farther away. Time was his enemy, more than the Trocha. They had to cross here, and soon.

The ping of tumbling metal tinkled from inside a trench. The boy soldier Rolón's head bobbed, asleep. He'd dropped his shovel when he'd dozed. And just behind the dozing boy, the irate officer stood. He'd have the boy beaten this time, for sure. Hilarión winced with pity, and waited.

Nothing.

Seconds turned to anxious moments. Hilarión watched, teeth clenched. But still, nothing happened. At length, Rolón lifted his head, picked up his shovel, and went back to digging. The officer stood with folded arms. He'd never been the wiser. But how?

The answer struck like a thunderclap. The officer hadn't seen the boy doze. The spoil mound had grown so high the officer couldn't see over it.

Hilarión scanned across the line. Most of the mounds were several feet taller than the men who'd dug them and the officers who'd overseen the digging. The Trocha was riddled with blind spots.

He focused, letting his eyes relax, staring dead ahead. Together, the spoil mounds, wall, and closest guardhouse formed a concealed, canal-like path heading east. Across the line, on the eastern side, the trenches had been started and spoil mounds begun. But no soldiers were digging or sentries patrolling, and no east-facing obstacles had been emplaced. Any attack, the soldiers were counting on, would likely come from the west. The eastern side was undefended. If someone could get behind the forward gunners, *and* get to the first spoil mound, *and* hide in the blind spots *and* cross the wall to the guardhouse, *and* do all of that unseen, he'd have a clear shot to the eastern woods.

Or was it a fool's errand? How could anyone get past the gunners, mere inches from his own hiding place—

"*¡Diez minutos!*"

The soldiers froze, then sighed. They let their bodies slacken. Inside the line, the sergeant bellowed, "Soldados... ¡Diez minutos!"

The men in the trenches stopped digging. They dropped their

shovels and grabbed their gear, then lit up their cigars. The workers slid off guardhouse roofs. Officers spurred their horses to stables. The sentries stopped pacing and trudged towards the barracks, joining the guards at the unfinished tower before shuffling north. The Trocha's vitality shriveled away, a world collapsing upon itself.

One of the gunners said, "Pensé que nunca llegaría." The other gunners crawled from their holes. Hilarión cinched himself in a knot. The gunners gathered their ammunition crates and draped their defenses with tarps. They trudged back to the Trocha, disappearing past the wall. A single sentry, slack-jawed and weary, was left to pace the forest's edge. He plodded past, eyes on the ground, Mauser slung carelessly over his shoulder. The stench of his body soured the breeze. His footsteps faded to the north. The line fell deathly silent.

Hilarión licked his lips. *Audentes fortuna iuvat*, his aunt always said, *Fortune favors the bold*. There'd never be a better time to see if it was true.

He raced across the open ground and flung his back against the spoil. He rolled along its inside edge, and pressed his body low. An errant soldier trundled past, then disappeared into the barracks. An evening wind kicked up, scattering some of the muddy spoil. The second mound was paces away. No one could see him. He leaned to lunge—

He jerked back. The sentry had returned. Hilarión rolled along the mound and squeezed against its east-facing side. The sentry's stench hung in the air. "¿Hay alguien ahí?" the sentry said.

Hilarión held his breath. The sentry shrugged and spat, then trudged off to the south. Hilarión exhaled. He'd need to time his movements better and move in the sentry's blind spots.

He watched the sentry disappear, then flopped onto his back. He slithered to the second mound. Someone inside the Trocha yelled, "¡Muevete rápido!" The Trocha was coming to life again, slowly. Soldiers clustered at the guardhouses: gobbling rations, calling at the latrine, readying weapons, stealing moments of sleep. Their voices flagged, too tired for jokes. They were still too exhausted to watch for intruders. He still had time, but none to waste.

Footsteps in mud sloshed from the south. The sentry came back into view. Hilarión sidled around the mound, out of the sentry's line of sight. The sentry plodded past, heading back to the north. Hilarión raced between the trenches, to the third mound. The stone wall stood mere feet away. He could reach it with his leg outstretched. He waited until two more minutes had passed and the sentry was shambling back away, south.

Hilarión heaved himself over the wall and scurried between the wall and the guardhouse. He paused at the threshold, wiped his brow, and spun himself through the guardhouse door.

He was inside the Trocha.

Bitter cigar ash and burned-up sulfur mixed with the scent of freshly laid plaster. The waning daylight streamed through the turrets. He crept farther inside, between sandbags and crates. The bags below the turrets were blood-stained. The guardhouse had already seen action.

"¡Dos minutos!" the sergeant yelled.

Hilarión's mind raced. War was monotonous: there was a good chance this opportunity came every sunset. He could get the M'Brae across. Here. The window of time was just wide enough, if only for ten minutes.

He turned to the east-facing doorway. Unfortified mounds were all that stood between himself and the eastern woods. Somewhere past those glistening eaves, Lightleaf Grove loomed tall, and rich. He refocused: he had two minutes to spare. He had to find the safest path, and get across and back. If worse came to worst, he'd find shelter in the woods—and a free path to Lightleaf Grove.

He stepped from the threshold. The first mound was only paces away. This time tomorrow, his arms would be brimming with treasure. He lurched—

"Nope." Two familiar arms yanked him back. She'd found him, after all.

xvi.

He spun around. "What are you doing?"

"Saving you from yourself," Ypriána said.

"I don't need saving. There's a window to the east. I need to see if I—er, if *we* can—"

"We can't. Not here."

She had no right to stop him. He stepped through the doorway. "We'll see."

"¡*Vamos!*"

He dove back inside. Voices chattered up the line, fast approaching the guardhouse. "Get down," Hilaríon said.

She stood her ground. "I guess we've seen."

"Esperen," another voice said. "Tenemos más tiempo."

He peeked through the turret. A stone's throw up the line, four gunners were walking their way. One of them ragged, "Otra noche en el interior de la caja." Hilaríon reached for his blade.

"¡Un minuto!" the sergeant cried.

The gunners stopped. They shrugged their shoulders and lowered their Mausers. "¡Un minuto!" they echoed. They slouched against the half-finished tower and lit up cigars. The path to the east was still clear.

Hilaríon rose to the balls of his feet and said to Ypriána, "Follow me—"

"¡A sus puestos!"

Voices rang all around. The soldiers, filled with evening rations, stepped from the barracks into the line. They lit their watch-fires and loaded their Mausers. They walked towards the cannons and Maxim-gun parapets, and hauled their long-scope rifles to rooftops. The Trocha was turning a deathtrap again. And he'd been gypped half a minute.

"Vamos," one of the gunners said. The others took lusty drags of cigars.

The window east was rolling shut, but it was still open just wide enough. They could get to the first spoil mound. Hilarión said, "We have to try."

"So does Phellhe," she said. "Don't die on the way back." She slipped through the west-facing turret and crouched. She was crossing back to the sugarcane field. And she wasn't waiting for him.

"Ahora." The gunners snuffed their cigars, then stepped off towards the guardhouse. He slid towards the turret and peered through the slats. She'd already cleared the wall. She was sidling between the trenches. He looked back over his shoulder. The east woods were tantalizingly bright. But she'd left him only one choice.

He wedged himself into the widest slat. Its plaster edges bit his spine. He'd have to squeeze through all the way. He gritted his teeth and pushed.

"La caja... la caja..." The gunners' footsteps clacked on stone. Hilarión wriggled his body forward. The stone scraped flesh off his back.

"Odio la caja..." The gunners, now, were just outside, approaching from the north.

Hilarión wrenched his back raw and bloody. The gunners rounded the doorway, laughing, "Odio toda la Trocha..."

He heaved upwards.

"Odio..."

His body slid free. He plopped to the mud below the west-facing wall of the guardhouse. The gunners hadn't seen him.

The din of a war-weary enemy rang. The soldiers filled the line. The window to the west was closing, as fast as the one to the east had just closed. "Damn her," he said. The regrets swirled like a riptide. Why hadn't he crossed to the east when he could? Why hadn't he walked off with the medallion, or killed her on Grijalva's command? But none of that mattered now.

He threw himself over the wall. He crouched behind the nearest mound, then slithered between the trenches. The sentry's returning footsteps grew louder. He rolled against the second mound, then sidled along a log pile. The sentry's boots sloshed in the mud. Hilarión flattened against the first mound. The woods were only paces away. The sentry hobbled by, then disappeared north. For a final, desperate moment, the way back west was clear. He darted into the trees.

The soldiers' voices echoed behind. Hilarión churned his legs. The pine trees loomed taller as each second passed. The forest's edge passed in a blur of brown. The woodlands glowed a fiery green, then drab to gray as night spread its veil. He ran until his lungs caught flame. The sugarcane field rose up around him. Ypriána bounded spryly ahead, like a coy doe in the rutting. He seethed in the pit of his stomach. The Trocha was far behind him now, and so was the treasure.

The hacienda crowned the horizon. They raced from the fields, past its rose marble portico, and into the vestibule. From the great room echoed Wresh's voice, saying, *"I'll* decide what happens."

"We have to wait for them," replied Necío's voice.

"We're not waiting," Phellhe's voice boomed. "I'll bet they're already—"

Hilarión and Ypriána burst into the great room. The M'Brae were clustered among broken furniture.

"—Dead," Phellhe said. "Where were you two?"

"Living," she said. "My apologies."

Hilarión grabbed her. "What did you think you were doing back there?"

She slipped from his grasp. "We're leaving before the phéa-sjant find us."

"Finally you see the light," Phellhe said.

She said, "We make for the hills."

Hilarión blocked the doorway. "That's a waste of a day with nothing to show. I found the way."

She threw open a window. "We'll head north, find someplace safe to cross, like we should have done before."

"Who says we'll find safer passage?" Hilarión grabbed her again. "Ypriána—"

"Guamá."

"Stop calling me that."

"Stop being Guamá."

"Listen to me!" He threw up his hands. She'd enlisted Guamá.

"Tick tock," she said. "That patrol's on the move."

He turned to the people. Their eyes swung trustingly to his. "We have a window," he said. "While the enemy's stretched thin and before that tower rises. I swear they'll never see us. I almost crossed—"

"Almost."

"No thanks to you. We have a day, maybe two, before they finish those trenches, or raise that tower. Then there'll be no window."

"That's the thing about windows," she said. "They slam. Shut."

"Behind us."

"Or on top of us," she said. "We're nineteen. What if only half got across? Or just a few? Then what?"

"Then..." He sighed. What had become of the bold wildling who'd raced up a hillside into the teeth of Mambí defenses, who'd dived headlong into a flood to save a man she didn't know? The treasure was slipping away. Was she testing him?

"Then pandemonium," she said. "We didn't charge into that gilded tunnel underground. We won't barrel across the Trocha now. We go as one—"

"No," Hilaríon said. "We take what we can, when we can get it. And we don't look back on what might have been."

She smiled patronizingly. "We go as one, or not at all. We'll arrive with our faces intact."

He seethed. He'd shove those words down her sanctimonious throat.

She opened the door. "Keep to the sugarcane. Stay low. With any luck, we'll get back to the hills—"

"¡Para Artemisa!" rang a voice.

"—unnoticed." She finessed the door closed.

Phellhe grabbed a heavy candlestick. Voices in the distance called, "¡A la Trocha!"

Necío pulled a curtain aside. "Guess we're out of luck."

Like a flood surging over the western highlands, the cane fields crawled with men. It was a legion of jaegers, the same ones who had sacked M'Brae-dah, streaming triumphantly out of the west. "Downstairs," Ypriána said.

They raced into the scullery and down a creaky stairway, then wedged themselves in the musty cellar. The thunderous passing horde shook the eaves, and rattled the dust from the baseboards above. Their polished boots and wagon wheels flashed through the cellar windows. They seemed an unholy swarm of locusts, let loose on an unrepentant land.

"Keep watch," she said. "Once there's a break to the west, we'll run. Stay awake and stay ready." She crouched at a west-facing window.

Hilaríon rankled in a nook. He picked cobwebs from his hair and batted silverfish from his legs. She'd begged *him* to come. *He'd* found a way across. But now he was shamed in a corner, like a misbehaving imp.

Wresh curled beside him. "Damned phéa-sjant," the old man said.

Hilaríon looked the old man over. Ypriána's caustic words came back. So what if only half got across the Trocha? What if only one?

He tapped Wresh's shoulder. "You want to kill phéa-sjant… taste Mambí glory?" The old man's eyes gleamed.

Hilaríon knew just what he'd do. The M'Brae would cross the Trocha here, every one of them. He'd see to it personally.

xvii.

Hilaríon crashed through the sugarcane. Nightjars trilled their evening dirge. The western sky bled sanguine rose, darker by the minute. Any moment, the sergeant would call out the soldiers' break. They had to be in place when that happened. He called behind, "Run faster." Even for an old man, Wresh was slow and doddering.

For two days and nights, the legions had streamed past the hacienda: shouting, pushing artillery, firing shots at the windows for sport. The M'Brae had hidden in the cellar. They'd taken turns, two-by-two, stealthily foraging for food and water. Wresh had clung to his hip the whole time. Then came the break in the soldierly tide, just when Hilaríon's shift had begun. It couldn't have been more perfect. He'd have them across, and his treasure in hand, no later than sunset tomorrow.

A wispy topknot crested the stalks. Wresh said, "I'm too old to run."

"Don't go soft on me now, warhorse."

Wresh puffed out his chest. "I won't."

Night was falling. Hilaríon said, "We won't get another chance."

"To do what?"

"Like I said. When we get there."

The sugarcane gave way to brush. The eaves of the forest loomed overhead. Danger could come from anywhere now. Wresh had to do exactly as planned. What Hilaríon was about to make happen would have to seem like an accident.

The tree trunks narrowed. The draws flattened out. Ahead, past the saplings, were light and commotion. Wresh gasped, "The Trocha—"

"Quiet." Hilaríon pointed to the berms, a stone's throw to the north. Behind the breastworks, the gunners' heads bobbed. They hadn't arrived too late.

The old man pulled something out of his pocket. He started towards the gunners. "Who's first—?"

"No!" He pulled Wresh back. The old man had a metal shank. "Not yet."

"We can kill them in their sleep."

"We're not killing, yet."

"But you said—"

"You'll get your chance, I promise. Just do as I say. Listen to me and we'll both get across."

Wresh said, "Across?"

"¡Diez minutos!" The sergeant's cry went up from the line.

Hilaríon cupped Wresh's mouth. The gunners rose and collected their ordnance. Tonight they seemed fresher, less lethargic. It had been two days since he'd seen them last. What else might have changed? Was the line still even passable? He was taking an enormous risk. But the treasure was just so close.

"Across?" the old man said again.

Hilaríon released his mouth. "That's right."

"But the others?"

"This is all for them. You've ever been fishing?" Wresh nodded. "You use bait to lure the fish," Hilaríon said, "so think of this as fishing. Ypriána needs coaxing. She's the fish and I'm the bait, only I'll be luring her to safety rather than into a trap. The people will follow. We'll all get across." He'd almost convinced himself.

"Then I'm supposed to... what?" Wresh said.

"Make her take the bait. Once I'm safely across you'll go back. Tell her you tried to catch up to me but I was already gone. Tell her you crossed east looking for me, then crossed back again, and tell her how easy it was to do it. That hacienda isn't safe and she knows it. And soon, that tower will be finished. She won't have a choice. They'll have to cross."

"Alright," Wresh said, "you go ahead. Once I see you've crossed, I'll go back. If anyone comes near you..." He ran his finger along the shank.

The old man was thinking too much. "No, no," Hilaríon said. "We have to do this together."

"Why?"

"Because, when you tell Ypriána what you saw, it has to sound like you mean it. You can't talk about crossing unless you've actually crossed. Make sense?"

Wresh nodded, but seemed unconvinced. The gunners hauled their Maxim guns back inside the Trocha. Hilarión said, "Listen, warhorse, the others need us. It's cross here or forget the treasure. We'll never find a better place. So just trust and follow me. Oh, and one thing more. This has to be our secret. No matter what happens, keep our pact to yourself. And another thing..." He licked his lips. "If, God forbid, you found yourself alone to the east, stranded—"

"Stranded?"

He cupped the old man's mouth again. "Then get as far as you could from the Trocha, east. Hide in the woods. Try to find Lightleaf Grove, if you can. But don't even dare try crossing back west. That would be your death, I promise. But do what I say and it won't matter."

The single sentry walked past the tree line. Wresh said, "I'm not sure."

"He's alone," Hilarión said. "He won't see us."

He prodded Wresh to the edge of the woods and pointed to the guardhouse. "That's where we're going."

The sentry's footsteps faded. Hilarión looked up. The tower was taller than two days before. The soldiers had added several more feet. But it still wasn't usable, yet. The Trocha was still passable. "With me," he said. "Stay close."

Wresh tensed his body. "Wait—"

He yanked Wresh from the trees. The old man dragged his feet. Hilarión pulled him across the open. He flung himself against the mound, then jerked the old man down beside him. "Make yourself small." He pushed Wresh's head low.

He peered past the spoil. The Trocha was still. The sentry trudged away. Hilarión grabbed Wresh's arm and led him to the second mound. The old man's face was ghostly white. His gray teeth chattered loudly. He pulled Wresh around the final mound, and lunged against the wall. Wresh buried his head in his hands. Hilarión peeked back to the trees. The sentry was gone away to the south. Hilarión peered over top of the wall. No one had seen them. He could feel the pull of the treasure. "*Now.*"

He heaved himself above the wall, then reached and pulled Wresh over. They scurried through the guardhouse door. He said, "Hide by the sandbags." The old man sank to the floor.

Hilarión laughed to himself. The plan was a masterstroke and Wresh had held firm. He could still reverse the roles: do what he'd actually told Wresh he'd do, and turn the old man back around. No—but it was tempting. The plan would never work with Hilarión trapped to the east.

He peeked between the slats. The soldiers were still preoccupied, slinging their rifles and downing their last swigs of spirits. "Now what?" Wresh said.

Hilarión's eyes scanned the barracks. Where was the sergeant? The plan hinged on him.

"Hilarión?"

"Shhh!" He had to be ready when two minutes was called. But the sergeant was nowhere.

Wresh said, "Why did you wait to tell me the plan? Why not tell me at the hacienda?"

Hilarión kept his eyes fixed ahead. "I couldn't risk it. You could've let slip."

"Or disagreed," Wresh said. "And what if she won't take the bait?"

"She will."

Wresh leaned in closer. "She knows you wouldn't really be stranded. She knows you could cross back west if you wanted."

"I already told you," Hilarión said. "That'd be—"

"My death? But you both got this far and back, alive. What if she doesn't bite?"

Wresh had picked up the scent of his lie. The voices at the barracks died down. Wresh pointed east. "You can cross now."

"Wait," Hilarión said. "I have to see what they do."

"What else do you need to see? If you're not crossing we ought to go back, before anyone finds us." Hilarión roiled: where on earth was that sergeant? Wresh said, "I'm talking to you."

"You'll get me killed," Hilarión said. "No more questions here."

"Get *you* killed? You brought me. You told me—"

"¡Dos minutos!"

"Finally," Hilarión exhaled. He pointed to the nearest mound. "That's where we're going. Get ready to run. I'll give you the signal. It'll be any second now. I'll cover you from the rear. When you get to the trees, keep going. Don't just stop at the edge of the woods."

"I'm not going first," Wresh said. "This is your plan. We go as one or not at all."

"Ypriána's wrong this time. She'll kill us with her caution. Get ready."

"Wait," Wresh said. Epiphany lit up his face. "Now I see."

Hilarión found his most innocent voice. "See what?"

"Now it all makes sense. The holes in the plan that you waited to tell me. How you ignored all my questions."

"I don't know what you're talking about, but now's when I need you most." He pushed Wresh towards the door. "Run and don't turn back."

"*I'm* the bait," Wresh said.

He pretended not to hear. "And don't stop for anything." He shoved Wresh past the threshold. "Ready."

"I won't."

"Ready!"

Footsteps crunched outside the guardhouse. He pulled Wresh back inside. A boyish head bobbed past the turret. "You brought *him*," a familiar voice said, "not me?"

Hilarión sighed. It was Necío. He pulled him through the doorway. "What are *you* doing?"

"¡Un minuto!" the sergeant bellowed.

"I crossed just behind you," Necío said. "What are you doing?" He looked as if he'd already guessed.

"Boy," Wresh said. "Go back and warn Ypriána. This devil's going to kill everyone. He tricked me. He's trying to get me to cross, alone."

"Para la caja," came voices outside.

Hilaríon pulled Necío low. The four guardhouse gunners stepped from the barracks. They stopped and milled about, then lit up their cigars. Their eyes and faces sagged. "Para la caja," they ragged. "Todas las noches, es a la caja." The window east was grinding closed. But the treasure was tantalizingly near. If he had to cross with Wresh, he would.

He shoved Wresh towards the doorway. "Necío," Hilaríon said, "go back. Tell Ypriána to bring up the others at sunset, tomorrow. Tell her it's safe."

"Don't do it, boy," Wresh said.

Necío glanced from one to the other. "Phellhe was right about you," Wresh said. "Two murderous birds of a feather."

"Thank me when you've got your treasure. Necío, tell Ypriána to wait for the window. We'll be on the other side." He pushed Necío towards the turret.

Necío said, "Let Wresh go back. Take me instead."

"Dale rápido," a gunner said.

Hilaríon threw up his arms. "We can't send Wresh back because he'll—"

"I'll tell them you're the monster Phellhe said. And Ypriána will slit your throat." Wresh lunged for the turret.

"¡Afuera, todos salgan!" Wresh dropped to the floor. Voices filled the air all around. "¡Por aquí! ¡En la formación!"

Hilaríon peeked through the turret. A stone's throw up the line, a squad spilled out of the barracks, ammunition belts across their chests and field packs on their shoulders. He recognized the soldiers. It was the patrol they'd encountered three mornings before. They were headed back to the sugarcane fields. Their capitán fumbled with his compass. He spun like a top until oriented. "¡Afuera!" he said again, pointing west.

"¡A sus puestos!" the sergeant cried out. The rest of the soldiers trudged out of the barracks. The Trocha rattled back to life. The patrol soldiers hoisted their packs. They fanned out and stepped towards the wall. Now, the way back west was blocked.

"¡Vamos!"

The four gunners drew their final drags, lifted their Mausers, and stepped towards the guardhouse. There'd be no crossing eastward now, either. If they tried, the soldiers would see them for sure. In the open, they were as good as dead. Even weak, exhausted men at point-blank were lethal.

Wresh and Necío trembled. Hilaríon reached for his blade. The Trocha rumbled all around. He could feel the enemy closing in. The plan was in ruins. And now, so was he.

xviii.

Or was he? He looked through the south-facing slats. Beside the guardhouse stood a shed.

"Odio la caja... odio la caja..." The gunners drew closer.

Hilarión's eyes scanned the angles. From the direction the gunners were approaching, they couldn't see past the guardhouse's north face. He had five seconds, maybe. They could get to the shed. "Out... out..." He pushed Wresh and Necío through the doorway.

The gunners' footsteps clacked. "El amanecer no va a ser tan rápido," one said. The gunners hadn't seen them.

Hilarión pressed them low. *Hasta la salida del sol,* the gunner had said. *Until the sunrise.* He'd had a hunch the window opened mornings, too. But sunrise was still hours off.

He nudged Wresh and Necío into the shed. The door creaked closed behind. "You *are* going to kill us," Wresh said.

He threw them burlap sacks. "Use these." They wrapped themselves and hunkered.

The Trocha's grinding nocturne screamed. The sun disappeared past the treetops. The soldiers lit their torches. A crackling glow spread over the Trocha and seeped through the slats in the shed. Beside them were barrels, covered in pitch. Hilarión's eyes settled on a word.

Pólvora. Gunpowder.

Beside the barrels were bundles of sticks, wrapped in paper and covered in sawdust. He needed no inscription. He'd seen them in the Mambí camps, always handled reverently, like relics, and feared like the angel of death.

Dinamita. They were inside an ordnance shed.

A bead of sweat ran down his brow. An errant or unexpected twitch and they'd be blown to pieces. "Don't move," he said. "I'll get us out."

"You'll only save yourself," Wresh said.

He peeked through the slat near the door hinge. The eastern woods were their only escape. The first spoil mound was mere paces away, the second only just past it. From the mound to the woods would be a quick lunge. They'd have shelter and safety all night. And when sunrise came, then what? For now, it didn't matter.

"La torre," the sergeant said. "¡Terminarlo!"

The pangs of rivets being pounded through wood rang loudly all around. Inch by inch, the tower was rising. Once finished, there'd be no hope of crossing at all.

He counted paces from shed to mound. They'd need at least five seconds. A diversion might do, but not just any diversion. It had to be big enough to buy him the time, but small enough to be promptly forgotten. Too small and it'd be useless, too big and the window would shut for good.

"¡Maldita sea!" Dust scattered. A soldier had leaned against the shed. "Dame un minuto."

The shed trembled. The dynamite rolled to the barrel's edge. Hilarión bit his quivering lip. The sticks came to a standstill.

"¡Cuidado! ¿Tú no sabes lo que hay dentro?"

The soldier pushed away from the shed. Hilarión released his breath. He glimpsed an oily rag and matches. His plan had been mangled, but no one was dying. He dropped the matches into his pocket and grabbed the rag from the shelf. "Be ready," he said. "When you hear them shouting, sprint to the mound."

Wresh said, "I told you, I'm not—"

"Run fast." He slipped through the door and dropped to the ground.

The soldiers went on working. Hilarión slithered between shed and guardhouse. Inside the guardhouse, the gunners were grousing. He wedged his body between the wall and west-facing side of the building. He pulled the matches and rag from his pocket.

"¡Mira como se levanta!" a soldier said.

The tower was quickly mounting the sky, almost to the treetops. They'd complete it in another day, two if he was lucky. But that was tomorrow's problem. He struck the match against the stone and touched it to the rag. A small flame smoldered. He puffed a draft of air across it. The fire spread across the rag. He placed it against the wall and sidled back the way he came.

He waited. The gunners in the guardhouse groaned. He could smell the burning oil. He could hear the fabric crackling. Filthy soldiers staggered past. They were hair-triggers, exhausted to tears. Their reaction times would be dulled, but why hadn't anyone—

"*¡Fuego! ¡Fuego!*" The gunners spilled from the guardhouse.

Muffled footsteps scampered behind him. Wresh and Necío had run. He turned and raced after them. He pressed himself against the spoil mound and peeked back towards the line. The soldiers had gathered at the fire. He waved Wresh and Necío on. They scampered to the second mound, then into the eastern woods.

The sergeant stomped to the guardhouse. "¡Malditos cigarros!" he cried. "Más cuidado para la otra."

Hilaríon sighed. The soldiers hadn't suspected foul play. Tomorrow, the window would still be open—

"¡Hay! *¡Hay!*" a soldier cried. "¡Allí, en los árboles! ¡A ellos! ¡A ellos!" Hilaríon turned. A soldier was pointing at them. "¡Hay, usted! ¡Alto!" He raised his Mauser. "*¡Alto!*"

Hilaríon hurried Wresh and Necío out of the open, into the trees. From the line, the Mauser barked. Its breath ripped the thicket around where they ran. Necío whimpered. Wresh groaned loudly. The soldier who'd fired on them gave chase.

Wresh whimpered, "Devil." They scurried ahead. The lights of the Trocha faded behind them.

"¡Alto!" the soldier's voice rang. "*¡Alto!*" He was hard on their tail. Their feet were leaving juicy tracks. Even a novice could track them.

The woods thickened, then all at once thinned. The ground swelled into a ridge, threaded by the corroded remains of railroad tracks. "Up there," Hilaríon said.

Wresh staggered. "Stop," he said. "I can't..."

"Help him." He flung Necío back towards Wresh.

"¡Alto!" the soldier railed, closing fast.

The track bent sharply, doubling back. The woods gave way to a plantation rail yard, long since reclaimed by weeds. A rusted locomotive lay on its side. The door to its cab was open.

"¿Dónde estás?" the soldier taunted, close behind.

They climbed the engine and into the cab. The firebox was empty. He pushed them inside, then hoisted himself. There was only enough room for two.

He told Necío, "Lock the door behind you. Don't open it unless I say." Wresh's labored grunts echoed in the metal. "And keep him quiet," Hilarión said.

Necío's head disappeared. The door groaned and trundled closed. It locked from inside with a squeal. Hilarión peeked from the cab. A stone's throw into the thicket, the wood gave way to marsh. He knew how to lose the soldier. But he'd have only a few minutes.

"¿Dónde... *estás?*" came the soldier's voice: louder, getting closer.

Hilarión ran up the tree line, then wiped his boots clean of mud. He jumped from trees to tracks, then stomped a conspicuous trail leading off them: from the rails, across the ridge, and into the foul-smelling marsh. He backtracked in his footprints, then made another trail.

"¿Dónde..."

Down the tracks, the soldier appeared. Hilarión scampered a third false trail, then slid beneath the locomotive.

"...*Estás?*"

The soldier searched along the tracks. Hilarión recognized him: Rolón, the scrawny boy, whose abuse at the officer's hand had revealed the way to cross the Trocha. "Sé que estás cerca," Rolón said. "¡Sal, sal fuera!" He stepped past the engine. "¡Hay! Te encontré."

"Rolón!" a voice called from the trees. A second soldier appeared. "Rolón, ellos nos necesitan en la Trocha."

"Entraron allí," Rolón protested. He pointed up the three false trails. "Créeme. Yo los vi."

"Los mendigos o vagabundos," the second soldier said. "De todas formas, yo no voy a entrar ahí. Vamos."

Rolón hung his head. The soldiers ran the opposite way.

Hilaríon exhaled. Against all odds, he'd salvaged his plan. He'd gotten across the line with two others, and kept the crossing-window intact. But if he was going to get all the M'Brae across, he'd have to make peace with Wresh.

He tapped on the firebox. The trapdoor swung open. Necío's soot-smudged face popped out. He was frantic. "We have to go back!"

"We can't until sunrise, and that's if there's even a—"

"We can't help him here!"

A chill ran up Hilaríon's spine. "Help him?" He peered inside.

The cold moonlight limned a crumpled form, curled in the pit of the firebox. Wresh held his three-fingered hand to his chest. A spreading red stain, like a blossoming rose, smiled up into the night. "Devil," he whispered, "you've finished me off."

xix.

The eyes scorched Hilaríon's every sinew. He tore a swatch from Wresh's shirt and pressed it to the gunshot wound. "Why did I listen to you?" Wresh said.

"Stay still." He pressed harder. The rag filled with blood. He tore another piece of cloth. "Breathe, breathe..."

Necío said, "Pull him out."

"That'd kill him for sure."

"Too late," Wresh said.

"Be still!" Already the shadow of death was falling. "At first light—"

"At first light it won't matter," Wresh said. A trickle of blood dripped out of his mouth. "I should've stayed with the others. Oh!"

He ran his finger along Wresh's neck. The old man's pulse was weakening. "Save your breath," Hilaríon said.

"I should've stayed in M'Brae-dah," Wresh said. "And you should never have come."

"I know," Hilaríon said, "I know." He tore another piece of cloth. But the blood gushed even redder.

Necío sobbed. Wresh dropped his head. "Golden days," he groaned.

"Stop," Hilaríon said, "please." He ripped another swatch.

"A thief is a thief forever," Wresh said. "You'll kill us all for treasure."

"I did what I had to," Hilaríon said. "Leaders make those choices."

Blood gurgled in the old man's throat. "Good for you, hilldevil," he said. "Now you're just like Phellhe." His mouth quivered, then settled agape. Wresh was dead.

A rage swelled inside him. A new pair of eyes glared hot. "Ypriána needed to be coaxed," he pleaded. "What choice did I have?"

He climbed from the firebox, then looked north, up the railroad tracks. La Habana was only two days' journey. He had only to keep to the shadows. He'd have nothing but the cloak on his back, but at least he'd be alive. Necío took his hand. "Don't."

"She'll kill me," Hilaríon said.

"She needs you. If you run—"

"She won't find me."

"But you'll wish she had."

Necío knelt and bowed his head. Through cracking voice its strains pealed out. Nothing had ever sounded so lush.

> "Our sires' yawning chasm spreads
> Parched our glories, myths untold
> Doubt devours my wasted heart
> Prayers unanswered, blood turned cold
> We'll be one in Ahr.
>
> Envoys of a better land
> In benthic depths, our sires' cry
> Leads me, weary wand'rer, on
> Roused my wonder, by and by
> We'll be one in Ahr.
>
> My journey's end, my fathers' fount
> Oft-rememb'red, never known
> A flame rekindled 'midst the dark
> To hold, to have in grace alone
> We'll be one in Ahr."

The song almost made him forget about Wresh. "That music haunts me," Hilaríon said.

"That means I'm doing it right," Necío said. "There's magic in its chords, you know. When the Ancients sang as one, it's said, they could draw miracles out of the sea."

Hilaríon looked back up the tracks. Necío was right: that road only ended in death, if at all. There, there'd be no golden days. He could still make good for what he'd done. "Take shelter," he said. "At dawn, we'll go back."

"*You'll* go back," Necío said, "and bring the others up. You'll finish this for Wresh. He still needs to be rescued..." He winked. "At least as far as they all know. Someday he'll take his revenge." He dragged the body out of the cab. He pulled the glove off Wresh's hand and threw it at Hilaríon's feet.

Hilaríon hadn't expected such shrewdness. "What did Wresh mean, about me being like Phellhe?"

"Some other time."

"Please," Hilaríon said.

Necío backed from the cab. "Those ruins where Phellhe found you... it wasn't by chance he was there." He cleared his throat.

"My father had gone. My mother and her own, and me, had stayed. When the phéa-sjant finally left, Phellhe called for everyone to rebuild M'Brae-dah. But my mother refused to join him. We went to the fringes to live apart, and to continue the search for the treasure. Phellhe didn't trust us, and why should he have? The lore, and the *lure*, of the treasure barred his way.

"Phellhe couldn't abide any disunity. He asked, then begged, then wheedled, then threatened that we come into the fold, and each time, Gnath refused. People began to laugh at Phellhe. What would-be chief gets stonewalled by doves? So he made other plans. Only, he didn't count on the winds.

"Phellhe and his henchmen staged a raid, I suppose to make us see how vulnerable we were on our own. They came at night, disguised as hilldevils. Most of us were sleeping. Phellhe struck only the outermost houses, believing, I think, they'd get out in time. Winds scattered the tinder. The houses burned. The people burned. Some tried to run, but there was nowhere to go. They fell to ashes, clutching each other."

Hilaríon remembered the ruins and shatter, and charred bones on the hillside. He remembered Phellhe's scars.

"My mother and I escaped, as did a few others. But after that there was nothing to stop Phellhe. He made himself Oíc, what you Vujoíe might call *prince*. He shut our doors to the outside world. The stories you've probably heard—that we're undead attercops? They were all spread by Phellhe, to frighten outsiders. He never confessed to what he did, but everyone knows it was him. *Leaders lead,* he'd always say. *Leaders make choices that no one else will.* But if that's what being a leader means, I'd rather just be a fool." He climbed back into the firebox. The door groaned shut behind him.

Hilaríon stood alone. What had he done? Had it been worth this poor man's life? He tried to think about La Habana. But somehow, its fruits didn't seem quite so sweet.

He dragged Wresh's body beneath the engine. Then he sat. The night breeze whispered through the trees. It sounded like the wails of a ghost. It sounded, almost, like the Gray Jaeger. But that monster had died in the caverns. No one could have broken that boulder. He was still inside that tunnel, dead. Wasn't he?

His mind tormented, he lay awake all night.

xx.

Hilarión raced through the western woods. Far behind, at the Trocha, the sergeant bellowed, "¡Dos minutos!"

Hilarión wiped the sweat from his brow, mixed with the blood from the scrapes on his hands. He'd been right about the sunrise window, and he'd gotten across unseen. But the Trocha grew stronger each day. The watchtower soared ever skyward. The M'Brae had precious little time. Necío and Wresh, in their haste and impudence, had blundered across to the other side: that was his story. For all her self-assuredness, Ypriána was reasonable. There was no way she'd deny them crossing, in light of what was now at stake.

He slipped inside the hacienda. From the cellar, Phellhe's voice boomed, "Forget him."

"Only he knows the way," Ypriána replied.

"He knows shit," Phellhe said. "He's been guessing and so have you. The phéa-sjant will kill us here. We'd be safer crossing the Trocha."

"Glad you think so," Hilarión said, descending the cellar stairs.

Phellhe looked him over. "Where are the others?"

"Alive," Hilarión said. "I think."

"You *think?*"

"I tracked them last evening, just before sunset." He held up Wresh's glove. "Their tracks led across the field, into the woods, then deeper. By the time I arrived, it was too late. I tried to find another way, but..."

Phellhe glowered, "But what?"

He licked his lips. Once he said it, there'd be no going back. "But they're on the other side."

The people fell to grousing and recriminations. Phellhe said, "You saw them cross?"

"No, but their tracks led out to the trenches. I would've gone farther, but the soldiers were guarding the line."

Phellhe raised a skeptical eyebrow. Hilaríon forced his most indignant voice, "What, you don't believe me? I searched the woods all night. I tried to find somewhere I could see them, or another way to bring them back."

"Strange, our paths didn't cross," Ypriána said. "I was out there, looking for you."

Hilaríon made no reply. He could hear it in her voice.

She knew.

"We should've seen this coming," Hetta said. "It's all Necío's talked about for days. If Hilaríon said the line could be crossed, it was good enough for him. *If only Ypriána would just trust Hilaríon,* Necío kept saying. *If only there was a way to make her.* Looks like he found a way."

Hilaríon sighed. Even miles away, Necío's faith had helped him, again.

"How'd they know how to cross?" Phellhe said.

"Crossing isn't the hard part," Hilaríon said. "Anyone could have figured out how. That's what I've been trying to tell you. Now, we don't have much time—"

"I'm not finished," Phellhe said. "So you *didn't* see them cross?"

"I told you, no. Now—"

"But you saw their tracks."

"Yes."

"You're sure it was their tracks."

"I'm sure."

"And the soldiers were back in place when you saw the tracks?"

He nodded.

"And the window is ten minutes?"

"Give or take." Hilaríon started up the stairs. "Now, we have to—"

"None of this adds up," Phellhe said. "You're telling me that in all of ten minutes you noticed they'd gone, found their trail, and tracked them to the Trocha, but by the time you got there they'd already crossed and gotten that far ahead of you?"

A pregnant silence fell. He'd underestimated Phellhe again. "That's, um…"

"That's the fog of war," Ypriána said.

"Or the lies of a swindler," Phellhe said. "If Wresh and Necío really did cross, and he thinks that's so easy, then he can go bring them back."

"No, no," Ypriána said. Her hand had been forced and she knew it. "We're not risking his life, or theirs, just to cross, cross back, then try to cross again. Their stupidity leaves us one choice. We'll have to go to them."

The people yelped and muttered. Some seemed excited but all looked scared. "We can't cross the Trocha," Phellhe said. "You said yourself, days ago."

"That was then," she said. "Wresh and Necío won't last there alone. We'll die if we stay here—that's what *you* said. Guamá has a plan. Does anyone here have better?"

"If the hilldevil knows how to cross," Phellhe said, "the hilldevil can bring them back. You vouched for him and made him our savior. You can go with him."

"You'd like that," she said, "both of us trapped or dead in a ditch. Whatever would you do? It's just as well. We have to cross somewhere. The faster we leave the better." She started up the stairs.

Hilaríon's racing heart settled. The plan was back on track. He could feel himself swimming through rivers of treasure. Wresh hadn't died for nothing. He whispered to her, "Glad you see reason."

"Oh, you're clever, Guamá," she whispered back, "but, then again, so is a rat." Hilaríon's hubris died on his tongue. Ypriána turned to the people and said, "Stay silent, stay low. At sundown we'll—"

Wham! An upstairs door slammed open.

"¡Traerla!" Voices rang through the floorboards. "¡Vamos!"

The eaves creaked. The timbers shook. Footsteps thumped through the upstairs hallways, then wended into the rooms. Soldiers were inside the hacienda.

xxi.

"Stay down, until they leave," she said. The M'Brae hunkered beneath the stairs.

Above, the soldiers plodded about. "Vamos a esperar aquí a los otros," one said. Hilarión peeked through a mud-crusted window. Already the mid-morning sun was beating. The dew was all but burned away.

The soldiers chattered like petulant chickens. "Odio este lugar," a scratchy voice said.

"No pasará mucho tiempo," another replied. Hilarión recognized the voice. It was the patrol capitán he'd eluded days before.

"En la última patrulla," a third man said. "Mañana todos verán nuestro trabajo."

The soldiers cheered. A chorus of clinking bottles rang out. The scent of rum wafted down through the floorboards. The soldiers weren't leaving. They were settling in.

Day wore on towards afternoon. Ypriána stood guard at the stairs. Hilarión roiled in the nooks. The window for crossing drew nearer and nearer. By nightfall, they had to get through. Another day and the watchtower would be finished. Then they'd never cross. And Necío was out there, alone.

"Ella esta aquí."

The front door opened. Footsteps wended inside. "Tengo un regalo," another voice said.

A faint noise seeped into the dark. It sounded like a muffled cry. "Yo primero," the capitán said. His voice faded up the grand staircase.

Afternoon bled to a soft orange gloaming. The soldiers clomped above. By their footfalls, Hilarión counted five. They were going up and down the stairs, one upstairs with the other four waiting.

Whatever the soldiers were doing, they were taking pains to keep it quiet. Once or twice, he could have sworn, he heard a sixth voice, crying in pain.

He couldn't stem the tide of questions. Would Necío be unharmed? Could the Gray Jaeger have escaped? What if they'd gone to the northern hills, as Ypriána had urged? Then would Wresh still be alive? He'd have to explain Wresh's death, but how?

Ypriána stepped beside him. "It's sunset now. We're going."

"Now?"

"Oh, I'm sorry. I must've confused you with Guamá. *He* is anxious to get across."

"But the soldiers."

She shook her head despairingly. "If only Necío and Wresh hadn't strayed." She ran up the stairs and slipped through the door.

The M'Brae held their breaths. Ypriána's lithe footsteps creaked through the floorboards, from the pantry to the scullery, then towards the great room. From a place just a few feet away from her, the soldiers' voices chattered on. Hilaríon clenched his jaw so tight he thought his teeth might crack. He hadn't bargained for so much intrigue, but it was his fault just the same. He couldn't stand idly by.

He pushed past the people and raced up the stairwell. He drew his blade as he ran through the dining room, then into the great room, ready to strike—

His feet screeched to a stop. Three soldiers and the capitán lay on the floor, splayed out like corpses. Ypriána stood between them. The cloudy forms of eight more eyes congealed in his mind's eye. "You killed them?"

"Sadly, not quite," she said. "But we'll be gone before they wake."

The eyes disappeared. He circled, blade held high. "You know there's a fifth."

"He's no danger now." The evening light was fading. "Get the rest up here—"

"*No!*" A woman's cry came from upstairs.

Ypriána raised her blade and crept up the grand staircase. Hilaríon followed. The sobbing continued. The dull sounds of thudding, like fists slamming flesh, thumped from a door at the end of the hall. "It's coming from in there," he said.

They crept closer. The floorboards creaked. The thudding stopped. "Ahora no," came the scratchy man's voice from behind the door. The faintest wisp of a whimper peeped out.

Ypriána turned the doorknob. It jangled but was locked. "Ya te lo dije, ¡vete!" the scratchy voice said.

Hilaríon looked Ypriána over. She was staring at but through the door, a picture of matchless serenity, as if contemplating some grand act she hated to do but saw no reprieve. It was the same as on the hilltop, before he solved the Seven Angels. He said, "We have to go."

She raised her blade. "Don't watch."

The scratchy voice boomed, "¡No he terminado mi parte—!"

A thunderous snapping of wood split the air. She'd kicked the door open and leapt through the frame. Hilaríon ducked against the wall. The scratchy voice shrieked, then turned to a gurgle. Hilaríon spun, then peeked past the door jamb.

The room was tiny: a bedpan filled with rancid piss, a fraying bamboo nightstand, a cot lengthwise against the far wall. It looked like servants' quarters. On the cot, sobbing, bruised, and huddled in the sheets, was a woman. On the floor was the naked body of a man. Ypriána's blade was lodged in his chest.

She pulled the blade from between his ribs and flung the blood against the wall. She grabbed the woman's clothes from the nightstand. She threw them at Hilaríon and said, "Bring her along."

"Bring her? We can barely cross with—"

"Bring... her... along." She disappeared through the doorway.

Hilaríon helped the woman dress. Up close she looked grand-motherly. Her skin was rough and almost greenish, like antique copper. She scrambled into her ragged clothes. In spite of what she'd just been through, her bearing was noble, her movements balletic, like a worldly, rusted dame. He hurried her down the stairs and past the rose marble portico.

The sky had darkened. The M'Brae were assembled. "Who's she?" Phellhe said.

"A fellow traveler," Ypriána said. "Any time now, tracker."

Hilaríon pointed eastwards. "Don't stop or make a sound." They raced through the field and into the woods. The shadows of the forest spread. The western sky grew crimson-gold.

He halted them south of the forward defenses. The gunners were snoring. The soldiers had been working hard. The logs had almost been fully emplaced and covered with barbed wire. The spoil mounds had shrunk several feet, the earthen breastworks finished. This would be their final chance. "Pair up," he said. "Any moment—"

"*¡Diez minutos!*"

The gunners rose and passed the berm, and wended their way inside of the line. On cue, the Trocha's discord shrank until it seemed a ghostly ruin. "Wait for my signal," Hilaríon said, "then do exactly as I—"

"*¡Lamparas de luz!*"

The woods, all at once, were bathed in light, as if the sun had burst. Wires whined behind the line. Above the treetops, commanding the view of the Trocha and woods, the finished watchtower loomed.

Hilaríon's heart sank. The Trocha, again, was invincible.

xxii.

"Well?" Ypriána said, sounding vaguely pleased.

He said, "We can't cross now."

"But Wresh and Necío need us." Her voice was doubly caustic.

The sergeant said, "Que intenten cruzar ahora." The enemy had a newfound zeal, born of their new advantage. Any moment, they'd sight the M'Brae. And when that happened—

"Wait," Hilaríon said. Just beyond the guardhouse, the wire for the watch-lamps' power gleamed.

Phellhe said, "We're turning back."

"Not yet," Hilaríon said. He scanned the visible Trocha. Though bathed in light, it remained in repose: guardhouses empty, a single lookout in the tower. The soldiers clustered at the barracks. Even the sentry, made useless by light, slumped at the latrine. The eyes glared hot inside his mind, hotter than the lamps. But Necío was out there. "We can still get across. Phellhe, I need you to—"

"No."

"Then Hrama, Jacinda, go up the line, just past the tower. Distract the lookout, then circle back. That should buy enough time for me." Jacinda and Hrama scurried off. Hilaríon turned to Ypriána. "Wait for the dark, then two by two."

She drew the medallion from her shirt and placed it in his hand. "Extra incentive," she said. Its sumptuous weight pressed into his palm. But this was her warning. There'd be no rejoicing. He draped it over his neck.

The soldiers in the barracks stirred. "Dos minutos," the sergeant said. Time was slipping, now less than two minutes. But if all went right, it'd be enough.

Up the line, Jacinda stepped outside the brush, laughing girlishly.

Her bodice dangled loose. The lookout pointed at her and said, "Tú."
Hilaríon ran.

"Tú!" the lookout repeated. Hilaríon dove behind the mound.
"Tú, muchacha... ¡Vuelve!" He trained his rifle on Jacinda. "¡Vuelve!"

Hilaríon crawled between the mounds. Hrama grabbed Jacinda's
hand and pulled her back into the trees. Hilaríon flung himself
over the wall. Some of the soldiers had stepped from the barracks.
"Vagabundos," the lookout said. He slung his rifle and gazed off north.
Hilaríon slithered along the shed, and spun inside the guardhouse.

"¡Un minuto!" came the command. The soldiers slung weapons
and made last head calls. The Trocha was coming to life again.
Hilaríon charged to the spoil mound. Behind him, soldiers bragged
on the tower, "¡Abajo Cuba Libre!"

The heat off the watch-lamps blistered his neck. He crawled to
the wire and lifted his blade. He might be burned to ash, he knew.
"Wresh," he whispered, "Necío." He drew a deep breath, exhaled
lustily, and plunged the blade down through the wire.

The pulse shook the blade. It juked from his hand. The watch-
lamps whined, then fizzled out. The Trocha fell pitch black. "¿Qué
pasó?" the soldiers said.

The severed wire crackled softly, spitting bluish sparks. Hilaríon
dropped a rock on the wire and covered it with earth. It smoked
beneath the dirt. The soldiers spewed out of the barracks. "¿Qué ha
pasado? ¿Dónde está la luz?"

The sergeant roared his loudest. The lookout shook the spotlight
lamps. The darkness thickened by the minute, the canopy obscuring
what was left of dusk. The din of cursing soldiers spread. Hilaríon
curled at the base of the mound. Maith and Aryei scampered past.
Ypriána had timed it perfectly.

The sergeant shook the tower. "¿Qué está mal? ¿Qué está mal?"

Hetta and Mabba ran past him next. Hilaríon felt a rush of
relief: already four had crossed. He hunkered low, against the spoil.
His foot caught the wire and knocked off the rock. The wire flipped
upon its side and barked a sharp, electric whine. "¿Qué fue eso?" the
sergeant said.

Hilaríon peeked at the guardhouse. Graciela and Revaj were waiting inside. He held his hand to halt them. "Por ahí," a soldier said and pointed towards the mounds.

"Rolón!" the sergeant said. "Debes averiguar... a ver si el cable está cortado."

"Sí, sargento," a slight voice answered. Rolón stepped from the soldiers' midst. He slung his weapon, cocked his head low, then disappeared past a pile to the north.

In only moments, Hilaríon knew, Rolón would circle back around. Now there was even less time. Hilaríon waved Graciela and Revaj across, then a moment later, Lanyan and Bolivar.

From behind the pile Rolón emerged. He paced slowly, checking the wire. "Tómese su tiempo," the soldiers mocked. "Tenemos toda la noche."

Rolón hastened. Hilaríon drew his blade. He could almost feel the fires of perdition, swelling up through the ground. If he wasn't already going there, this latest debacle had sealed his fate. Rolón would have to be silenced. The smallest loose end could ruin them all.

"*Rolón!*"

The boy stopped inches away. The wire burped a shower of sparks. Rolón rounded the mound. He looked down onto the sparking wire. "Aquí está—"

Hilaríon throttled him down. He shoved him up against the spoil and laid the blade against his throat. "Dígales que usted está equivocado," Hilaríon said. "Diles que no está aquí." He pressed the blade more firmly. "*Tell them.*"

Rolón drew quivering breath. "No, no," he called out, "lo siento. No está aquí, después de todo."

"Tell them you'll keep looking," Hilaríon said.

"Lo encontraré," Rolón said.

The sergeant replied, "¡Encontrar!"

The soldiers kept grousing, milling about. The lookout rattled the lamps again. Shadows gathered over the east. Hilaríon held the blade in place and threw more earth on the wire. "Antes, eras tú," Rolón said. "So it *was* you. Why'd you come back?"

"Don't talk."

Hrama and Jacinda rounded the spoil. Rolón wrenched his hips. Hilarío turned the boy onto his chest. "Don't move."

"We'll see."

"Open your mouth again, I swear on Christ I'll—"

"Kill me?" Rolón said. "I hear that twenty times a day." He drew breath to scream. Hilarío smothered his face.

"Rolón," the sergeant said. "¿Lo encontraste?"

Hilarío said, "Tell them—"

"No."

"Rolón!"

Hilarío covered the boy's mouth again. To track meant to know when to mimic your quarry. "Estoy buscando," he said, in a voice like Rolón's. "Creo que está muy cerca." That hopefully would buy some time.

The sergeant groaned, "¡Apurate!"

Chropher and Unish ran past. Rolón said, "You're good."

"I am."

"But not good enough to save that old man."

Wresh's eyes took flame. Hilarío snarled, "Bastard—!"

"Rolón! ¿Qué dijiste?"

He'd cursed so loudly the soldiers had heard. "Estoy buscando," Hilarío said. "Es difícil ver en la oscuridad."

"Le daremos una antorcha," the sergeant said.

"No!"

The rusted dame scurried past, followed closely by Sunovín.

"No?"

Hilarío said, "No, er—ahora puedo verlo... y la pólvora está cerca—"

"Date prisa, Rolón!" The sergeant stormed off in a hail of curses.

Rolón said, "Close call."

"What did I tell you?" He ran the blade along the boy's throat.

"You don't have it in you," the soldier boy said. "Or you wouldn't be sneaking in blind spots."

Hilarío dug his thumb into Rolón's eye. "Speaking of blind..."

"You can't stay forever. You can't let me go."

"Someone needs to pay for Wresh. Might as well be you."

"He was following you when he died," Rolón said. "So really you killed him."

Wresh's eyes took sudden flame, among all the other eyes, plaguing his heart. Hilaríon felt himself slipping away, into a dull and reckless fugue. "Bastard boy," he snarled, "I didn't!" Hilaríon raised, then plunged his blade—

No. The face he saw belonged to Wresh—to Lux León, Elídio and Concepcíon, Fenn, and all his Mambí legion. He pulled the blade from Rolón's face, then cracked the butt against the boy's skull. Rolón withered, out cold. Hilaríon said, "I didn't kill him."

Chay and Phellhe scampered past, followed by Ypriána. "Rolón!" the sergeant bellowed. "¡Ahora!"

Hilaríon reached for Rolón's Mauser. "Leave it," Ypriána said. "You want Phellhe at the trigger?" He dropped the rifle. They slunk around the mound.

"Rolón!"

He peeked back. The sergeant was walking towards the wire. He pushed from the mud and into the woods. "Rolón!" came the distant voice, "Rolón... ¿dónde estás?"

The forest darkened, the ground softened. The air swelled thick with mist. The sounds of the Trocha melted away into a meaningless din.

Ypriána raced ahead. Hilaríon caught up to her. "Wresh and Necío first," he said, "then treasure." Regardless of Ypriána's suspicions, he had to keep living the lie. Wresh was alive as far as he knew.

Necío stepped from the shadows. Hilaríon exhaled, never so glad to see someone alive. Necío motioned excitedly. "It's here... this way! I already sent the others. Come!" Necío ran off into the forest. Ypriána followed.

For a moment, Hilaríon lingered. The people would soon ask after Wresh. His consequences would be grim, but lying could only make them worse. His stomach churned. He pressed his chest. His load felt lighter, his clothing less bunched. He reached inside. The twine dangled free.

The medallion was gone.

"Missing something?"

Hilaríon turned. The rusted dame leaned against a tree. She held out the medallion. "You need this where you're going."

He snatched it back. "I've arrived where I'm going."

"That's what M'Brae always think."

He tied the medallion back onto the twine and asked, "How do you know who they are?"

"When it's time, I'll tell you everything." She pointed towards Ypriána. "But she can't hear. *She's not who she says she is.*" She sauntered off after the others.

The trogons resumed a prattling soiree. Hilaríon watched the rusted dame walk, until she'd disappeared past the bramble. How could this woman know about M'Brae—or Ypriána? For a moment, he missed the life of a thief. The intrigue of questing was more than he'd guessed. But it would all be over soon. Wouldn't it?

He trailed behind the others. The shadows lengthened, then faded. The land swelled like a gathering tide, then dropped into a hollow. The others were gathered at the rim. Necío pointed below. "There!"

The hollow was filled with cinchona trees, bursting with rose and silver blooms. They shimmered in the moonlight, their leaves like tiny gems. And set in the ground between the trees, a stone slab like the cap of a vault peeked out from the moss.

Lightleaf Grove. The treasure.

Hilaríon yelped, and threw his body down the hill.

xxiii.

"Come on," he said, "the treasure!" He grabbed Necío by the arm and scrambled down the slope. He could feel the pleasures of La Habana, now his for the taking.

He raced to the slab. On its face was an array of ridges and bumps and tiny indentations. He pulled out the medallion. Its serrated edge matched the rough-hewn pattern. He fitted its frills into the holes and pushed against the stone. The slab creaked, then shook, as if a latch had been disengaged.

He slipped his fingers under the stone's edge. It budged the slightest in his grip. He motioned the men to help him. They pulled as a winch. His heart throbbed with anticipation. He'd gotten the people across with their lives—mostly—and gotten them to the treasure. Leaders make the difficult choices. And leaders would savor the best of the spoils.

The stone slid upwards. The men gasped for breath. Hilaríon said, "A little farther... pull!"

They heaved it from the ground. Hilaríon peered into the vault. Any second now, he knew, the glitter of the priceless horde would shine up through the gloom.

The dust settled. It was no vault. Inside was just another slab.

The people groaned. "You didn't think it'd be that easy?" Ypriána said. She seemed unsurprised.

A rage swelled up inside him. "*Easy*? Hither lies the priceless trove?"

"But laced with visions fast uphove," Necío said. "So that's what that meant."

"Color me disillusioned," Ypriána said.

Necío leaned into the hole. "It really isn't here, only more instructions." He wiped the dust and read,

"Now stripped and ground the Lightleaf hide
Its bitter potions drunk in haste
The grinding road through mangrove hacked
To threshold of the watery waste
And 'gainst the Westbound Flood to keep
A way of kings away below
Where Tumbled Bark o'erspreads her slough
'Twixt rivers twin in southbound flow
And there in shattered hulk to claim
The princely ransom, kingly prize—
The gotten gains of ages past
A maudlin feast for callow eyes."

"No end of riddles," Hilaríon said. The eyes of Wresh burned holes in his mind. La Habana seemed so far.

Necío said, "A way of kings? The Ancients would never send us *there.*"

"Not much of a prize," the rusted dame said. She strolled into the hollow.

Phellhe said, "How do we know she's not one of them?"

"I'm no *phéa-sjant*," she said. "Dragooned like many others. My name is Oriel. I can guide you where you're going."

"How do you know where we're going?"

Necío added, "And how do you know what phéa-sjant means?"

"Clever guesses."

"I think we can trust her," Hilaríon said. What she'd already said had piqued his interest. Whatever she knew, they'd need to know, too.

"Good enough for me," Ypriána said. She patted a tree trunk. "For now, you heard the rhyme. Strip the bark, then crush it to powder and drink it with water. Take as much as you can. We'll need it where we're going."

"Where is Wresh?" Phellhe said.

The people looked around. Hilaríon's stomach writhed in a knot. The truth would come out, sooner or later. Better it be through him. "Wresh—"

"Wresh went to fight," Necío said. "We crossed paths with a Mambí patrol. They kept us safe by darkness, then slipped away at daybreak. Wresh went with them. He'd waited his life for a chance like this. He said his share should go to the children. He trusted we'd see it done."

The M'Brae chattered in agreement. "It's what he wanted," Hetta said. No one paid it a second thought. Hilaríon let go his breath. It was over.

The people scattered, collecting bark. Ypriána said, "Guamá and I will take the first watch."

Necío said, "That isn't his name. Why do you keep calling him Guamá?"

"You've heard the last of Guamá," she said.

✳   ✳   ✳   ✳

Night deepened. The M'Brae snored in camp. Hutias and bull-dog bats began their nightly chorus. Land crabs scuttled through the leaves with crackling racket. The woods were safe. The soldiers wouldn't bother patrolling this far, and they had their hands full, digging. To the west, the sound of clanging spades and errant gunfire echoed from the devilish Trocha. But they were well clear of all that now. Ypriána had to be grateful. Didn't she?

He paced along the tree line. The canopy of Lightleaf Grove rustled like chimes in the breeze. *You've heard the last of Guamá*, she'd said. Those words loomed like storm clouds. And what had Oriel meant? *She's not who she says she is.* If Ypriána wasn't who she said, what did that make her? What did that make *him*?

He clutched the medallion. She'd forgotten to take it. The woods to the south yawned wide and inviting. No one would see or stop him. He'd have the medallion for his own. It wasn't the treasure but it came a close second. Days ago he'd have killed for it. Better with a little less loot than dying by her hand, pleading his case.

He looked around. The forest was dark. The tree frogs could not have been louder. It was as good a chance as he'd ever get. He stepped towards the trees—

"Nope." She pressed her blade into his throat. "His body," she said. "Where is it?"

He swallowed. "Whose?"

She jammed it harder. "*Where?*"

Between the pink cinchona boughs, Arcturus danced its golden jig. But stars weren't saving his life this time. He nodded towards the northwest. "Walk," she said.

He stumbled through the woods. She held the blade against his back. She was leading him off to some dank oubliette. "Ypriána," he said, "I can explain—"

She scraped the blade across his flesh. He winced. She said nothing. The locomotive rose, at length, above the thorny bramble. Wresh's body lay where he'd left him. Already the crabs had begun their feast. He said, "It's here."

"Don't run," she said, "or I'll kill you." She dragged Wresh's body from beneath the engine. She pushed Hilarión down beside it, and laid her blade against his neck. "Bury him."

He hesitated. "But I don't have a—"

"*Bury him now.*"

He cupped his hands into the loam. He clawed them hard beneath it. The roots and errant bits of shale snagged the tips of his fingers. He tore at the ground with painstaking vigor. His palms bled raw, his wrists burned hot. The tears welled up inside his eyes. He could feel the stone of bedrock below. He cleared the silt from the hole and exhaled.

"Deeper," she said.

"What?"

She lay the blade behind his ear and cut a hairline slice. He plunged his hands beneath the stones. He ripped it twice as deep. He dragged Wresh's body down, filled the hole with earth again, and turned to Ypriána.

She looked the grave over. "Dig one more. Not as deep."

Bile spurted into his throat. He clawed a second pit. He reached in to clear the bedrock—

"That's enough." She drew him up to his knees by the blade. "Feel familiar?"

He thought of the hilltop, where he'd guessed the Seven Angels. Hours before then, he'd been ready to kill her, and yet she'd spared his life. She could have killed him many times. Why would she kill him now?

"I was born for greatness," she said. "But there was no way to put out the fires. We left before the phéa-sjant came. It was either that or perish."

He squirmed. She wrenched the blade. "We fled far into the west," she said. "We tried to make lives for ourselves. But we never forgot M'Brae-dah. One by one the others died—hunger, sickness, war. My mother and I were the last. And before she died, she gave me a gift... and a choice." She lifted the medallion. "She entrusted this to me. I could keep it for myself, she said—trade it for riches, live out my days like a queen in some Eden. Or I could honor my birthright. I could lead us to the treasure. It was so much more than a prize. It was a torch to a bolder world. But what I had to do, she said, I could not do alone.

"He will come to *you*, she said. You'll know him when he spares your life. He'll be drawn to you. No matter where you go he'll follow. He will always find the way. You may save the M'Brae, but always he'll save *you*. Only he, and he alone, will make you what you're meant to be."

He remembered Phellhe's words. "A Steeled Elect whose heart is true," he said.

"I didn't believe it," she replied. "I didn't need help. Then I met you. You couldn't kill me. You tracked me into the hills. Try as I did to lose you, I couldn't. Then I realized why. And when you found the Seven Angels, I knew my mother had been right. I made my choice, Hilaríon—or Guamá, whichever it is. Now it's time to make yours."

She kicked him square between the shoulders. He lurched into the grave. "We go as one, or not at all," she said. "The weak aren't pawns. The strong aren't special. All of us will share the treasure. Every one of them—the elders, the children, the whore—will reach the end of this journey alive." She pulled him up. "Are you the steel to my elect?" She rolled his sleeve. On his arm glistened his hilldevil brand. "Or are you one of *them*?"

"I go with you," he said.

"Good." She slapped the blade into his hand. "Cut it out."

He winced. "What do you mean?"

"*Cut it out.*" She glared with relentless eyes.

Hilaríon clenched his rattling jaws, and slid the blade beneath his flesh. He pulled it along the length of his arm. The brand peeled away like the rind of a fruit. He sagged at his hips, spent in pain. She said, "Throw it in."

He flung the ribbon of flesh in the grave. She knelt in prayer above them. She whispered low and blessed herself, then sprang to her feet with a jaunty smile, as if the last hour had never occurred. "But you managed to get us across the Trocha," she said. "Not just anyone could have done that." She draped the medallion over her neck, then turned and walked away.

Hilaríon clutched his bleeding arm. Who was this wildling, Ypriána? Each answer begged a new question. Each question pared back a bit of himself. Each bit of himself having been pared back seemed to re-form in her likeness. He shivered. He'd forgotten, momentarily, about the eyes.

He wiped the blood away from his arm. He'd have a mangled scar forever, but never a hilldevil brand again. The new look suited him better. He tore a swatch from his cloak and bandaged it, then stepped off after the woman.

xxiv.

They pushed to the east. The clamor of war and pillage faded. In its place rose the music of herons and toads, and dewdrops dripping from majagua leaves. The piney mulch gave way to loam, the hardwood stands to mangrove. The M'Brae crushed and boiled the bark, and drank it with their food: water snakes and millipedes and fish too slow to evade them, but never enough to leave them filled. Oriel kept their spirits high. She could juggle and dance like a jester, or throw her voice three places at once. He laughed at her antics when the others laughed, but otherwise kept a shrewd eye. Whatever secrets Oriel knew, she held them to herself.

The sun sank over a dreary horizon. The Westbound Flood lulled black, and still. A mist rolled off the temperate sea and found them huddled in camp. "Sadness finds a home here," Necío said. "It drips from the sky. It pools at our feet."

"Good we're near the end," Hilaríon said. They *were* near the end, weren't they? He handed Phellhe a draught of Lightleaf elixir. The big man pushed it away. Hilaríon swallowed the final drops. "How far to this Tumbled Bark?"

"Two days on the north bank," Oriel said, "then south between the rivers twin."

Ypriána said, "And down into Ha—"

"Don't say it!" Necío said. "Never say its name."

The air grew stickier, the mood seemed to sour. Hilaríon quipped, "I wonder how many bearers I'll need for my cut of the treasure." No one laughed. Necío began to tremble. Hilaríon said, "What is it?"

"Don't you hear?"

"Hear what?"

"Listen."

Hilaríon cupped his hand to his ear. Above the fire came a faraway sound, like lowing beasts. "They're calling each other," Necío said. "They sense we're near."

"They're animals," Phellhe said.

"Nothing here's what it seems. My mother—"

"Your mother filled your head with lies. There's no curse on Ha—"

"Don't!"

"—Yanrinol."

A meaty roar brayed the darkness. Necío said, "I told you not to speak that name. Why would the Ancients send us here?"

"It's a test, like everything else," Ypriána said. "No one would chance the Kings lightly."

Hilaríon said, "Chance the Kings?"

"That's just an old ghost story," Phellhe said. "It frightens children and fools. Then we grow up. We're supposed to grow up."

"Forget it," Hilaríon said.

"A sweet luxury, forgetting is," Oriel murmured, but only Hilaríon heard.

Necío said, "We'd have been wiped out if not for Líj." He cleared his throat.

Phellhe rolled his eyes. "Story time."

Necío prodded the fire. "Long before the Vujoíe came, before our very sires, this land belonged to the first peoples. This land belonged to the Esèh.

"The Esèh were mystics. They'd dwelled in these swamplands ere time was born. They'd been formed from the water itself, some say. Their minds were nimble, their wills made of stone. Tall and lordly, their skin was bronze, their hair the veils of running rivers, their eyes all the shades of the dawn. For days on end, the legends hold, they'd gaze on their watery reflections, and weep.

"But for all their beauty, the Esèh were proud. They gave themselves sway over all plants and beasts, and the power to name them, that they might be masters. Those which they loved they gave beautiful names, and to those they feared, or hated, gave none. For ages they reigned and, alone, decided what thrived. But the Esèh's world was about to change, for a new people had come to these shores—the M'Brae."

Faint crunching rose from the darkness. Hilarion said, "Did you hear that?"

The fire crackled softly. The treetops swayed in an evening breeze. The eleuths resumed singing. The swamp abounded with sounds. There was no use worrying over one.

Necío went on, "Now, when our sire first came ashore, he was poor, and weak, and humble. He asked only what space and food the land, and the Esèh, could spare. The Esèh laughed and called him *jhaga*, a beast to be hunted for fun. So like any tarpon or quail, our sire made sport for the Esèh, dying on their blades and hooks. And from afar the Esèh laughed, and went on admiring their reflections.

"But our sire was clever, full of will. He pulled himself from the brink of death and spread out from the strand. His footprints pierced the veil of the swamp. His ambitions soared above the trees. The Esèh stopped laughing, and watched as the M'Brae grew strong. They doubled their efforts to stem our tide, and push us back to the strand. But the M'Brae, hardened by days of little, had become a rolling force. There was no going back. Our time had come."

Hilarion heard another crunch. He'd tracked long enough to recognize a padded footfall. "Listen—"

"I'd like to know," Phellhe said to Ypriána, "what happens after. Where will we go?"

She ignored him. Her arms, like mythic bowstrings drawn, glowed orange in the firelight. Silence regathered. The footfalls—if they had been footfalls—altogether ceased.

Necío continued, "So at the peak of their wisdom and might, the M'Brae dreamed to raise a city, worthy of their remade selves—the City of Ten Thousand Fires. Made in the image of cities of yore, its spires were white and reached for the heavens. In every window, beneath every archway, our sires set a candle, and their fires could be seen for miles at sea.

"And the Esèh raged that the M'Brae would dare. They massed their forces and made open war. Their warriors leapt from the treetops and sprang from the depths of the mire. They harried the M'Brae in woodland and waters. And our sires resisted, defending their city, but they could not hold back the Esèh's fury. Defeat, and death, seemed all but certain."

"Just like now," Phellhe said.

Necío said, "Have faith."

"Your mother chased it from me."

"You believed her, once."

"And then I grew up. We were fine until you swindlers came. How many died so she could keep looking? Fenn and Wresh are just the beginning."

The fire popped. Necío went on, "So death and defeat seemed certain, but the cause was not yet lost. No one knows for sure how he did it. But Líj saw the Esèh with fresh eyes, and saw their fatal flaw. At once he knew how the war could be won with neither arms nor numbers.

"So Líj went forth from the city alone, armed with a sealskin sack and guile. He found where the Esèh dwelled. He slipped past their guards and into their midst. And, with the swiftest of swipes, he stole from the Esèh their almighty weapon, brought it back to the city, and hid it within its walls for all time."

Hilaríon's thoughts drifted. Phellhe was no fool: a bully, perhaps, but keen. Necío nudged him and said, "Want to *ask* me anything?"

"Ask you?"

"Storytelling's collaborative," Necío groused. "You're supposed to ask me. The Spoils of Líj. Want to know what it was?"

Hilaríon nodded. He could swear he'd heard another footstep.

"So would I," Necío replied, "yet, sadly, no one knows. But for the Esèh its theft was an untold disaster. Back to the nethers they slunk like worms, leaving the land to our sires. The City of Ten Thousand Fires rose, dwarfing all else for miles. And the Ancients entered the city in triumph, and in mockery called across the waters, daring the Esèh to take it back. But that was a fateful decision, for—"

"How can we spit on our forebears like this?" Phellhe said. "We'd all be dead or never born, but they held M'Brae-dah together."

"Big of you to share credit," Ypriána said.

"I'll thank you not to lecture me. Your family fled to save themselves."

"You saved no one," she said, "just delayed fate. The world has to die to come again, bolder. Weapons swapped for wisdom. No one goes without. That's what treasure will bring."

"The Bronze Titan will burn this land," Phellhe said. "The Butcher will slaughter the people. There'll be nothing. But there *was* a treasure, once. It was called M'Brae-dah. We let them have it, too." Phellhe stormed into the darkness.

Necío grumbled, "For the spirits of the Esèh lived on. They accepted our sires' invitation. They resumed their war on the ones who'd broken them. Some took the form of monstrous beasts— massive, swift, and sharp of eye, mad with a craving for M'Brae flesh. Some took the form of airy midges—swarming, relentless, ever thirsting for their enemy's blood, their bite the kiss of fever and death.

"And our sires fled their glorious city, for which they'd shed so much blood. Weakened and humbled, they stole into darkness, to the cracks and fissures of this land, never to return to the swamp, never to regain their former strength. And the swamp, and the sea, and the spirits of the Esèh reclaimed the City of Ten Thousand Fires, and took it for their own, and hold it even to this day, it is said—waiting, for the children of Líj to return and receive their just due. Long gone and long forgotten, the Esèh live on. They are the Kings of this realm—*cocodrilo* and *mosquito*, the Toothed King and the Winged King. Whose bite is the deadlier?" He made his hands into claws. "Both."

"I know a story like that," Oriel said, "but different."

"That's M'Brae lore," Necío said. "You'd never have heard."

"Later," she said, "I'll tell you mine." It sounded strangely like a threat.

Hilaríon lent his ear to the darkness. Swamp owls hooted from hollows in pines. Almiqui peeped in crusty leaves, rooting for succulent grubs. Whatever had made the footfalls had gone. And Phellhe's blunt words still rankled. "What if Phellhe's right?"

"*Está en lo cierto,*" a woman's voice said. "He is very right."

They sprang to their feet, drawing blades. Phellhe shuffled back into the firelight, clutched from behind by a pair of arms. One held a knife to his throat, the other a knife to his crotch. Whooping rang out all around. Amazons, draped in leather armor, their faces masked and painted, jumped from the darkness, surrounding the camp, leveling wooden pikes at the M'Brae.

"Hilaríon Soto," their leader said, "this is a night you'll remember, for sure." She lifted her mask.

It was Lux León.

xxv.

The Amazons herded the M'Brae together. Hilaríon stared in disbelief. Lux León had survived after all and now was leading female Mambíses. Necío said, "You've got the wrong man."

"Like dancing fuck I do," Lux said. "Who's in charge here?"

Phellhe said, "I'm M'Brae Oíc."

"And I'm the Queen of Sheba. You're on Cuba. That makes you Cuban. That makes you a combatant. *That* makes you a Mambí, unless you're a loyalist, in which case that makes you dead. Now." She pressed the knife back into his crotch.

"That's Mambí freedom," Ypriána said.

"I'd be careful," Lux said. "Everyone here's expendable. And you won't be needing *this*." She pulled the medallion off Ypriána's neck. "I'll lighten your load, in the name of the people."

"The people are thieves."

"No, just borrowers. We'll pay you back in liberty." She put it around her neck.

"We're passing through," Phellhe said. "We have nothing to do with you, or Cuba Libre."

"Wrong again," Lux said. "This fight's about freedom. We all have a stake in winning."

Hilaríon laughed: he'd heard that before. He'd taught her to say it. "That dream's dead."

"Thanks to you, it might be," Lux said.

"We have nothing you want," Phellhe said.

"How'd you cross the Trocha?" Lux said.

"Carefully," Ypriána quipped.

"Hah!" Lux said. "Now you have something I want—the truth. Carefully, with my old capitán? More likely it was recklessly. There's a pit of noses, eyes, and ears at Cacarajícara says—"

"That's enough!" Hilaríon said. The memory was caustic.

Lux looked the M'Brae over. "I am in need of stevedores," she said. "Boats are coming, fast ashore. Those who choose to help, many thanks. Those who don't, you'll help even more. No free rides in free Cuba." She smacked Phellhe's cheek. "Get them moving."

Phellhe ordered them in line. An Amazon told Hilaríon, "Not you." She confiscated his machete and led him past the trees. "Wait here."

A squall set in from the north. Lightning flashed across the sky. The treetops shook in a cold, wet wind. He found himself alone, with Lux. He said, "How did you—"

"Don't," she said. "Not now."

"I watched you."

"What?" she said. "Die? I watched you run."

He said, "It was all just, so... not what I expected."

"That's what battle is, capitán—the unexpected."

He thought about the hillside. "About your husband..."

"He still doesn't know. I ran from him. I was running when you met me. I'm still running. Only now I'm running *to*."

"To what."

"To a world without him. Or you."

"Lux, Elídio is..." He stopped. "Your husband is..."

"What?"

"Stupid."

A smile fell across her face and just as quickly vanished. "A year ago that might've made hay."

He stepped closer. "Pretend it's last year."

She pulled back. "It's a new world, capitán. We don't have room for dabblers."

"Dabblers?"

"Whatever lie you sold these fools to make them follow you, it's over. They belong to Cuba Libre now. You too. And you're worth a lot."

"She'll come for me."

"That wildling? Not if she knew the price on your head, alive. Every Mambí in Occidente is looking for the Coward of the Faceless Legion. You're famous. That's what you wanted."

"You craved it just as much."

"But I grew up, Hilarión. Watching you run made me see. The cavalry isn't coming."

Lux had changed. The old charms weren't working. "I can help you," he said.

"I'm counting on it. We're small fry here. You're a big scalp."

He said, "You won't kill me."

"I don't want to. You're worth far more to me living."

"What price?"

"Price-*less*, capitán, price-*less*. Why would I need a reward? In the world we're building it'd mean less than shit. But gratitude from on high? There's the rub. And I know something no one else does.

"In Playa Majana, seventy miles west of here, there is a port. And in that port there is a dock. And at that dock, bouncing in its moors, is a boat. And in the bottom of that boat, probably disguised as a fish box, is a trapdoor. And beneath that trapdoor—you guessed it— there is a secret crawlspace. And that secret crawlspace is the center of the world because in two days' time, *he's* going to be inside. And he's going to be coming *here*. The Bronze Titan."

A cold sweat broke at his temples. The Bronze Titan was eight feet tall. He'd carried his warhorse from battle. He could kill ten men and fuck ten women before the morning dew had dried. "Here?"

"The Butcher's gambit is working," she said. "The Mambíses can't cross the Trocha en masse. But outflanking it by sea? He's coming to scout a landing. And he doesn't know it yet, but also to collect *you*."

This certainly wasn't the old Lux. "But what if I could—"

"You can't."

"Hear me out. What if I could do you better? These people are after a treasure. It's here, in the swamp, not far. This wildling thinks I'm some kind of prophet, that only I can find it. I don't know what she's talking about. But I know it has to be real."

She scowled. "In a million years, Hilarión, I wouldn't have thought you could drop any lower, but somehow you proved me wrong. Bravo, capitán. That's the biggest fish tale I've ever heard."

"But it's not," he said. "I've tracked all my life—I know how to read people. These rubes believe every word. This treasure is real, or they think it is. Think of what the Bronze Titan could do with it."

"And you'd let me take it?"

"As long as I get mine, and these people get enough to live... except for that big man. Nobody likes him. The rest belongs to you."

She raised an eyebrow. She was thinking—or faking. "Why would I trust you?"

"Why would I trust *you*? If I'm lying you lose nothing. If you throw me in with the Bronze Titan, I'm mincemeat. I'd stand in your shoes. Would you stand in mine?"

A moment passed in silence. "Alright, capitán," she said. "You want these people to get their just due?"

"They shouldn't have come this far for nothing."

"Then I've got just the plan." She drove her knee into his crotch. The pain exploded in his balls. "I'll take the credit for capturing you, and they can have the reward. Everyone wins except, well... you."

He doubled over, groaning, "Wait..."

"That'll be treasure enough. I'm sure they'll all be happy to hear."

He reached for her. "No."

"And *she'll* be happiest of all. You never change, Hilarión. Treasure won't buy you peace—"

"*No!*"

A bloodcurdling scream split the air. "Sol," Lux said. She ran from the glade. Hilarión followed. Lux pushed the mangrove fronds aside, then shrieked and stumbled back. Among the branches was an Amazon's body, the one who'd led him to the clearing and taken his machete. She'd been spitted through her head.

A reptilian hiss sliced the chorus of raindrops. "*Cerca,*" it said, "*Cerca... o lejos?*"

xxvi.

The Gray Jaeger sprang from the dark. His blade caught the lightning that shattered the sky. His eyes, like a hunting hawk's, burned white. Hilaríon turned to run. His foot caught on a root, spilling him face-first to the mud.

Lux leapt to Hilaríon's side, blade drawn. The Jaeger swung. The force of his strike shattered Lux's blade. She crumpled onto Hilaríon's back, miring their bodies into the muck.

The rainfall doubled. The Jaeger sheathed his blade. He pressed his boot to the dead Amazon's face, and tore the pike from her skull. Hilaríon struggled to get to his feet. But Lux's quivering held him down.

The Jaeger raised the pike aloft, aiming it at Lux's heart. "Juntos otra vez y para siempre," the Jaeger said. "Esto es lo que querías—"

"But not what *I* want," came Ypriána's voice. A glint of metal flashed from the shadows, cleaving the Jaeger's pike in half, as Ypriána leapt into their midst. She kicked the Jaeger in his ribs, then wheeled her blade at his head.

The Jaeger hollowed backwards, then thrust the broken pike through her legs. Ypriána spun to her back. The Jaeger swung the pike at her face. She caught it and pulled him towards her. The pike sliced her ear. Blood trickled down her face and neck. The Jaeger vaulted over her and landed in a crouch.

Hilaríon threw Lux aside. He grabbed the other half of the pike. The Jaeger swung at Ypriána's head. Hilaríon parried the strike. He hooked the pike through the Jaeger's arms. The Jaeger released his grip on the pike and Hilaríon flung it away.

In a flash the Jaeger drew his blade and swung at Hilaríon's head. Hilaríon raised his own pike in parry. The Jaeger's blade lodged into it. Hilaríon let go the pike, still spitted on the Jaeger's

136

blade. A shaft of lightning lit the grove. Thunder rent the sky. The Jaeger struggled to wrench the blade free. Hilaríon drew back his fist—

"*Make it stop!*" From the camp Mabba's voice cried, "Make the storm stop!"

The Jaeger cocked his head towards the sound, like a shrike honing onto its prey. He ripped the blade out of the pike and ran off towards the child's voice. Ypriána raced after him. Hilaríon turned to reach for Lux and take back the medallion, but Lux had already gone. He grabbed the pike and followed Ypriána.

The mangrove spread its tendrils. Thunder pealed like cannon fire. Lightning turned the woods pale blue then blotted it into darkness. Where the Mambí camp had been was empty, save for embers and Amazon bodies, hands still gripping pikes and blades. They'd never seen the Jaeger coming.

A man's voice yelled in the distance. A chorus of screams rang out in its wake. Ypriána raced off towards them. Hilaríon grabbed a dead woman's blade and willed himself on Ypriána's heels.

The shrieks of the hunted filled the night, the number of voices steadily dropping. The rainstorm hammered all the harder, pummeling the soil to gluey mire. Hilaríon raced through the tangle of mangrove, trying to keep Ypriána's pace. The rain slashed down in heavy sheets. He doubled over, gasping. The sky was too black, the ground too soft. And she was too strong a runner.

"Ypriána!" he called. "Where—" He stopped himself. The Jaeger could be anywhere. There was no use trying to catch up to her. His best defense was silence.

He forced himself onward and splashed through a stream, by its looks the first of the twin rivers spoken of on the slab in Lightleaf Grove. The mud of its banks had been trampled: the others must have passed this way. Lux would be headed wherever they'd gone, and she still had the medallion. If she fell, the quest was over. There'd be no prize of any stripe.

Hilaríon stumbled on into the night. The swamp rang with a chorus of screams, distant behind the pelting rain. The trees thinned and shrank, then disappeared: he'd passed beyond the mangrove. But the darkness was still impenetrable.

Weariness took him. He let his head drop.

✻   ✻   ✻   ✻

The first light of dawn tinged the east. The downpour had slowed to nettling rain. Hilaríon rubbed his groggy eyes. A putrid waste of stunted trees, scrub, and water spread before him. And like flotsam off the sea, the swamp was filled with woven baskets, rolling, tumbling, and blowing about. Some lodged in hammocks, others on sawgrass. Others rode the whispering tide, lapping at the strand. The sight was otherworldly. He bent and lifted one. Between its woven cords of straw, beads and bits of shellfish gleamed. The craftsmanship was flawless.

Sobbing rose from a hammock, "Gone... all gone." Hilaríon parted the toothy sawgrass. Lux was curled in a heap. "Every last one," she said. "It should've been *you*. You led that devil to us."

He scoffed. Whether or not it should have been him, his wits had saved his life, again. He raised his machete under her throat. "Something borrowed, please." He nodded towards the medallion.

"What's it to you?" she said.

"Golden days."

She handed the medallion over. "Yours or hers?" she said. "It won't be long, and neither will *she*."

Dawn bled away. Black, pregnant rainclouds rolled in from the south. The M'Brae emerged from the mangrove together, arms sagging and eyes bloated, but otherwise none the worse for wear. Why had the Jaeger spared them? Was he taunting Hilaríon?

Ypriána came last, neck caked with blood from her mangled ear. Someone was missing. "Oriel?" Hilaríon said. Ypriána shook her head.

Another pair of eyes glowed warm. Oriel had perished, taking her secrets. Who knew what she had had to share? They should never have involved her. Ypriána took back the medallion. "My regrets to liberty," she said.

"This is the final straw," Phellhe said. "We're leaving. We'll be safe in the Mambí camp."

"At the river mouth," Lux said. "We can get there by dark."

"That's where the Jaeger hit us," Hilaríon said. "Your fighters are dead."

Lux said, "There are more on the way."

"We're finished with you," Phellhe said. "The Mambíses will protect us."

Ypriána said, "Like they did last night?"

Phellhe said, "For long enough. We'll help them, then decide what to do." He took a lumbering plod to the north. Lux rushed to his side.

"We're not going north just to turn south again," Hilaríon said. "The treasure's too close."

"The treasure you wanted to give me," Lux said, "if I let you go? Minus your share, of course."

Lux was playing for keeps. But he'd taught her how to do it. "No," he said, "I said I'd split my share with you. That was after you demanded it all, and after you said you were going to kill Phellhe."

Phellhe spun to Lux. "You *what?*"

She squirmed, "I didn't."

"The Jaeger did us a favor," Hilaríon said. "We're closer to the treasure. We crossed the first of the rivers at night. The Tumbled Bark is east, a day if Oriel was right."

Lux said, "The Jaeger didn't do *her* any favors."

"We can honor her, then," Hilaríon said. "Treasure now, Jaeger later." He stepped to the east. The people followed.

Phellhe yelled, "Stop!" The people kept walking. "Hilldevil," he railed, "I've indulged this long enough—!"

A hush fell over Phellhe and the people as all their eyes settled on something behind him. Phellhe backed away. Hilaríon turned.

In the hammock sat a rawboned man, weaving an ornate basket. His skin was the color of lichens, or copper left too long to the rain. Only inches shorter than Phellhe, but nowhere near as bulky, his lankiness gave him a willow-like aura, drooping in a midsummer's breeze. His face was gaunt with bony cheeks, his hair fell about his shoulders unkempt, less mane than fraying cloth. Mud dribbled from his wiry arms.

From far away, then closer, a plaintive chorus filled the air, sounding like seraphs on the march. From behind the hammock, more rawbones emerged. Their voices pitched like wailing loons and rolled like dripping nectar. Necío said, "Our Ancients' tongue, sung as it was meant. I'd never hoped to hear it."

The chorus swelled and soared anew, then just as quickly faded. "How can they know our language?" Phellhe said.

"Because your sires taught ours," a woman's voice answered, "before your sires wiped ours out." The rawbones parted. The voice was Oriel's.

xxvii.

She stepped from their midst, more druid now than rusted dame. Necío said, "Who wiped who out? The Ancients only wanted somewhere to live."

"So do locusts," she said. "And *jhaga* means *little brother.*"

Necío said, "It can't be. *You* can't be. The story says."

"Stories are weapons, wielded by winners. The stories keep them winning, making monsters of the losers."

Necío sulked. Oriel said, "Yours is a name that begs laughter, Necío, but hides a trove. You've never liked your name. Before long, you'll have a name to be proud of."

He grinned. "A new name?"

"By and by," she said, "but you'll have to earn it in blood."

Phellhe pushed Necío aside, and said to Oriel, "Who are you, really?"

Oriel dangled her arms like a wraith and said,

> "In darkest depths of vilest mire
> With blackest sin upon their heart
> And M'Brae blood upon their lips
> The Kings wait.

"Isn't that what your fathers warn, when children misbehave?"

Ypriána said, "The Esèh were killed."

The rawbones hissed. "*Esèh*," Oriel said. "Your sires' gift to mine. Would they'd never been so kind."

Necío said, "That *is* your name."

"That's your problem, fool, not my name."

Fear pulsed from the M'Brae faces. The rawbones could break them handily. Hilaríon would have been happy to run. But Oriel still knew something he needed. "What do you want?" he said.

"Now, you're of many names, aren't you?" she said. "One for every face you meet. Who knows what to call you?"

"How about finder of gold?" he replied.

"A princely moniker," Oriel said. "For shame princes are but leeches with land. Let's gather what you've earned."

The Esèh encircled the M'Brae. They slogged off together into the waste. Swamp deer bounded from their path. Hummingbirds, like speedy gems, darted past their faces. Storm clouds gathered overhead: another squall was coming. Lux, with nowhere else to go, stalked just out of reach. Every so often, Hilaríon thought, he could see a savage, yellow eye peeking from the muck.

Baskets drifted among the flats. Necío swiped one as he walked. "Why so many?"

Oriel said, "It's all we remember."

"What have you forgotten?"

"Who could say?" she said. "That's what forgetting is."

Hilaríon peeked at Ypriána, then turned to Oriel. "Tell me all you know," he said.

She laughed, "That'd take all year."

"About Ypriána."

"I already told you. She's not who she says."

"Then who is she?"

"Before we part, I'll tell you. No more questions now."

Morning turned to afternoon, afternoon to evening. They closed in on another hammock. Oriel pointed and said, "In there." The rawbones spread out, as if blocking the others' escape.

Ypriána stepped towards the trees. Oriel stopped her and said, "Not you." Ypriána pushed her aside. Oriel pushed back and said, "I don't invite you further."

Ypriána held out the medallion. "It's mine."

Oriel said, "It's been passed around."

Cracks spread across her implacable calm. "Like you?" Ypriána said. "You'd still be in that bed."

"You'd never have gotten across the Trocha." Oriel looked at Hilaríon. "You go."

Ypriána's hand drifted towards her blade. Oriel said, "What about weapons swapped for wisdom? A bold world?"

Ypriána's fingers danced on the hilt. "We still have to get there, don't we?"

Hilarío n stopped her. To argue was pointless. "Wait here," he said. They were at the journey's end. Weren't they?

Ypriána curtsied. "Shall I, then?"

He called to Necío, "Come with me." Oriel let him pass. Ypriána seethed. Hilarío n pushed the leaves aside and sank into the thicket.

The sprawling fronds enveloped them. Dragonflies buzzed around their heads. Moisture off the forest floor hung leaden in the air. Hilarío n hacked through the bramble, his mind awash with questions. "What was that about?"

"Esèh insolence," Necío said. He spat a mouthful of gnats. From the distance came a throaty sound. It might have been a roar— or a laugh.

Hilarío n said, "They don't like being called that."

"Who cares what they like? They hunted us. It's good the treasure comes from them."

"But why would she treat Ypriána that way?" He thought of her sinewy, naked body, glistening in the sunset. "The medallion is hers."

"It's *ours*." A branch smacked his face. "Argh! What does that witch expect us to find—?"

"*That*," Hilarío n said. The rotting, upside-down hulk of a boat rose like a ridge above them.

The Tumbled Bark.

It soared past the treetops, a sheer wall of wood. Its masts lay shattered across the ground, its timbers draped with mosses. It looked an ornate barrow, long reclaimed by the festering swamp. Necío peeped a childish squeal. Hilarío n let the image take him. He'd make La Habana in less than a week.

Necío disappeared inside through a porthole. Hilarío n dropped to his knees and followed. The mud in which the boat had sunken had hardened into a densely packed floor. The stagnant air inside the hulk was thick with the stench of rotting hardwood. The dark was absolute. He swept his hands along the ground but couldn't feel a thing.

He reached into his pocket. He still had matches from the Trocha. He felt for a stone and struck the match to it. A tiny flame sparked. He held it to his face.

He staggered back. Glaring from the rotting wood were multitudes of eyes, pupils like daggers, trained on his heart. He fell to the dirt.

The chamber was barren.

Necío touched the flame to a sprig. "It *has* to be here," he said.

Hilaríon felt something rough beneath him. His hand closed on a knobby rod. Halfway submerged in the dirt was a scepter. He said, "Over here."

Necío brought the light and drew the scepter to his face. It was pocked with foreign carvings, and made of human bone. Necío read it to himself. "We should never have come," he said.

"Where is the treasure?" Hilaríon said.

A sound tore through the earth, like a thousand horses screaming. The hulk swayed in its muddy moors. "The treasure," Necío said, "is *us*."

xxviii.

"What did you say?" Hilarión said.

Necío shouted over the chaos, "The treasure—*their* treasure—is us."

A crack spread bow to stern. The eyes flaked to dust. The ceiling timbers broke to shards and rained into the hold. They squirmed through the porthole and back to the hammock.

The rainclouds gleamed metallic gray. Icy hail screamed down in waves. The Tumbled Bark boomed its death-rattle, then caved beneath its weight. From the north, a gathering droning sound whined across the gloom. There was no sign of the Esèh. Ypriána said, "They're gone."

Necío said, "Not for long." He slapped the scepter into her hand. She read aloud,

> "In fest'ring staves the truth now writ
> Not shape nor size the prize to hold
> Bestowed but once ere taken sack
> By pillage fraught with death untold
> In swinish lust astride this land
> Your ancient sire who bore all things,
> Doth grant you now a regal tithe—
> A chance at last to walk with kings
> Through Sabal Gate to grassy sea
> In promenade through rankest mires
> Their sumptuous gauntlet just deserts,
> To City of Ten Thousand Fires
> And there the Broken gather near
> In ancient sin by your hand wrought
> Restore them fast the Spoils of Líj
> Lest Vexing Heirloom fall to naught."

Necío said. "They mean to hunt us."

"Not if we find the spoils," she said.

The droning grew louder. The water of the tide pools chattered. Hilaríon said, "They won't kill me. I'm not M'Brae."

Ypriána said, "They'll kill you worst. *They think you're the Steeled Elect.*"

The droning reached a fever pitch. The people clutched their ears. A sooty shroud was falling fast, like witchcraft on the wind.

The Winged Kings had come.

"Cover your mouths!" Hilaríon said. "Cover——!"

The swarm broke across them. The midges bore their bristling fangs. They spiraled into mouths and ears. They tore through hair and chewed through clothes. Their tiny talons ripped at eyes.

"The elixir!" Ypriána cried. "Drink what's left!" But no one could hear her.

Hilaríon slithered into a pool. The people dove behind him, submerging all but the tops of their faces. The midges perched on M'Brae chins. They sunk their dagger-barbs in cheeks and dug their claws in noses. "Out," Hilaríon said. The left bank was firmer. He pointed. "This way."

They stumbled towards steadier ground. The midges cut them off, and hovered in front of Hilaríon's face. He lurched leftwards. The midges stopped him. He spun to the right: the midges went with him. He leaned forward. They rushed at his eyes and brandished their spindly beaks like spears.

He took a step backwards. They sheathed their beaks. He drew back further. The midges in front of his face broke off and rejoined the larger swarm. He only could go where the midges would let him. "They're driving us," he said.

"Where?" Ypriána said.

In the distance, past the rolling swales, were two identical palms. It had to be the Sabal Gate. "There, by deadliest path."

The midges fanned out, droning with rage. But they kept their distance. Hilaríon draped his cloak over Maith. He gathered the M'Brae children in close and formed the adults in a ring around them. A cold rain mixed with icy chunks battered them from a green-black sky. The thunder bellowed its guttural dirge. The people, like turtles, drew heads inside clothes. Hilarío led them, head held high. The scattershot water pelted his face. He pressed on just the same.

Ypriána hacked at the swarm. He said, "It only makes them mad." He guided her blade into its sheath.

The M'Brae trudged across the waste. The midges took wing and darted away. Their droning mellowed to a lull. The Sabal Gate loomed high above: two massive palms, their broad leaves tattered and draped in Spanish moss. Hilarío said, "We've come—"

He stopped. A child was standing between the palms. His flesh was blue: translucent, even. The wind seemed to whip through his body, unbroken. Hilarío knew he'd seen him before.

"Go through," Ypriána said.

A chill ran up Hilarío's spine. He knew where he'd seen the boy. He'd been a child soldier, at Cacarajícara—where he'd died. Hilarío said, "Not yet."

The whine of the midges intensified. She glared. "When would be good?"

He peered past the boy. More faces appeared—more than he could count. Each one was different, yet all were the same. They stared with burning eyes. The torment welled inside him. They were his slaughtered Faceless Legion. He drew back. "We're not going."

Ypriána said, "The scepter said."

"The scepter didn't mention *them.*"

"Who?"

"You can't see them?"

"I see two trees and a thief who's lost his mind." She fingered her blade. "Remember what I warned you."

The whining rose to a grinding roar. The midges fanned among them. They dropped in front of M'Brae faces, brandishing bloodthirsty beaks. The phantom faces leered. Hilarío's stomach seized in knots. Ypriána took his hand. "Whatever you've done, it's led you here. We need the capitán now," she said.

Perdition was waiting, either way. The Gray Jaeger's question was unanswerable: he was running away from, yet towards the same thing. But treasure would surely sweeten the meantime. It *had* to.

"Inside!" he said. The midges alighted, the Legion vanished. He rushed the people through the palms. Their faces were pocked with rashes and whelks.

Necío staggered at the rear. "I saw them, too," he said.

Hilaríon took him by the hand. He wouldn't have wished that curse on anyone, Necío least of all. "Then that's all you'll ever see," he said, and charged into the Sabal Gate.

xxix.

Silence reigned. He opened his eyes. The swamp stretched around for leagues on end. The air sat frightfully still. He could hear the blood pounding inside his temples. He was alone. The others had vanished.

"*Hilarión,*" a voice said.

Hilarión's skin turned gooseflesh. The voice seemed to come from inside his bones. It thundered across his ears.

"*Finder of gold.*"

His legs quivered uncontrollably. His ankle gave out. He stumbled.

He made no splash when he broke the water. The bottom seemed like miles below. Five massive forms, like giant fishes swathed in gray, trundled in inky depths. He flung himself from the pool.

"*Guamá,*" the voice said, closer.

A golden fog descended. The mists swirled thick in front of his face. The droplets dangled in front of his eyes, like the shards of a shattered mirror. He peered into the glassy haze. The face looking back was not his. "Walk," it said. He tried to turn. A cry split the stillness, "*Walk.*"

He bit into his lower lip. The blood seeped into his mouth. He willed his throbbing legs from the muck. The voice began to sing,

> "Where have you gone, o weavers of spells?
> Your fathers' scepters splintered shards
> Your breathless incantations lost
> I cannot hear your voices.
>
> Where have you gone, o divers of pearls?
> 'Neath moonlit seas your treasures plucked
> Your knotted flanks like tideswept stone
> I cannot feel your hands."

The music seemed a saccharine dirge, terrible and lilting. He couldn't stand to hear it sung. He couldn't bear to shut it out.

Through the fog, a tiny figure flashed, then another, and another. The laughter of children filled the void. At their heels ran the shadows of willowy adults, laughing and chasing the children. The voice sang,

"Ere the gun and bloody spear
And ere the barren farlands' lust
We plunged the shallows, twirled the winds
And heard a name in every gust.
Ere the spade and grinding wheel—
An endless spring, of boundless lease
We sang with spoonbills, danced the swales
And lived here in a dream of peace."

The laughter faded. The fog grew thicker. Hilaríon trudged ahead. The ground gave way to tidal marsh. A figure climbed from the water and flopped like a mudfish. The song went on,

"Like shrouds from blackest nether world
The sails upon the horizon loomed
The M'Brae sire crawled ashore
And into harrowing earth, entombed.
The haggard flotsam M'Brae begged
Lest death devour his dwindling swarms
To nectars rare we touched his lips
We took him in our bounteous arms."

Necío had told this same story. Hadn't he?
The figure staggered to its feet. Its gaunt frame swelled then split

in two: one man and one woman. The marsh winds stirred the fog.
The figures went on splitting. He was surrounded by shadowy beings.

"Then the M'Brae raised his head
Whelped from dust by patient hand
His windward gaze turned leeward leer
His long legs splayed astride the strand."

The shadows of the willowy ones rose among the shorter figures.
The figures joined hands and sang. The song continued,

"We sang as one, our throats entwined
'Midst Ringing Rings our questions shared
The light of Wonderwhy relit
The timeless seaborne secrets bared.
We bowed in thanks to teeming earth
For fickle chance had deigned to spare
Once dark imposter, now beloved
Our M'Brae brother clasped so near."

But this wasn't Necío's story, at all.
The figures vanished. The voice resumed,

"But swirled the pitiless winds of change
As bellows to a warlike spleen
The bilious upstart babe no more
The child from the home-hearth weaned.
The stripling's love for shepherd fades
And wonder of the swaddling sands
Once trickle now a raging tide
His bullish tendrils grope—for land."

Four new figures loomed through the fog. Two shorter ones stood with folded arms. Two willowy ones begged on bended knees.

"On secret sacred sunswept isle
His mind's-eye conjures princely spires
Then yoked, his masses' gall to build
His City of Ten Thousand Fires.
Now comes our chance to beg a'knee
Let hallowed grounds be hallowed aye
But cocksure fledglings hear no plea
His ivory towers slit the sky."

The shorter figures turned away. The ones who'd pleaded wept. The fog bled deathstrike-red. From the marsh rose the spires of white marble buildings. The weeping gave way to the clamor of toil. Atop each spire and from each window, a torch flame twisted in the winds. It seemed a cluster of white-hot stars, against the vastness of space.

The City of Ten Thousand Fires.

The rains whipped into a squall. A chorus of screaming rose from the fog. Countless figures, tall and short, seemed to grapple and clash all around.

"And desperate pleas to plaintive wails—
Our one-time brother's thoughts go red
In M'Brae minds our souls made beasts'
In knelling tales our truths now shred.
Thus raped and scorned our legacy
The vain foe moves to round the rout
But flush with carnage comes to learn
Our flame is not so fast stamped out."

The spires vanished. The marsh fell silent. Alone, through the fog, a single man stood, holding a sealskin sack. The voice sang on,

"He came alone, not blade nor sling
The deft fox in the gath'ring gloom—
A devious heart, a sealskin sack
His footfalls soft a tramp of doom.
For Líj the grievous mole had spied,
Wellspring of our boundless sway
Then like a surgeon-highwayman
Tears our ruddy soul away."

Now, the sack was full. Líj raised it over his head. A leviathan, like the ones in the pools, appeared above Líj's head. It devoured the sack, and Líj, then turned Hilaríon's way.

Hilaríon's heart pounded. The leviathan was monstrous: as big as the earth and the seas, it seemed, and hungry as the rigors of time. It trundled towards him, mouth agape. He closed his eyes, collapsing. "No—!"

There was only silence. The leviathan faded into the mists. It had been but an illusion. But the mire was now filled with shadowy bodies, some dead, others dying. Their death-groans ground the silence away. The voice sang,

"Shorn of honor, slashed of self
Our essence minced and scattered wide
Triumphant M'Brae carves his halls
Upon our bones, our mangled pride.
But thus made beasts in M'Brae eyes
Our broken spirits find new breath
Kings rankling mad for M'Brae blood
To make us countrymen in death."

The fog began to lift. The air felt clear and cool. A swooning sensation of flight overtook Hilaríon. He could feel his body drifting skywards, like goose-down in an updraft. The swamp spread wide beneath him, the rolling woods and plains to the north, the mountains to the east. He could almost see the curve of the earth, the living planet, ringed in blue. Below him was the city. Then he fell.

His body spiraled every which way, legs and arms flapping like winnowing straw. "It's not real," he said through clenched teeth. "*It... can't... be... real...*" But that did nothing to slow his descent or ease his all-pervading fear.

He hurtled towards the city. In its center rose an ornate dome, supported by pillars. He leveled off and soared between them. The voice said,

"In eighth room of the north-most spire
Through riddled hatch 'neath monster's grin,
To turn aside—to decimate
Thine own untreasured M'Brae kin."

He sped down a marble corridor, then into a spiral stairwell. He slowed and came to rest at the bottom, atop a wooden trapdoor. He looked closer. Beneath its handle was some form of writing, too old and faded to decipher. He wondered aloud, "Riddled hatch?"

The voice climbed to a crescendo and sang,

"Where have you gone, o tender of fields?
Thine wisdom churned to halest root
Thine yeoman now a vagabond
I cannot remember your voice.

Where have you gone, o giver of names?
Your verve's free fountain parched to dross
What words dreamt fast but ne'er bestowed?
I cannot remember your name."

"Giver of names," Hilaríon said, "I cannot remember your name... your name." His mind drifted back to Necío's story about the mystical Esèh. *Those which they loved they gave beautiful names, and to those they feared, or hated, gave none.... Líj saw the Esèh with fresh eyes, and saw their fatal flaw. At once he knew how the war could be won with neither arms nor numbers.*

The Spoils of Líj. It all made sense.

His fingers closed on the trapdoor handle. He pulled—

"Hilaríon?"

He was beneath the Sabal Gate, rain lashing his body in sheets. The M'Brae were gathered around him, staring. Ypriána snapped her fingers. "Come back," she said. "Wake up."

He looked for the trapdoor. "Where did the city go?"

"City?" Lux said. "You stepped through the trees a second ago."

Hilaríon looked the people over. They seemed like living flesh and blood. He poked their sides to know for sure. They leered and moved away from him. He was, for sure, back in the swamp. It had all been but a phantasm.

Or had it? Necío was gazing blankly, off into the distance. Hilaríon recognized that look. Necío had seen it, too.

Hilaríon said, "I know what they want."

"Oh, he's been bitten deep," Lux said. "Your bark won't help him now."

"No," he said, "I know what it is."

"Know what?" Ypriána said.

"The Spoils of Líj," he said. "What we have to find is—"

The earth thundered. Water splashed from ground and sky. The palm trees swayed, then groaned aloud, then toppled from the muck. A massive sinkhole opened wide and gulped the people into it. A chorus of bellows, savage and bestial, cracked from the sloughs all around them. The Toothed Kings were on their way.

"Good time for an almighty weapon," Ypriána said.

Hilaríon answered, "Not this one. There's nothing *we* could do with it. The Spoils of Líj is the Esèh's true name."

xxx.

The crocodiles burst from the mud and lunged. They were bigger, even, than Hilaríon had pictured, their hard scales marbled black. Their eyes were yellow, burning orbs. Ypriána twirled her blade about in a sweeping, fantail wake. It clove through the monsters' leathery flesh. Their treacle-blood pooled as their dead bodies twitched.

The M'Brae thrashed at the sinkhole-walls, trying to climb but toppling down. Phellhe and Hilaríon drew their blades and stepped towards Ypriána. "No," she said, and pushed them away. "Help the others."

The lightning cracked. The beasts regrouped. Hilaríon said, "But—"

"Help the others!"

The beasts spilled over the rim of the sinkhole, roaring as one and shaking the earth. The panicked people scattered. Ypriána stood her ground. Phellhe and Hilaríon, joined by Lux, formed a line against the beasts, protecting the huddling M'Brae behind. Ypriána lopped off the beasts' heads and skewered them with her blade. What ones evaded her buried away, snapping at M'Brae legs from below.

Phellhe and Hilaríon hoisted the others: children first, then Maith, then the rest. With a scream, Sunovín vanished into the mud, a crocodile's jaws locked around him. Where he'd stood was but a crack in the earth, dotted with pieces of fabric and blood.

The green skies broke, the squalls resumed. The crocodiles retreated. Ypriána clambered from the hole. The people fixed terrified eyes on Hilaríon. He could only stare at the sinkhole, dumbfounded. In his mind, Sunovín's eyes caught flame.

"Stay away from the water," Ypriána said. "Roll with them if they take you. Strike the eyes or the nose, if you can."

Hilaríon regathered his wits, and stepped in front of the people. "Get in line—"

"Line?" Ypriána shoved him aside. "Wedge formation, children inside. I thought you'd know that, capitán." She pushed him, Phellhe, and Lux to the points of the wedge. "Make yourselves useful and guard the flanks." The people clustered in formation and stepped off into the swamp.

The winds howled louder. The ground grew softer. The rain chattered with fresh, unbridled vigor. The sky was so black they could hardly see on. The gathering beasts rumbled low from the shadows. Ypriána strode at the point of the wedge, carving the air with her blade as she walked.

Lightning cracked across the sky and bathed the swamp in light. The M'Brae braced themselves. All around them, everywhere, a snarling morass of reptiles spread. Their gaping maws were ghostly white. Ypriána said, "Keep moving." The people dropped their heads and followed.

The wedge gained speed. The Kings gave chase. Inch by inch, they crept from the gloom. Their eyes like warning lanterns flashed. They snapped at M'Brae heels. The rain tore down in icy walls. The Kings leapt in pairs at the staggering M'Brae, daring them to stand. Ypriána raced about, a frantic angel of death. She hacked and skewered whatever she could, but the monsters were relentless.

The mud gave way to silt. Hilaríon splashed in cool, shallow water. The eastern horizon was clear and flat. The Kings were driving them into a lake.

"Form a line!" Ypriána said. Hilaríon, Phellhe, and Lux stood fast. Ypriána grabbed Hrama and Jacinda, then joined them. The others stood in the shallows.

The phalanx of Kings snapped at their front. Others, underwater, slipped to their rear. The line collapsed into a ring. Adults hoisted children high and clutched each other's arms. They flicked their legs at snapping snouts and sidestepped whipsaw tails. But the monsters' talons found their marks.

The water reddened. Phellhe shouted, "What now?" Ypriána

gaped as if to speak but, at length, said nothing. The Kings roared together. The ground below shook. Phellhe cried louder, "Woman! What now?" But still, Ypriána said nothing.

The Kings tensed to strike. The people shrieked. For once, Ypriána seemed helpless, and wholly out of ideas. Hilaríon pushed her behind him. He raised his blade above his head. The Kings hurled their bodies. He swung—

"Yélé -t-M'Brae o fehnoé vame
Fa-yil thu zélé ephvachû rah'yoghû..." [1]

A mighty voice rose, like fire and honey, splitting the ears as it lifted the soul. It coursed through the people, an electrical rhythm, like no sound he had ever heard. Graciela, the mute, was singing.

All at once, the beasts backed away. They splashed from the water onto the shore and tumbled about like worms in the sun. Graciela kept her throat aloft. The storm relented, the black clouds parted. Moonlight limned a clump of trees on an island in the distance. Hilaríon shouted, "Keep moving!"

"We can't swim that," Phellhe said.

"We won't have to." Already the water had receded. A narrow spit was surfacing. The tides would be their saving grace. "Wait for the ebb—"

"We wait for the ebb!" Ypriána shouted over his voice. "Until then, protect the song."

She ran to Graciela. Phellhe, Lux, and Hilaríon took positions, defending the people. The monsters writhed, just out of reach. They barked like frustrated hunting hounds. But they didn't dare cross the surf. The song held them at bay.

The M'Brae took each other's hands. The rains began to lift. The tides rolled out, the spit arose. The sand was solid enough to pass. Hilaríon waved the people on.

---

[1] "The M'Brae story's writ in song

What wonders follow fast the throng?"

Ypriána took Graciela's hand. Her face was wet and flushed crimson. She coughed between bars but kept up the song. Ypriána led her at the rear. The trees of the island ahead loomed taller. The Kings gave chase from the water, on all sides. But the spit was just wide enough.

Graciela fell, coughing bloody phlegm. The song disappeared. The Kings moved in closer. Ypriána pulled her standing. Graciela hacked the blood from her throat and resumed her harried singing. The song, though strained, rang out again,

"Yélé -t-M'Brae o fehnoé vame
Fa-yil thu zélé ephvachû rah'yoghû..."

The tide rose higher, drowning the spit. A piercing whine broke from the skies. Midges descended like venomous mist. The people ducked and covered their eyes. The midges gnawed their necks and scalps. They flew at Graciela's face.

Graciela crumpled. The song fell dead. The Toothed Kings bellowed a song of their own. They crawled atop the shrinking spit, to bar the last safe path. There was no way to fight them, and nowhere to go.

Hilaríon looked to Ypriána. She clutched the medallion, hanging her head. She seemed to be surrendering. Her blade went limp. She closed her eyes. The Kings would devour them all, unless—

<u>xxxi.</u>

"Tell them you'll kill me!" Hilaríon said. He backed his body into hers and pressed his throat against her blade. "A dead Elect's worthless. No spoils for them." She hesitated. "Do it!"

"Imposter, don't make me!" Ypriána shouted, pulling the blade deeper. The beasts fell silent. He could almost see it in their eyes. They didn't trust that she wouldn't kill him.

She waved the others onward. Phellhe led them to the island. She dragged Hilaríon by his neck while he pretended to try to escape. Her cheek felt soft against his. The bewildered Kings followed. The tides rolled in and covered the spit.

"Not yet, not yet," came Oriel's voice. She was standing on the shore when the M'Brae arrived. The Kings disappeared in water and sky. "Ere sunrise comes," she said.

"For shame," Necío said. "We're not our sires and they're not us."

"Then lay no claim to their leavings," she said. She turned to Hilaríon. "If this is the last time we meet, finder of gold, I have a promise to keep to you. If you hear nothing else, hear this.

> "The Ancient sire who chased the dawn
> Before this fallen world departed
> A mighty treasure stowed away
> And left a mightier dragon to guard it."

He'd barely heard the words she'd said, much less comprehended them. But Oriel was already gone. Ypriána pushed him away and said, "Clever of you."

"Like a rat?" Hilaríon snarked.

Graciela panted, dripping with sweat. The others offered syrupy thanks. Phellhe snarled at her, "Where did you learn that?"

She said, "Same as you."

He looked thunderstruck. "I don't sing— Oh! *M'Brae do not sing.*"

"We're lucky *one* does," Hilarión said.

"Don't let me hear it again," Phellhe said. "And just how do you steal a name, hilldevil?"

"Easy enough," Necío said. "You see, when lies pile up, by and by—"

"Fool," Phellhe said, "I don't care."

"You should," Ypriána said. "We have until sunrise to find it."

The island heaved skyward in ridges to the east. Hilarión recalled the vision. "It's past the hilltop, then down to shore."

She bowed deferentially and said, "After you." Hilarión couldn't help but feel that he was being mocked.

The M'Brae shuffled up the hillside. Their flesh was pallid, covered in welts, their eyes bulged thick and dreary. They hadn't the strength to lie down and die. Some of them wept for Sunovín, but not one of them complained. *They believe the treasure is real*, he'd said. He'd told that to Lux as a bargaining chip. But he'd been more right than he knew. "It's only a little farther," he said. A twinge of shame came over him. Since when did he find it so foul to lie?

Phellhe straggled at the column's rear. His size seemed to hang on his bones like dead weight. Hilarión looked closer. The big man was shivering, his flesh golden-brown. Hilarión had seen it before, in the Mambí camps. The men had called it swamp fever. The doctors had called it *malaria*.

They crested the crown of the ridge. Gentle grass like shearling wool blanketed the ground. The people were spent and needed rest, if only for a few hours. "Make camp," Ypriána said. They flopped to the ground. Hilarión followed. The tender grass against his neck felt a sweet caress. Between the knitted mangrove boughs, the mid-summer constellations gleamed—

He gasped. There were faces in the trees.

Two rows of statues, hewn of wood, loomed above the campsite. Hilarión counted ten of them. Some were taller than the others. The shorter figures each clasped sextants, the taller figures conch shells. All of them had mouths agape, as if frozen in intense debate.

Hilaríon looked the campsite over. Necío was missing. Telltale footprints led from the camp and disappeared past the statues. He stepped off after the trail. Aryei scampered beside him and said, "You had to have seen it this time."

Hilaríon said, "Seen what?"

"That glower that could wake the dead. The way she looked at you."

He stopped. "Glower?"

"From Ypriána," Aryei said. "The first was when that Esèh woman let you and Necío pass, but not her. I saw it again when those beasts closed in, then again when you said to climb to the hilltop. She'd always looked your way three seconds—no more, no less. But then it was ten, through snarled lips, and most recently—"

"That's quite an imagination you have. I'd rest up, if I were you." He walked off, brooding for an anxious moment. Could Aryei have seen something no one else had?

The woods gave way to a stony cliff, beetling savagely into the marsh. The ground widened into a crescent hollow, expiring onto the strand. Nestled in the hollow were four concentric, man-made rings. The topmost three were incomplete, hugging the contours of the cliff. The lowest and largest formed a circle from the shore into the shallows. Together they made an amphitheater. He remembered it from the vision. "I know this place," he said.

"The Ringing Rings," came Necío's voice. He was sitting atop the cliff.

"You heard them, too?" Hilaríon said.

"I walked with them," Necío said. "They told you where to find the spoils, and me I'd better hope you do—that I was a fool, true to my name. I'd suffer if they got me. I did what the Ancients most abhorred. I took answers without questions."

Hilaríon sat. "You just repeated what you'd been told."

"And what I'd been told was wrong. So really I stole their name, same as Líj, my mother, and everyone else who's shared that tale. A lie gains strength with every retelling. It brutalizes all the more. I didn't know they were lies. But did I bother to ask for myself?"

"Who would have?"

"The Ancients, that's who. Asking's what made them who they were. We weren't always ruled by fear. There was a time we welcomed others, instead of shutting them out. There was a time we cherished learning. I used to ask my mother what magic had made the Ancients great. She said no magic at all, except for the magic of wondering why. Anyone can have answers—there's nothing at all to that. Anyone can remember what someone else says. Anyone can filch beliefs, but it's asking questions that pushes us forward. Questions make the difference, not answers. That's what the Esèh reminded me. It was here that our sires gathered to trade questions. That's how they honored one another."

Necío looked despondent. Hilaríon took pity. "You'll make good. You can even start now. I'll trade you my questions for yours."

Necío smiled. "Then I go first. Um... where were you born?"

"Camagüey, in Oriente," Hilaríon said. "My turn." In the moonlight Necío seemed especially boyish. "How old are you?"

"Not yet a man."

He laughed. "And when will you be one?"

"When the steeples are drenched and the cocks drowned away. It's what my mother told me. She'd pinch me if I asked too much. She said someday I'd learn what it means. But I couldn't wait for her to tell. Turns out, I'm twenty-five."

Hilaríon would never have guessed. He and Necío were the same age. "Why did you lie about Wresh?"

"We'd all be dead if it wasn't for you. One mistake doesn't change that. Why did you fight for Cuba Libre?"

"My aunt fought in the first rebellion. She taught me how to track. I knew I'd regret it if I didn't follow." A pang of regret shook Hilaríon. His aunt had seen the best in him, even when he couldn't. She reminded him of someone else. "Is Ypriána who she says?"

"She has the medallion, and she found you. You've gotten us farther than anyone's ever. That couldn't be by chance."

She's not who she says she is. It was a warning Hilaríon couldn't ignore. And now even Aryei had suspicions. But Necío couldn't give him an answer. Neither, probably, could Ypriána. Necío said, "Did you and that red-haired Mambí, you know..." He winked.

"War makes strange bedfellows. What's the treasure going to be?"

"So many stories," Necío said. "Some say it's of the Old World—Cathay, Bessarabia, or Kipchak's Golden Horde. Some think it from the New World, the Olmecs or the Incas. It's colossal if ever colossal was. Were you really a hilldevil?"

The scab on his hilldevil brand tingled. Necío was probing deep. "They needed a tracker," Hilaríon said. "I needed... something to do." He rose.

"Wait, just one more round of questions, please?"

The croaking bitterns in the reeds kept time with trilling grebes. For a moment, the world was filled with song. Its beauty haunted him—like something else. "That wan madrigal," he said. "What is it?"

Necío patted the ground, grinning. "That's a story unto itself." Hilaríon sat back down.

Necío cleared his throat and said, "So the light had burst across our world. We'd clambered from the seas. We were a new breed altogether. There was nothing like us anywhere. But we were not alone.

"No one knows where They came from, or when. Even now, no one knows who They were. But They saw something in us and reached out to us, alone, out of all living things. They taught us how to speak. Our voices raised, our hearts entwined, our splendid strains rang out as one. They led us to a place we could dwell together for all time, a place where strand, sea, and sky came together and the warmth of summer reigned."

"Ahr," Hilaríon said.

Necío nodded. "We call them The Ones Who Came Before. No one knows their true name. In Ahr, They gave us Their greatest gift—the way, and the will, to ask questions. For ages, we lived in harmony. Both our numbers were great as the stars. Now, They're always depicted as five."

Hilaríon thought of the hilltop statues, and the faces above the swirling mud. There'd been five of each of them.

"Buoyed by our will to learn, the M'Brae struck across the globe.

Our shipwrights built indomitable crafts, the likes of which had never been seen. Our pilots probed the sprawling seas. Our traders bartered foreign wares. Our scribes made homes in distant lands, sharing whatever knowledge they gained and bringing back what they had learned. We advanced and the world advanced through us. Our might was based not in weapons or wealth but the will to ever ask questions.

"And whether or not it was meant to be," Necío said, "wealth did follow knowledge. We amassed a fortune beyond all reckoning, the envy of the ancient world. It could fill nine ships and part of a tenth. Pharaohs and rajahs thought themselves poor to look upon our treasure. We were the greatest power the world had seen, or would ever see.

"But things were not so well in Ahr. The Ones Who Came Before looked upon their erstwhile children, and saw in us a strange, new creature—one they did not recognize. By and by our voices faded. We could no longer sing with Them. They would no longer sing with us. We turned our backs on Ahr, and the brethren who had made us whole."

Hilaríon rolled his eyes. He'd heard fall-of-man stories like this before.

Necío continued, "We grew rich and full of hubris. We forgot Their mighty gift. We turned from our past, with all we had learned. We turned from our future, and all that could be. We grew staid and fat with self-regard. Lesser captains helmed our ships, lesser teachers shaped our minds. Our days were whiled in repetition and rote recitals of the known. Our learning, squandered, dwindled. Our fortune, wasted, disappeared. We became a sinful, fallen race, adrift in a sinful, fallen world. And The Ones Who Came Before disappeared, never to be heard from again.

"But some say in death our souls seek Them out, that when we die, They come for us, and lead us to that beauteous place where strand, sea, and sky come together, where we can dwell in peace. That's why we sing when one of us dies, so They might hear and remember. Those of us who aren't so lucky—well, that's another story."

It sounded so outlandish. The closer Hilaríon got to these people, the less he believed they were real.

"My turn," Necío said. "What happened at Cacarajícara?"

The eyes burned hot. "Time to get moving."

Necío said, "You have to make me a promise, though. Whatever the treasure is, you have to do something good with it, even if for yourself. Too many people have bled for it. It has to be more than a prize."

"Good advice," Ypriána said. She was standing behind them. "Ready?" Necío stepped towards her. "Not you."

"Look after the others, Necío," Hilaríon said. "You're in charge. We won't be long."

She said, "We won't?"

Away in the distance, below the dawn, the peaks of the city rose from the waters. They looked the bastions of olden times, which he'd heard of only in books—Byzantium, Babylon, glittering Rome—far across the seas, their burnished heights stretching towards an elusive God. A sanguine laugh died in his throat. Somewhere beneath that tangle of spires, the Spoils of Líj awaited. "On second thought," he said, "make yourselves ready."

Necío said, "For what?"

He said, "For anything."

They staggered down the hill. At the shoreline bobbed a wooden boat. Hilaríon climbed inside, and Ypriána followed. She cut the mooring rope. The boat drifted from the strand. The sky oozed an ominous pink. They had less time than he'd thought.

She threw him an oar, then dipped her own. They rowed away from the shore and out to the City of Ten Thousand Fires.

The placid water rippled. The Kings were swimming beneath them.

xxxii.

The east grew brighter. The strand disappeared. The lake sprawled fast to every horizon. He looked below, into the water. In the faint morning light he could make out the crags of ruined rooftops and slime-coated walls. They were passing the city's outskirts. The homes had been planned in orderly rows, all regular length and width. The M'Brae had hewn it with pride. But it hadn't been theirs to build. It was gorgeous stolen goods.

"Which one?" Ypriána said. He raised his head. The east was brighter.

He looked the skyline over. He could still see the virgin spires, fresh inside his memory. He married the ruins up to the vision, then pointed to a spiral dome atop a colonnade. "That one."

"Better be right." She guided the boat towards the dome.

The battered hulks of rotting buildings rose like atolls in their path. "Keep calm," she said. "Don't tempt them."

"Who—?"

The tops of the ruins were crawling with crocodiles. In the splotchy light of the rising sun, they seemed gargoyles, sprung from perdition. Some seemed to smile, others to laugh. The eastern sky was flecked with gold. The M'Brae's chances of delivering the spoils before sunrise grew slimmer with each passing moment, and the Kings knew it. She gave the oar a hearty pump. The boat trundled deeper into the city.

Warm winds off the waters swirled. She steered the boat between the columns, beneath the dome, into a rotunda. In the center was a marble step-pyramid. The stench of death and rotting flesh hung stolid in the air. "This must be their pantry," she said.

They dragged the boat to the topmost rung. Ypriána threw off her cloak and pulled her boots from her feet. She drew her shirt off over her head and sidled from her pants. Her sinewy arms and shoulders seemed cut from dappled marble. In the silence, beneath the soaring dome, no god in any hereafter's halls could hold a candle to her.

Between the pillars, a shaft of light crept. Somewhere past the east horizon, the sun sped ever closer. Outside, the crocodiles surfaced. A cloud of midges trundled past. She fastened her blade in the crook of her back and asked him, "Where to now?"

He scanned the rotunda. At the pyramid's base, all but submerged, were four identical corridors, each oriented in a cardinal direction. Each ended in a tower, rising out of the water, capped with a crumbling battlement. He remembered what the vision-voice said. *"In eighth room of the north-most spire."* He oriented to the sun and pointed down the northbound hall.

The crocodiles grumbled. "Take heart," she said. "They'll probably only eat one of us." She drew breath, dove, and disappeared.

Oriel's warning reverberated. *She's not who she says she is.* Of all the places to be betrayed, this seemed like the worst. But, so far, she'd earned his trust. He blessed himself and followed.

The sludge of the marsh engulfed him. He held his breath and bobbed ahead. The water was dark but passable. Fishes and water snakes brushed by his legs. The tendrils of slimy marsh-grass grabbed him. The corridor-ceiling was pitted with nooks which held small pockets of air. He sipped quick breaths as he pressed along. Tracking through water was easy enough. Quarry always left a sediment-trail, turning the water cloudy.

Out of the grime her face appeared. One of her eyes was closed, the other wide in apprehension. Her flesh seemed ghostly white. He motioned to her but she didn't move. He reached to grab her—

He bit down on the scream in his throat. *This must be their pantry,* she'd warned. He was staring into the mummified face of a dead and bloated deer.

A fleshy corpse slid past his neck. His cheek brushed against a waterlogged rat. He kicked his feet, groping for the surface. All around, the rubbery forms of half-devoured turtles and fish floated, like some demonic stew. He thrashed to the surface, retching—

"Light, up ahead," Ypriána said, surfacing beside him. Some yards away, the water brightened. Dawn was spreading from the east. A massive door stood at the end of the corridor, wooden and bound with iron struts. They swam to the door. He pulled on the handle. The door didn't budge. She told him, "Get behind me."

They ducked back underwater. She grabbed the handle and winched with her legs. The door creaked ajar. She squeezed herself into the crack, then heaved it wide. He slipped inside behind her. The door closed with a groan. They were inside the top of a tower, fully submerged, except for a ceiling nook. Below them, the tower was wide and hollow and disappeared into a black abyss. Built into the walls were steps. It was the spiral stairwell from the vision, just as he remembered. They treaded water. He said, "Below, there's a trapdoor, and behind it—"

A roar shook the tower. Two ponderous jaws closed around him. A massive shadow thrashed between them. He heard a voice rasping, unable to scream, begging for its life.

The voice was his own.

The water turned red. Teeth ripped his flesh. The air rushed from his lungs. A monstrous beast was dragging him under. Its strength was overpowering. Surrender was taking him whole. There was no resisting—

"Hilarión!" she cried. "*Strike the eyes!*"

He jammed his thumbs in the crocodile's eyes. It clenched its jaws tighter. He pressed his thumbs deeper. Its jaws went slack. He pushed away. Its teeth ripped at his flanks. He slammed his fist into its snout. Ypriána pried the door open, pushed him through, and pulled it shut behind them. The beast's weight lurched against the door. The temple shook at its foundations.

She dragged him to the ceiling. His head was light, his body numb. His mind ran in meaningless circles. "A mightier dragon," he blathered, "mightier... dragon... Oriel said..."

"You're in shock," she said. "Breathe." He inhaled—once, twice, then five more times. He concentrated on her face. His flesh had been torn but not badly. He pulled a tooth from his side. "Keep breathing," she said. "You'll live."

"Not for long if we don't get the spoils. It's down that shaft. We have to get past him."

"Easy enough." She drew her blade. "Winch the door. When his head comes through..." She twisted the blade.

Hilarión grabbed the door handle. The M'Brae were counting on him: he couldn't fail. He pressed his legs against the wall and heaved the door ajar. Inches from where their faces peeked through, the dragon floated, perfectly still. It snorted bloody mist. It wasn't being tricked.

He looked back down the corridor. The sky was brightening, sunrise approaching. They'd precious little time. He looked in Ypriána's face. For an instant, her eyes seemed thick with fear, same as on the spit, just before Graciela's song. But then her face hardened with resolve. She pulled the medallion off her neck and draped it over his head. "I can buy you time," she said. "Don't wait up for me." She grabbed onto the handle.

"What are you doing?" He reached to stop her. No one could face that dragon alone.

"I'll catch up to you," she said.

His fingers slid along her back and brushed against her hips. He was back in the stormy days of his youth. As a child, he'd reached for his aunt the same way, as she'd left for war.

"It has to be this way," she said. "I was more right about you than I knew." She pressed her lips against his own, then winched the door and slipped through the gap.

A roar shook the stone. A crush of water slammed the door. Then it was quiet. He pried the door open. They were gone.

xxxiii.

He filled his lungs with air and dove. The water was murky and heavy with silt. Light through the turrets limned the trapdoor below. It was too far away. He needed more air.

He kicked back to the surface. The walls were pink with light through the slats. Time was slipping away. He inhaled deep, to the pit of his belly. He could still see Ypriána's face. But she'd never have let him waste precious time. He'd look, or mourn, for her later. He grabbed his nose and flipped down through the murk.

He pumped his arms and legs. The wounds from the dragon's bite still burned. He grabbed the turrets and pulled himself downward. The trapdoor was closer, but still out of reach. He hooked his legs and strained his arms. His fingers brushed the handle ring—

His cheeks deflated. It was still too far.

He scrambled to the surface, gasping. He'd never be able stay under long enough. He still had to get to the door, and then he'd have to open it. And after he'd opened it, then what? Sunrise was moments away.

A stone block splashed into the water, narrowly missing him. He looked to where it had fallen from. Time, decay, or the beast's brute strength had caused the spiral stairway to crumble. Its bucket-sized blocks were wobbly. Four were ready to fall. He could ride them to the bottom.

Hilaríon drew a deep breath, then wrapped his arms around a block. He laid his feet against the wall, ready to heave away. He'd make Ypriána proud. The block lurched into his lap. He hurtled to the bottom.

The block struck the deck with a thud, clear of the trapdoor. The light through the turret was brighter now, though the water was murky. He fumbled for the trapdoor handle. His fingers brushed against its frame. He felt his way down the wooden grain. His hand closed on the handle ring. His air was waning. He yanked.

It was locked.

He ran his hand below the ring. He could feel a shallow indentation. He pressed his palm against it. It was shaped just like the medallion. He reached for the lanyard on his neck—

The medallion was gone.

Hilaríon's heart beat raw. The light through the turrets glowed brighter. Time was fading. The medallion was missing. And he was out of breath again.

He kicked to the surface. Now there were only three blocks left, and even less time to use them. A panic took hold in the pit of his chest. Without the medallion, his pains would be useless. He grabbed the next block and sank to the bottom.

He pulled himself down to the door by the ring and locked his feet below the blocks. The medallion had to be nearby. His head grew light. The horror spread. He plunged his hands beneath the muck and ripped at the stone and tangled grass. His air was running out—

There! Something shimmered bluish-white. He plucked the medallion, then dug through the mud to the trapdoor-lock's indentation. Etched in the iron was writing: the illegible glyphs of the M'Brae, but beside it the common tongue. He remembered it from the vision. There was just enough light to read what it said.

Ringing Rings
Vengeful Kings
Ones Who Came Before

The phrases sounded familiar. And his air was almost gone. He pressed the medallion into the indentation and pulled against the ring.

Nothing.

He yanked with all his strength. The trapdoor didn't budge. He strained to press the medallion deeper. It clicked what felt like a notch to the left and lifted from the lock.

Hilarión's cheeks deflated. He grabbed the medallion and thrashed to the surface. He hacked the water from his lungs. The medallion had turned and clicked. He thought of the boxes the nobles of Camagüey always used to hide their jewels.

The trapdoor was a safe. The writing told the combination. He reached for a stone—

"No!" The two remaining stones toppled. The first one sped away to the bottom. The second struck a ledge and wavered. He lurched and hooked his fingertips on its edges. It plummeted fast as he grabbed hold. Dread crackled across his body. He hadn't drawn a deep enough breath.

He sped to the bottom, grabbed the handle, and pushed the medallion into the lock. It spun both left and right. But which way to turn it? Either guess was as good as the other.

Ringing Rings? He'd seen for himself. He turned the medallion four clicks left. *Vengeful kings?* Two clicks right. Each ticked off smoothly. Lastly, *Ones Who Came Before.* Thank goodness he'd been attentive. He spun it back five clicks to the left. He grabbed at the handle ring.

Nothing.

He snorted. A spurt of bubbles popped from his nose. He spun the medallion back to the center, then laid his palms against the door. He wouldn't get another chance. Four clicks right, then two clicks left, then a final five clicks right. He yanked on the handle. The trapdoor flung wide. Lungs burning, he grabbed the medallion and floundered down into the vault.

Through the water, far away, he heard the faintest sound of rumbling. His head lulled lighter. The rumbling gave way to a full-throated growl. The dragon was coming back. But Hilarión wasn't leaving empty-handed.

He groped about the stony walls and squirmed his hands in every nook. He squeezed his lips to keep his breath. The vision-voice played a loop in his mind. *In eighth room of the north-most spire, Through riddled hatch 'neath monster's grin...* He looked up through the trapdoor hatch. The light was growing brighter, less reddish now than gentle gold. He had only precious moments.

He clawed away the slime and weeds. Staring from the wall were two giant eyes. He cleared more mud and looked again. Carved in the rock was the image of the leviathan who'd swallowed Lij's sack.

'Neath monster's grin. And now, his air was all but spent.

The primal roar rang out again. He reached below the leviathan's eyes, to where its mouth would be. A panel was loose. He squeezed his fingers into its edges and heaved it from the wall. Where the panel had been was an alcove. Inside was a sealskin sack.

He grabbed the sack. His cheeks deflated. He tucked the sack beneath his arm and clambered from the room. The trapdoor slammed behind him. He hunched against the sunken blocks, then pushed up towards the surface.

A violent current now swirled through the tower. Light streamed through the turret. Something flashed from far below—massive, black, and gaining speed. The beast was ascending behind him.

He broke the surface, gasping for air, and lunged for the corridor door. The light of dawn was spreading. He could still get back to the step-pyramid. He could still get back to the boat, and the shore. He could still deliver the spoils in time.

He heaved the door open and wrenched himself through, then ground it shut behind him. A crush of water slammed against it, from the other side. The beast had broken the water's surface. The temple shook like a boat in a storm.

The dragon lurched against the door, popping it off its upper hinge. Hilarión swam through the mummified bodies. The roars grew louder. The currents lashed. The sound of twisting metal groaned. The dragon was breaking through.

He churned his arms and legs even harder. The grisly pantry passed behind. He'd nearly cleared the corridor. The pyramid was close at hand. He could make it there, alive. Only a second or two ahead...

The telltale crack of metal sang. The water surged around his head. The beast had broken through the door and now was headed up the corridor.

Hilarión thrashed his arms like mad. He curled his legs beneath him. His hands brushed against the welcoming marble. He pulled the spoils-sack from his breast and placed it on the step above. He'd outrun the nightmare beast.

He scrambled from the water. The sun was close but not yet risen. He'd still a few moments left. He could still get back to the others. He grabbed the boat to free it.

The Gray Jaeger fell upon him.

xxxiv.

His boot cracked against Hilaríon's jaw. Hilaríon saw stars. He rolled down the terrace, face smacking each step, and stopping at the water's edge. The sack was just out of reach. Hilaríon reached. The Jaeger pounced. Hilaríon's fingers closed around it—

The Jaeger plunged his blade. Hilaríon swung the sack like a flail. It cracked against the Jaeger's knee. The Jaeger crumpled backwards. Hilaríon dragged himself to the boat, the Jaeger limping on his heels. Hilaríon threw the sack in the boat, then grabbed and swung a wooden oar. The Jaeger parried the strike with his blade and trapped the oar against it. He yanked the oar free and spun it around, then flicked the butt-end in Hilaríon's face. Hilaríon's nose exploded with blood. He tumbled onto his back.

The Jaeger stood erect. He chopped the oar on Hilaríon's shoulder. Pain erupted down his back. The leering Jaeger spun the oar. "*Cerca,*" he said, "*Cerca... o—*"

Bristling jaws engulfed the Jaeger. The massive dragon surfaced behind him and dragged him to the depths. The water burst an angry red. The Jaeger railed, then gasped, then gurgled. Then both demons disappeared. The tide lapped playfully at the stone.

Hilaríon climbed inside the boat. His eyes scanned every inch of the temple. "Ypriána!" he called. He could still feel her lips. She was an element of nature, like fire. She couldn't be dead. "*Ypriána!*"

The crown of the sun was breaking the water and he had an arduous row ahead. There was precious little time remaining. *I'll catch up to you,* she'd said. This was not the end.

He dug the oar through the rippling current, tumbling onto his back. The boat lurched left, then right, then floundered. He clutched the sides to steady himself, and squeezed the sack between his legs.

The boat banked hard against a pillar. The waiting crocodiles raised their heads.

Hilaríon pulled himself to the beam. He wedged his feet inside the prow and threaded the oars through the rowlocks. The crocodiles bared their teeth and slid from the rooftops into the lake. The boat trundled grudgingly out through the pillars. He thrust his arms forward then throttled them back. The boat sped into the west.

He ground the oars with all his might, and locked his sight on the rising sun. The boat wended between the crumbling temples. The walls and rooftops smeared to a blur inside the corners of his eyes. The crocodiles slithered along as he passed. The pink sun swelled as it climbed. He tightened his grip and tensed his legs. He threw his body into the row, each and every sinew pulsing, bringing him closer to the shore, and the treasure closer to him. "Come on," he said, "come on..."

A flotilla of snouts surfaced around him, like Men 'o War in formation. They growled in unison. The flimsy wood of the rowboat shook. Hilaríon shouted, "I dare you!" He dangled the spoils over the gunwale, and twirled it like a heavy sling, as if to bash against the boat. The sun poked higher into the sky. Past the mist, the island where the M'Brae were waiting was coming into view.

A crocodile surfaced starboard and bit down on Hilaríon's oar. The wood snapped in two with a meaty crack. The paddle-end spun away. The beast dove beneath the boat. The craft floundered. He grabbed at the remaining oar. Another crocodile lunged to bite it. Hilaríon yanked it clear of its mouth. The beast sank away. But now he had only one good oar.

The sun rose brighter. He looked to the west. The island was still some distance away.

The flotilla of bristling snouts returned. They snorted pungent mist from their nostrils, like prehistoric beasts.

Hilaríon drew the oar from the rowlock. It still had the cleft where the Jaeger had struck it. He knelt in the prow and paddled, pumping his arms like a seaman possessed.

The crocodiles fanned out around him. They seemed to multiply:

two, then three, then four or five, each taking the place of another. The dawn's light glittered off their scales. The lake burst into every color, like a lovelorn artist's palette. He looked back east again. The sun had passed its widest girth. It was more than halfway risen. Oriel hadn't said what she'd do if sunrise passed without the spoils. But who knew what she was capable of? "Faster," he said, "come on..."

His heart raced. His head lolled weightless. Each passing thought splashed fuel on his fire: the M'Brae, the treasure, and Ypriána. The water parted beneath the prow, and left a fantail wake behind.

From the island rose a desperate sound. He could make out some of the voices. The M'Brae were stammering in fear. The Esèh were shouting above them, laughing. They were preparing the final sacrifice.

"No," he cried "Not yet!"

The crocodiles tightened ranks. They poked their heads above the water. They lashed their whipsaw tails. Hilaríon looked back. They were closing distance with the boat.

He paddled harder still. He passed the outskirts of the city. The boat keel bumped on ruined rooftops. The paddle tangled in curly reeds. The shouts from the island grew louder, and frenzied. The sunrise seemed to gather speed. Only a sliver remained submerged below the horizon. "Wait!" he yelled. "I'm almost—"

The sky darkened. From the ruins spewed a swarm of midges. They drew down on the trundling boat, hovering, ready to strike. They licked their beaks against his ears.

The crocodiles snarled. Hilaríon looked east again. The sun seemed to perch upon the horizon, like a melon on a knife-edge. There were only seconds left. And the island was at least two minutes away. *"Wait!"* he roared as loudly as he could, *"I'm here!"*

The beasts with gaping jaws converged. One of them surfaced beside him and snapped. Hilaríon cracked its skull with the oar, but others took its place. The sky glowed golden-red. The island was only a stone's throw away. *"Oriel"* he screamed, *"wait for me!"*

The midges descended. The crocodiles leapt from the water. He jumped to a stand inside the prow, and raised the oar above his head. He squeezed the spoils between his thighs. He thrust the oar across the gunwales. But the midges only filled his hair and gnawed his sunburned face. The crocodiles swiped at his arms and heaved against the timbers. They'd held back long enough.

The M'Brae chatter turned to wails. The sun cleared the line of the horizon. Hilaríon's time was up. He dropped the oar and grabbed the sack. He closed his swollen, besieged eyes. Somewhere—everywhere, perhaps—Ypriána hung her head in shame.

XXXV.

A chorus of voices rose from the island. The crocodiles sank from sight. The midges droned into the sky. The heat of the newly risen sun pressed like a sledge on the back of his neck. He let his arms, still clutching the sack, fall against his sides. He dropped his head in surrender.

The music of the dawn broke across him, like rain. He closed his eyes. From somewhere past the stolid mists, the Esèh were greeting the sun.

> "Our sires' yawning chasm spreads
> Parched our glories, myths untold
> Doubt devours my wasted heart
> Prayers unanswered, blood turned cold
> We'll be one in Ahr."

The current seemed to ebb away, pulling the craft in its arms. The boat changed course and gathered speed. It trundled westward, into the shallows. The mists off the waters burned dry as he passed. The Ringing Rings came into view. The Esèh voices rang louder, carried on the sultry air.

> "Envoys of a better land
> In benthic depths, our sires' cry
> Leads me, weary wand'rer, on
> Roused my wonder, by and by
> We'll be one in Ahr."

The last of the vapors broke. The sunlight streamed across the lake. The M'Brae stood upon the strand, arm in arm with the Esèh. Their hair and faces shimmered clean, their clothes were crisp and new. Behind them soared the amphitheater, its majesty shining brightly still, like cloud-topped towers across the seas, built in the times of heroes.

The Esèh filed from the strand and filled the uppermost rings. Their plangent voices intertwined.

> "My journey's end, my fathers' fount
> Oft-rememb'red, never known
> A flame rekindled 'midst the dark
> To hold, to have in grace alone
> We'll be one in Ahr."

Hilaríon remembered the madrigal's meaning. The Esèh were singing the M'Brae to peace, those who'd fallen in battle with them, trading blows for the rights to a swamp. Their faces glowed with sincerity. They were singing for Sunovín, too.

The chorus faded into silence. The Esèh stood like statues. Hilaríon's boat came to rest in the sand. Oriel was waiting there. The silence of the morning reigned, broken only by prattling moorhens. "Hilaríon," Necío said, running towards him. "The spoils! You found them!"

"Too late." He yanked a crocodile tooth from his ribs.

Oriel tugged Hilaríon's cloak, revealing the dragon's bite pattern. "I'd say you made good."

"Not before sunrise."

"But when it counted most. You could have quit but you pushed ahead. You honored yourself, and us."

Oriel's babbling seemed even more farcical. "If you say so."

"To question is to invite pain," Oriel said. "Your sires taught us that."

Hilaríon's head swam. His body ached, his legs burned. He couldn't remember when last he'd eaten. But he still knew why he'd come to this place, and why he'd suffered all he had. "Where's my treasure?"

Oriel laughed, "Mine first."

Necío looked around. "Where is Ypri— Oh." His face sagged. "Is she—?"

"No," Hilaríon said, "she *isn't*." Of course she wasn't. Was she?

He peered back east. The city's spires skewered the sun, like a burned-out forest's silhouette. Ypriána *had* to be out there, somewhere. He was alive, his body intact, and he'd delivered the spoils in time. He could still find her. He flung the sack at Necío. "Finish this—"

"Not so fast," Oriel said.

Hilaríon grabbed the oar. "I can save her."

"She doesn't need saving."

He said, "She's alive, then?"

"I didn't say that."

"So she's dead?"

"I didn't say that, either. I said she didn't need saving, unlike you and me. Now—"

"*Then where is she?*" His anger swelled. Oriel was playing coy and wasting precious time.

"Who could say?" she said.

"You could," he snarled. "I'll be pulling teeth from my side for a month. I'm fed up with riddles. Tell me plainly, for once in your life, is she dead or not?"

"They're only riddles now," she said. "It'll all make perfect sense, in time."

"Christ!" he said, "I don't have time for—"

"If you try to save her now, you will never, ever see the treasure. That much I can promise you. She's passed beyond your help, or mine."

"So she is dead, then."

Oriel only shook her head. "The woman you know won't return."

He closed his eyes. He could still feel her breath on his face, and recite every word she'd last told him. He could feel the strength of her body, like stone, pulling him from the dragon's jaws.

Oriel smiled reassuringly. "It's best it happens this way." She motioned towards the sack. "Finish this."

He glanced at the city, then back to the strand. Time was wasting, Ypriána perhaps waiting, in spite of Oriel's admonition. But the treasure had waited far longer. And he had come for the treasure.

The Esèh in the rings leaned in. The M'Brae on the strand stood back. Hilaríon reached into the sack. His hands closed around something large and metallic, rough and spiky at one end but smooth along its sides. He pulled the sack away. He lifted the spoils into the air. In his hand was a conch shell, wrought of silver, but shimmering red and gold in the dawn. The Esèh raised their arms. From far across the windswept swales, the sound of lowing beasts rolled on.

There was writing in the silver. It was all just meaningless scratch to him. He held it out for Necío. Necío stifled an anxious gasp and raised the shell aloft. The people, together, leaned in to hear. Necío read aloud,

> "To thrust for King a Slave will make
> As foes no longer, brothers aye,
> So learn we once and evermore.
> Your name is Guanahatabey."

His voice reverberated. The final word he'd spoken—*Guanahatabey*, the Spoils of Líj, the elusive talisman on whose airy back empires had risen and died—danced among the Ringing Rings, like music in the dawn. Then all was silent. Not even the birds or insects chattered. Hilaríon looked around. The world seemed to curdle to stillness.

Oriel beamed a cathartic smile. The Guanahatabey joined hands, and raised their voices in thundering song,

> "From past the swales to Whispering Woods
> And wellspring of tomorrow's vine
> One germ above, one spore below
> Their choice to make, unmade, be thine
> A citadel resplendent gold
> Of sweet-perfumed patricians proud

Though trussed upon a shunted blood
All prelude to a fitting shroud
To where stargazers pondered aught
On Gilded Peak, its trove concealed,
When Trodden Seed take root on high
Your Vexing Heirloom's fruit revealed."

Oriel stretched taller. Her figure seemed to straighten. The green rust seemed to flake from her body, revealing the warmth of coppery flesh. Hilaríon looked to the heights above. The others had sloughed the blight, too, as if their burdens had melted away. A surge of pride swelled—

His hubris died. The realization crashed. The treasure, as yet, was still far away. His golden days would have to wait. Again.

Or would they? He fondled the medallion.

Necío handed the shell to Oriel. The M'Brae gathered at the strand. The song of the Guanahatabey faded to whispers, then vanished altogether. They were gone. Necío said, "Where are they?"

"Everywhere," Oriel said. "They have their treasure, and their peace." She kicked a basket from the strand. It flopped into the surf and sank.

Necío said, "About my new name?"

Oriel clasped his shoulder. "I never promised you a new name, Necío. I meant you'd come to love your own. Trust yourself. See what's right in front of you. The cocks and steeples are not far off."

Necío gasped, "How did you know—?"

"And you, angel," Oriel said to Graciela. "Test your bounds. Share what you learn. Let the awakening start with you." Graciela bowed her head.

"Wait, what's this?" Necío said. He reached into the sealskin sack and pulled out a metal shank, short but thick and oval.

Hilaríon recognized the shape. He took the shaft and fitted it inside the medallion's hole. It clicked into place. The medallion was now a glittering key. He said, "I'm guessing this unlocks something."

"Your wit is boundless," Oriel said. "Now be on your way. Not yet friends, no longer foes."

The tide had shifted eastwards. In the shallows bobbed more rowboats. Inside of them were sacks of fish and boots of crocodile hide. The M'Brae and Lux climbed into the boats. Hilarión glanced up at the sun. It had soared well clear of the horizon. An hour ago its movement meant everything. Now, it was just a very bright star.

They pushed from the shoreline into the lake. Hrama rowed and Necío steered. Hilarión wedged himself in the prow. He hadn't the will to complain.

In the distance rose the purple line of the mighty Sierra del Escambray. They looked like the sweeping profile of some drowsy, supine giant. Hilarión had seen them before, in his youth. They'd been wild, untamed badlands then. He'd been warned to keep his distance. Now he was speeding into their gullet.

He smoldered. Seven Angels, Lightleaf Grove, Tumbled Bark. And now what? Gilded Peak and Trodden Seed? More riddles, more obstacles, more promises of a treasure just always out of reach. His patience was wearing threadbare. Ypriána had died—or hadn't—that he should find them all a prize. Her admonition echoed. *I'll catch up to you.* He had to trust her instincts. But how much longer could he wait? La Habana's strains soared louder. He couldn't resist them much longer.

Something large bumped the boat. He looked over the gunwale. The carcass of a massive crocodile tumbled in the surf. Its scales were sooty black. Where its toothsome head should have been was only a bloody stump. It looked like the dragon that had bitten him raw, and dragged the Jaeger down to his death. But this beast had been beheaded.

He looked back west across the swales. The spires of the ruined city peeked from the lake like fangs. It would hide its secrets well.

They beached the boats on the eastern shore, then stepped from the marshland and out towards the foothills.

xxxvi.

Phellhe sen Vaal knew in his heart he was the true M'Brae Oíc. He'd earned that honor in blood. He'd saved the M'Brae, beguiled by swindlers. He'd led them into the hills and brought Mambíses to their side. He'd battled the phéa-sjant from Golgaj's walls, and watched the enemy beat a retreat in violent disarray. He'd restored the people's homes and crops. He'd purged the leeches from their ranks. They'd survived because of *him*.

Hilaríon was a swindler, just like Bollísh and Gnath had been swindlers. He'd destroy them with his greed. But time was running out for Phellhe. Hilaríon's prestige grew every day. The people were losing themselves—singing, even! They needed Phellhe more than ever, whether or not they knew it.

Nighttime seemed a balmy quilt, like the cool and piney dark of M'Brae-dah. The lights of the Vujóie cities glimmered, fireflies in the valley below. They'd pass into the mountains soon. Phellhe drew a lingering, wistful breath. He hadn't felt like himself in days. His head rolled light and fraught with pain, like storm clouds gathering over the sea. Would he ever see his home again? He couldn't wait any longer. But he couldn't do it alone.

He watched Lux scamper from the camp. The others snored, asleep. Hilaríon was sleeping, too. She stopped at the trees and glanced at Hilaríon, then turned and passed the wood line. Phellhe stepped from behind a tree—

"Christ!" she said, startled.

He held out empty hands. "The same shadow falls on us both."

She looked at him quizzically. "Drink the bark."

"Elixir won't cure what ails us."

"There *is* no us."

"You know who I'm talking about."

186

"He's your problem now," she said. "You'll see his colors soon, or won't have eyes to see them with. Or a nose, or a mouth."

"I know his colors," Phellhe said. "He'll get us all killed. Unless..." He made a slashing motion across his throat.

"What's stopping you? That wildling's gone." She stepped past him.

He pulled her back. "I'm not finished with you."

"But I'm finished with you."

He felt his knees buckle. "I can't do this without you," he said.

"Then you can't do it."

"Please." He pulled her closer. "It may already be too late." He tried to lock his knees. They only wobbled more. "The farther we get from M'Brae-dah, the less likely we'll ever go back." He grabbed a tree to steady himself. "You can help me."

"But I won't."

He leaned into the tree. "Lives are... at stake."

"In Matanzas—yes. Morón and Oriente. I've wasted enough time. I'll look for your graves at the end of the war."

Phellhe's world began to spin. What should have been a pitch-black sky swirled swarthy beige. Vomit tossed inside his throat. The trees began to whisper and hop, and the ground was not where it should have been. Then out of the madness a single thought popped.

M'Brae-dah.

"He went back for her," Phellhe said. Lux stopped.

Phellhe went on, "Or would have." He gathered his wits. "That woman stopped him. But in his heart he went back. He's still going back, even now."

She turned around.

"He watches for her," Phellhe said. "He can't take his eyes off the shadows. Is she dead? Is she coming back?" He brushed his hand along her hair. "And here you wait, so... available."

"You think I'm a fool," she said. "I rue that day."

"All the days?"

"Fuck yourself."

"Same as he did?"

She swept him down. He let himself fall. She held her blade against his cheek. "I'm not much for shaming."

"I'm not the scalp you want," he said.

She pushed her blade back into its sheath. "So do it, then."

"Would that it was that simple," Phellhe said. "Killing him is easy. But what would happen next?"

"Go back to your home," she said. "What else? That's what you've wanted, isn't it?"

"Back through the swamp and across the Trocha? That'd be suicide. We might as well keep pressing forward."

"Then get rid of him and find a safe place to ride out the war. Show some backbone. Make them follow."

"Backbone's not what I'm missing," Phellhe said. "I have nothing to offer them, do I? I never dangled a treasure before them. I thought by now they'd see his greed, that he's played them all for fools. But with him dead and no one to lead, it'd be pandemonium. We'd all be scattered. Then M'Brae-dah would really be dead."

She nodded. "He's worthless dead, anyway. Alive, the Mambíses would pay. Whoever brings him in..." She stared off into the sky.

He said, "What is it?"

A newfound zeal was on her face. "How much do you want to see him dead?"

"As much as you'd like to see him in chains."

"Then maybe we can both be winners."

He drew closer. "Tell me."

"There's a place in these mountains—not far, it looks, from where we're headed. Siguanea, it's called. Mambíses built it in the first rebellion. It's been rearmed. The enemy's never set foot inside."

Siguanea. He'd heard its name years ago. She went on, "If we could get your people inside, keep them there, and get my brother and sister Mambíses to help..."

"We'd have to separate him from the others," Phellhe said. "Draw him off temporarily."

"Your people won't go on without him."

A fiendish thought flickered to life. "Unless they're being chased," he said.

"Chased by who?"

"The only thing worse than him," Phellhe said. The fog in his head began to lift. He paced around the clearing. "If we could just get the people inside Siguanea before Hilaríon knew what had happened. If we could lead him off, alone, then—"

"Then I get the credit when we take him," she said, "*alive.*"

Phellhe's skin turned gooseflesh. He'd be a latter-day savior. He'd do his family's legacy proud. Children in a thousand years would still be singing his praises.

He looked Lux over. She was all-in. "He's a tracker, you know?" Phellhe said.

She looked at her boots. "I'm aware."

xxxvii.

The M'Brae mounted the gnarled, knobby highlands. The sultry breath of the brown floodplain expired in windy hilltops. The sawgrass faded in prickly scrub, the drooping mangrove gave way to pines. The soft world turned to stone.

They kept to the ill-used hillside trails. They willed their weary bodies on. Morning brought identical vistas, clones of the pathways they'd traversed before, at earlier breaks of similar days. Sunset found them, sore feet and bowed backs, clambering into makeshift camps. With nightfall came the biting chill and plaintive lowing of the wind. It sounded, at times, like calves at the slaughter. It sounded, at times, like voices.

Scattered about were strange monoliths, bowed like billowing mainsails, too numerous and evenly spaced to have been dropped by chance. They'd seen them in the foothills first. They'd grown in number the higher they'd pushed. Hilarión could almost swear he'd seen misshapen faces floating among them. But the tracker in him knew better. Fatigue and darkness dulled the senses.

He chafed as never before. There'd been no sign of a Gilded Peak, or a Trodden Seed. The treasure might have been oceans away, or right beneath his feet. He was none the wiser, or richer. Was Ypriána coming back? Oriel hadn't said she was dead. The more he dwelled on Oriel's words, the less clear they became. *The woman you know won't return,* she'd said. But if she had survived, shouldn't she have caught up by now? They'd already come to the base of the peaks. If she didn't find them soon—

"Something out there?"

He snapped around. "No."

Necío said, "You keep watching the trees."

"No, I don't."

Necío looked askance. "Alright, then."

A distant sound like voices howled. Necío shuddered, then quickly tried to hide that he had. Hilaríon said, "You heard that?"

"Heard what?"

A prickly silence descended. Chatter from the M'Brae camp faded. The jungle ahead loomed dark and primeval. Once he stepped off, there'd be no escaping. He could feel the tension in the air, the moment of truth drawing nearer. "So, Lux was a coward, after all," Necío said, "leaving before it got tough."

Lux had stolen away days ago. "Or smarter than the rest of us," Hilaríon said. "This hilltop's good ground. Dry, good visibility. Nice spot to lay roots."

"I don't think we're safe here. You heard Aryei. Three mornings, three sightings. Ghouls draped in gold, staring out from the trees, who vanish the second he sees them."

"Eyes play tricks in the dark," he said. But countless real dangers did await them. The thought of trudging another treasure-less day made him ill. "Runaway slaves made these trails. They fled into the highlands. Then they turned hilldevils. But that was years ago, I think."

"Then we're safe where we're going, as long as you're with us. You were a hilldevil. You know how they think."

Necío wasn't getting his drift. Hilaríon said, "Aren't you tired of danger?" The west woods loomed a beautiful morass, perfect for any escape. If he was going to do this, he had to soon, before they'd pressed too far.

"I've seen that look in your eyes before, Guamá. Don't forget what I told you, and what I didn't tell them."

Hilaríon sneered. "Wresh's eyes were open." He took a step towards the trees.

Necío said, "Ypriána's, too."

But it was time to give up the ghost. The M'Brae weren't his problem, anyway. "Ypriána's dead," he said. The words escaped his lips like a eulogy. He patted the medallion. He was off to golden days—

Phellhe burst from the trees. "Hilaríon, come quickly! He's gone, just vanished!"

"Who?" Hilaríon said.

"Aryei," Phellhe said. "Someone's taken him."

He roiled, mere seconds from freedom. But something didn't make sense. Why would Phellhe ask *him* for help? "Wait."

"Now." Phellhe grabbed Hilaríon's arm. Looks of panic and relief took turns on Necío's face. They raced back to the camp.

The people were searching the tree line. "How do you know he was taken?" Hilaríon said. "Maybe he just wandered off."

"Not possible," Phellhe said.

"No?"

Phellhe pointed between two pines. "He was last seen here."

The forest seemed darker and much less inviting. "Seen by you?"

"Not me."

"Who was on watch?"

"I was," Hetta said sheepishly.

Hilaríon felt a rage inside. He could have been half a mile away by now, the M'Brae forever behind him. "Look at me," he said.

She kept her head down. He said louder, "*Look at me.*" She raised her head. "You fell asleep, didn't you?"

She shook her head. "No."

"Don't lie to me."

"I didn't, I swear it. One moment he was there. The next moment, Phellhe and I had gotten to talking. He asked me if I'd seen anything strange, and just as soon as that happened—"

"You let us down," he said. "If you were one of my soldiers, I'd— Wait. How long had you been talking with Phellhe?"

"Just a few minutes."

"Are you sure?"

She sobbed, "Maybe longer."

"And then you noticed the boy was gone?"

She nodded. He looked at Phellhe. The big man was combing the tree line. Something wasn't adding up.

"Hilaríon," Mabba said, "Phellhe, Necío, over here." She stood at the forest's edge.

He led Hetta towards the trees. "It's not your fault," he said. He tried to sound reassuring, whether or not he meant it.

Mabba pointed to the ground. Hilaríon scanned the bramble and swept his hands along the mud. Someone had indeed passed this way. From the look of the mud it was less than half an hour.

Hetta's eyes filled with tears. "It was *him*, wasn't it?"

"Quiet," Hilaríon said. The tracks of a youngster led off in the darkness. He leaned in closer. The tracks of a larger adult lay nearby. "You were right."

Hetta clutched her face. "He took him, didn't he?"

Necío said, "That Jaeger's dead—"

Hilaríon cupped Necío's mouth. "You'll start a panic. We don't know yet." He looked at the bigger prints. They'd been pressed deep into the mud. In spite of their size there was something unusual. They'd been awfully easy to find.

"The Jaeger took him?" Phellhe shouted.

The people gasped. Hilaríon threw up his hands. "They didn't need to hear that."

Phellhe said, "They deserve to know."

"They deserve some peace," Hilaríon said. He looked at the dappled woodlands behind. The angel song of La Habana wafted through the trees. He'd have been well on his way, medallion in hand, if only he'd been a mite quicker. "We all deserve some peace."

"Forget Aryei," Chropher said. "That fool's gone."

Necío said, "I'll remember you said that if you're ever lost." He looked at Hilaríon. "What now?"

Hilaríon looked the M'Brae over. Their eyes held nothing but confidence in him: Aryei was as good as found. They'd never suspected he wanted to run. But only a tracker could save the boy now. La Habana would have to wait, again. "Keep alert," he said, "and quiet. I'll find Aryei."

"I'll keep watch," Phellhe said. "The rest of you stay in camp." He swung resolutely towards the west.

Hilaríon pointed east. "The danger comes from this way, I think. Unless you know something I don't."

"Uh, no," Phellhe said. He turned back. Hilarión watched the big man's eyes. They glowed with something other than fear, more like anxious mischief. Phellhe knew something he wasn't letting on. But there was no time for more questions.

Distant wailing came again. Necío trembled but composed himself. He said, "I'm going with you. They couldn't have gotten far."

Hilarión looked, again, to the trees. He remembered the warnings he'd heard in his youth. *The Devil fears to tread the Escambray. He doesn't know what he might find.* But if Necío could be brave, so could he. "Don't leave my side for a second," he said, "or you'll never get out alive." They raced off into the darkness.

xxxviii.

Lux León missed Hilaríon's touch, even if she'd never admit that. He'd trace battle plans on the draws of her shoulders while she faked being asleep. Elídio had been just an ordinary grunt but Hilaríon was a capitán. He'd seemed so very different. But he'd left her to the wolves when he ran, then left her again for a wildling— a dead wildling. She churned her legs faster. The wolves would soon be coming for *him.*

"Keep up, stubby," she called to the boy. "We're only as fast as your chicken legs."

"My name isn't stubby," he said, "it's Aryei. I'm named for my—"

"I don't care. Run."

She scanned the tree trunks ahead. Moonlight limned her marking. She'd cut them into the trees by day, to show the path by night. The jungle had been unforgiving. She'd raced in circles a day and one-half before she'd found Siguanea. Once proud, it had shrunken to an outpost, manned by a skeleton crew. The Mambíses warned her not to take chances: the woods were too vast, her plan too risky. But Hilaríon's scalp was too big to pass up. And when she strode back into Siguanea, the Coward of the Faceless Legion wriggling under her knife... the thought was thrilling. She dragged Aryei into a turn, then looped back into her path.

"We're going in circles," Aryei said.

"Shut it."

"No." He doubled over, panting. "You said we'd be there by now."

"I said *about* half an hour."

"It's been half an hour, and three minutes and seventeen seconds more."

"You're counting?"

"I'm the next best thing to a clock," he said, "and I'm very sharp."

"Well, I said about half an hour—"

"Twenty-six, twenty-seven, twenty-eight..."

"Ugh." Why had Phellhe not warned her?

She loosened the straps around her feet and pulled the paddles off her soles. It was becoming harder to run on them. They ruined her balance in the dark. But the rabbit trail was shaping up beautifully. By the time Hilaríon knew what had hit him, it would be too late. He'd have blundered into the ambush, and she'd be ready to pounce. Some Mambíses had laughed at her plan, but she knew what was what.

"Thirty-three, thirty-four, thirty-five..."

She sighed, "Listen, little clock-boy."

"Aryei."

"Aryei, Hilaríon needs our help with the treasure."

He stopped counting. "Not your help. He doesn't trust you."

"He sent me to bring you, remember?"

"You left us, after the swamp."

"I never left. It, *ahem*, only looked that way. He sent me ahead as a scout."

"That's not what he told us."

She found her most saccharine voice. "I told you all this before, remember? That's why you agreed to come with me." The sweet-talk made her stomach whirl but she had little choice. "Hilaríon's found the treasure. You told me you'd come help. We don't have time to waste."

"Then why are we running in circles?"

"It's, um... hard to find my way in the dark."

"You're following those marks." He drew the mark in the air with his finger.

Had they been that easy to spot? If this whelp could see them, who else might? But even if Hilaríon could find them, she'd have long been in position by then. "Aryei, there are no—"

"Something is following us!"

"—Marks. What did you say?"

A look of terror glazed the boy's eyes. "Something is following us." He pointed past her shoulder.

She wheeled around. Before her loomed a thicket. Somewhere past the canopy, a growl of thunder broke the calm.

Her heart leapt into her throat. Inside the thicket, something moved.

✳   ✳   ✳   ✳

Hilaríon charged through the forest. With any luck he'd find the boy, then make for La Habana. He could taste the rums and Turkish leaf, the perfumed napes of sun-kissed necks. But the trail had been easy to follow—too easy. Something wasn't right.

Necío kept pace. The trail abruptly doubled-back, then branched off from its arc. It reminded him of Ypriána's, only she'd had far more skill, if no more scrutable intentions.

He stopped at a thicket. The soil was trampled. "This doesn't make sense," he said. He crumbled the mud in his fingers. "They stopped here."

"Together?" Necío said.

"Just for a moment." He pointed. "Aryei stood here. The other stood there. They faced each other."

"Like they were talking?"

"The boy didn't run. He wasn't in danger. Or he didn't think he was."

"Or he knew not to bother," Necío said. "He's not really going anywhere, just looping."

Hilaríon glimpsed a gracile footprint. "I'd say *he* might be a *she*."

Necío said, "Did they meet up with a woman?"

Hilaríon's heart raced. Could Ypriána have returned? It wouldn't be the first time she'd led him on a chase. But why hadn't she come right to him? And what was she doing with Aryei?

Necío said, "Look at this." He pulled the bramble back. In the mud lay several barefoot prints, long but shallow. Whoever had made them had stepped about lightly. And each foot had six toes.

"Someone picked up their trail," Hilaríon said. "Some*thing*, anyway."

The tracks led from the thicket and came to a halt in two sharp depressions, then resumed in shallow prints. The prints had been made by balls of feet, shadowing Aryei's trail. The six-toed stalker had stood and waited, then tiptoed after them. A fine strand of fabric dangled from a branch, glittering golden in the moonlight. "Whoever it was hung back in the shadows. He waited until they'd gone far enough, then set off after them."

He peered into the distance ahead, then behind. The mystery was thickening, growing by the minute. He'd been counter-tracked before. He knew what it looked like, and this wasn't it. His quarry was either insane, or had pre-planned every move. Was Ypriána out there, alive? And if not her, then who?

Necío said, "Thank you."

"Not until we find her—*him*, I mean. Keep your head up. Danger comes from everywhere." They stepped off after the trail.

✻   ✻   ✻   ✻

Lux drew her blade. "Cuba Libre?" The moonlight was poor and intermittent. Somewhere in the distant gloom, a nightjar trilled its dirge. The faintest little groaning sound wafted from the trees. It might have been a creaking limb. But the wind was standing still. "Cuba—"

She bit off the word. The Mambíses had refused to leave Siguanea. And by now, a Mambí would have answered. Aryei whispered, "Golden ghouls."

She looked closer. She could almost swear she saw a man, prominent but deformed, peeking from behind a tree. "Hello?"

Nothing.

Her blood ran cold. Something was there. Could it be Hilarión, already? She'd given herself an ample head start. No one could have tracked her that quickly. She'd heard these lands were haunted, but she'd dismissed that as myth. "Come out."

The shadows grew longer. Wind rustled the branches. The profile twisted then disappeared. Surely, it was nothing: jagged bark, fungus, or the spoil of a hutia's nest. She'd wasted precious minutes. "No one there," she said. Aryei looked unconvinced. She pulled the paddles onto her soles and tightened the straps on her feet. The Mambíses were waiting in Siguanea. And Hilaríon would be closing in. "Don't fall back again."

They struggled up the hillside. The ragged greens gave way to pine and soared above like watchtowers. The ground pitched in a tide of loam. The monoliths seemed to double, then triple, dotting the forest like scattered gravestones. The moon disappeared past veils of cloud. They'd been running far too long. By now they should have turned again. Where was her next marker?

"One hour," Aryei said. "Twice what you said."

"Be quiet." Nothing looked familiar. "We must have missed the last—"

"So we *are* following marks."

"Ugh, just come with me," she said. Time was wasting and with it, the plan.

He tugged her cloak. "Backwards, now?"

"Shut up."

She ran, then trotted, then walked. They stumbled into crevices and batted saplings from their eyes. They backtracked in their footprints. To use the big stones as landmarks was futile. There were far too many of them to keep track. Where could that marker be? She shoved the boy ahead. "Thanks for not pushing," he said.

"You can thank me when you have your treasure."

"Tell me what the treasure is."

"Heaven forbid I spoil the magic."

They passed trees and crossed draws she swore they'd passed and crossed before, only to realize they hadn't. She dragged the boy up ferny hillsides, looking out at the forest ahead and behind. Hoping for familiar sights, all she saw were strange ones. She groaned silently to herself. This was all Hilaríon's fault.

"One hour and one-half," Aryei said.

The moon peeked from the clouds. In hiding it had climbed higher. Hilaríon would be hard on her trail. And Phellhe—forget

Phellhe. The M'Brae weren't her problem. There was no denying she'd lost the markers. Now she had to be bold. She looked at the stars. "Northeast," she said. "This way. We're close."

"We're lost."

"Free Cubans can never be lost."

The forest closed in from all sides. Its claws reached out to waylay them. But Siguanea had to be near: it was well-hidden, not invisible. She fingered the hilt of her blade. Once she arrived, she'd ditch the boy, then take her place to spring the ambush.

Aryei slowed. "Tell me what the treasure is. Hilaríon must've told you."

Every moment counted. There could be no more stopping. "Aryei—"

"Until you tell me, I'm not moving." He wedged his foot beneath a root.

She had to keep the plan on pace. She'd be damned if the clock-brat ruined it. "Aryei!" She yanked him. He stumbled to the mud, howling. She said, "Get up."

"I can't. My ankle's twisted."

Lux pulled the paddles off her feet. She took his injured leg in her hand and slowly rolled it back and forth. Aryei winced. "This hurt?" she said.

He stopped wincing. "No."

"How about now?"

"Not really."

"Pretending, are we?" She gently bent his foot towards his shin. "And now?"

The boy cried, "It's here!"

"Then it isn't broken—"

"Not that," he said. "It's here—*he's* here. It's following us again."

A blur of gold flashed in the shadows. She shot to her feet. "Who's there?"

She drew her blade. She could feel the blood in her temples like hammers. She peered into the gloom. Deep in the thicket a stone's throw away, something was moving: barely, back and forth, like the chest of a slow-breathing hunter. "That's what they do," Aryei said, "the ghouls."

She cupped his mouth and crouched atop him. The thing in the thicket billowed gently, until it stopped altogether. Whatever it had been was gone. All there was were boulders and tree trunks, and the rustling of leaves in the wind. It had been nothing, same as before. They had to get to Siguanea soon, and not a moment to spare. "We're safe," she said.

"We're not. They melt to the shadows, but they're never gone. He's still near, I know it."

"Aryei," she said, "there are no ghouls. Now let's get going before Hilarión thinks we're not coming."

"I'm not going anywhere." He jumped to his feet, landing hard.

Lux said, "So you *were* pretending."

"You know all about pretending. If we're not being followed, there's time. Tell me what the treasure is and where he found it. Tell me his exact words." He slid his feet back under the root.

A wasted minute, here or there, and the plan would fall to ruins. "He said for me to bring help."

"He'd have asked for Necío."

"He said to bring someone spry, and trustworthy."

Aryei laughed. "You picked me? Not Hrama or Jacinda? What kind of fool are you?"

Her final sliver of patience cracked. She snarled, "There is no goddamn treasure! And Hilarión is dead."

"Dead?"

"Soon enough, he will be." She lifted Aryei clear of the root.

He said, "But the other M'Brae?"

"They're Phellhe's problem now. At the rate that fever's taking him, he'll be dead in a week and them with him. You're safer with me. You ought to be grateful."

Aryei sobbed. She raised his chin. "A year from now there won't be M'Brae... or Guanahatabey, or even Cubans. All there'll be is women and men. Together. Equal. Free. And I'll have been to thank—"

"*Esta tierra será quemada antes de ser libres,*" a familiar voice hissed.

Lux's skin turned gooseflesh. Her knees gave way. Aryei leapt aside and ran. "Help!" he cried. "Somebody!"

The rustle of brush underfoot crunched loudly, all around, from every side. Shades of gold bled from the night. Cloaked figures were encircling her.

xxxix.

Phellhe looked at the moon. It had climbed since last he'd glanced its way. Time was wasting. Hilaríon wasn't stupid: in no time at all, he'd guess the plot. Where was Lux? She should have returned by now, disguised as the Gray Jaeger. It shouldn't have taken this long. Could something have gone ill?

He paced the edge of the woods. He wiped the sweat from his lolling head. The fever was getting worse. He could almost swear there were fiendish faces peering from between the trees. But he was only seeing things. The midges' bites had dulled his mind. There'd be tonic in Siguanea. But would he ever get there? Where on earth was Lux?

He'd made it clear, he'd thought. The longer the M'Brae were outside Siguanea, the worse the chances they'd ever get inside. They'd never go anywhere on their own, and they'd never follow him. They'd wait for Hilaríon's return or they'd have to be shocked into action. Phellhe had relented, agreed she could ambush Hilaríon first. Had she double-crossed him?

He looked the people over. Every last one was sound asleep. This is how it should have been: in Golgaj, asleep without care, proud Mambíses manning the ramparts, and he in command of it all. Hilaríon had taken his place. They'd forsaken their Oíc for a bandit—a hilldevil! In spite of a few small regrettable ills, he'd done them all much good. He'd make them remember.

But where was Lux? His whole plan hinged on her. He couldn't wait any longer. There was too much at stake.

He peeled his cloak and drew his dagger. This would sear, but the illusion would hold. The people needed a Jaeger attack. He'd give them what they needed.

He chomped down on his knuckle. He pressed the blade into his flesh and carved it across his chest. The blood trickled down and pooled in his clothing. He splashed the blood across his face and screamed from the pit of his belly, "Awake! The Jaeger—*he's come!* He's come! Awake!"

The people began to stir. "Run!" he shouted, louder and louder. "Run! The Jaeger! He's here!"

The people's whimpers turned to screams. They scrambled to their feet. He pointed between the two tall trees, the direction Lux had told him. "That way!" The people took off running.

Phellhe wiped the blood from his eyes. Pain had never felt so good. He'd be Oíc again within the hour. "Run! Run—!"

The word died in his throat. Through the trees behind him, what appeared to be golden ghosts were approaching.

✳   ✳   ✳   ✳

Hilarión pressed on. Necío kept close to his side. Their quarry's trail grew frantic. It plunged down into a muddy gorge then looped back out the way it came. It double-backed to the top of a hill. If it *was* Ypriána, what was she doing? Necío said, "Stopped again?"

A trail told a story, if one could read. Now their quarry's turns were sharper, their forays more but smaller. To the novice eye the trail would seem pell-mell, but Hilarión knew better. Before, the quarry had known where they'd been going, albeit by circuitous path. Now, they were flailing, looking for something. "They're lost," Hilarión said.

Necío said, "And six-toes?"

The stalker's tracks had vanished. They'd already vanished three or four times, only to reappear later. The stalker had shadowed at a distance but hadn't done much else. For now he was just a distraction. "Don't worry about him." Necío looked unconvinced.

Hilarión peered closer. The woman's footprints had returned, and now there was something he hadn't noticed. The left boot heel was split left to right, and made a distinct imprint. It wasn't the same as Ypriána's, from the hillside near M'Brae-dah. But Ypriána had doffed those boots before she'd faced the dragon. She could be wearing anything now.

Necío said, "I think I see—"

"Wait." In Hilaríon's mind a story was shaping. Aryei hadn't been kidnapped. He'd been lured away by someone he trusted, at least long enough to have gotten this far. He'd been taken for a reason. He was good at keeping time: he'd be useful in the woods at night. It *had* to have been Ypriána. She'd been sure enough of her trail at first, but then she'd gotten lost. But even when she'd known her trail, where had she been headed?

"Hilaríon."

"What?"

Necío pointed up a tree. "A marker, I think."

Just before the fork of the tree were two diagonal scratches, hashed by a vertical line. He ran his hand across the mark. The wood was moist but not saturated. Recently doused by rain, it was drying. Whoever had carved the mark could have missed it. Ypriána would not have made such an error. "It can't be a mark."

"It looks like one."

"The mind sees what it wants," he said. "Anyway, she missed it."

"She?"

"Whoever. We need to find Aryei."

They started down the trail again. It led into a ferny hollow. It rambled on in fits and starts. The moon climbed ever higher. This wasn't like Ypriána, to be so scattershot. But the terrain was rough and the moonlight scant. Anyone could have gotten lost.

Necío said, "I see it again." Etched into another tree, barely visible in the bark, were parallel lines hashed vertically. Again, the wood was wet but drying; again, the trail looped past it. Ypriána would not have made this mistake, and certainly never twice. Necío pointed back the way they'd come. "What direction is that, between the two markers?"

"They're not markers," Hilaríon said.

"Trust me."

Hilaríon looked at the stars. "Southwest," he said. They were wasting time.

"So he's headed northeast, or would have been if he'd seen the markers," Necío said.

"Anyone who knows to use markers knows not to carve them in wood in the rain, and anyway not eye-level. And no one would dead-reckon a place like this."

"You mean Ypriána wouldn't."

"I already told you, Ypriána is—"

"Dead," he said, "I know. But I know you don't believe that."

Necío, as annoyingly usual, was right. He'd let her go, pinned his dreams to La Habana. She'd stormed back into *his* life. "We need to keep going."

"We need to think," Necío said. "What's northeast of here?"

"More mountains, more jungle. A tangle like you've never seen."

"Then why would they be headed there? You said yourself there were hideouts."

"*Were* hideouts."

"Where would a Mambí go?"

He spat. Necío was fast becoming dead weight. "There was Siguanea, years ago." But Ypriána would never have heard of it. He'd been a capitán and knew only rumors. "Stop wasting time."

"I'm not," Necío said. "You think it's a woman and maybe you're right. I'm telling you, it's Lux."

Hilarión said, "She's long gone. Off to sing to the Bronze Titan, no doubt."

"It makes sense," Necío said. "Lux wanted you prisoner. Who-ever took Aryei wants you to follow. You said yourself the trail's too easy. How else to trap a tracker? She's headed to Siguanea, drawing out the trail."

Hilarión said, "That's clever, but no. If Aryei's in danger, you're making it worse."

But Aryei wasn't in danger, because he was with Ypriána. Who else would Aryei trust? Who else would leave a trail to be tracked? Ypriána was an enigma. But for all of Oriel's doublespeak and all of his own misgivings, it was coming to pass as she'd promised. *I'll catch up to you*, she'd said. She was reaching out to him, leading as only he'd follow.

"Don't you see?" Necío said. "Lux is using Aryei like you used Wresh, as bait."

"Necío, it's not—" The word, like a grub, bored into his brain. "—Bait." He sighed.

It couldn't be Ypriána. She'd never use someone as bait.

He hung his head. The scope of his failure began to unfurl. In his rush to get it over with, he'd blundered down a rabbit trail. He'd been soft when he should have been steadfast, slipshod instead of alert. He'd ignored what he hadn't wanted to see: the demand for help, the distracted lookout, the certainty of danger from the west. He'd seen the clues but missed their sum.

Phellhe.

"It isn't Ypriána," Hilaríon said. "Ypriána's dead."

Necío gasped, "Can I worry now?" He pointed. Fifteen sets of six-toed tracks converged in the mud where they stood. All about were prints of knees and wet depressions shaped like hands. Crushed in the prints were pieces of cloth, each a different shade of gold. Aryei's tracks took off at a lope.

Hilaríon drew his blade. If Aryei was still alive, all that could save him was speed. "Keep up with me," he said. He sprang to the shadows.

The ground grew rougher, swathed in pine. The tracks grew harder and harder to see. He pumped his arms and leaned ahead. How could he have let this happen?

The trail grew wide and frantic. Aryei had run, but the stalkers had followed. They'd walked but still gained time. Their feet had lightly kissed the green: they'd anticipated being tracked. Hilaríon could see their trail, but a novice like Necío never could.

"Faster, Necío!" he called back. Necío drifted farther behind.

He ran harder still. The greens crushed in the footprints were wet. Aryei was only moments ahead—at least what was left of him would be. He could claim the boy's body, if nothing else. At least he'd be buried with dignity.

"Necío! Hurry!"

He clasped the medallion under his cloak. More eyes were coming into view. But what was one more pair of eyes? What were sixteen more? The medallion would turn the eyes to coins, their torment to gold bullion. "Get ready, Necío," he said. "Almost—"

He stopped. He was alone. "Necío?"

The woods stood still. Nothing swayed or stirred. Life itself seemed to harden to stone. In the hollow of the air, he could hear the distant howling again. It sounded like people crying for help. "Necío?"

He shuddered. Through the trees, watching him, were five massive pairs of eyes.

<u>xl.</u>

L ux crashed through the monstrous woods, branches whipping
at her cheeks, thorns biting at her legs. She could hear Aryei's
scuffling footfalls behind. He was no longer trying to escape her, but
following. "Cuba Libre!" she railed, "*Cuba Libre!*" Someone had to
hear. Siguanea *had* to be near.

The voices seemed to spring from the soil and hang like soot
on the wind. They dropped from the trees like rancid fruit. They
filled the night, a grim ensemble, words she couldn't understand and
loathsome in their strangeness.

> "Gold and gild, gild and gold
> So much alike, so very cold..."

She fell to the ground. Whatever demons held these woods, they
were closing in on her. It was all because of Hilaríon. "Help!" she
screamed. "Cuba Libre—!"

"*There!*" Aryei said, pointing frantically. Through the bramble, a
fire flickered red.

Lux flung herself towards the light. Aryei shuffled at her side.
The voices soared to a throaty crescendo, then faded into silence. The
forest gave way to woodland edge. Ahead was a clearing with watch-
fire burning, and behind it thatch-roofed huts.

Siguanea.

Lux rolled her eyes in ecstasy: against all hope, she'd reached safe
haven. The plan was still intact. She was going to live, Hilaríon to pay.

"Um... Lux?" Aryei said.

"Quiet. Find a hut," she said. She had to get in place. With the
time she'd wasted running amok, Hilaríon had to be close. He'd still
never know what hit him. She drew her machete.

"But Lux—"

"But nothing." He'd used her like a penny-whore but the final laugh would be hers. Hilaríon's head would rot on a spit while she would live a brand-new day—

"*Lux.*" Aryei tugged her cloak.

She snapped, "Didn't I tell you to get to a—"

The words died on her lips. The scream in her belly collapsed on itself. She withered to her knees. She could force but the faintest whisper, "No."

The clearing was deathly still. All voices had gone silent. A Mambí standard lay in tatters, shredded across a blood-stained bush. Scattered about the cabins and huts were butchered Mambí bodies. Siguanea had been razed. She recognized the handiwork.

It was the Gray Jaeger.

"Dead," Aryei said, "all dead." He yelped like an infant, "Help."

She wrapped her hand across his mouth. "We're past all help," she said.

Bile frothed inside her spleen. It was the same as Cacarajícara, and at her camp in the swamp. Hilaríon! This was his fault, too. Even if she couldn't barter his life, she still could take his scalp.

Bramble rustled in the woods. Someone was headed their way. It had to be Hilaríon. She grabbed Aryei and raced into the largest hut.

✻   ✻   ✻   ✻

Hilaríon stumbled backwards. The eyes were enormous, hewn in stone.

He stepped into a cedar stand. The rainclouds had parted, if just for a moment. The moonlight pooled in the sheen of the leaves and scattered like dew on the trees. The starry sky through the boughs above seemed a glittering ocean. He forgot the chase and the missing boy, the medallion and La Habana. A feeling of peace came over him, as if he'd strayed into a dream.

Breaking from the earth, as if breaching from the waves, were five leviathans of stone, each long as a locomotive. They looked like giant fishes, same as the vision he'd seen in the swamp. Crumbling and shorn of fins and flukes, they seemed less like their living selves than corpses, cloven by time and forgetfulness. He ran his hands along their hides. Who could have carved them with such loving hands, then left them to rot in a gorge? Their eyes seemed to peer into his own, as if begging him to remember. He knew who they were supposed to be.

The Ones Who Came Before.

An ill wind whispered past his face. A chill ran from his feet through his head. A solitary raindrop, harbinger of storms to come, plopped against his nose. All was ghostly calm.

Then the skies broke, and the Gray Jaeger pounced.

<u>*xli.*</u>

Necío rounded the cluster of trees. The forest thinned to saplings. He could see several stone's-throws ahead. But Hilarío
wasn't there.

"Hilarío?" he whispered. Wind snaked through the lonely wood.
The scrawny branches creaked. Somewhere past the canopy, the din
of rolling thunder grumbled.

Necío dropped to a knee. Hilarío had been only paces ahead.
Even in this nightmarish tangle, he'd kept Hilarío's pace—mostly.
He couldn't have gotten too far away. He whispered again, *"Hilarío."*
But there came no answer.

The sky groaned on. He waited. There was no sense chancing
some random path. Hilarío would reappear soon: he'd probably
stumbled in the dark, or chased a fruitless tangent. But he'd soon
regain the trail. Wouldn't he?

The heavy air burst and chattered with rain, by and by pooling
over his shoes. Time enough had passed. Something had to be amiss.
Then Necío remembered: Hilarío still had the medallion. By now,
he could be well en route towards his precious golden days. Had it all
just been a highwayman's con? A panic welled inside him—

No. He wasn't that mewling runt anymore. He smothered the
fear in his chest. He could track well enough, on his own. He could
find Aryei then retrace his steps. Hilarío was gone, Ypriána dead,
Phellhe succumbing to fever. The treasure was as good as lost. But the
people could still survive, through *him*—

"Help." A whimper, like a fledgling bird, came from past the
thicket, "Help."

Necío said, "What?"

"Help—" it came again, cut short. Something had stifled its cry.

"Hello?" Necío said. Footfalls shuffled in the distance.

To act brave was to be brave. He stood. "Whoever you are, come out," he said. "Maybe I'll let you live."

Nothing.

These woods would drive the sanest man mad. He scoffed, "Guess I showed him—"

"Help."

He wheeled around. Not a stone's throw to the north, something large loomed from the woods. Past the knotted stand of trees lay horizontal planks, overhung with thatch.

A cabin.

He took a step closer. Beyond it stood similar cabins, painted brown and draped with vines, all well-disguised in brush. Somewhere near, the dying embers of a fire threw veils of light against the trees.

"Find me," peeped the voice. It was coming from a cabin.

Sweat pooled at his temples. The howling voices on the wind— he knew exactly who they were. His mother had warned him daily. *Beware the Wailing Vale,* she'd said. *Beware the ones who guard it.* But he was the closest thing to a Oíc now, even if by default. Someone was in danger. He knew better than to run.

He grabbed a branch for a makeshift club and tiptoed towards the sound. A cold breeze licked his cheek. The cabin loomed tall above him, like a ramshackle crypt.

The voice inside began to wail, "Find me.... Help..."

He pressed his hand to the door. Its rusty hinges groaned. It trundled open, revealing a barracks.

"Find me," came the voice.

He sidled past sleeping berths. The floor boards creaked beneath his feet. Weapons leaned in smart intervals against the grimy wall. Boots stood in pairs under the beds. No doubt Mambíses had been here, from the looks of it very recently. Not lightly did soldiers leave weapons about. He didn't have to be one to know that.

"Help." He was getting closer to the voice.

Necío raised the branch. He could almost swear, above the creaks, that he heard another voice. It seemed to mutter, almost growl, *"Say it again."*

And then, as if on cue, the little voice sobbed, "Find me."

At the end of the room was a doorway. He drew up close beside it. "Here," the voice said, "in here." He pressed his palm against the door. It swung inwards at his slightest touch. Any chance of stealth was gone.

"Help."

He stepped into a storeroom. Someone was cowering in the corner, behind a pile of wood. He pulled the planks aside. A smallish figure cringed beneath.

Aryei.

Necío heaved a grateful breath, then whispered, "Did you give *us* a scare." Aryei's face was pale, his eyes pink and swollen.

Aryei said, "I'm sorry." For a moment a light returned to his eyes, only to fade and flicker to black. "She made me do it."

Necío pulled back. "Who made you do what—?"

"*Die, traitor, die!*" A figure lunged. "Die, you demon Judas, die! They're dead because of you!"

A blade tore through his flesh. The tearing of muscle and snapping of sinews rumbled through his body: up, then down, then back again, like an arc of lightning. The figure cried, "There's nothing for me anymore!" The force of the strike slammed him backwards. He could feel the blade burst through his flank and lodge in the wood of the door. "Die, you demon... die—" The figure raised her head. "Oh."

It was Lux.

Necío gasped. The pain was too horrible even to speak. He let his arms drop. The branch fell from his hand. Lux said, "Um, I thought you were... never mind." She wrapped both hands on the hilt and yanked, as if to withdraw the blade. Necío retched. He hadn't the strength to cry out in pain. She'd skewered him to the wood.

A voice cried in the distance. He recognized Phellhe's husky tenor. "We'll be safe here. Wait... what?"

Raindrops peppered the cabin roof. Lightning split the sky. In the blaze Necío could see it all now. In single-mindedly following Aryei's voice, he'd failed to notice his surroundings. Bodies lay in blood-soaked bunks and pinned against the walls. Some were spitted fast on pikes. Their jaws hung agape, their eyes peeled wide, same as the Amazons in the swamp. It was the Gray Jaeger's butchery. And Hilarion—where was Hilarion?

Lux flung blood from her fingers. Necío's head lolled and swam. All at once, Lux's youthful face morphed into a scowling middle-aged woman. Necío's heart leapt for joy. At last, his mother had returned! They had so much to talk about. "I've made the most wonderful find," he said. He reached out to hold her.

She pushed him away. "I'm sorry," she said, pushing Aryei through the doorway. "I didn't mean to... I didn't want to..." The front door crashed behind her.

Necío's head rolled onto his shoulder. He hadn't the strength to lift it. He could feel himself slipping away. But his mother was not a patient woman. And there was never time to waste. "Gnath, I'm coming, straight away."

He smiled. What new adventures lay in store?

✳   ✳   ✳   ✳

Hilarion lurched aside. The Jaeger's blade whined past his head. He reached for his machete. The Jaeger kicked him in the chest. He fell to his back, his arm lodged beneath him.

The rain squalled in droves. The Jaeger dug his boot heel into Hilarion's gut. Hilarion thrashed to free his arm. The pressure forced the breath from his lungs. The Jaeger drove his other heel against Hilarion's hand. The crunch of wrist bones crackled.

The Jaeger reared his savage head. His face and neck were pocked with welts where crocodile teeth had ripped. The witchcraft that had buoyed him had faded to mere spite: he was less hellhound than wounded cur now. Hilarion could almost swear he could see the Castilian nobleman's son ere death and battle had mangled him. "*Cerca*," the Jaeger said, "*Cerca... o lejos?*"

Hilarion made no answer. What was left to say?

The Jaeger seemed to swell skyward, stretching like a fast-growing weed. "*Lejos, entonces*," he said. He plunged his blade—

Hilaríon rolled. The Jaeger stabbed between his legs. The blade sliced his thigh above his knee. The Jaeger pulled the blade away and stabbed at Hilaríon's face. Hilaríon flicked his head aside. The Jaeger stabbed a third time. The blade lodged between Hilaríon's fingers, slicing the web of his hand.

Hilaríon rolled and stood. He feinted with his right fist, then swung through with his left. The Jaeger coolly dodged the strike, then clove down with his blade. It grazed the tip of Hilaríon's nose. The pain sang through Hilaríon's face. The blood lapped into his mouth.

Hilaríon threw his head forward and spat in the Jaeger's eyes. The Jaeger snatched Hilaríon's face and hooked him by the nostrils. He dug his bony fingers deep. He grabbed the Jaeger's wrist with both hands. The Jaeger sliced a bloody gash below Hilaríon's elbow.

Hilaríon reached for his arm. The Jaeger pulled his hand away. Hilaríon fell, head snapping to the ground. The Jaeger held his blade aloft.

The eyes in Hilaríon's mind burned red. At last, the reckoning was at hand. "Just finish it," he said. Whatever gruesome death was coming, he'd earned it.

"Usted eligió esto," the Jaeger said. "Usted lo eligió, día a día."

"My best," Hilaríon lied.

The Jaeger paused. For an instant, he let his shoulders drop. His coat sagged loose on his body. From the folds of his clothing an odd object dangled. Hilaríon looked closer. It was a piece of human flesh, stretched and pinned across a brooch. A pang burst in Hilaríon's chest. He remembered their fight near the Amazons' camp. It was a cloven piece of ear.

Ypriána's ear.

The Jaeger swung—

Hilaríon kicked the Jaeger's knee. The Jaeger's leg snapped sideways, spinning him onto his back and knocking the blade from his hand. Hilaríon scrambled to his feet. The Jaeger lunged after his blade. Hilaríon swung with all his strength. The Jaeger reached to block the strike, but Hilaríon found his mark. The Jaeger's eyes went glossy white. He wilted to a knee. He drew his coat open and glanced at the brooch. "Moldeado en elinfierno," he said.

Hilaríon said, "Where is she?"

The Jaeger smiled. "Muerta." But his eyes belied more.

"*Where is she?*"

"Tú vas a ver—" The Jaeger grabbed, then swung his blade. Hilaríon hollowed backwards. The blade just barely grazed his chin.

Hilaríon slammed his fist into the Jaeger's chest. He closed his fingers around the brooch and tore it fast away. He grabbed the Jaeger by the throat. He tried to draw his own machete but could not reach where it hung from his waist.

The Jaeger writhed. Hilaríon tightened his grip on his throat. The flesh on the brooch was still moist, not more than two days old. Its outer edge was jagged, cut from someone struggling. "Where is she?" he said.

The Jaeger's eyes swelled red. Hilaríon throttled relentlessly. The demon gulped deeply, then said, "Es ella—"

A sound like a knot of wild pigs croaked from close behind. The Jaeger broke Hilaríon's grip, then scurried off into the shadows. Hilaríon slid the brooch in his pocket. A ring of figures, draped in gold, was encircling him. The clearing was filling with strange troglodytes.

xlii.

They snorted and sniggered like swine. Beneath their golden tatters, their lifeless eyes were gray. Their flesh was the color of spoiled meat. Each of their hands had six fingers, each of their feet six toes. They held their arms wide, as if to embrace him, and intoned as they surrounded him,

> "Gold and gild, gild and gold
> So much alike, so very cold..."

They formed a perfect ring around him. He waved his blade to fend them off. They kept up their advance. Their noses were crooked and dripping with ooze, horrid to look at, like corpses bewitched.

A withered crone stepped from the ring. Her golden tatters were made of silk, crowned by a fraying headdress, as if she were a fearful queen. She grabbed Hilaríon's arm. He whipped back his blade. He'd free her from her misery—

No. The Jaeger was escaping.

He shoved his way through the troglodytes. He could feel their bony bodies, the fishy grips of their hands on his. He broke from their midst and tore off running. They set off after him, intoning,

> "Gold and gild, gild and gold..."

The storm renewed its fury. The rain gushed down the spouts of leaves and turned the forest floor to paste. Hilaríon kept his eyes to the ground. The trail was soft and hard to spot. The Jaeger had known how to mask it well. He hadn't run haphazardly.

The troglodytes moaned. Their footsteps shuffled. Their cloaks flashed golden in the dark. They weren't just behind him now, but ahead and all around.

The trail hooked, then flattened, then bolted downhill. The Jaeger had picked up speed, no longer bothering to disguise his path. His strides were deep and confident. He'd known where he was going. Hilaríon squeezed the Jaeger's brooch. Ypriána would not have surrendered her ear lightly. What happened in those final hours, only the Jaeger knew. But Hilaríon had to know, too.

Up ahead the forest thinned. Moldy tree trunks crisscrossed the ground, as if the area had been cleared to make room for a wreckage yard. Strewn about were telescopes, copper pipes and leather books, their pages torn and drifting. Mounds of what looked like coconut husks rose to treetop-height. Scattered between mounds were the shattered frames of ornithopters, human-powered flying contraptions, large enough to bear a man skyward. They looked like primordial thunderbirds. Their bat-like wings reached from the heaps, still stretched across with sheepskin.

A wistful twinge shook him. He lifted a page. He'd seen books like this in his youth. The page was a chart of constellations, the sizes and colors of the stars. Aldebaran, Betelgeuse, Sirius and Procyon: he remembered them all. Once he'd cherished books like this. Who would have defiled them?

"Gold and gild. Gild and gold..." The troglodytes were coming.

The Jaeger's path led up a mound. He couldn't let the trail go cold. He ran to the base of the mound and jumped, and flailed for something to grab. A cascade of husks and debris toppled down, pushing him to the ground again.

"Gold and gild..."

He scurried back onto the mound and grabbed a thunderbird wing. He hoisted himself upwards—

The wing cracked lengthwise. He came crashing down.

"Gild and gold..." The troglodytes were closer, still.

Hilaríon winced. The pain of brutal weeks at quest was finally catching up with him. His body was breaking. He'd will himself on, nonetheless.

He grabbed the broken halves of wing and laid them one above the other. He stepped onto the nearer one. It bowed at the center but held his weight. He crawled onto the second wing, then grabbed the first and flung it ahead. He climbed from the second onto the first, then turned and repeated the drill. The crest of the mound loomed closer. He mounted and switched the wings three times more. He was almost at the summit—

A troglodyte loomed from the crest above him. The wing skittered down. Hilarion clutched the piece beneath him. The force of his backwards lurch shook it loose. His knees wheeled into his face. He spun head over heels down the pile.

"Gold and gild, gild and gold..." The troglodytes converged. They had him cornered against the mound. There were too many now to hold off with his blade. He grabbed a wooden ornithopter-beam. It cracked as the contraption crumbled, revealing a hole in the wreckage.

He slithered through the hole and into the wreck of an ornithopter, its rib beams like a cage above. All around was dust and grime. Earwigs pranced along his arms. Spider webs choked his eyes and mouth. But the rib beams kept the debris from collapsing on top of him. And the troglodytes did not pursue. He strained his body farther along. A faint light shone ahead.

"...Gold..." The voices fell to silence.

He clambered from the crawlspace. The raindrops pummeled his face like stones. The Jaeger's trail was gone. He'd have to guess aggressively. A good tracker could inhabit the mind of his quarry. To the Jaeger, wounded and on harsh terrain, the way of least resistance would have seemed the surest path.

He raced off into the morning twilight. The mounds of trash rolled on. Each was filled with oddities rotting: statues dismembered, lanterns junked, ornate tapestries torn to strings. Some might have been royal relics, bearing witness to glorious pasts, and some seemed perfectly meaningless but elegant just the same. He forged his way through the wreckage then stopped. He'd come to the rim of a gorge.

The rain had slowed to a piddling mist. He could see in the distance for miles on end. To the north, the land dropped away to a wide, sprawling valley, honeycombed like a rabbit warren. Slung over it was a craggy peak, capped by a glass-domed observatory. The mountainside was hollowed away, as if it had been excavated, in some laborious, unfinished venture. It had to be the Gilded Peak. He wondered aloud, "What is this place?"

To the south the land tossed in green, ferny hills, then flattened to meadows down to the sea. A legion of clouds hung over the water, stowing, somewhere, daybreak behind it. Between him and the coast there was nothing to stop him. Freedom was only an hour's descent.

He looked at his feet. Daybreak pooled in the trough of a boot print. A trail of prints led towards the peak. It had to be the Jaeger's.

He sighed. Tracking the Jaeger wouldn't be difficult. In the Jaeger's weakened state, a hand-to-hand fight might even be feasible. But even though her ear-flesh was moist, there was next to no chance Ypriána had lived. And Hilaríon wanted no part of that mountain.

Golden days. It was time.

"Gold and gild, gild and gold..."

From the tree line a stone's throw away, the M'Brae burst from the woods. On their heels were troglodytes, driving them like stone-age hunters, towards the beetling cliff. Hilaríon ducked behind a monolith. Their terrified shrieks rang through the hills. Those not dashed to death in the gorge would be trapped below and cornered. His would be a bird's-eye seat to the M'Brae's final act.

They formed what stalwart line they could. The troglodytes pressed closer. Tiny Mabba slid down the cliff, then Hetta jumped after her. Phellhe raised his fists in defiance. His chest and arms were caked with blood. This would be Phellhe's exeunt, too. In Hilaríon's mind, the eyes—

No. Hadn't the eyes shamed him enough? Because of them he'd been swindled, chasing ghosts in a broken land.

The troglodytes lunged in a wave toward the M'Brae. The M'Brae spilled into the gorge. They were dead now. All of them. Probably. Weren't they?

Hilaríon looked at the Gilded Peak, then the beckoning, un-guarded strand. Either place held a prize of some stripe: vengeance for Ypriána, or freedom. But golden days could abide no guilt. If

Ypriána was truly dead, somewhere, she was watching him. And Ypriána would have gone.

He slid into the gorge.

xliii.

He snaked between the boulders. The rain made running rivulets and lithe cascades of outwash silt. The opposite wall of the canyon rose, blotting the fledgling dawn. The gorge below him was brown and cracked, a sliver of putrid waste. Across the way, the M'Brae clustered, having survived the fall, it seemed. But a troglodyte was bearing down upon them.

Hilaríon scrambled to firmer ground. The troglodyte shambled towards the M'Brae. Hilaríon ran behind, then stabbed at the creature. It turned and parried his strike. It re-grabbed his wrist, then punched his elbow. His arm went numb. He dropped his blade.

Hilaríon grabbed its throat with both hands. The troglodyte dropped its weight to a crouch, then threw up its elbow and spun. Hilaríon's grip broke apart. The troglodyte spiked its thumb to Hilaríon's throat, then drove the heel of its palm to his chest. Hilaríon fell to his back, gasping.

The troglodyte stared blankly. It grunted and turned, exposing its back, and shuffled on towards the M'Brae. The M'Brae formed a protective line. Hilaríon doffed his cloak and hung it on the end of his blade. He strode behind the creature's back and raised his makeshift dummy. He flicked it against the creature's left side and feinted to the right.

The troglodyte spun and grabbed the cloak. Hilaríon swung and shattered its jaw. The troglodyte stopped, dazed. Hilaríon drew the blade from the cloak and plunged it into the creature's back. He could feel its bone and sinew snap. The troglodyte dropped to its knees. Hilaríon pulled the blade away and kicked the creature down to the mud.

The M'Brae stepped forward. He waved them back. The troglodyte wrenched around in the dirt. Hilaríon placed his hand on its head. It squeezed a drawn-out, plaintive moan. He ran his fingers under its jaw. Its pulse had stopped. "It's dead," he said.

"What are they?" Hetta said.

Pain broke across Hilaríon's body, worst at his joints and sensitive places. The troglodyte had known just where to strike and how to turn his bones. "Relentless," he answered.

He looked to the edge of the cliff, above. The other troglodytes had gone. The walls of the gorge where the M'Brae had fallen were smooth and lined with moss. The base was overgrown with ferns. Other than some scrapes and bumps, the M'Brae were none the worse for wear. He marveled and said, "You're all unharmed." He could still make a break for the unguarded strand—

"All but one," Jacinda said, pointing. Crumpled, bruised, and panting for breath, Phellhe looked like a broken man.

Hilaríon said, "Is Aryei still missing?"

"We'd hoped you'd found him," Hetta said, "and Necío."

He looked around. Necío was missing, too.

A crystalline flash below caught his eye. Underfoot, something shimmered. The storm had turned the gorge to marsh. Beneath the water were glittering gems and precious golden nuggets.

The treasure.

One by one, the M'Brae saw and burst into excited chatter. They dropped to their hands and knees and cheered, splashing about excitedly and making piles for themselves.

Hilaríon exhaled lustily. It was even more princely than he had imagined. He scooped a heaping handful of nuggets. All of his pains had been worth this moment. The legend all along had been true. Fenn, Wresh, and Sunovín—and even, perhaps, Ypriána—hadn't died in vain. And La Habana would make everything right—

The water bled golden in his hands. The nuggets were only painted rocks, same as in the caverns. The gems were weathered flakes of quartz. The stones were blobs of tin. The entire valley was littered with trinkets but all of them were worthless. He flung the trinkets onto the ground. "Naturally," he said.

The people groused, toppling their treasure-piles. Hilaríon

stared at the waterlogged ground. Among the trinkets lay two vials, blown of golden glass and corked, filled with clear liquid. He sniffed, then tasted: it was Lightleaf elixir. One of the M'Brae must have dropped—

"What on earth?" he exclaimed. He couldn't believe his eyes. A boot print bloomed in the nearby mud, by the look of it only minutes old. And its heel was split left to right.

Aryei.

He took off running. The pregnant one, Maith, said, "I need to tell you.... Wait!"

He called back, "Just a moment." The trail was fresh and easy to read: two sets of tracks, a woman and child. Aryei and his abductor had fled, but weren't trying to hide their route. Nor had they been chased.

The gorge deepened, widening still, and opened in a field of sage. The field was filled with the strange monoliths, arranged in a figure-eight, like some pagan altar. Inside the stones was an old walnut tree, its branches spread like gnarled claws, reaching towards the cliff-tops. The trail led to the base of its trunk. And standing atop the thickest branch, grinning nervously was Lux. Aryei clung beside her. "Happy returns on your treasure hunt?" she snarked.

"Better," Hilaríon said. "So it *was* you. Necío was right."

Aryei said, "Necío's dead."

The word struck like a poleaxe-blow. *Dead.* Necío had trusted him, kept his secrets, covered his sins. But Necío had paid the price. Why hadn't he ordered him not to follow? He'd have been be off to La Habana and Necío alive. Another pair of eyes glowed hot.

"She tricked me," Aryei said. "She told me you'd found the treasure."

The M'Brae shouted curses at Lux. "I can explain," she said.

"What was the plan?" Hilaríon said. "Draw me into an ambush?"

"Why don't you ask Phellhe?"

He turned. Phellhe was sallow, drenched in sweat. The fever was taking him, a would-be hero reduced to a cripple. It was fitting torment for his sins. But Wresh, rest his soul, had been right. Phellhe and Hilaríon were one and the same. "Phellhe stood against those ghouls. Did you?"

"My weapon seems to have been... misplaced."

Aryei said, "It's in Necío's gut—"

Lux wrapped her hand around his face. "Out of the mouths of babes," she said. "Hilaríon, you have to see this from where I'm standing."

"Hard when you're way up there, with leverage."

"You know all about leverage," she said. "I want out of this valley, alive. No tricks."

"Send the boy down and I won't kill you."

Lux laughed. "Since when do you care about anyone else? Like I said, you don't fool me. It's only a matter of time 'til you run."

Lux was more right than she knew. He said, "You can't stay up there forever."

"Try me." She tickled under Aryei's arm. He whimpered and regained his hold.

The M'Brae gasped. Hilaríon said, "She won't."

"You aren't giving me much choice."

Lux had been his protégé: before long, she'd have been his lieutenant. He'd fallen for her boundless hope. Now, she was just like him. "What happened to you, Lux?"

"*You* happened, capitán. You broke me, you bought me. And I know something you don't, about someone you want. I saw your wildling, Hilaríon. You can still save her."

He could picture Ypriána's body, beaten and bleeding from her ear. Was Lux for real? If this was a trick, he'd used it before, most recently with Lux's husband. "Ypriána's dead," he said.

"No," Lux said, "she's not."

"She is to me." He reached for the tree trunk. "I'm coming up now—"

"Wait," she said, "don't."

The foil was to keep her talking. "I don't believe you."

"But you ought to," she said. "She's alive and unspoiled, and waiting for you."

He stepped from the tree. The devil was always in the details. "Why should I believe you?"

"She stands atop a towering plinth," Lux said, "displayed like a monument, imprisoned like a stylite of old. Her unspoiled face and unblemished flesh gleams like silk in the moonlight. Those monsters have her. I can tell you where. There just might be enough time."

He hung his head. Ypriána was dead, after all; Lux still a novice liar. He stifled his disappointment. "You really did see her?"

"Let us down and I'll tell you more. Oh, and my price just went up. Give me your machete. And give me something borrowed back." She pointed at the medallion.

He clasped it over his heart. "Not this?"

"That," she said. She jostled Aryei. "Oh, and Hilarión, if you don't like what I have to tell you, you can always come with me." She blew him a kiss.

He snickered. Lux had sealed her own fate. He stuck his blade into the ground. "Come down."

"I knew you'd see it my way." They shuffled their way down the limbs to the trunk. Aryei jumped and ran to the others. Hilarión held Lux at her hips, and gently lifted her down.

"It almost restores my faith," Lux said. "Maybe you really *have* changed—?"

"Unspoiled face and unblemished flesh?" He slammed Lux up against the tree and pulled Ypriána's ear from his pocket. "Make sure the person you're trying to con hasn't already conned you." He yanked the machete out of the ground and pulled it under her throat. Lux shut her eyes. Her game was done.

"But you *do* have something I want," he said. "Necío's life for my cowardice. I've waited enough. Now, say it."

She swallowed hard. "No."

"We're even now," he said. "Release me from Cacarajícara."

"Go to hell."

He twisted the machete. A line of blood pooled on its edge. "Release me now."

She gritted her teeth. He couldn't have guessed it'd anguish her so. "Alright," she cried out, "for Christ's sake, I release you! We're square. Just let me—"

"Look!" Mabba pointed. "There!"

Perched atop the rim of cliff, chattering in their filthy tongue, were upwards of twenty troglodytes. There was no space for the M'Brae to run and no chance of parley, now that he'd killed one. They were cornered with nowhere to hide.

A flash of motion caught his eye. He looked down. A snake was slithering over his boot. It was hued bright milky white, as if each scale was dipped in gold. He held still lest the snake be venomous. But Lux seemed not to see it. She struggled, railing, "Let me go!"

The troglodytes began to chant,

"Gold and gild, gild and gold
So much alike, so very cold..."

Hilarión let go of Lux, mesmerized by the snake. It moved like gentle music, powerful but fluid, elegant in its effortlessness. Like Lux, the M'Brae seemed not to notice it. But he couldn't take his eyes off it. "Hilarión?" Chropher said. It slithered past the M'Brae feet and seemed to disappear through stone behind them.

Hilarión looked closer. Where the snake had gone was a camouflaged fissure, cut into the cliff-side, wide enough for the people to pass.

"Gold and gild, gild and gold..."

Hilarión marveled, pointing into the fissure. "Lanyan, Bolivar, Chropher, help Phellhe," he ordered. "The rest of you follow. I'll be along." He sheathed his blade.

"Thank you, capitán," Lux said. "I knew you'd do right."

He grabbed her by the face. Necío had been his friend, or the closest thing he'd ever had. Justice had to be repaid. "Your husband's final thoughts were of you. You ran from the very thing you sought. He's dead because of *me*."

He shoved her away. The M'Brae streamed towards the fissure. The skies swirled black and belched cold rain. The troglodytes' chanting rose to a thrum. He followed the M'Brae to the rock wall, then glanced behind as he let them all pass.

Beneath the tree, Lux stood alone. He could see the terror in her eyes, same as at Cacarajícara. But she'd abandoned him this time. The eyes in his mind had diminished by two.

xliv.

He squeezed into the fissure. The rock seemed to clamp around him. It felt like the pass in the underground tunnels, only now he was walking upright. He struggled forward until it was wide enough, then worked his way to the front of the M'Brae.

Maith tapped him and said, "It's happening now." The ragged dress she'd worn for weeks was soaked across her thighs. By nightfall, there'd be one more M'Brae—if they lived to see nightfall.

Hilaríon asked, "Can you run?" She nodded weakly. "Hetta, Mabba, help Maith," he said.

Chropher said, "Where are we going?"

"Where they can't get us." But he'd be damned if he knew where that was. "Single file. Absolute silence." He waved them on ahead.

The fissure widened inches enough to let them pass unhindered. The light of morning dappled the crags. The troglodytes swelled in sound and pitch, like a fast-approaching wave. Hilaríon kept his head on a swivel. An attack could come from any direction. Being pummeled by boulders from above seemed the most frightful prospect of all. But there was no sense worrying. There'd be no surviving that, anyway.

The sky grew brighter. The passage banked each way and back, like the entrails of some serpentine beast. The people tumbled and toppled about, and helped each other onto their feet. Fleshy leaves loomed overhead. They were passing deeper into the jungle, below a eucalyptus grove. Runoff seeped along the rocks. It made their footsteps sound like splashes. They could only slog along.

The sun climbed towards high noon, baking fog inside the pass. Hilaríon slowed the column. Phellhe, still propped by the boys, was straggling. His skin was even paler now. His bulk was slowing the others.

Aryei said, "I've seen this place. We passed this way before."

Hilaríon looked around. They'd taken many forks and twists, too many to remember. The rocks here *did* seem familiar, but all of it had looked the same. There was no way to tell and less time to try. He pointed to a lump of trinkets cut to look like rubies. "Aryei, take those. Drop one every five minutes. In case we have to backtrack." Aryei filled his satchel until it overflowed. Hilaríon gave him a wry grin and said, "Next time, it'll be treasure." He waved the people onwards.

The fissure narrowed. The air grew cooler. They slowed to a shuffling crawl again. The sky rolled gray and overcast. The fog in the passage swirled about, tinged with sour sweat. The passage opened into a valley. Hilaríon felt a rush of relief, envisioning his dash to freedom. Here, the M'Brae could camp in peace, while he stole away in the night—

"*What?*"

He couldn't believe what he was seeing. They were back where they'd begun.

A stolid mist embalmed the gorge. The monoliths that poked from it seemed islands in a tempest. Lux was nowhere to be seen. Chropher leaned against a stone. It wobbled and split, and fell to the ground.

Blurs of gold flashed in the mist. The crackle of labored breathing rose. The shuffling of six-toed feet crunched a stone's throw away.

Hilaríon said, "Stay calm." He motioned the people back to the fissure. The heavy mist swirled, concealing the probing troglodytes. He could hear their tatters flapping away and smell their rancid bodies. They sounded close enough to touch. But the mist masked their presence, and his from them.

"Gold and gild..." Their voices flagged.

The vapors re-gathered. Hilaríon whispered, "We'll try again."

Chropher said, "It's just a blind maze. You try dragging Phellhe along."

"Chay and Unish," Hilaríon said. "Your turn. Help Phellhe."

"We won't go on," Chropher said. The people seemed lifeless:

limbs dangling, eyes blank, wills breaking. Maith and Phellhe were fading. The troglodytes would find them soon.

Hilaríon flinched. Twisting among their feet was the snake. It shimmered even richer than the first time he had seen it. He pointed. "Watch out!"

"For what?" Chropher said.

It slithered away down the fissure, vanishing beneath the mist. Hilaríon looked their faces over. They hadn't seen the snake. They *couldn't* see the snake. He couldn't tell them. They'd think he'd gone mad. He said, "These passages were made by men. Who'd go through the trouble to build a blind maze? We must have missed something. We'll try again, unless you want to stay here." Chropher looked away. Hilaríon said, "I didn't think so." Maith hunched over, clenching her teeth. There could be no wrong turns this time. "Hrama, Jacinda, cover the rear. Aryei... red rocks, every five minutes." They moved out at a trudge.

The fissure banked and looped again, same as he remembered. The runoff slurped around their feet. A steady stream of gripes flowed from Chropher's mouth, then from the other boys. So far nothing seemed different.

Afternoon dribbled away. Late-summer squalls rolled in and out, dousing their clothing, turning the fissure under their feet into a fast-moving stream. The sky bled golden, then silver, then pink. There seemed no end in sight. The riddle of the maze seemed unsolvable. "Guamá," Chropher said.

Hilaríon ignored him. The boy groused louder, "*Guamá.*"

"Not my name."

"How much longer?"

"As long it takes."

"I can't keep walking."

Hilaríon pointed him towards Maith, bowed but still unbroken. "Observe," he said. But Chropher was right. They couldn't wander aimlessly forever.

He halted the column. The people leaned against the rock face. Their eyes throbbed with exhaustion. Between two slabs, almost invisible from where he stood, was a narrow slit in the rock wall. From the angle they'd passed the first time, they'd missed it. This had to be where they'd gone wrong before. "Inside," he said. He waved them through.

The passage banked in a narrow, arcing turn. They slogged through it sideways, single-file. They seemed to be doubling-back on themselves. Whether or not they'd made any progress was impossible to tell.

Aryei said, "Look." The ground ahead was covered with red rocks. Dropping stones was useless now.

"Find another color," Hilarión said. But there were none to find.

The sun began its western slide. Evening spread its arms. Chay and Unish groaned under Phellhe's weight. The big man drew to Hilarión's side. "What are you waiting for? Just tell them I was behind it all. The waiting's worse torment than fever."

It was tempting to Hilarión. Necío was dead, no doubt, in part because of Phellhe. But Phellhe had only precious days. Cosmic justice would soon take its course. And Ypriána's eyes were watching. "Drink this." He slipped Phellhe an elixir vial.

"Witchcraft," Phellhe said.

"It wasn't when you cleaned my arm."

Phellhe took the vial. Maith staggered past, face twisted in aguish. Phellhe surreptitiously passed her the vial. Then Maith gasped as she looked up. Atop the cliff were troglodytes.

Hilarión whispered, "Down in place." The M'Brae sank to their bellies, Maith to her back. Ahead, the cliffs drooped. Atop them, four troglodytes stood. A figure lay on the ground between them.

"Now what?" Chropher said.

"Wait until they leave." Hilarión moved for a better look. There was something about that figure.

The troglodytes fanned out. Each grabbed a limb and hoisted the figure. Hilarión's heart slammed into his throat. The distance was great, the twilight resplendent, but there was no mistaking it.

The figure was Ypriána.

"Stop!" he yelled. The troglodytes hurried off. "*Stop!*"

The stone where the cliffs bowed was easy to climb—easy enough for him, anyway. He scrambled up the rock-face. The troglodytes shuffled fast away. They seemed to be headed towards the Gilded Peak, by the look of it still a day's journey off. He could overtake them handily. But this had all the markings of a trap. And he had the M'Brae to think about. He'd brought them too far to abandon them now.

He looked around, chiding himself under his breath for not thinking of doing so sooner. He could see from his lofty vantage that the fissure was nearly at its end, opening into a nearby valley: their destination, at long last. He'd lead them there, then take up the chase. Four six-toed fiends, stumbling under a body's weight, would be the easiest thing in the world to track.

He climbed back down. Chropher said, "So much for quiet."

Hilaríon said, "We've arrived." He took off at a canter. The M'Brae willed their feet along, Maith valiantly keeping their pace.

Twilight had dissolved in dusk, and night was creeping near. His pulse raced: Ypriána. The troglodytes wouldn't haul off a corpse. Why not just kick it into the gorge? She *had* to be alive. A fresh vigor, born of hope and triumph, drove his every hurried step. Ypriána was as good as rescued, and he as good as the hero she'd hoped for—

He stopped. The web of sweat that doused his hair turned droplets down his neck. "This can't be possible," he said.

They were back among the monoliths. They'd gone in a circle, again.

"So very cold… so very *cold*…" And the troglodytes were waiting.

Phellhe collapsed. Maith clutched her belly. From past the mist that filled the gorge, the golden-clad figures of troglodytes rose. He looked wistfully at the Gilded Peak. There'd be no hiding, slipping away, or mounting rescue missions. The moment of truth had come.

Aryei tugged his cloak. "Hilaríon?"

"Not now," Hilaríon said, looking down. The snake had returned. It hissed, then slithered inside the fissure. Whatever it had tried to show him, he'd failed to comprehend. Phellhe was dying, Maith giving birth, the troglodytes closing in. He couldn't risk the fissure again. "Make a ring," he said. "Grab rocks, sticks, and dirt. Hold them off as long as you can."

Aryei said, "That isn't the way."

"What do you know?" he snapped. Aryei had wasted enough of his time. "If you hadn't been so gullible—"

"Then I wouldn't know how to beat them. *They're blind.*"

xlv.

Necío watched the sun go down, across a vast and swelling sea. The chase was getting the better of him. All of his best-loved stories and songs—he'd lived out every one of them. He'd seen them with new eyes: discerning, ever questioning. But Gnath had drifted farther away. She'd talked _to_ but not _with_ him. The greatest question was shrouded still. Why had she named him _fool?_

Nearby grunting caught his ear. All at once he was back in M'Brae-dah. Pigs were rooting, gobbling fruit. Somebody was feeding them. "L'o naj,"[2] a voice said. It was Gnath's.

He held out his arms. She took a step back. "Don't give up now," she said. "He needs you." Necío gasped. The fruit underfoot had turned to snakes, flicking their tongues against his heels. "Keep going," she said. "Help him fit the pieces together. Think you can handle that, fool?" She shoved him into the water.

Falling, he screamed, "No—!"

He opened his eyes. A brassy moon hung in a gauzy sky. "Gnath?" he said. She was gone. He was alone, surrounded by palms and ferns, his limbs splayed on a slab.

A withering pain sang through his gut. He clutched his side. Two lines of sutures, like a railroad junction, crisscrossed his pasty flank. The pain was sharp but tolerable. But where had the stitches come from?

The distant sound of a woman screaming echoed through the night. A rush of fear came over him. He remembered the terrible howling sound, echoing across the hills. But something about this voice was different. He could swear he'd heard it before.

He wiped the sleep from his eyes. By and by, it all came back. Lux

---

[2] "You're closer than you think."

had stabbed him in a rage, then run away with Aryei. She'd left him to die. He should be dead. He'd been right about Lux, after all. He had to tell Hilaríon.

Where *was* Hilaríon? For that matter, where was *he*?

He sat up. A tangle of jungle dripped all around him. Rocky walls soared high above. Last he recalled he'd been in a cabin. Now, he was in the trough of a gorge. Someone had to have carried him here. His limbs were numb, his knees stiff, his head was thick with fog. He'd clearly been drugged, but by who?

"Ooooohhhh...." Came a voice.

He reached for a branch beside him. "Hello?"

A man, a woman, and four little children were busy gathering things from the ground. Their bodies were draped in sheaves of moss, their waists thick with bulging satchels. They warbled and oohed at the sight of their quarry, plucking them from the ground with glee, then placing them tenderly into the satchels. He couldn't quite see what they were gathering. In deference to their choice of clothes, Necío decided he'd call them *mosslings*. He asked, "Do you know how I got here?"

They raised their heads, then looked away, as if too coy to speak. Their eyes, like colorful saucers, bobbled inside their fair-skinned faces. They had the aspect of overgrown babes, like the porcelain dolls of the Vujoíe his ancestors had sometimes brought from the cities. He pointed to his sutures. "Did you do this?"

The little ones looked at the adults. The man and woman blushed. "Thank you?" Necío said.

A flash of yellow caught his eye. Between his feet was a golden nugget. He lifted it to his face. Its lustrous sheen and weathered edges looked a perfect gem. "The treasure?" he said, and bit down upon it.

It was just a painted rock. "Guess not." He rolled it in the palms of his hands.

The glade fell deathly silent. The lilting coos of the mosslings had stopped. The six were standing arm-to-arm, staring with hateful eyes. Their gazes cut through him. They clutched their sacks. Where once they'd looked so innocent, now they seemed more beast than man. Necío followed their eyes to the stone and, holding it out, asked, "You want this?"

The distant voice wailed again. This time there was no mistaking. The voice belonged to Maith. "It *is* them," he said. He dropped the stone and hobbled towards the sound.

He peeked back over his shoulder. The mosslings were clawing each other's faces, battling over the worthless stone.

✳　　　✳　　　✳　　　✳

How could Hilaríon have missed that? "Blind," he said, "as in—"

"They can't see," Aryei said. "It's all a giant echo chamber—mountains, woods, and maze. They made it with those tall stones. They don't *have* to see." Hilaríon remembered the Guanahatebey song. *Whispering Woods*, they'd said. It was so outlandish it had to be true.

Their groaning intensified. The foe was bearing down on the M'Brae. "We can use it against them," Aryei said.

Maith screamed. Hilaríon said, "You don't think they'll hear that?"

"Leave it to me," Aryei said, and hurried Graciela away.

Hilaríon led Maith under the tree. "Mabba," he called, "let Maith's head in your lap." Hetta came and clasped Maith's hands. He turned the hem of her skirt—

"No." Maith pulled away.

He gently put his hand back. He'd helped Mambí midwives in the field. Time hadn't faded those memories. "I know what I'm doing," he said.

He lifted the dripping skirt. The last shafts of light from the fast-setting sun were hardly enough to assist him. He still had Ypriána's flint and steel. He dug through his pocket, then tossed them to Unish and said, "Light a torch—"

> *"Yélé -t-M'Brae o fehnoé vame*
> *Fa-yil thu zélé ephvachû rah'yoghû. . ."*

All at once, Graciela's lilting strains rose across the valley. They bounced against the monoliths and danced among the canyon walls. They soared to the slopes of the Gilded Peak and sent stones tumbling down the cliffs. The troglodytes grunted in bewilderment, scrambling sideways, helter-skelter, and toppling each other in their fugue.

Maith let out an ear-splitting shriek. Her flesh was taut. The child was close. "Push, Maith, push," Hilaríon urged, "harder, push harder, and breathe—"

"Hilldevils!" Phellhe shouted, his wilted body springing to life. He convulsed, swinging wildly. "Hilldevils in M'Brae-dah!"

Hetta said, "What's happening?"

"Fever's burning his mind," Hilaríon said. "Keep Maith breathing. Deep in, short out. When the head crowns, call me." He raced to Phellhe's side.

Phellhe railed, "A good tricking? I'll give you tricking!" He swung at the tree.

"Phellhe," Hilaríon said, "stand down. The phéa-sjant are in full flight, thanks to my brothers and you." Phellhe stopped swinging. Hilaríon raised the last vial of elixir. "To health and to our triumph."

Phellhe took a sip. "I don't remember—"

"Another draught." He tipped the vial into Phellhe's mouth.

Phellhe swigged it all. "Cuba Libre."

"Thanks to you." He lowered Phellhe against the tree.

Graciela's music pitched, then plunged and rolled with gusto.

"Yélé -t-M'Brae o fehnoé vame
Fa-yil thu zélé ephvachû rah'yoghû . . ."

"Heavenly music," Phellhe said.

"Like angels."

Phellhe nodded. "Yes, like angels, like... *Seven Angels.*" His lips curled. "You—!"

"Hilaríon!" Hetta shouted.

He ran back to Maith. "Crowned yet?" He grabbed a torch from Unish, who'd managed to find something dry to ignite. The sound of approaching snorting rose. The song was flagging, the foe regrouping.

He pressed Maith's stomach. Now, she was tighter. Once the child's head came through, the rest would be much simpler. "Maith," he said, "you're nearly there." He wedged a stick between her teeth. "Bite on this and push." She let go a primal scream. "Harder," he said, "again."

She heaved. The arc of a buttock popped from her womb. The child was breech. "Keep breathing," Hilaríon said. But breech birth was an ordeal, even in the best case. A false move or two and both would die.

"Hilaríon!" Aryei called. Graciela's voice was sputtering.

Hetta peeked between Maith's legs. Hilaríon whispered, "Don't tell her. No pushing until I get back."

He ran towards Graciela. Phellhe swiped at him but missed, then set about pummeling the tree. "Unish, keep Phellhe near," he said. "Climb the tree if you have to. If he wanders off he's dead." He raced past the monoliths into the gorge, then peeked over his shoulder. Unish was taunting a weary Phellhe, the big man giving chase.

Aryei, beside Graciela, pointed into the darkness. The troglodytes were closer. Atop the cliff, perched like a hawk, was the terrible withered queen. Graciela fell to her hands and pleaded, "No more."

To deliver the child, Hilaríon needed more time. Graciela had given all she had. He couldn't ask any more of her. But she'd never claimed to be anyone special. She'd only mimicked Necío's mother. Music was in the M'Brae blood. He needed every throat.

He said, "Give me two more minutes." She grudgingly resumed singing. He raced back to where the other M'Brae were hiding. "Sing with Graciela. The Guanahatebey showed you how."

"No one can sing like them," Chropher said.

Maith screamed. Graciela coughed. Hilaríon said, "Surprise yourself." He herded them past the monoliths. One by one with fretful glares they gathered next to Aryei.

Chropher said, "But men don't sing. It's shame to sing with women."

"That's what Phellhe told you," Hilaríon said. "That world's behind you now."

The people looked each other over, and then awkwardly joined hands. One by one, they cleared their throats and raised their voices skyward,

"Yélé -t-M'Brae o fehnoé vame
Fa-yil thu zélé ephvachû rah'yoghû..."

The valley shook. The song took flight. The M'Brae children, men, and women, a motley throng of altos and tenors, melded fast in harmony. The chorus was bracing, like nothing on earth. Necío, rest his soul, had been right. Even stunted, sung by rubes, there was magic in its chords. He turned to Maith—

"Swindler!" Phellhe throttled him down.

"I couldn't stop him," Unish said.

Phellhe straddled Hilaríon, balling his fist. "This is for Fenn, Wresh, and Sunovín..." His eyes pulsed red with rage. But even in his fevered state, Phellhe's dark shame was clear.

Hilaríon said, "You can put out the fires. You'll be free!"

Phellhe stopped mid-swing. "Free?" A weight seemed to lift from his face. He smiled. Then his eyes rolled back. He dropped, convulsing, to the ground.

Maith screamed. Hilaríon loosened Phellhe's collar and belt, lest the big man hang himself. He said to Unish, "Tell him stories... he's back in M'Brae-dah, manning the ramparts, fighting the jaegers. Fan his will to live." He dashed back to Maith.

"Yélé -t-M'Brae o fehnoé vame
Fa-yil thu zélé ephvachû rah'yoghû..."

The song intensified. He could feel it like electricity, filling the valley with glorious music. He turned back to Maith. Her face was sallow, limbs flaccid. The child's buttock was still peeking out. It would have to be born in the breech.

He rolled his sleeves: he'd turn the child. He'd seen it done before, in the Mambí camp at Hoyo Colorado, months before Cacarajícara. He'd been warned it was a last resort, better to cut the child out. But that would be impossible. He lacked the instruments to clean or bind the wound. He said to Hetta, "Steady her." He slid his fingers inside her womb and felt along the infant's thighs. Its legs were folded to its shoulders, head between its knees.

"Yélé -t-M'Brae o fehnoé vame. . ."

The harmony began to falter. The enemy's grunts grew louder. He'd be bold or bury parent and child. "Maith," he said, "close your eyes. You've come this far, you can go longer."

"How much longer?"

"The rest of your life," he said. "You're a mother now."

He pinched the infant's heel. It squirmed and broke his grip. He pinched the heel again, and pressed his palm against Maith's thigh. The infant kicked. Maith arched her back. He spread his thumb across both feet. Its toes flexed into his palm.

". . .Fa-yil thu zélé ephvachû rah'yoghû. . ."

More voices dropped out, panting. The song was fading, the M'Brae failing. He drew the infant's legs towards him. Fluid spilled across the ground. He pulled the infant's feet from the womb, then its legs up to its hips. Maith roared in pain. Behind its legs, the umbilical cord trailed. The infant's hips were crushing it. Every second inside Maith, its chances of living slipped further away.

He curled his hand about its thighs and pulled the infant downwards. He cupped its buttocks in his palm and spun it belly-down, then drew it further through. Its back was fleeced with downy fuzz, its little spine was knobby. The cord was wrapped around its neck.

The song fell dead, the M'Brae exhausted. Maith's wailings echoed unrestrained. Hilaríon tightened his grasp on the infant's ribs. The M'Brae streamed towards him, between the monoliths. Behind them loomed a golden line.

"Gold and gild, gild and gold. . ."

"Make a ring," Hilaríon said. Aryei, Jacinda, and Hrama formed a wedge around him. The others ran into the fissure. He tugged the child out to its shoulders. He could see the base of its tiny neck, obscured by the compressed cord.

"So much alike, so very cold..."

The troglodytes were a stone's throw away. He cradled the infant in both hands and gently spun it to the left. Its right arm popped outside the womb.

"Gold..."

Aryei said, "You have to get up."

He licked his lips. "Not yet." He twisted the infant to the left.

Nothing.

"Gild..."

The defensive wedge tightened. Hilaríon turned the infant with force. Maith shrieked. Mabba hugged her. The infant's right arm was trapped in the cord. Its head was still inside the womb. "Push!"

"Gild..."

The wedge collapsed. The fiends, any second, would fall upon them. Hilaríon stroked the infant's shoulders: Maith's child would enter a new, bold world. When Ypriána returned, he'd personally hand her the newest M'Brae.

He laid his hand on the infant's neck, and dug the thumb of his other hand into the bottom of Maith's bloody womb. He could feel the infant's tiny face, its quivering lips and wiggling nose. He hooked his thumb against its chin and drew its head through Maith's hipbone. The crown of its skull popped through. He slipped his finger beneath the cord and looped it from its shoulders. The infant's other arm popped free. He pressed the infant's chin again and cupped its head inside his palm.

"Gold..."

"One more second," he said, "one more—"

"Hilaríon, now!" Aryei screamed.

Maith roared. Hilaríon pulled. The child slid into his arms. Maith let out a final, gratified moan. Hilaríon rolled and grabbed his blade, then spun to his feet and swung.

The chanting dwindled into the shadows. The troglodytes had shrunk away, as if they'd never been there at all. All was silence once again, behind the jungle's thrum.

He held his blade inside the flame. "Hold tight," he said, "Almost done." He sliced Maith's umbilical cord in two, then tightly tied the end off. The infant flapped his arms. "Keep him warm, then feed him."

"Him?" Maith said.

He handed the child to his mother. "Your son."

Hilarion heaved a lusty sigh. Aryei's wits and all their voices had kept them alive, long enough to welcome one more. But Phellhe was slipping away. And the enemy would return before long.

The gibbous moon rose. Its light filled the waterlogged basin. Beneath its frigid glow, the beads and trinkets and gold-painted rocks shined like flotsam in a shallow sea. Hilarion rubbed his eyes. Hunger, fatigue, and restlessness had melded into a toxic brew, blunting the edge of his senses. But he could almost swear in the ghostly light he could see man-shaped shadows, scurrying from the folds of the valley, gathering up the glittering kitsch. "What *is* this place?" he said.

"I think I know," a voice said. He spun around.

It was Necío.

xlvi.

The stars shone crisply, burning white: Deneb of the Northern Cross, Altair in the Eagle, all crowned by Vega in Lyra. The Milky Way seemed a trail of ash, the entrails of a burning world. Autumn was coming, summer expiring. They'd been on the road three months now. Hilarión had never thought he'd have lingered so long. By now, he should have had something to show for it.

The troglodytes had slunk like slugs back to the dark eaves. Hilarión scanned the rim of the gorge. They were up there, no doubt, listening, too shamed or confused to press on. But they'd regroup, and soon. Stuck here in the low ground, no one was safe. They had to get out of the gorge.

A tender wheeze, the sound of new lungs, whispered beneath the tree. He crept to the makeshift nursery. Exhaustion had taken Mabba and Hetta. They lay on the ground like drunkards. Maith was propped against the tree, newborn clasped against her. Hilarión dabbed the sweat from her face. She said, "He's finally sleeping."

The infant was hale and ruddy. The sight of infants made him smile. His aunt had had a baby girl, Paola. Influenza had carried her off too soon. "What's his name?"

"Selwin," she said, "for his father. But no middle name yet." She blushed. "I was thinking about _Hilarión._"

He looked away. He'd have been halfway across Matanzas by now, or nearing the port of Júcaro, if he'd done what he wanted. He didn't deserve such an honor. "How about Wresh?" he said.

Sadness, then pride, flashed in her eyes. "Selwin Wresh. It suits him."

"He'll know his roots." He dabbed her final beads of sweat. "Do your best to keep him quiet."

Phellhe sprawled beside the humble fire. His eyes were black and sunken. Even in the evening cool, the sweat clung to his brow like dew.

Necío tended him, running cloths along his face and humming gentle ballads. Necío said, "We're losing him."

"We lost him weeks ago. Too proud to drink the Lightleaf hide. What he drank tonight won't be enough."

"How long?"

"A day? A week? Who knows? But there are healers, you say?"

"I told you," Necío said. "Overgrown children, draped in moss, collecting painted rocks. They didn't seem keen on sharing."

Hilaríon said, "And they saved you?"

"They must've. One minute, Lux is carving me in half. The next..."

"You saw them do it?"

"When I woke up, they were there. All I know is I'm alive."

"Aryei told us you'd been killed."

"Lux was as surprised as me. Her strike was meant for *you*."

"Urged by him, no doubt." He pointed at Phellhe. His body seemed especially big. "We'll never get him out. Unless these healers of yours show up, maybe we ought to find someplace secluded..."

Necío's eyes popped. "Guamá?"

"I've done all I can. I'm thinking of everyone."

"Everyone includes him."

"You said he was a monster."

"Maybe so," Necío said, "but he's *our* monster."

He racked his brain for an acrid retort. Necío's mercy was absolute. They were all lucky he hadn't been killed. "So where are we?"

"I thought I knew," Necío said, evasively. Something in his eyes said more.

"Tell me," Hilaríon said.

"To ignore before you run?"

"I'm still here."

"For now."

Hilaríon drew out the Jaeger's brooch. "Ypriána is alive," he said. "The Jaeger had her, now those ghouls. She's waiting for me. I can feel it."

Necío said, "You're under her spell."

The thought was absurd. There was only one spell over him. "We need her to find the treasure."

"The others won't move to save their lives. I'd worry more about that."

"I'll worry about both. It'd be helpful to know where we are."

Necío grumbled, "If I must." For a moment he seemed a venerable bard. As if intoning an ancient skald, he sang,

> "I am the shunted mountain
> My timeless wonders shattered shards
> My spore turned grasping wildmen
> Because I might hold treasure.
>
> Thrust above the stony swells
> As watch-lamp o'er a grassy sea
> Below, beyond my keen gaze falls
> Nearer to the firmament.
>
> Rising out benighted dale
> Refugees from erstwhile sin
> In twos and ones, then star-struck droves
> They mount upon my spine.
>
> Then freed from world in doubt—"

He stopped. "Then freed from doubting world... no, wait. Then doubting world.... Oh, my mother would pinch me," he said. "I've forgotten the line. Then..."

"Then freed from world in thrall to doubt," Phellhe said. The big man winched himself seating and sang,

> "Then freed from world in thrall to doubt
> They carve the grand leviathae
> Pilot peace-kites zephyr-borne,
> A harvest twice as fruitful.

I am the shunted mountain
My timeless wonders shattered shards
My spore turned grasping wildmen
Because I might hold treasure.

The ills what ravage bone and flesh
Shrink to nethers 'neath their gaze
And, probed the depths of heart and sky
Dreams let loose to soar.

The world past each horizon rots
Unasked questions, truths ignored
My spore keep bright the living light
A shrine to wonderwhy.

But evil creeps into the fold
A darkness well disguised as light
The lambent lure of gleaming spoils
In whispers, then commands.

I am the shunted mountain
My timeless wonders shattered shards
My spore turned grasping wildmen
Because I might hold treasure

Then smelted scalpels into spades
The aqueducts turned hoisting rigs
And peace-kites warped to hunting-hawks
To comb the land for veins.

Now pierced, my hide, by wolfish blade
Fancy swapped for lockstep toil
Sapling groves and grottoes razed
Leviathae thrown down.

Then frozen fast like ambered moth
Time the unmoved mover waits,
The wisest cast into the cracks
To suckle life from dust.

I am the shunted mountain
My timeless wonders shattered shards
My spore turned grasping wildmen
Because I might hold treasure."

Necío marveled. "You know that song?"

"You're not the only one your mother confided in," Phellhe said. "You see what a blight that treasure is, or even the thought of it? Healers and growers, artists and builders, clever enough they learned how to fly? Even they succumbed."

"The wisest resisted," Necío said. "They were pushed into the cracks of the land. The greedy ones ruled above them, or so I was told. But really who knows? I won't make that mistake again."

"Too late," Phellhe said. "Fenn, Wresh, and Sunovín, all dead because of stories. Were we worse off in M'Brae-dah?"

Hilaríon looked across the camp. The M'Brae were the worst he'd ever seen them. Those not sleeping or dressing their wounds gnawed raw fruit or sipped rainwater. The youngsters looked haggard, the adults huddled like urchins. Hrama and Jacinda, once hale, had faded, hunched over an overripe melon. There was no denying Phellhe was right. "No," Hilaríon said. "But that won't get us out of this gorge."

Phellhe looked at Hilaríon's chest. The medallion shimmered in the firelight. "Will *you*, Hilaríon?"

"Look!"

Shrieks rang from the camp. The M'Brae leapt to attention and scattered. A cluster of people, draped in moss, streamed through their midst on shuffling legs. They gathered at the base of the tree. Their eyes were wide with fear. "The mossling healers," Necío said.

"Gold and gild, gild and gold..." Troglodytes suddenly poured over the cliff.

Aryei said, "We can hold them off again." He reached for Graciela.

"She can't sing anymore," Hilarión said, "and neither can anyone else. We have to…" His mind whirled. The gorge was filling with troglodytes. The cliffs were too high to scale. "We have to…" They had no weapons and not enough numbers. Their strongest man, Phellhe, could barely stand up.

"So much alike…"

He looked at the fissure. The snake was coiled in front of it. But he couldn't risk it again. "We have to—"

"What?" Chropher said.

"I don't know!" He'd uttered the words no leader could speak.

The snake hissed loudly and rattled its tail. But Hilarión's will was firm. That path led nowhere. "No," he said. The snake hissed louder. He shouted, "No!"

"Who are you talking to?" Necío said.

"Tell me you see it."

Necío looked bewildered. "See what?"

"There! That golden…" He could hardly believe his own voice. He sounded raving mad. "Snake."

Necío's eyes flashed. "Snakes are a very good omen. You Vujoíe think they're devils, but we M'Brae know better. Snakes were pathfinders in the wild."

"So very cold…" The troglodytes tramped closer.

The hair at Hilarión's temples tingled. "Pathfinders?"

Necío said, "That's right, you see—"

"Wait." He stared at the medallion. The moonlight obliged: its stunning detail came to life. The serpents of silver were twisted about, some without heads and some without tails, and some with more than one of each. But one serpent, thicker and longer than all, burst from an oblong egg to the right, and gaped its maw widely, far to the left.

"Gold and gild, gild and gold…" The troglodytes were almost upon them.

But the way out was at his fingertips. It had been all along. *Pathfinders in the wild.*

The medallion was a map.

xlvii.

"So much alike, so very cold..." The troglodyte phalanx gathered speed.

"Unish, the torches," Hilaríon said. "The rest of you, shoes off and carry them." The chase wasn't over, not by damn sight.

Unish started the torches. Hetta bound Selwin to Maith's chest. The M'Brae pulled their shoes from their feet and rushed into the fissure. Hilaríon propped Phellhe up. "I can walk," the big man said. "Help the others."

He studied the medallion with new eyes. The cluster was a devilish hex, a latter-day Gordian Knot. Where the true path led, who knew? For now, the wrong paths would help more. He said to Necío, "Lead them where the pass banks south and joins with two from the east. Wait for me there. I won't be long."

Necío looked at the mosslings. "And them?"

Hilaríon counted twenty-one mosslings. They'd slow the M'Brae escape for sure. But they'd make quick prey for the troglodytes. And they had saved Necío's life. "Why not?"

"Gold and gild..." The snapping of branches by six-toed feet crackled near the walnut tree. Necío waved the people on. Hilaríon waited. His eyes adjusted to the dark.

The first troglodyte stepped into the pass. The creature was female, stunted and gray, but not much older it seemed than himself. She cocked her head and listened. He could see the milky orbs of her eyes but she, as yet, hadn't sensed him. Five more appeared behind her. Hilaríon slithered down the pass. The troglodytes followed, like hounds on a scent.

The fissure by darkness was even more treacherous. He let his elbows brush the walls, rasping softly as he passed. The troglodytes kept close behind, marking him by his sounds. He hastened and dug his elbows harder. The foe was doing just as he'd hoped.

The fissure narrowed to a junction. The right-hand pass led to Necío, the left to the morass of dead-ends and wrong turns they'd fumbled inside ere nightfall. He held his breath. Too soft, they might miss him; too eager, he'd belie his game. He clacked the heel of his boot on the stone. It echoed through the southbound pass. The troglodytes spun and charged towards the noise. Hilaríon ran. They'd taken the bait.

A crag jutted overhead. He swiped a handful of stones and climbed. The troglodytes shambled past beneath. He waited until they'd gone far enough and threw a stone down the fissure. It echoed as it struck distant rock.

The troglodytes raced towards the sound. Hilaríon threw another stone, farther than the last. It shattered against the cliff-side. The troglodytes pressed deeper. He heaved the final stone away. A faint tinkling chimed. The ghoulish chanting faded.

The moon peeked out. He checked the medallion, tracing the length of the Pathfinder-Serpent to where it burst from the oblong egg. If all had gone according to plan, Necío and the others would be near, only a few twists and turns away. He pulled off his boots and climbed from the crag. His feet squished in the mud. He stuffed his boots beneath his arms and sidled up the pass.

Anxious moments passed like hours. A faint orange glow tinged the passage ahead. Hrama and Lanyan were standing guard. Necío had listened well.

Hilaríon replaced his boots in the torchlight. Phellhe was leaning against the rock face. The shadow of death was upon him. The others clustered in a ring, Maith with Selwin at the center, surrounded by moon-eyed mosslings. For all the trials the M'Brae had passed, they hadn't yet been broken. They were not the same peasants who'd fled from their village, quailing and praying for mercy. The slag was hardening. Hilaríon whispered, "Follow me."

The torches crackled softly. The mist off the jungle rolled through the passage, then just as quickly seeped away. The M'Brae kept a steady pace. The mosslings trudged behind. Hilaríon checked the medallion again. The Pathfinder-Serpent looped in a coil. That had to mean something. But what?

The night sky glittered. The passage widened. Hilarion slowed and looked around. He could see no branches or tunnels to take. The walls of the cliff were rutted with grooves but otherwise nothing was different. He knocked at the stone. "Help me find it."

"Find what?" Phellhe said.

"The coil. It's got to be here."

The M'Brae searched around the walls. The mosslings stood and watched. Hilarion pulled at the seams of plates and pushed against the crags. Something had to reveal the way. The map was clear, unless it was wrong.

Voices echoed down the passage, "Gold... gold... *gold*..." The troglodytes had discovered his feint and now were hard upon their heels. He had moments to find it, whatever it was, or it was back to flailing inside the maze.

Phellhe said, "We have to move."

"Not yet." Hilarion ripped at the ground. An underfoot hatch, perhaps? "We can't miss it this time."

"Gild... gild..."

"Damn it!" There was only mud. He slammed his palms against the wall.

A trickle of pebbles rained from above. They streamed along the cliff-face and vanished past the ruts, then reappeared, spilling at Hilarion's feet. He looked up. The groove in the cliff formed a crude sort of ramp that led from the ground to a switchback. The ramp hooked into the stone, then vanished. In the dark, fleeing quickly, he'd never have seen it.

The Pathfinder-Serpent's coil.

"It's here," he said. He hurried Necio up the ramp, then Maith, and then the others. They shuffled through the switchback.

"Gold and gild, gild and gold..."

Hilarion helped Phellhe up the incline, then paused at the switchback's edge. The troglodytes passed swiftly below. Hilarion scampered inside. The passage hooked in another switchback, then opened into a parallel fissure. He ran down the ramp to the head of the people. He oriented the map as he stood and motioned the people onward.

The first rays of dawn spread tawny arms. The people kept his hurried pace. Against the ruddy eastern sky, a massive shadow loomed. They were headed towards the Gilded Peak.

Selwin mewled. Hilarían recognized the cry. Mother's milk was the only cure. Silence was worth the extra few minutes. He said, "Feed him quickly."

Maith pressed him to her breast. The others took up fighting stances. Phellhe leaned into Hilarían's ear. "Leave me."

All was quiet, save for the infant's suckling. Hilarían pulled a dried fish from his cloak and ate it. It might as well have been manna, so famished he was. Phellhe said again, "Leave me."

"No."

"I can hold them off."

He finished the fish. "Now who's choked with hubris?"

"I told you it had to be smoked out," Phellhe said. "Let Wresh be forgotten. Let my death mean something."

"Your life should mean more."

"You still think she's coming back, don't you?"

Ypriána was seared in his thoughts. He'd gone too far to give up now. "I'm bringing us back to *her*."

Necío cried, "Look!"

Troglodytes lined the cliffs overhead. In their arms were pails: it was the worst that Hilarían had feared. They were going to dump something horrible on them: boiling water, or worse.

The M'Brae scrambled from the walls. Selwin shrieked a hungry cry. But silence didn't matter now.

Smiles spread across the mosslings' faces. They raised their arms and danced about, as if in the throes of a faith-healer's rite. The troglodytes raised their pails. Hilarían cried, "Get down!" He threw himself on Selwin and Maith.

A deluge of baubles cascaded around, pooling on the ground like hailstones. The mosslings dropped to their hands and knees. Their nimble fingers went to work, gathering gems for their satchels.

More troglodytes appeared. They raised their pails and dumped them. A silver shower rained through the fissure. The mosslings squealed, their heads thrown back. Hilaríon shouted, "Run!" The M'Brae scampered out of sight, save for Necío, but the mosslings went on gathering.

Hilaríon lifted a bauble. A mossling woman wrenched his wrist. It fell from his grasp. The woman grabbed it. He looked at Necío. "Now what?"

Necío pointed up the fissure and said, "*Jae-cün ephvachu.*" The mosslings barely turned their heads. "I said there was more up ahead," he said, "but I don't think they care."

A third line of troglodytes appeared, pushing barrel-sized boulders and chanting, "So much *alike*... so much alike..." The boulders teetered at the rim.

"Forget them," Necío said.

Hilaríon said, "But we can save them."

"I don't think they want to be saved."

"So very cold... so very *cold*..."

Dirt scattered from the boulders. The mosslings went on gathering. They would all be mashed to paste. What would Ypriána have done? Hilaríon grabbed two mossling children. "*Everyone* wants to be saved," he said. He turned up the passage—

"Yoooooooohhh..."

An unearthly howl rang over the fissure: voices in torment, wailing as one, drawn on the waning train of the wind. The cliff-stone trembled. The troglodytes scattered. The mosslings scurried up the pass, the same direction the M'Brae had run. Necío quivered, holding back tears. It was the sound they'd heard in the foothills and forest, only now it was close enough to feel.

The passage tapered as they ran. Hilaríon stopped to study the medallion. They'd reached the tip of the Pathfinder-Serpent's tail, where it burst from the oblong egg. "Wait here," he said, and grabbed a torch.

Necío stopped him. "Please don't go. Beware the Wailing Vale."

"The what?"

"Those who never make it to Ahr. If they can't share the treasure, they'll see no one else does."

A chilling breeze, the dry season's envoy, wafted past his temples. The grisly voices cried again. The sound could turn a man to stone. But he'd been sent this way. Hadn't he? "Look to the others, Necío. I won't be long."

The passage opened to a ledge, then dropped to a basin of grasses. They billowed in the twilight breeze, a fathomless inland sea. A voice moaned, then another. They were coming from below the grass.

He looked at the medallion again. He was but a borrower. The vale was for the Steeled Elect. And that was Ypriána.

"Yoooooooohhh…"

And yet, beneath the waning stars, the vale seemed welcoming, its forbidden essence tempting him. He'd come too far to lose his nerve. Who knew where Ypriána was, or if she'd ever make it this far? And she'd left him in charge.

He clambered down the ledge and leapt. His feet crunched in the sodden ground. A stone's throw away was an outcropping, commanding a better view of the vale. He took off running towards it. The towering grasses brushed his face, like virgin hands at play. Their pungent vapors filled his nose. The mountains rose above him stout, dwarfed by the Gilded Peak. He climbed atop the outcropping. From his perch, another stone's throw ahead, he could see that the stalks of grass were moving. There was something there.

He leapt from the outcropping and approached. He cupped his hand to his ear and listened, risking no movement, not even to breathe. The breezes waned, the grasses froze. The toads, snails, and spiders settled in their tiny tracks. All was still, a petrified world, waiting for the din of sound. But there was only silence.

He scoffed. There was nothing, same as every other turn along this foolish quest. Ypriána was dead, Phellhe would be soon. By and by, he'd follow. The only treasure was around his neck.

The M'Brae were gullible rubes. Why go back to them? He'd been killed, for all they knew. Golden days, at last, were his.

Breeze tussled his hair. He turned to the east. And then the voices came again.

"Yoooooooohhh…"

Whimpers, cries, and ghastly shrieks came from below, around, and through him. His blood ran as ice. He turned and fled, rushing against the driving wind. It pushed him to a standstill, motionless.

The earth below gaped in a sinkhole. Hilarión closed his eyes as he plunged, voices howling in his ears; a landslide of grasses, roots, and mud as the world fell to shadows, and silence.

xlviii.

Hilarion opened his eyes, unsure, for a moment, where he was. He felt along his chest. The medallion was still there. He lifted his swimming head and pressed his hands against the ground. It was spongey, though it looked like rock, soft and well-disguised. It had been meant to cushion his fall.

Then he remembered. He was beneath the Wailing Vale.

An icy gust filled his eyes. A sound, like a serpent, hissed from the darkness. There was something beside him.

He said, "Who's there?" It didn't answer. He yelled, "Get back!" It didn't move.

He thrust his blade into the shadows. It struck something hard in a hail of sparks. "Who are you?" he demanded. It wheezed like a drowning animal. Red streaks of dawn glimmered down through the ceiling. Hilarion prodded the thing with his blade. It was made of stone, but it *breathed*. In the spreading light, it came into view—

He stumbled backwards, heart pounding wildly. Peering from the gloom was a face.

Morning spilled through the sinkhole above. Its rosy flush filled the cavern. He shuddered in the sunlight, terrified and transfixed. One by one, faces burst from the darkness: men and woman, elders and infants, mouths gaping wide in the throes of song. The light revealed hundreds, no two alike. Among them were leviathans, rolling through a fiery sea. The walls, carved as waves, rippled about the cavern, catching the light, throwing it far, and snatching it up again. All around appeared as motion, the nimble twists of a brazen flood. He thought of Necio's story. The faces were those of the Ancients, among The Ones Who Came Before.

In the valley, the wind began to gust. From the pillars, ceiling and walls, from the very stone of the cavern itself, the chorus rose again, resounding through the underworld. The Wailing Vale was nothing but wind across hollow pipes.

His eyes adjusted to the light. The faces were in full bloom now, limned by the morning sun, their every crack and imperfection clear. Some of them were mounted to bodies, the bodies to arms, all pointing one way. He followed the way they were pointing.

The cavern spread into a bright antechamber. In the center was a mound, illuminated through the ceiling-holes like an enormous trophy. From a wide and sprawling base, it spiraled to a crumpled spike, like an old magician's hat. Its silhouette was familiar. It was a miniature Gilded Peak.

His hairs stood on end. Like the scepter in the swamp, it was made of human bones.

He drew nearer. Femurs, ribs, and gaping skulls made up its ghoulish rise. Its base was a thicket of greenery: moss, ferns, and violets, growing lush. They stopped abruptly at the bone, save for a single, narrow thread, spiraling up the miniature mountain to its shank of a peak. Atop the peak was a single flower, shaped like a golden bell.

The wind howled through the valley above. The sound of wailing came again, no longer sad, but joyous. All clues had converged upon this place. The Pathfinder-Serpent had shown him the way. The song sung by Necío and Phellhe had told why. *To where stargazers pondered aught*, the Guanahatebey had said. *When Trodden Seed take root on high.* And the miniature mountain, draped in a green vine and capped by gold, had been the final piece. All of it had seemed like a dream, a jumble of notions running together, watercolors in rain. But now, he knew what he had to do.

The mosslings were the Trodden Seed. They had to take root on high.

He had to lead them atop the Gilded Peak.

✻   ✻   ✻   ✻

Necío sat at the lip of the valley. The grasses of the Wailing Vale billowed in the breeze below. Now and then, the voices cried. They seemed to come and go with the wind. But they'd kept the troglodytes away. Every M'Brae was asleep, even little Selwin. The sun climbed over the eastern ridge. Hilaríon would return, he knew. But would he be the same?

The mosslings played with the glittery stones. They rubbed them along their necks and kissed them. The exiles of the shunted mountain: they'd been the stuff of legend. In truth, though, he'd expected more. Their attachment to trinkets was unseemly. But they *had* saved his life. He hardly noticed the pain anymore. "Thank you, again," he said.

They blushed and went on groping. He drew back his shirt, revealing his scars. "How'd you learn how to do this?" he asked. Their skill was too great for modesty.

A woman mossling rose, then gathered a handful of stones. She pointed at Necío's stomach. "*Fhayé.*"

"Yes, *fhayé*," Necío said, repeating the Ancients' word for *heal*, "but how?"

She lowered him onto his back. "No," he said, "I just want to—"

She dropped the stones along the wound, then rubbed them with her elbows. The rocks ground into his skin. A drop of blood seeped from the sutures. "Stop… stop!" he said, "That's good."

The mossling smiled. "Fhayé."

He grumbled, "Says you." The wound throbbed.

He couldn't quite place it, but something about these strange people rankled. He grabbed a handful of stones and arranged them, blue for the upper left shoulder, red for the lower right knee, three silver across for a belt. His mother had taught him the stars of the Hunter, as the Vujoíe called them. But he'd arranged them incorrectly for a reason. Surely, the mosslings would catch the mistake. "Orion," he said. The mosslings ignored him.

This was as easy as they came. Any amateur would spot the error. He'd mislaid red and blue. "Orion," he repeated.

"*G'daev*," the mossling said. She pushed the stones into a pile and scooped them into her satchel.

He griped, "Some stargazers—"

"Necío." He turned. Hilaríon stood at the lip of the gorge, tall and lordly in the sun. He strode past the sleeping M'Brae. There was something new about him, a power in his gait, a confidence born of certainty that Necío had longed to see.

Hilaríon drew a slate from his cloak. "Everything you need is here. I'm no master, but this should do. Be speedy and silent. I'll be waiting."

Necío took the slate. It looked like battle plans. "Huh?"

"Bring every last mossling," Hilaríon said. "And take this, too." He lifted the medallion. The mosslings cooed. He draped it over Necío's neck. "Use it well."

"Use it, how?"

"It's all there," he said, pointing to the slate, "down to the smallest detail. Remember, speed and silence. *To where stargazers pondered aught.* That's where we'll find what we came for."

He looked back over the mosslings, still ogling the medallion. What stargazers didn't know Orion? Something had to be amiss. But what did it matter now? What was about to happen would change his life. He wished his mother was here to see.

Hilaríon stepped into the fissure, then bent down and gathered a handful of tin. Necío said, "Where are you going?"

He stuffed the trinkets into his pocket. "To save Ypriána," he said.

xlvix.

The silver waning gibbous moon perched upon the crest of night. Hilaríon winched himself up the rock-face. Far below, the Wailing Vale seemed a distant, billowing plain. His joints throbbed and his weary legs seared. The climb had claimed the better of two days. But now, the observatory was only just a short ways off. Past the terraced trough of the peak, he could make out movement in its windows, all of them glowing a foreboding yellow. The troglodytes would be inside, at least as many as he could hope for. Timing would be everything. Necío had to succeed in his task.

He crept towards the nearest tall listening-stone. From head to toe his body ached, his stomach roiled with hunger. But Ypriána was near. Whatever his sufferings, hers were worse.

He placed his hands against the stone. It shifted but stood fast. It was larger and heavier than earlier ones, that much the better its fall would do. He hadn't been able to topple them all, but he'd done enough. By the time the troglodytes found what he'd done, it would be too late for them. He wedged his feet beneath the soil and pressed his shoulders backwards. He gritted his teeth and winched his back. The big stone slammed into the ground. Its death-groan ripped across the vale. He toppled two more listening-stones, then shuffled the final paces ahead.

Above him loomed the observatory, threatening yet melancholy: no doubt once the soaring haunt of some philosopher, but now in the clutches of benighted ghouls. Like the books and ornithopters, the troglodytes had done their worst, their bestial ignorance writ large.

He slipped inside an open door and into a corridor. At the end of the hall was light from the dome. The corridor was lined with cells. The air was filled with stifled sobs and muffled sounds of groaning.

He tiptoed past. Inside each cell were strange contraptions, resembling miniature steam pump engines, uttering rubber and copper tubes. The contraptions whirred rhythmically, odorless and nearly silent. He marveled. The craftsmanship was otherworldly, like something from beyond the stars. The tubes hooked into mounds of cloth strapped to nearby cots. He stepped for a closer look—

He recoiled. A hand reached from the cot. Hilarío regathered his wits and drew near. The cloth-mound quivered and gurgled. Hilarío pulled the blankets aside.

Bound to the cot was a withered male mossling, his flesh like purple, rotten burlap stretched across a skeleton. He moaned and groped for Hilarío's hand. Hilarío gagged, replacing the blankets, then stumbled back to the corridor. The whirring contraptions were torture devices. Would the journey's horrors ever cease before he found some treasure? Necío had to be on time.

He tiptoed the length of the corridor, then stepped through a doorway. The glass dome spread above him. Its struts and seams were hewn of brass. A band of stone below the dome was carved depicting the zodiac. Surrounding the rotunda, stacked with doting precision, the walls were lined with reams of books and diagrams. He hadn't quite expected this. Its elegance transfixed him. He said, "Where stargazers pondered aught..."

"And ponder we do, and always will," a voice said, "for aught is a shifting shoal."

A massive telescope, supported by upright stone leviathans, stood at the center of the rotunda. Its shaft tapered to an observation platform. And standing there, beside the eyepiece, draped in golden, fading silks, was the withered queen.

Everywhere was stillness. The zodiac-carvings seemed to glower, warning of impending ills which he was powerless to stop. Troglodytes had gathered behind him, filling the corridor from where he'd come. They spread out, lining the rotunda walls, sealing off any escape. Hilarío looked at the crone. "Where is she?"

"Shifted with the tides," she said, "like the heavens, by and by."

Riddle-speak no longer shocked him. He took a step closer. "You couldn't see that, even if it was true."

"We remember well enough. The shapes and ripples of the world are all the same as what came first. Eyes are redundant. Patterns hold."

He looked up the length of the telescope. At the point where the two leviathans' snouts came together was a palm-sized circular plate with a keyhole. It had to be meant for the medallion. The plan all depended on Necío now.

He stepped deeper into the rotunda and said, "I want to see her." The troglodytes stirred.

"Why?" the crone said.

"To know she still is."

"She is."

"Show me, then," he said.

The crone pulled the hood from her head. She was less frightening than he'd expected. Set beside a gentle nose, her cloudy eyes still flashed hues of brown, her teeth full and white in a curious mouth. She seemed less ghoul than dowager. "What were you told?" she said.

"Not to seek her."

"And what do you see that no one else does?"

He could still feel Ypriána's lips on his, breathing life into his mouth. He hadn't had to see. "Eyes are redundant. Patterns hold."

"Small, empty man," she griped and motioned towards the eyepiece. "Tell me what it is you see."

He hesitated, then peered inside. A single point of light shone back. "A star," he said. "Where is she?"

"Look again," she said. "What really do you see?"

He looked. It was an ordinary star, but even the blandest of stars held magic. That magic had never left his eyes. "Light," he said, "and heat. A furnace to fire a distant world, past the veil of time. Better? Now where is she?"

She pointed at the eyepiece. "There."

"Enough games."

"Ah, but you enjoy them so. The heavens play a confidence game against which we are callow marks. The light of the stars we see this night was born ere you or I, or the stone of this peak or this looking-glass' gold. The eyes make fools of the mind. You see what *was*, long after it was. The star is dead, yet you see it alive, shining in splendor as ever. She is the same. Let her go."

The metaphor was lyrical, dwarfed only by its bombast. "*You couldn't.*"

The crone slinked her hand beneath his collar, tugging on the braided twine. Once she'd discovered his ruse, he'd be out of time. "Incentive," she said, "from golden days. The world might never know your steel. Let her go. Unborn thousands thank you."

He'd been warned this same way by Oriel. Phellhe had spoken warnings, too, and even Aryei had had worries. He had to shrug at the sound of another. None of them knew her like he did. "I'm taking her," he said. "And I'm taking *them.*"

The crone's mouth curled. "Them?"

"Your captives in the cracks."

"Is that what they told you they are? Captives?"

"They scratch for quartz and bits of tin. They wear rags and drink from pools. They didn't have to tell me."

She replaced her hood. "Cracks are for worms and worms for cracks."

"And treasure for the Trodden Seed."

"And answers for questions, not questions for answers."

Dawn was spreading from the east, Necío's moment of truth fast approaching. "We were sent here to save them, from you," he replied.

She said, "They squirm in cracks for a reason."

"Spoken like a master of slaves. I'm taking them. Their nightmare ends now."

"Ere yours begins."

"Hardly. Healers in a war-torn land? That's treasure itself."

She laughed. "You might wear the robe of a Levite, boy, turn staffs to snakes and bleed water red, but until you learn to trade questions for answers, you'll have no treasure in this life."

The number of troglodytes had swelled twice-over. Now he counted roughly forty. Had Necío been waylaid? There was no more time to waste.

He jingled the medallion. The troglodytes perked at its sound. "Rank hubris," the crone said, "to bring that here. Sad, you too succumbed." She slapped her hands against her sides. The troglodytes stepped from the wall, towards him.

Hilaríon stood his ground. "You couldn't before and you won't now."

She said, "Before, there was promise."

Two ghoulish arms clasped him from behind. He held perfectly still. The crone plunged her hand inside his collar and pulled out the medallion. "The world's busiest killer," she said, "treasure—" She recoiled, then ran her gnarled hand down the disk. "Trickery," she hissed. She ripped it off his neck and threw it to the floor.

Hilaríon looked at the mosslings' tin he'd melted and hammered into a counterfeit. "The stars don't play the only confidence game." He waited for her to call off the others.

The chirrup of a mockingbird, welcoming the morning, jingled from the mountainside. The crone grinned with scorn. "Ever a step behind, you'll be. We may be blind, but you don't see." She slapped her side. The troglodytes clutching him tightened their grip.

This wasn't part of the plan. He said, "Hold on a moment."

"If you insist," she said. "A moment's far too short."

The foes' hands groped along his limbs, then tightened on his wrists and ankles. He thrashed but could not break their hold. "Wait—"

The old crone grabbed him by the jaw. She drew a handful of stones from her cloak. The troglodytes wrenched and drew him four ways. He gasped, ready to scream. She cupped her palm against his mouth and dumped a handful of trinkets inside. "*The choice to make unmade be thine.*"

The troglodytes racked him again. His throat and windpipe filled with stones. He could not breathe or shake to dislodge them. He could feel his bones and sinews stretching towards their breaking points. He writhed but the enemy held him down. More stones slipped past his tongue to this throat, suffocating him.

"What we have is better than treasure," she said, "with or from the likes of you—"

The observatory shook. A rumbling boomed across the peak and knocked him from the troglodytes' grip. Surrounding the observatory, an angry tide of mosslings streamed.

l.

They smashed the glass and spilled inside. The troglodytes, overwhelmed, froze. Without their listening-stones, which Hilaríon had toppled, they hadn't heard their chattels approaching. The mosslings' fury, long suppressed, swelled as they swamped the rotunda and carried off the withered queen.

Hilaríon whipped his head about, expelling what stones he hadn't swallowed, and wiping the spit from his face. The troglodytes scattered, mosslings pursuing. Behind them ran the M'Brae. Necío threw him the medallion. Hilaríon said, "Keep all of them inside. Just watch what happens next."

Necío shouted, "*Ianthé rah'ephvachu!*" [3] The mosslings stopped dead and turned to Hilaríon.

He raised the medallion over his head. "Treasure!" he cried. The mosslings cooed in unison, then resumed pummeling their captors.

He hoisted himself upon the telescope. It was too wide to hook his legs around. He clamped his thighs vise-like. The mosslings grappled with the troglodytes, herding them back inside the rotunda. The telescope widened. He winched himself on. The terrifying sensation of climbing with nothing beneath, save for a back-breaking fall, took him whole. The keyhole was still well out of reach. It was no use. He slid down and leapt astride a leviathan.

"Hilaríon, hurry," Necío said. The troglodytes were regaining their bearings.

The arch of the leviathan's back was steep, hewn from onyx, slick as rain. He locked his feet above its fluke and reached out for its tiny dorsal fin. He hooked his hands around the fin—

It cracked off in his hands. He tumbled to the floor.

---

[3] "Keep them here!"

He mounted the stone a second time. He grabbed the broken dorsal stump and winched his body upwards. He cinched his knees around its back and strained to pull himself along. His legs slipped and flailed. The stone, like the telescope's metal, was smooth. He slid back to the floor again.

The troglodytes now were fighting back. He looked up at the keyhole. Only a bird or a ladder could reach it. Only a ladder—

"Necío! Tell them to stack themselves."

He looked perplexed. "*Shuré oib-éa.*"[4]

A group of mosslings peeled to the telescope. They tilted it vertically, holding it steady. Others wedged their bodies between the scope and leviathan-stones. Hilaríon watched them work as a team, with urgency and precision. Still others mounted up their backs, until what had been an empty space was filled with a mossling-ladder. "*G'daev,*" the mosslings chanted. He recognized the word for *loot*.

He hoisted himself on their backs. They groaned as he pressed his feet on their shoulders. The mossling-ladder wobbled but held. Other mosslings formed a line and kept the troglodytes away. He winched himself atop their backs and reached out for the key plate.

Hilaríon paused: he had come a long way, indeed. By now, he'd have been in La Habana. But then the M'Brae would have been dead, the mosslings still enslaved. The best escape had been the one not made. He pressed the shaft inside the keyhole, and turned the medallion clockwise.

The rotunda shuddered on its base. The stone of the mountain around it split. Like an unmoored skiff adrift in a storm, the observatory swayed, then lurched. The mossling-ladder toppled. Hilaríon wrapped his arms around the snout and clung with all his strength.

The mountain belched a raucous groan. The troglodytes clasped their ears. The bedrock heaved an ear-splitting crack. The floor of the observatory trundled downwards, driven by the mosslings' weight, as the mountaintop shivered to spoil around it.

---

[4] "Climb atop each other!"

The people railed. The floor hit bedrock. The telescope swiveled to east-northeast, knocking Hilaríon from his perch. He clasped the medallion as he tumbled onto the pile of mosslings.

The face of the mountain crumbled away into an avalanche of boulders. The sky was resplendent, lit by the sunrise. Ahead rolled yellow, treeless plains, vanishing past a golden horizon. The people stood, regaining their bearings. The sinking rotunda had revealed a shaft, and carved into the stone were words. Necío read,

> "Now safe on high the Trodden Seed—
> Shall weeds devour the stripling shoots?
> Naught but time and patient hand
> Shall tempt its germ to multitudes
> Where badlands droop to milky brine
> From tawny moors, the distance closed
> The azimuth of the mariners' joy
> And by and by, a question posed
> For treasure is what treasure must
> A flame to blaze a life ahead
> Of fallen earth, a final length
> Your Vexing Heirloom's path to tread."

The disoriented troglodytes staggered about, tripping over one another and slicing their feet on shards of glass. The mosslings herded them from the rotunda and pushed them over the cliffs to their deaths. Hilaríon watched them, part with horror, yet part with pride. By his own hand, the mosslings were free. And even if the treasure was not, Ypriána had to be near.

Necío said, "All I had to say was that you'd give them loot. All their fear vanished."

Hilaríon looked around. "Where's Phellhe?"

"We had to leave him. And there's something I need to tell you."

"Later," Hilaríon said.

"But you really—"

"Help me find her. She's here." He could feel Ypriána at his fingertips.

Necío said, "We may have been mistaken."

The observatory rumbled and listed slightly onto its side. The terrible din of a death rattle, overlaid with ghoulish laughter, crackled nearby. The withered queen lay on the floor, beaten almost beyond recognition, sprawled across a wooden trapdoor. Her headdress lay in pieces. Hilaríon knelt beside her and draped her tatters back over her body. He almost pitied the bitter ghoul, defiant to the end. But the crone had one more thing to do. Hilaríon said, "Where is she?"

She raised her battered head. "She'll be the least of your worries."

He laid his blade against her throat. "I can save you from the mountainside."

"You couldn't save them from yourself."

"Who's taking the treasure? And the Trodden Seed?"

The crone pointed towards the sound of the mosslings, shoving her spawn off the mountainside. "That seed's not so trodden. The treasure's glint blinds you, fool, as it blinded them. Are you happy with your choice?"

"My choice?"

Necío said, "About that mistake..."

"The choice you'd already made," the crone said, "ere you were told you'd make it."

"I never made a..." A glint of gold flashed. A heap of shattered vials gleamed, the same type that had held the elixir. "...Choice," he said. He peered down the corridor, shattered and twisted and deathly silent. Rubber and copper tubes dangled, some dripping blood, some chemicals. Sterile blades and bottles of leeches rolled underfoot like flotsam.

The observatory was a healing-house—or *had* been.

The crone said, "Now you see. You might have chosen differently."

Hilaríon said, "But the wisest were pushed into the cracks."

"What's wise won't linger in cracks very long, and time can't be trapped in amber."

The mosslings were smashing medicine bottles and ruining surgical instruments. They were tearing pages out of books and urinating on star charts. Again, the observatory rumbled. A burst of dust filled his eyes. The ceiling glass was fracturing, branching into spindles. But Hilaríon knew what he'd seen. "You ghouls would have killed us—"

"Ghouls? That's all you see? None of us touched a hair on your head. Who saved you from the Jaeger? Who sent you down the mossy cliff? Who spurred you on when spirits flagged? Who found the boy and healed his wound? Who came to birth your woman's child? Who brought elixir that your man might live?"

"Who failed to say they came in peace?"

"The fool's retort, the dunce's plea. It was all laid bare before you, but all you could see was our ugliness."

"No one could have sewn that wound or birthed a child without eyes," he said. "You should have told us who you were."

She said, "Would you have believed? We made the art and the great machines. *They* threw them into the gullies to rot. We mapped the stars and the human form. They laughed and looked for gold. We preserved what our sires had learned, so well that even as we lost our sight, we could still feel our way inside of a man just as if we still could see. *They* cast *us* down. They ripped the mountain to shreds. Then they dwindled like worms to the cracks, but we rose higher, past them. They ruined themselves with their greed, same as you M'Brae will do."

Hilaríon swallowed hard. The crone was lying. Or he'd utterly failed them all. "I'm not M'Brae."

"It doesn't matter what you are. They're your problem now."

The observatory lurched. The ceiling glass tinkled, another shower of dust rained down. A fissure like a fault line started at the opposite end of the observatory's ruins and slithered across the floor in an arc, slicing the rotunda in half. Hilaríon said, "You tormented them. You kept them dumb, in squalor, with *this*." He pulled a trinket from his cloak.

"We played the role they made for us. We saved them from themselves."

"But why?"

"Lust for gold is lust for gild. There is no difference in them.

Both set fire to the mind. Soon, the body follows. They were past all help. We told them what they wished to hear, gave them what they longed for, kept them living in spite of themselves."

"I don't understand."

"You will. You'll live out your tragic choice, but it will outlive you. This is what happens when you take answers without questions. Plant your Trodden Seed, M'Brae. See what takes root, and grows." She keeled aside. Her palm fell open. Inside it was an iron key. Hilaríon prodded her. She was dead.

The mosslings dragged her body off and threw it down the mountainside, then went back to gathering: sextants, field-glasses, leather-bound tomes—just so many baubles to them.

The split widened. The north side of the rotunda sank. "Get them out," Hilaríon said. "I'll find you at the bottom." Necío dithered. "Go!" Hilaríon said. "I won't leave her again."

Necío raised his hands and yelled, "*Jae-cün ephvachu!*" The mosslings filled their satchels with trinkets and streamed away down the mountainside. They were the same words he'd used inside the fissure: only the lure of loot would move them. They were mated to each other now, M'Brae and mosslings made one. Leaving them would not be possible. But Ypriána would make it right.

He pushed the ghoul's key in the trapdoor-lock and swung the trapdoor open. Beneath it was an oubliette. Inside was Ypriána.

His heart leapt. He gathered her into his arms. Her frame was gaunt, her face sallow, her legs and feet bare. She was draped in faded orange rags, little more than an oversized shirt. But her ear had been repaired, new skin grafted onto the old. The troglodytes had been surgeon-artists, but he'd exterminated them.

He lifted her from the oubliette. Slowly, she opened her eyes. "You found me," she said. "That wasn't the plan."

The whine of twisting metal squealed. A shower of dust and slivers of glass tinkled from the ceiling. The telescope popped from between the leviathans and thundered against the floor. The rotunda was collapsing.

_li._

The brass web above them split. Shards rained down. He threw her beneath a leviathan's fluke. It shivered the falling glass to whits. The observatory tore in half. Its backside scattered down the mountain. What remained lurched forward, throwing them against the wall. The stone leviathans wobbled.

He pulled her to her feet. The floor was strewn with glass. He tugged off his boots and held them out. She looked at them disdainfully, then pulled them onto her feet. "Too big."

He said, "Or you're too small." He hurried her through the doorway, into the terraced trough.

Behind, the leviathans crashed to the floor. The rotunda listed. The stones and telescope lurched against its leading edge. A cascade of glass poured into the trough. The broken rotunda slid further, then stopped. The stone on which the structure had perched buckled and rolled in a rockslide.

Ypriána stumbled among the rocks. Hilaríon positioned himself behind her, shielding her as best he could from the coming onslaught. The listening-stones that lined the slope toppled. Glass gnawed through his stocking feet. Below, past the trough, the mountain bowed violently, beetling over a glassy pool. There was no sign of the M'Brae or mosslings. Necío had led them to safety.

They scrambled along in the flood, down the mountainside. A beam of brass webbing rolled from the rockslide and slammed against their legs. Hilaríon spilled onto his back. Ypriána fell headlong. The beam slid down the length of her back and pinned her at her neck. Hilaríon lifted an end of the beam. The tumbling shatter swamped him. A heavy rasping scratched from behind. A listening-stone was bearing down on them. It trundled upright like a billowing mainsail.

"Crawl out," he said. She arched her back. The tide of shatter surged. It spun the beam against her head and drove her to the dirt.

The listening-stone sped closer. He squatted to hoist the beam. The listening-stone's shadow fell over her body. A boulder smacked his knee. He buckled to the ground. The footing was impossible, the sliding stone too close. He dove upon her and put up his arms—

A figure rushed from behind them. It threw itself against the stone, striking a sideways, glancing blow. The stone held upright but wobbled, then slowed, then settled harmlessly.

It was Phellhe.

The big man clutched his shoulder, mangled by striking the stone. But a vital spark flashed in his eyes, same as the would-be hero from Golgaj. "Together," Phellhe said. He propped his good arm on the stone and wedged himself against it. Hilaríon wrapped his arms on the beam and hoisted it from Ypriána's back. She drove her feet against the stone's base. Hilaríon pressed against its center.

The stone pivoted on its base, facing uphill, like a shield. The torrent of debris broke around and beside them: shanks of glass, stone, and copper pipe, made projectiles in the flood. But tucked in the fold of the stone they were safe, like mariners in the prow of a ship.

An earsplitting groan at the mountaintop thundered. The first of the leviathans dislodged. It rolled down the terrace and into the trough, and split beneath its weight. The pieces tumbled end-over-end. The snout-end caught a patch of spoil. It dragged, then slid to a stop. The fluke-end bounced aside, downhill, and clipped the listening-stone. A telltale crack snaked down the seam. Phellhe winced but leaned in deeper.

The telescope lolled into the trough and settled at the bottom. Behind it burst the second leviathan. What remained of the dome and rotunda collapsed and gushed away downhill. The leviathan slid down the telescope shaft, gathering speed and spinning.

Hilaríon braced. Ypriána pressed harder. The leviathan slammed against them. The force of its impact broke their stone-shield and flung the three onto their backs. The stone-halves rolled in the tide of debris. It swelled around the leviathan and nudged it from the trough.

Hilaríon jumped atop the leviathan, then reached for Ypriána. She scrambled onto the stone. Boulders, metal, and fragments of glass whipped by their sides and over their heads. Hilaríon grabbed a fluke with one hand, and reached for Phellhe with the other.

The tide surged again. The leviathan lurched. The current devoured and spit them downhill. Phellhe thrashed inside the avalanche, then vanished over the cliff.

The leviathan floundered each way downhill. Ypriána leapt from its fluke to the ground and out of the way of the rockslide. She curled beneath a jutting ledge. Hilaríon jumped to the opposite side. The current caught him in its sway and heaved him to the edge. He dragged his legs. His momentum waned. He turned to rise—

A stone glanced his chest, spinning him sideways, knocking him backwards. He grabbed the beetling lip and held on. Below, the pool gaped, its greenish waters trimmed in white by the froth of falling boulders. He could feel the strength in his grip giving way, the sinews in his fingers failing. "Here," he said. Ypriána crawled towards him.

The cascade of pebbles and glass broke across them. She grabbed his arms and arched her back. The last gasp of wreckage heaved and rolled, slicing her back and the top of her head. Rivulets of blood ran down her arms. She clutched him by his wrist and hauled him partway up the ledge.

The rock gave way. He lurched towards the gully. She pulled again, jolting him higher. Something shiny smacked his face and settled in the crook of his neck—a slice of glass, or quartz, he guessed. He flicked it aside, then swung his arm towards her. "Take my hand," he said.

But she didn't.

He said, "Pull me up!"

She knelt. Her eyes were neither wide nor bright but resigned, like a vanquished warrior. He hadn't been struck by glass or quartz. The medallion had popped outside his shirt. And she was staring at it.

"What are you waiting for?" he said.

She reached her arm. He stretched to meet it. But she pushed his hand aside. He reached again. She batted it down, gaze fixed firmly on the medallion. He grabbed at the crumbling lip of the cliff. His fingernails dug into the dust. He felt himself sliding. "I can't—"

"I know," she said. She grabbed the medallion and let go of his wrist.

He thrashed his arm to grip the ledge, scattering stone to the pool below, until he hung but by his fingertips—and Ypriána's grace. He said, "Not part of the plan?"

She answered, lightly, "No."

He looked below. The water was deep, the road ahead long, the fate of the M'Brae uncertain still. He was bound to them and them to him. There'd be no forsaking them.

He swung his dangling arm towards her hand, and clamped his hand around hers. She pulled back. He held firm. He dug his thumb into her wrist. Her eyes were dead, same as at the hacienda stairs and before she'd faced the crocodile. He pried her fingers, grabbed the medallion, then released his grip—and fell.

The visage of Ypriána shrank. Only she was not Ypriána. She was something else.

But he'd been warned. And as he tumbled into space he thought, *Should I have listened?*

<u>lii.</u>

He smashed into the water. His neck whipped sideways, limbs buckling, until he slammed into the lakebed. The mud swirled thickly around his face. Any higher and he'd have been dashed to his death. He churned his arms to keep from sinking, then kicked towards the light with searing lungs.

He thrust his head above the surface, drawing deep, renewing breath. The morning was resplendent. The golden dawn had given way to cloudless, indigo skies, reflected in the rich mountain pool. The Gilded Peak had crumbled. Where once its observatory gleamed sat a pitiful stump. *Answers without questions.* It had sounded so banal, but the consequences were real. A body was floating beside him.

Phellhe.

Hilaríon dragged him to the shore and rolled him to his back. "Phellhe," he said, "can you hear me? Come back. The fires, they've gone out!"

Spittle spilled from the big man's lips. "You killed Wresh."

"Save your breath," Hilaríon said. He'd said the same to Wresh.

Phellhe said, "You killed Wresh, but so did I. They were never mine to save. Where M'Brae are, M'Brae-dah is. Ypriána had it right." He gasped for breath like a dying fish. "I lied to you. From the very first, I knew. I knew all along." He sang,

> "A ruthless path through living earth
> A Steeled Elect whose heart is true
> *A timeless hymn proclaimed at last*
> *Ere all is lost, a hope for you."*

Hilarión remembered the haunting couplet Phellhe had sang in Golgaj, now augmented with another. He'd demanded to know about rivers of treasure. From that loose-lipped confidence, all had flowed.

Phellhe pressed the medallion on Hilarión's neck. "The M'Brae belong to no one, hilldevil. The fires will never be out. The fires are you and me."

His grip slackened. For an instant, Hilarión might have sworn, a grateful smile curled his lips. But it was only the rigor of death. The big man, Phellhe, was gone.

Hilarión bowed his head. An icy Castilian blade licked his neck. "He aquí, el fruto de la perfidia," came the Gray Jaeger's voice. The demon had outlasted him.

Hilarión let his head sag. The eyes caught flame: Wresh and Phellhe—the troglodytes, even—savoring his grief forthwith. The Jaeger swung his blade. "*Lejos*—!"

"¡*Alto!*" Across the pool, an officer shouted, "Aqui no. Tráelo junto con los otros. Para Morón."

"Él no," the Jaeger hissed.

"Todos ellos."

A battalion of dragoons surrounded the officer. Behind them, wrists bound, were the M'Brae and mosslings. "Deje que la guerra mate, no nosotros," the officer said.

The Jaeger slid his blade away. "Yo soy la Guerra."

Hilarión feigned a stumble, then rolled. The Jaeger said, "Levántate." Hilarión snaked his hand through his shirt. He snapped the medallion off his neck and slipped it in his stocking. The Jaeger pulled him onto his feet and kicked Phellhe's body into the pool.

Hilarión threw the Sierra del Escambray one final glance. The naked nub of the Gilded Peak seemed a gelded hope. And somewhere, he knew, Ypriána was watching—not from the hereafter but in hiding, planning her next move.

liii.

Ash hung thick in the air like plague. They trudged across the battle plain. War's numbing roar was everywhere: rifles barking, dragoons thundering, the distant whine of naval gunfire belched from filibustering ships. The soldiers stalked along their flanks. Alone, at the rear, rode the Gray Jaeger. Astride his pale, bony mare, he looked the dreaded Final Horseman, harbinger of end-times.

Occidente seemed a tawny, scorched Elysium. Past the clouds, Hilaríon knew, daybreak came and turned to noon, by and by doffing the sun for night, but no one was the wiser. Every so often, the sides of his eyes betrayed the length of the refugee train. Phellhe was dead, Ypriána unknown, but now the M'Brae and mosslings were his.

Ypriána. Her name was like an incantation, stark and sugar-sweet. Had she really reached for the medallion? Exhausted and desperate, perhaps he'd erred. She'd looked like she was reaching for it, but all he had were images—impressions, really, muddled and vague, like an etching too many times erased. He'd misremembered things before. Surely, he might have done it again.

The ivory spires of Sancti Spiritus pierced the morning mist, a floating mirage of feminine grace amidst the doomsday hellscape. Columns of refugees slinked from its walls. He'd loved this land, and cities like this, enough that he'd been willing to die for them once. His aunt had been his paragon. She'd answered the clarion-call. She'd been so much like Ypriána, and yet nothing like her.

"Where are they taking us?" Hetta said.

Hilaríon said, "To a camp."

Necío said, "Why don't they just kill us?"

"That *is* killing us, slowly."

"Savages," Hetta said.

Hilaríon said, "He's called the Butcher." The Butcher was a

279

grotesque dwarf, as short as he was vile. Ypriána would have taken his head. Why hadn't she taken Hilaríon's hand?

"Hagan el campamento," an officer said. The soldiers herded them into a ring. Pickets took places at their flanks. An icy rain chattered out of the sky, soaking their clothing, chilling their bones. Servants pitched the officers' tents. M'Brae and pickets alike shivered blue. But Hilaríon was worlds away.

She'd led him to M'Brae-dah. She could have killed him anytime. Instead, she'd dragged him into the ruins, then saved his life on the hilltop. She'd asked—no, *begged*—him to help find treasure. She'd followed his lead in the underground caves. Whether or not she'd ever admit, she'd followed him over the Trocha. She gave him the medallion and said she'd return. She'd all but told him his coming was prophesized—that *he* was the key to the treasure, not her. Where had it all gone wrong?

A sanguine sunrise brought no comfort. The soldiers threw them moldy bread, then spurred them on with bayonets. Maith and Hetta took turns carrying Selwin. Chropher let Mabba ride on his shoulders. The mosslings shuffled in lockstep silence. The absence of trinkets would soon drive them mad.

Morning turned to afternoon. The plains gave way to knolls. Their refugee train, now five hundred strong, augmented by people from despoiled towns, shuffled along on exposed feet and nauseous, half-starved bellies. The road wended through leafy draws, then slithered up a hill. Hilaríon chopped his stocking-foot steps. The rope bindings gnawed his wrists raw.

Atop the hill the trees had been felled. Cannons and field-guns dotted its crest. The land rolled forth in forested knolls, then flattened to a treeless plain, dotted by burned-out villages. To the northeast ran a tangle of railroad, converging on a sprawling town ringed by fortifications. Past a screen of bristling redoubts and railroad-mounted Maxim guns, a veil of barbed wire lay three layers deep, and behind it wooden fences. Patrols with attack dogs stalked through each ring. It was as if the Trocha had been dragged from the west and wound about this unfortunate town. Plumes of smoke beyond the rooftops belied desperation within. The prisoners were burning their dead.

That was their destination, Morón. He'd heard its horrors spoken of.

To the northwest gaped a wooded dale and past it, a white-hued lake. Woodlands wrapped around the lake, then thinned in scrubby dunes. Beyond them, Hilarión knew, was the sea. He'd have long been in La Habana by now. Golden days would have been his.

Part of the plan? What plan? Why resent him saving her? Why entrust him with medallion and people, only to toss him to his death? Who could blame him for rescuing her? She'd said she'd catch up to him, but who'd have taken her words to the letter? And even if that wasn't part of her plan, had he deserved to die for it?

Necío and Aryei chattered. "That had to be milky brine," Necío said.

Aryei said, "And the azimuth of the mariners' joy?"

"North," Hilarión said.

Necío said, "You've been listening?"

"It's you or my unwelcome thoughts."

"The treasure's at the north-most point of that lake," Aryei said.

Where they were going, the treasure might as well have been on the moon. But to tell them now would only sow panic.

Afternoon sagged. The rainclouds re-gathered. The dirt road turned to cobblestones and widened in a cart-path. They passed through smoked-out peasant farms. Tools and utensils littered the roadside, abandoned, no doubt, by families in flight. Bodies of cattle, horses, and men moldered in the overgrown fields. The mosslings leered at shiny debris. The M'Brae kept their eyes ahead. The slag was all but hardened now. They could, at least, take pride in that.

But Hilarión couldn't stem the tide. The crush of questions drowned him. The withered queen had spoken of stars and of their deaths, by and by. She'd warned him to let Ypriána go, that unborn thousands would thank him. And yet, they'd saved her life—even healed her mangled ear. Had the troglodytes had their own death wish? Surgeons, artists, and alchemists, their spite had sealed their fate. A word or two of explanation and they'd be with him now, the mosslings still skulking in cracks in the hills.

The farms gave way to cottages, the cottages to courtyards, then the courtyards to buildings, charred and waterlogged. Carts of hay and dried tobacco lay overturned in byways. Save for the cawing of crows in the eaves and wandering dogs in the alleys, the scene was devoid of life. The cart-path narrowed to one lane, then opened into a square. The hulk of a village church loomed tall, surrounded by trash heaps and huts. A golden belfry, braced by pillars, crowned its whitewashed roof. Upon first blush it almost looked like the submerged temple in the swamp.

But Ypriána! There was no reprieve. It was as if her blade was still under his throat, but infinitely more maddening. Ypriána had vanished in that temple; facing a dragon, welcoming death. But death had not complied. She'd survived the Jaeger, then been healed, then been reunited with them. She'd preached, self-righteous, after the Trocha. She'd gained from his audacity, then moralized on playing things safe. She'd bragged of how she'd chosen the people, fulfilling a birthright, forsaking herself, only to leave them to capture and torment. She'd done nothing but lead from behind. What reckless blunders had gotten him here? They'd all been duped—or worse.

He looked the ruined village over. It was inauspicious ground. What was left of the Mambí capitán within would've sworn it would make for a perfect—

"*Ambush,*" Necío whispered.

Behind the churchyard fence, a band of highwaymen crouched in wait.

liv.

Hilarío crashed to the here-and-now. Ypriána could go to hell. "Run into it," he said.

Necío said, "Into it—?"

"*Ug'que!*"

Rifles crackled. Smoke filled the air. The highwaymen rushed from their places of cover and slammed into the column. Hilarío spun Necío aside. Soldiers and captives alike scattered, running. Officers bellowed and rattled their sabers, then dropped from saddles, dead. The surviving soldiers tried to form a battle-line. A squadron of mounted highwaymen swept down upon them from the north. Hilarío and Necío ducked into the church.

Inside was a shambles: a refuse-pile ran the length of the aisles, flanked by rows of broken pews, capped at each end by statues of saints and wooden bursts of martyrs. The pile was mostly ruined furniture, stacked to the height of a very tall man, rounded by farming tools, saddles, and harnesses. Whoever'd sacked the village had taken no chances.

They dove past a pew. Shards of stained glass lay on the floor. Necío wedged a piece between his knees and cut the bindings off their wrists. The clamor of skirmishing rang from the square. They peered through a crack in the masonry. The horsemen had rolled the soldiers' flank and put them to flight from the village. "*Ug'que,*" Necío said. "That's M'Brae language."

"Makes sense," Hilarío said. Only partisans used such outmoded rifles. "Follow me—"

The church-doors whined open. Hoof-beats clopped against the stone. He recognized the horse's gait. It was the Gray Jaeger's mount.

They dropped. The Jaeger lingered in the doorway, then spurred his horse down the left-side aisle. Hilarío squinted in the light from the door. The pile was high enough to screen them. They slithered down the length of the pew, then hooked around the pile. The mare snorted, tossing its head. "Light on your feet," he said, and lunged—

He jerked to a stop. The Jaeger was back in the doorway.

A rope beneath Hilaríon's foot ran to a chandelier, wedged like a cornerstone beneath the refuse. Commotion could draw the Jaeger in, enough to open space to run. He tugged the rope. The pile groaned. The Jaeger turned his head to the sound. Hilaríon pulled with greater force. The pile spilled across the pews. The Jaeger dismounted and slapped his horse's rump. The animal sauntered out of the church. He slammed the doors closed and wedged the handles, then lifted a scythe from the pile.

Hilaríon peered down the length of the church, shaped like a supine crucifix. Where the wings came together stood an altar and pulpit. The debris was still tall enough to hide them. The gunfire outside still covered their sounds. But there was still only one way out, and that was past the Jaeger. Hilaríon pointed to the altar and mouthed, "We'll double-back." They crept behind the pulpit.

The crackle of Mausers intensified. He could see through the window-holes. The soldiers had re-formed their line, swelled by re-inforcements. The popping of partisan guns had slowed. The smoke had all but cleared. The engagement was waning, and with it the covering sound of gunfire.

The Jaeger's footsteps crunched in the spoil, punctuated, here and there, by the thumping of wood on stone. "What's he doing?" Necío said. Hilaríon peeked. The Jaeger was stalking towards them, lopping off heads of martyrs and saints. They struck the floor like ten-pin balls. Necío said, "Should we split up?"

"Only if you want to die, or—"

Tap... tap... tap...

The Jaeger drummed the scythe on the pulpit. The vibration of iron on stone sent shivers up and down Hilaríon's spine. The Jaeger could still terrify him without so much as a spoken word. And that was before the question that haunted. *Cerca o lejos?* Towards or away? Hilaríon still didn't know.

The Jaeger gave a final tap, then stalked off down the left hallway. Hilaríon continued, "Only if you want to die, or escape while he kills me. This way."

They sidled around the base of the pulpit, out of the Jaeger's line of sight. The way out was clear, except for the doors. He'd have to unwedge them. The Jaeger would then have time to pounce. Send Necío ahead while he, himself, held off the foe? Hilaríon was weaponless. He'd make short work for the Jaeger, then Necío, alone, was as good as dead.

He looked the other way. Past the altar was a vestibule, with stairs leading up to a belfry. A bell-rope dangled in the shaft, too long and light to climb. It was a dead-end, but at least he'd hold the high ground...

Epiphany spread across Necío's face. "He doesn't know there are two of us."

He followed Necío's gaze. Even on the gray-blue stone, gauzy smudges of blood were clear. He'd forgotten his stocking-feet. He'd been leaving tracks. "Keep it that way," Hilaríon said.

Necío said, "How did Odysseus pass the Sirens?"

Nothing could be less apropos. "Huh?"

Necío toppled a candlestick. It slammed against the floor. The Jaeger's footsteps stopped, then turned.

Necío cursed, "Damn wobbly thing." But the noise had sealed their fates.

Hilaríon's stomach twisted in knots. "Wait 'til he follows me, then run," he said. He pushed past the altar and lunged for the stairwell. Motion flashed in the side of his eye: the Jaeger was in hard pursuit. Now Necío could safely escape, even if he was a clumsy fool.

Hilaríon scurried up the stairwell. It might have been a cannon-barrel, so narrowly it squeezed him. The Jaeger's footsteps clapped below. He hoisted himself past the topmost step and into the musty belfry.

A cast-bronze sanctus bell hung from the dome, above the shaft leading down to the vestibule. Swallows fluttered in the eaves.

In the village square the skirmish had settled. The partisan fighters that remained took pot shots from behind the church. The soldiers went on pursuing their captives and gathering dead comrades. Like rhythmic drums, the Jaeger clomped, slowly stalking up the stairs. But now, there were two sets of footfalls.

Necío.

Hilarión ripped a board from the wall. A muffled cry came from the stairwell. From past the bend, a figure emerged: not Necío, but an urchin girl. The Jaeger held her to his chest, scythe pinned to her breast. "¿No ves?" the Jaeger said. "Ellos estaban escondidos, también."

Hilarión *hadn't* seen more people hiding. He'd led the Jaeger into their sanctuary.

"Tú ha sido cegado por el resplandor. Esto lleva al dolor, pero no el suyo propio." He ran the scythe along her stomach. "¿Cuántos más?" the Jaeger said, "¿Cuántos más?"

"Don't," Hilarión said. He dropped the board. The Jaeger kicked it down the stairs, and pushed the girl down after it.

The Jaeger stepped into the belfry and prodded Hilarión towards the window. It was too small for Hilarión to clamber through quickly, whether he'd even survive the fall. The Jaeger said, "Quiero que ellos oigan."

Hilarión raised his arms in surrender. The Jaeger tapped Hilarión's breast. "¿Dónde está?" he hissed. He was looking for the medallion.

Hilarión could feel its cold on his leg. It was still inside his stocking. "Safe," he said.

The Jaeger drew the scythe to strike. Hilarión stared at the sanctus bell, outsized for a village church, probably brought from an Old World cathedral. At least his end would come before God. That had to count for something—

The bell-rope juked; the bell lurched sideways. What was it Necío said? How *had* Odysseus passed the Sirens? The question made sense, now. Hilarión smiled.

Necío had become a man.

Hilarión covered his ears. The bell struck its clapper. The

stentorian roar of its voice pealed out. It shook the scythe from the Jaeger's hands and sent him writhing to the floor. From the vestibule, Necío peered up, grinning.

The bell sang its august hymn. Hilaríon kicked the Jaeger's head and drove his heel to the back of his neck, still plugging his ears with both fingers. The Jaeger withered, ears trickling blood. Hilaríon kicked the scythe down the stairwell, then followed it into the vestibule. The stone of the tower pulsed with the sound. Necío gave a final tug.

"Sirens and candlesticks?" Hilaríon said. "You could've just told me."

Necío replied, "Wresh's revenge." He pulled a pair of boots from the floor. "Don't ask me where I got these." They raced outside the church.

Past a graveyard, a wood spread its eaves. They rushed past the tree line into a thicket, and ducked behind a stand of pines. They could see through the brush to the village square. The soldiers had recaptured the M'Brae. As quickly as they'd sprung from the flanks, the mysterious partisans had vanished. Hilaríon pulled the boots on his feet. "We have to go back," he said.

Necío said, "Soon."

"Now."

"Why fall on the sword?"

"So *they* won't."

Necío blocked his path. "You said yourself they're going to a camp. So there's time."

"Time for what?"

"A better decision. Not to mention..." He pointed north. "The treasure's just this way."

The M'Brae were in danger. But unarmed, Hilaríon was of little use to them. Any moment, the Jaeger would pick up their trail. And the treasure was just so close. How better to spite Ypriána? "This time, don't get lost," he said. They stepped off into the woods.

The sun, a lazy fire-galleon, sank across the west. The woods were bright and easy to pass. The land rolled on in draws, filled with figs, then plunged into the dappled dale they'd seen from the crest of the knoll. The ground was pocked with hoofprints: the partisans had ridden this way. Even though they'd ambushed the soldiers, their loyalties were still unknown. "Keep to the rough," Hilaríon said.

Necío echoed, "And rocks and firm ground."

The terrain flattened, the woodlands thinned to holly trees. Hilaríon dragged his weary feet. The thought of the treasure, hidden so close, sent chills along his body. And yet the people were inside Morón or, in no time, would be. How would he carry their shares to them? Could he even claim it without Ypriána? Her name was both bellows and icy douse, stoking his anger then snuffing it out, in a maddening dance of uncertainty. Why hadn't she taken his hand?

The woods abruptly ended. The trees gave way to a milky white lake. A knot of flamingoes digging for shrimp squabbled in the shallows. Terns wheeled overhead. The sea was near enough to smell. Already, night was falling. In the azure quilt of the billowing dusk, he could make out the contours of the Great Bear, and follow it to the North Star. He traced a line down to the horizon. The northernmost point of the lake was near, a mere half-hour's walk. He pointed. "It's there."

The red sun slipped into the nethers. Necío bounded a stone's throw out front. The wide lake shimmered bluish-white, just like the medallion.

By and by, the strand widened and curved in a spit, and thrust from the shore to an islet. The islet was lined with flowering bushes, in the middle of which stood a vine-draped pergola, arching above a sculpture garden. The sculptures were dazzling, hewn from rich marble. Hilaríon had seen the scene before. It was the same as the hilltop outside M'Brae-dah: five leviathans hand-in-fluke with five smaller figures. He'd come full-circle.

They raced to the islet. The bushes were fiery heliconia, bright like birds of paradise, filled with hummingbirds. Between the statues, the ground gaped wide and dropped to a narrowing stairway.

Hilaríon stopped at the head of the stairs. For what seemed like forever he'd pictured this moment. And yet, it was nothing like he'd envisioned. La Habana and all its charms were nigh. And yet he couldn't rid himself. Ypriána besieged his every thought. Without her, the moment was incomplete.

Necío said, "Are you ready?"

He hesitated. "You be for the both of us."

Necío grabbed a driftwood branch. Hilaríon handed him flint and steel. He sparked a flame in kindling straw, then touched it to the branch. A warm glow danced about the pergola. They took their first steps, reverently.

The stairs led to an underground vault. Its tall iron doors were wedged tightly shut. Its heavy lock was battered in two and each door dimpled inward, as if they'd been slammed by a percussive blast. Necío pulled on the handle. It broke off in his hand. They snaked their fingers into the seam and pried the doors apart. The doors let out a plaintive moan, like a giant strongbox hinge.

Necío held the torch aloft. They stepped inside an octagonal vault. Its walls were draped with tapestries. The floor was rough and undulating, dotted with lumps and strange formations, like a tiny mountain range. Hilaríon reeled to keep from falling. He panned his gaze around, then back, and then both ways again. The vault was completely empty, save for a single coin, in the center of the floor.

And why shouldn't it have been this way? Nothing else had been as promised. Nothing else had been as it should. The Vexing Heirloom had lived up to its name. Hilaríon was utterly dumbstruck.

He bent to lift the coin. It was fixed to the ground, immovable, but he could see an inscription upon it. Necío cleared his throat and read, "*Huath-ux bafhé-g'daev.* Not all treasure hunts—"

"*Pah'ada,*" a voice said. "Bear fruit."

They turned. A middle-aged man stood behind them. He was dressed in raggedy partisan garb, an antique rifle slung on his shoulder, a dueling-pistol at his hip. His cloak was torn and made for a woman. But his bearing was that of a warrior. His eyes commanded unwavering respect. He said,

"Not all treasure hunts bear fruit
Not all gild revealed for gold
But fortune overflows the vault
When Vexing Heirloom's secret told."

The stranger stepped closer. "You look just like your mother," he said. "I see you've gotten her recklessness, too. Necío, you're my son."

lv.

Aryei shuffled in the dark. It was worse than when Lux had kidnapped him. His hands were bound behind his back. The soldiers prodded with bayonets. The smell of burnt cloth from his shirt filled his nose: a ball had missed his neck by inches. But he wasn't feeling lucky. The maw of Morón gaped nearer and nearer. If what Hilaríon said was true, it might have been better to have been shot.

"*Yûl-t-r'ephvachu,*"[5] a man whispered, ducking among the mosslings. Bindings sat loosely on his wrists. His face was smudged with powder. He had to be one of the highwaymen. He said again, "*Zhar!*"[6]

"Me?" Aryei said.

"You."

"¡No hablen!" A Spanish officer leveled his pistol.

The strange man whispered, "Stay close, when we reach the gate."

Aryei said, "Why?"

"They'll put a rifle in your hands."

A barbed-wire fence, the height of two men, loomed like a palisade. The soldiers halted the column. An officer yelled, "¡Abran!" Over the growls of slavering dogs, a guard-captain answered, "¡Entren!"

Guards unlocked the wooden gate. The soldiers herded them inside. Aryei looked around for the stranger. He had no reason to trust the man, but even less to trust the soldiers. The strange man whispered, "Not this gate."

"Tú, camina," a soldier said, pushing Aryei forward.

"Él va a hacerlo bien," another said. Aryei locked eyes with the stranger and nodded.

They passed the next gate in similar fashion. Wagons piled high

---

[5] "Stay close to me"

[6] "Boy!"

with corpses dotted the wasteland between the fences. Guard dogs strained against their leads. Even in the cool of night, the stench of death hung in the air. The third gate drew nearer. Aryei's heart raced. Hilaríon, he knew, would come. But when?

The soldiers prodded them into the town, mocking, "Bienvenidos." The orange glow of sustenance-fires might have been welcoming someplace else. Refugees huddled in clapboard lean-tos, boiling rations and cleaning their clothes. Feral cats scuttled about their feet, mewling for scraps and drops of milk. Tall buildings, once graceful, stood covered in soot. From inside them came the screams of children and despondent groans of elders, railing in that peculiar pitch that only comes with hunger. Their cries blended with the braying of mongrels. Not a single refugee turned to look as the M'Brae passed through the gate. They were all too weak and resigned to their fate.

A soldier grabbed Aryei's hair. "Ven conmigo, muchacho." He pulled him down an alleyway. Another soldier followed. Aryei looked back but the stranger was gone.

He ripped himself from the soldier's grasp. The soldier re-grabbed Aryei's neck. The second soldier raised his rifle and aimed the butt at Aryei's head. Aryei bit the first soldier's hand. The soldier howled. The other swung—

Arms pulled Aryei backwards. The soldier stroked his rifle-butt into the other soldier's face. The first soldier fell, clutching his nose. The stranger, having reappeared, pushed Aryei behind him. The second soldier spun the rifle and lunged at the stranger bayonet-first. The stranger coolly dodged the strike. He shouted a startling cry at the soldier, who dropped the rifle, recoiling. The stranger swept the soldier's legs and threw him to the ground.

"With me," the stranger said. He pushed Aryei up the alley, then into a carriage-house. He propped a wheel against the door, then heaved a wooden coach aside, revealing a floor-hatch. Outside, the soldiers' voices railed. Aryei stepped towards the hatch. The stranger stopped him. "No."

The soldiers slammed against the door. The wheel fell to the floor. The stranger pulled Aryei into the shadows just as the soldiers raced inside. "¡Ahí está!" they said, pointing at the hatch. They lit a lantern and disappeared below.

"Easy dupes," the stranger said. He pushed Aryei back through the door to the alley.

Already the M'Brae had dispersed. Near the gate were throngs of guards, scouring the byways with torches and lanterns, searching high and low for the stranger. The stranger pulled him through a refugee-crowd and into a rickety shanty. They ducked beneath a window. "No one saw us, I hope," Aryei said.

"It wouldn't matter if they had. No one helps the phéa-sjant." Soldiers skulked past, then vanished. The stranger exhaled. He was a middle-aged man with leathery skin and dark, commanding eyes. "They arm young men to fill their ranks," he said. "That's why I couldn't leave you alone." He held out his hand. "Lin Créa-Rohr. Child of the sea."

"What?"

"M'Brae, like you." He winced. His flank was bleeding. He *hadn't* dodged the bayonet.

Aryei pretended not to see. "You snuck in with us?"

"I'm not as patient as my general. Soon there'll be nothing worth saving." He pulled back his cloak, revealing a pouch filled with medicine bottles. "I can do more good here." He gathered a handful of rags from the floor and tied them end-to-end. He wrapped the poultice around his chest. "This way."

"Where are we going?"

Lin said, "To M'Brae-dah."

"M'Brae-dah?"

"You'll see."

They sidled down grimy byways and squeezed through twisting alleys. It reminded Aryei of the mountain fissure, only there the humid air had been fresh and he had been amongst friends. Lin held his flank as he hurried along. An ever-swelling trail of blood dribbled from his poultice. The buildings around them rose higher, like granite-faced hillocks. One of them had a giant clock-face. Its hands had stopped, but Aryei's mind ever whirled at breakneck speed.

It had been twenty-six minutes and fifty-four seconds since he'd set foot in Morón.

Lin said, "Twenty-seven."

Aryei marveled, "How did you know?"

"You're not the only one," Lin said.

The soaring structures fell away to brown and stunted bungalows. Refugees crowded in doors and on porches, their clothing short and threadbare, their faces long and sallow. Gaunt women nursed infants on wizened breasts. Children threw stones at gutter-rats. The bloated bodies of cats and horses rotted in the silent streets. The smell of death was everywhere. Aryei pinched his nose.

Lin stumbled. Aryei helped him up. His poultice was saturated. "I'll change that," Aryei said.

"No need," Lin said. "We're here." He pointed up a gentle hill. Aryei draped Lin's arm over his shoulder. "I see my son in you. I think you two will be friends."

All his life he'd eschewed friends, kept to the fringes and to himself. Hilaríon and Necío had changed all that. They, like the stranger, had risked their lives—for the others, and for him. If having a friend meant being a friend, this new world was rife with chances to take.

They crested the hill. Through the pain Lin smiled with pride. "This is where we live," he said. "M'Brae-dah as it *should* have been—"

Lin gasped. The hilltop was deathly silent. Nothing moved or made a sound. The cluster of houses and buildings was still. Most of the windows were shattered away and household items littered the streets. Most of the homes had been looted. On the walls of those not burned or wrecked were scrawled vulgar broadsides in the Vujoíe language. Lin gasped, staggering backwards. In the commons lay a pile of bodies, some festered and some recently heaped, all their eyes and mouths agape.

Lin dropped to a knee. His gaze told all. The bodies were his kin.

From the shadows emerged a group of refugees. They knelt with Lin and joined hands, sobbing.

✳   ✳   ✳   ✳

Necío flinched, as if he'd been punched. "Your son? Then that means you're—"

"Bollísh," another partisan said, entering the vault, "Ioh'othé rah'éa."[7]

Necío said, "Save whom?"

"Huath s'éa!"[8] Bollísh ordered. He turned to Necío. "Warms my heart you know our tongue. That's one thing your mother and I agreed on." He motioned them up the stairs. A squadron of partisans was waiting. He pointed towards two rider-less horses. "Keep up, you two."

Hilaríon said, "Going where?"

"Second crack at saving our kin."

"Give us rifles, then." He pointed at one of the partisans, carrying captured Mausers.

"Be happy with the mounts," Bollísh said. "I don't know you that well enough."

Bollísh spurred his horse to the south. The other riders followed. Hilaríon looked at Necío. "Is that man really your father?"

Necío stared emptily after him and shrugged. "He knows about my mother." He struggled up onto a chestnut colt and rode after the others. Hilaríon mounted a coal-black mare and reined her nose to the shadows.

The squadron rode in silence. Their hoof beats fell in unison, neighs and whinnies muffled. The woodlands passed in a leafy blur. He recognized the way they'd gone: dale and orchard, graveyard and village, by and by back to the bald-headed knolls.

Flood-lamps bathed the plain in blue. The land, a bellicose machine, spun with the motion of war and internment. A refugee column was wending through the harrowing entrance gates of Morón. Bollísh looked through a spyglass. He grunted and ordered his riders, "Fall back."

"Just like that?" Hilaríon said.

---

[7] "We can still save them."

[8] "Everyone" or "all heads"

"We'd be in range of their Maxim guns, easy marks for counterattack. I'd hoped we'd have found them farther south. The gate to Morón swings only one way."

Necío said, "But you were M'Brae-dah's greatest general."

"*Am* its greatest. I chose my battles."

Hilaríon said, "But no plan for this?"

"Not without one hundred men, horses, guns, and surprise, which we'd lose the second we charged. I have kin who've been trammeled inside there for months. I can't risk trying to free even them." He wheeled his horse down the knoll.

The squadron retraced the way it had come, down through the orchards and into the dale. The silver crescent moon rose high. The riders slowed to a canter. Ahead, through the brush, were flickering watch-fires. Pickets stepped from the trees. "G'daev," one said. Hilaríon remembered their word for *loot*.

Bollísh answered, "Gnath." Necío winced. Their password was his mother's name.

The riders dismounted. The pickets took the horses' bridles and led them towards the fires.

"No blindfold?" Hilaríon said.

"If my son trusts you, so do I," Bollísh said.

Necío said, "How do you know that?"

"Soon enough. First, you need to indulge me."

The draw in the hillside gave way to a glade, filled with redoubts, trenches, and tents. The air was thick with the scent of lamb stew. Horses swayed in makeshift pens. Troopers chewed rations under the stars. Scattered among them were familiar faces: Revaj, Lanyan, Chay, and Mabba, with Selwin in her arms. Beside them were mosslings, combing the ground. Mabba burst into tears. She handed Selwin off to Revaj, and jumped into Hilaríon's arms. He kissed the top of the little girl's head.

Necío said, "This is all they saved?"

Bollísh said, "Be thankful they tell me there were no losses."

But there *had* been a loss. Hilaríon said, "About the treasure..."

The general laughed. "*Now* I know you well enough—*all* too well, really. No concern for the others? Instead you ask what I already answered?"

"You also already said it was hopeless."

"Unless we get guns, mounts, and men. Curious to know how we'd get them?" Bollísh ran his blade down Hilaríon's chest and drew out the medallion. "They'd love this."

Hilaríon pulled it away. "You too, I'm sure."

"Not for the world."

"Who, then?" Necío said.

Bollísh's drift was clear. "Mercenaries," Hilaríon said.

"Not mercenaries," Bollísh said. "Partisans like us."

Hilaríon said, "Partisans fight for their dreams, not loot."

"To fight for their dreams, they *need* loot," Bollísh answered.

"But not you," Hilaríon said, "with your pistol that can't even shoot ten yards?"

"Stout hearts fear no soldier of fortune. I won't lay a hand on *that*." He pointed to the medallion. "My wife's love, my son's embrace, my home—all lost in search of it. Not having it ruined everything. Think what having it would bring."

"It would bring treasure."

"I already told you, there is no treasure."

"Never was," Necío said, "or was but now is lost?"

"Most assuredly, never was," Bollísh said.

Hilaríon said, "And only your word as proof."

"You couldn't be more wrong." Bollísh walked off towards a tent and motioned them to follow.

Hilaríon pulled the flap aside. The tent was filled with artifacts. Fish and lizards preserved in gin bobbed in jars on wooden plinths. Ferny terrariums with live salamanders stood on shelves beside harquebus-pistols and mounted skeletons of birds. In the corner was a suit of conquistador armor. Balanced on its arms was a telegraph. "Headquarters or museum?"

"Salvage from Morón," Bollísh said. He unstacked a pile of trunks and flung the largest open. Inside were more curiosities. He spoke as he rifled, "The heirloom legend has always been with us. M'Brae have always heard of the treasure. But by the time you were born, Necío—and, yes, I promise, you are my son—the story of the key had passed into myth. A few of us had heard of it… some of the elders, your mother, and Phellhe. But no one knew how it would work, or even what it would be. So while your mother combed stories and songs, I was busy ransacking the village. That's when I found it." He lifted a canvas bundle, then gently unrolled it along a table. Inside was a metal and glass cylinder, hollow and domed at both ends. "Do you know what this is?"

Necío said, "A bottle?"

"True," Bollísh said. "And it's also the wedge that split M'Brae-dah. See anything unusual?"

Hilaríon held it to his eyes. Bits of cork rattled inside. Bollísh took it back. "Sealed on both ends," Bollísh said. "Nothing gets in or out. And yet, if you look hard enough, you can see bits of rust on the metal and a chalky film on the glass."

"Ships in a bottle," Hilaríon said.

"Correct… and not just ships. The cork's so decayed you can hardly tell. The small bits are boats and the larger ones—"

"The Ones Who Came Before," Necío said, "leading the others' souls to Ahr. I've heard of toys like that."

"Vujoíe have their crucifix, our Ancients had these," Bollísh said, "And it was once filled with water. White, fresh water…

"Months passed. I thought nothing of it. It was early sixteenth century, probably brought by the founders. Otherwise, it was junk. But then something happened I didn't expect." He cleared his throat and pulled up two stools.

Hilaríon rolled his eyes and sat. "No question, he's your father."

Bollísh handed them bowls of stew. He continued, "M'Brae-dah has a twin. Cacoch, it's called, deep in the hills. It was almost impossible to find. And there was hardly anything left of it, except…" He reached in the trunk and pulled out a scroll. He unrolled it on the table, revealing what looked like a gravestone rubbing. Between lines of M'Brae glyphs was a sun over a crosshatched lake. "Necío, can you translate?"

Necío leaned over the parchment. "Elyesh san Vaulx," he said, "son of Christ and the sea."

Bollísh said, "The Ancients liked to hedge their bets. Go on."
Necío, squinting, struggled to read,

"Where milky brine finds sunny sea
A long-awaited tryst shall be."

"Seeing this," Bollísh said, "I remembered the cylinder. I couldn't ignore it any more. The white lake was somehow linked to the treasure. I had to find that lake. Gnath thought I'd gone mad."

Hilaríon said, "Who could blame her?"

"I don't need to tell you what happened next. Your mother accused me of walking out. I told her she wanted me gone, that much more power for her. My men and I struck out on our own. Based on the carving we guessed it'd be north.

"When we got here it was buried. The north bank was all one muddy berm. It took us close to a year to find it, digging every day. My men are loyal and determined, but a strange thing began happening. They started arguing with each other, about who owed who what, what each planned to do with his cut. There'd never been talk of cuts before. These men had fought for each other for years. They'd hacked their way across this land, battled the enemy, buried their comrades. But the closer they seemed to get to the treasure, the less I recognized them. They'd have killed each other before too long. It was just as in M'Brae-dah, but worse. I thought of calling off the search, but they'd have mutinied.

"The door was impenetrable when we found it. I sighed relief but the men wouldn't have it. We blasted it open with dynamite. And that's when we found our greatest gift."

Hilaríon leaned forward. Bollísh, like his son, had a talent for being obtuse. "And?"

"The explosion was enormous, bigger than we'd planned. My men ran shouting from the shaft. Ten were badly injured. I tried to help, but they were fading. That's when I looked up. The blast, you see, was heard in Morón. The townspeople had come running. They carried my men to their clinic. Their doctor and nurses healed their wounds. Not one of my men died. Some of them you met today. If that kind of love isn't treasure enough..."

Hilaríon groaned: more sleight-of-hand. "But you didn't rebury the vault."

"Better a shrine," Bollísh said and looked away.

"How certain are you?" Hilaríon asked. Lies, to the tracker, were always apparent. There was something Bollísh hadn't said.

Necío said, "Why didn't you go back home?"

Bollísh said, "There was nothing to go back to."

Necío cried, "There was me!"

"It wasn't that simple."

"Wasn't it?"

Bollísh now seemed more world-weary grandsire than battle-hardened warrior. "What you say and how you say it gives me comfort I did right."

Necío looked at Hilaríon. "Now I understand how you feel."

"Death by riddles," Hilaríon said.

"I knew you'd come," Bollísh said. "When the war moved west, I knew M'Brae-dah's days were numbered. I set watches on the roads. I hoped you'd find the way. I'd almost... well, I'd even hoped..."

"Gnath's gone," Necío said, "Not quite six months." Bollísh hung his head. Necío said, "Blame yourself."

"Blame her mulish heart. She stayed behind to spite me. But she held all the M'Brae back. We were meant to come to this place."

A rage like Hilaríon had never seen burned in Necío's eyes. "A bottle and a gravestone?" Necío said. "That's how you know we're supposed to be here? Do you even know what you missed?"

"I sent messages back," Bollísh said, "telling Gnath where we were, begging her to come along, that here there was something better than treasure."

Necío shot to his feet. "You mean Gnath knew about this place all along, and that there was no treasure? You didn't tell me? *She* didn't tell me?"

"She told you all you needed to know. It broke my heart that she never followed, but in time I came to understand. Following my footsteps would have meant nothing. The story had to unfold like this. You had to come the way you came."

Necío pouted. "Easy for you."

"There was nothing easy about it," he said. "I couldn't force what had to be learned. And I couldn't go backwards, out of love for my men. We made a life for ourselves in Morón—which brings me back to where I started. That..." He pointed to the medallion. "You want to do some good in this world? Or do you want to be rich?"

Hilaríon said, "You have men with rifles."

"And you still think you're on a treasure hunt."

"I did what Ypriána asked."

"All the more reason to give up the ghost. Ypriána dar Se? The torment that child lived through... who could say what she might be capable of? Better we never have to find out. This is the end of the line, I promise. If I were you, I'd take that medallion, the closest thing to treasure you have, and use it to help the others."

"Or keep what I earned," he said. "Golden days."

"Not in my camp," Bollísh said.

Hilaríon leapt from the stool. The M'Brae and their occult bunk were the biggest mistake of his mistake-ridden life. That he'd lingered this long with them made him fume. He grabbed a machete hanging from a rack, and the twin of Bollísh's dueling-pistol. "That won't be a problem."

He stormed into the night, towards the woods to the west. As he walked, he looked back. Mabba, holding Selwin, was watching him.

lvi.

Aryei unfastened the bandage. What blood remained was dry and black around the greening wound. He laid his hand against Lin's chest. His flesh was warm, his heartbeat racing. He dabbed the wound with medicine, then placed another bandage upon it.

Lin's eyes flickered. "Bring the horses," he muttered. "It's a half-day's ride to the southern sea and mother longs to watch the ships." His apparitions were worsening, fast.

It'd been four days and all of ten minutes since they'd entered Morón. They'd found shelter among the ruins that once housed Lin and the other M'Brae. Jacinda tended the elders. Hetta handed out bits of bread. The children played tag in burlap sacks while their boiled clothing dried. Others lay like routed soldiers. Of the M'Brae and mosslings who'd left the mountains, only twenty had escaped the ambush. The rest, like him, were trammeled, along with Lin's extended kin. Leading them all up the hill had been work, but here at least the air was crisp, the roving gangs below unlikely to harass them.

Light returned to Lin's eyes. He pushed Aryei's hand away and said, "Don't waste it on me. The wound's too deep."

Aryei remembered what he'd been told. Hilaríon's brush with Phellhe in Golgaj had already become the stuff of legend. "Think if Phellhe hadn't done the same for Hilaríon."

"Their work was just beginning," Lin said, "but mine... Twenty thousand and six days is a good enough life for anyone."

Aryei finished tying the bandage. "Don't despair," he said with feigned cheer. There had to be *something* to cling to. "The Armorican filibuster you said was coming?"

Lin said, "It would've come by now."

"But you said—"

"Where facts flee, rumors dare."

"Then *he'll* come," Aryei said, "I just know."

"Your Hilaríon?"

"He always comes."

"For treasure."

"For *us*," Aryei said. He hesitated, then added, "First."

Lin shivered. "And if he thinks there is no treasure?"

This wasn't time for squabbling. "He'd still come. The treasure's real."

"You've seen it?"

Aryei looked away.

"How will you know when you've found it?" Lin said.

He tugged at his satchel, remembering Hilaríon's sunny words, collecting fake rubies in the mountains. "When this overflows."

Lin's shivers turned to tremors. The other M'Brae barely raised their heads. Death had lost its novelty. "What if it's always been with you? You just needed to see in a different light."

Aryei looked around the camp. Graciela chattered with mosslings. Back home, she'd been a strange, shunned mute, but here she was a songstress. The mosslings no longer scraped for jewels, nor kept silent, to themselves. Chropher chased the children, laughing. He'd once tormented youths like this, but here he was a brother.

In the auburn glass of the medicine bottle, Aryei saw his own reflection. He'd once been a whelp, scared of his shadow. He'd cowered from the bigger boys. He'd fallen fast for Lux's wiles. But in that, he'd learned the troglodytes were blind and how to hold them off. He'd earned his people's respect that day, Hilaríon's most of all. No loot yet overflowed his pouch. But Lin's words still rang true.

Lin pulled a package from his cloak. "This belonged to my son," he said. "I had it from my father, and all the way back to the first of M'Brae-dah." He handed it to Aryei. "All your answers are in here."

Aryei unwrapped the package. Inside was an antique copper box. Its casing was well-worn and smooth, its lid shaped like Ypriána's medallion. "How can answers be in here?"

But Lin did not answer. Lin was dead.

A chill breeze swirled about the camp. Aryei thought of M'Brae-dah. He hadn't thought about his home, much less missed its rustic charms. The hillsides would be drenched with rain, the drab woods filled with finches, sojourners from the icy north like jewels amidst the pines. It seemed a weary world away, obscured now by the mists of time.

He pinched the rusty box lid. It squeaked and inched ajar. He couldn't see anything inside. He squeezed until it groaned open. A tinny melody chimed out. It was a music box.

Now, the people turned their heads. One by one, their faces changed from dour to determined. The elders took the others' hands. As if upon conductor's cue, they raised their voices fast as one, entwined with the metallic chords.

"Our sires' yawning chasm spreads
Parched our glories, myths untold
Doubt devours my wasted heart
Prayers unanswered, blood turned cold
We'll be one in Ahr…"

The world and all its pains fell away. The song was magical. It filled the hollow void of night and swathed the prison camp in hope. Aryei raised his voice with theirs, and prayed Hilaríon would hear.

lvii.

Dusk found Hilaríon submerged in thought. Chatter from Bollísh's partisan camp danced like bells among the trees, reminding him how close they were, even as he was worlds away. Everything was worlds away. His mind was a storm of questions.

What was left of the man he thought he'd been was coming undone in front of his eyes. He was wearing a stranger's boots. His hands, cracked and red, were unrecognizable. The scent of his cloak was a poignant bouquet: ash from M'Brae-dah, muck from the swamp, sulphur from the Trocha. His hilldevil brand was a rubbery scar. Most all he'd been was left behind, and yet the piece stood incomplete. Ypriána had turned, then stolen away, taking the grand design with her. He was the rump of a stunted vision. But it wasn't he who'd paid the price, just as the Jaeger had told him. Wresh lay in a shallow grave, Fenn was drowned and Sunovín eaten. Phellhe, who'd saved his life twice-over, moldered on the bed of a bright mountain lake. He'd saved one race, destroyed one more, and restored another's pilfered glory. Ypriána had turned from her destiny through some great sin of his. What she'd given, he'd taken away. The people were trammeled inside Morón. The chances they'd survive were grim. Then the M'Brae would be extinct. He should never have started down this road. All he'd found for himself were more eyes.

"Rain and mud," Hilaríon said. Necío sat beside him. "We were badly outnumbered, but we had a plan. We'd play to their pride, let them think we were running. So we harried them for days. We shot at their column as they marched up the mountain, headed for Cacarajícara. We dug in halfway up the slopes, then dug more trenches at the summit. We waited in the lower trenches. By the time they got to where we were, they were red with anger. But I was the one full of pride.

"I was farthest to the left, anchored on one side to the south hill but otherwise in the air. The order came to feign retreat, withdraw to the heights by darkness to lead the enemy into a trap. Only I saw something different—a chance to turn the Butcher's flank, to roll up his right and get to his back. I would be a hero, like the Taíno leader Guamá, whose name I'd revered as a boy. So as the other Mambíses withdrew, I ordered my legion to charge downhill. Only I hadn't bothered to reconnoiter. If I had, I'd have known about the mud.

"It had rained for days. The water had run off the hill to the slope, and turned it into glue. The slope was a perfect killing field. It should have been the enemy's. Instead, it was my own.

"Lux led the charge—she was brave that day. I can't blame her for her bitterness. It should have been me leading, but I hung in the rear. By the time I realized what I'd done, they'd already been overrun, shot to ribbons by Mauser fire, or spitted on bayonets. They looked to me... for aid, for an order, even for just a rallying cry to know their deaths would mean something.

"I'd already turned. With a ghost of a glimpse I peeked back behind. They were watching me, every one. Then the jaegers drew their knives. I could hear my Mambíses, begging, then screaming... I've been running ever since that day. The treasure would make it right, I thought. I tried to outrun all of it. But what the jaegers did to me, I've done to all of you." He rose and patted the medallion. "It's best this way, for everyone."

Necío said, "Ypriána will find you."

Hilarión looked away. "I hope."

Rustling footsteps came from the bramble. Bollísh stepped from the trees. He looked Hilarión up and down. "So much for golden days."

Hilarión said, "Try back in five minutes."

"Someone's been sneaking into camp at night, feeding the infant, singing him to sleep. Any idea who that might be?"

"Saint Philomena?" Hilarión said.

Bollísh laughed. "What if I told you the treasure was real?"

"You already said it wasn't."

"That was before I knew. Both of you, follow me. I promise it'll be worthwhile."

The purple dusk gave way to night. He led them through the woods. The chorus of katydids kept time with their footsteps. The woods expired at the beach. Before them was the spit. Bollísh bowed. "After you."

The heliconias were still. The hummingbirds had gone to sleep. The statues, standing hand-in-hand, seemed less marble than living flesh, welcoming nightfall. He led them to a spiral stair, then motioned them to climb. It opened to a balcony, overlooking the sculpture garden.

The night sky was resplendent. Each star shone in its very own aspect, no two alike, far beyond numbering. From the east came the flash of the Leonid meteors, tumbling through the vastness of space, ending their timeless journeys in flame. The breeze still held a hint of salt, the tempting kiss of the sea and its wiles, so tantalizingly near. In the distance glowed the lights of Morón, hiding its murderous resolve beneath a veil of baby-blue. Life, and the earth, seemed to hold perfectly still, poised on the brink of some grand revelation.

"We're all rich men, Hilaríon," Bollísh said, "and you are most of all."

"By and by," Hilaríon said.

"That's what the Hollow Man said," Bollísh said, "the hollow, haunted man. *I've nothing but ghosts of the men I've killed, of gifts not used, of rights made wrong, but by and by I'll be rich.*"

"Ghosts and regrets?" Hilaríon said. The eyes in his mind glowed warm.

Bollísh said, "He had nothing to lose, everything to gain. He went off after the treasure. He knew he'd someday find the prize."

Bollísh's voice was soothing, like a honeyed cradlesong. The journey—*Hilaríon's* own journey—had to mean something. Bollísh's words had struck the mark. Hilaríon needed to hear what came next. "I'm listening."

"Good," Bollísh said. "The Hollow Man listened, too, to the naysayers, trying to warn him away. *It's just a myth*, they said, but he knew better. He set out alone in search of the treasure. In time, others followed. In time, they came to trust him. He knew he'd someday find the prize.

"The Hollow Man asked questions. At first he asked about the treasure, what it might be and where. But in time he came to ask for the asking. He came to learn more than he'd thought. He came to love learning itself. He knew he'd someday find the prize.

"The Hollow Man made many foes. He overcame all, at a terrible price. His followers began to doubt, then abandon him. Most were just weary of endless searching, but some lost faith, and called him a fraud. He grew old, and weak, and tired. And still, he knew, he'd someday find the prize.

"The Hollow Man came to the end of his life. He was poor, and broken, and alone. He made ready for his death. With his last remaining strength, he did what every M'Brae must. He raised his voice in song. He had to for himself, you see. He was alone. But because of all this man had seen, and because of all the trials he'd passed, and because of all the things he'd learned, he could sing with all the voices of earth. And the madrigal he sang was so beautiful, The Ones Who Came Before appeared to pay him final homage."

"But this great honor meant nothing to him. He boiled with rage at such a fruitless life. He demanded to know why he'd found no treasure, having battled and bested the quest's every turn. He cursed The Ones Who Came Before. He called Them cheats and liars, as he himself had come to be called. He defied Them to admit, at last, the treasure was just a myth."

Hilarion sighed. The story had crossed into absurdity. He'd wasted precious minutes. "Well, did they?"

The wind picked up, rustling the trees, painting ripples across the lake. Bollish said, "Listen. What do you hear?"

"Katydids and frogs."

"Listen harder."

Hilarion lent his ear. Past the waters and trees, beyond the stubby bare-topped hills, across the brown and shunted plain, a hint of a sound drifted in on the breeze. It started in a whisper, then rose to a hum, then altogether swelled and took flight. Inside Morón, the M'Brae were singing. Their seraph voices filled the night, weaving a tapestry of sound. The song was dour yet joyous at once, uplifting in its exuberance, haunting in its pain. It was the wan madrigal as he'd never heard sung. Its magic beggared all belief.

"And The Ones Who Came Before bade him turn," Bollísh said, "and look back over the road he'd traveled. And from where he stood, he could see that road, stretching all the way back to the day he took his very first step. And from where he stood, he could see the people—those who'd followed and those who'd refused, those who'd turned away and even those who'd turned upon him—happy and healthy, among their children, their minds and lips overflowing with questions. And in his final moments, the man understood what his life had been for. The man understood what the treasure had been. And he went to his rest a truly free man—free and hollow no longer."

The chorus soared to its crescendo, then faded into silence. All, again, was still.

"Ghouls and attercops?" Bollísh said. "Listen to them now. You did that, Hilaríon. Isn't that treasure enough?"

Necío clasped Hilaríon's shoulder. Standing beside his lordly father, for the first time Hilaríon saw the resemblance. "In Bollísh's camp were minstrels," Necío said. "Before they departed they put on a play. I usually can't sit still very long. But something was different this time.

"The play told the story of a king, great in his time but now in old age, dividing his kingdom among his three daughters. The first two strut and puff about, proclaiming everlasting love. But the third, who loves him, tells the truth. She says she loves her husband more than he. This, the King doesn't want to hear. He takes her slice of the kingdom away and gives it to the other two. Needless to say, tragedy falls. It might have been avoided.

"But the king, you see, had a friend—in the end his only friend. This friend was neither royal nor noble, no more than a low-born clown. Yet he spoke the truth when the king wouldn't hear, but when most he needed to. When all the flattering courtiers bowed and filled the king's ears with lies, this friend warned the king of dangers to come, brought by his own insufferable vanity. And when the king had divided his kingdom, and when his daughters had turned him away and out into the storm, who but this one and only friend stood by the broken king's side?"

Necío embraced Hilarión. "I know what my father says is true. I know who you are because I know who *I* am. All my life I never knew. I thought my mother had marked me for shame, giving me a spiteful name. *When the steeples are drenched and the cocks drowned away*—those were the words of the king as he raged in the storm. She'd hidden my destiny in plain sight, for me to discover it when it was time.

"The name of the friend was the Fool. No more than a humble jester, he held a mirror up to the king and showed him his misdeeds. But when those misdeeds bore fruit, he refused to forsake the king. He stood by his side to his bitter downfall. *A Steeled Elect whose heart is true.* I know now what that means."

"You can still make it right," Bollísh said. "There is a plan to save them all. You can still deliver a treasure, Hilarión. You can see that your people live." He held out his hand.

His people? The words pierced. But Hilarión's people they'd become.

He thought of his aunt. She'd taught him to track but also to care. When they'd buried Paola together, even in her grief, she'd smiled. He'd loved the child, too, she knew. She'd told him she was glad for him, that his education was complete, that someday he would do much good because he'd tasted loss.

His people? He thought of the Mambíses, Grijalva, and Montez. Searching for something, he'd found them, each. For a time, the world made sense. For a time, there was always something in reach; he'd never have to look behind or stare off longingly into the sunset. But fears unanswered must someday be tamed. One he betrayed, the others defied, and in the end the guilt was the same. The eyes never let him forget what he'd done. They'd made him human, all along, for monsters see no eyes.

His people? He thought of Phellhe. He'd tricked Phellhe into spilling his secrets. But Phellhe had been running from fires ere Hilaríon ever saw eyes. Phellhe had clutched his people tight. Yet, Phellhe had never left their side.

His people? He thought of Necío. He'd shunned the gangling bore from the first, but Necío had not conformed. He *had* held a mirror to his vice. He *had* stood steadfast at his side. In the bottomless well of his prolific mind, *he* had saved the M'Brae by keeping alive their lore. Carrying a nation's flame, he'd held Hilaríon highest of all.

His people? He thought of the M'Brae themselves. From desperate dash across the downs, to tunnels underground, he'd stayed. Medallion in hand, Wresh underfoot, he could have escaped, but he didn't. Medallion in hand, Ypriána taken, he could have made his getaway. Medallion in hand, Aryei kidnapped, he could have taken his leave but he'd stood. He'd pined aloud for golden days but lingered on in dark ones. Even now he'd refused to depart before Bollísh had spoken his piece. Even now he was searching for reasons to stay. He'd ever been searching for reasons to stay.

His people? He thought, at last, of Ypriána. Her treachery had been his grace, her perfidy his salvation. She'd warned him away from seeking a prize but promised him a treasure. She'd promised to return to him, yet chided when he'd fulfilled her pledge. She'd hung a medallion around his neck, then tried to kill him for it. And yet she'd saved his life. The medallion was a torch, she'd said; the treasure so much more than a prize. She'd been more right than she'd ever know. The Vexing Heirloom had delivered. The journey was its own destination, the seekers the treasure unto themselves.

He'd be Ypriána now. He'd be what she should have been.

The eyes took sudden flame, then vanished. He inhaled lustily. He lifted the medallion off of his neck and gave it one last look. It was but a hunk of metal now. He lobbed it towards Bollísh.

Ypriána plucked it from the air.

lviii.

Bollísh reached for his pistol. A chorus of hammers cocked from the spit below. A squad of Mambíses surrounded the pergola, rifles trained upwards. Hilaríon didn't know whether to grimace or blush. His wits tossed adrift at the sight of Ypriána. All he could wheeze was, "I offered my hand."

"I did better," a woman's voice said. Ypriána stepped aside. Behind her, atop the spiral stairs, stood Lux. Her coat and trousers, once smart, were frayed.

"I had no idea, Guamá," Ypriána said. "If I'd known what they'd have paid for you, alive…"

"Then we'd all be dead," Necío said.

She rubbed her eyes. "Yes, about all of you…"

Hilaríon said, "Leave them out of this."

She pointed to the shoreline. Just outside the stand of trees, a Mambí company stood in formation. Among them were Bollísh's men, with the M'Brae and mosslings saved during the ambush. Their hands were bound with rope. "They were in longer than us," she said. "This is for their good. They just don't know it yet."

Lux prodded all three of them down the stairway. She snatched the pistols from them as they passed. Mambíses took them by their arms. Ypriána raised a torch overhead and led them into the vault below. "There is no treasure," Bollísh said as the Mambíses pushed them to their knees.

Ypriána strode to the far wall. "Moment of truth," she said.

Bollísh repeated, "There *is no* treasure."

"Come now, generalissimo," she said. "We both know that's not true." She pushed the tapestry aside. Behind it was a keyhole. She fitted the medallion-key. The thrum of a lock disengaging clanked. She threw aside four more tapestries, releasing four more locks with the key, until she came to the final one. "Perfect number six," she said. She turned the key inside it.

The sound of rushing water hissed. The vault filled with steam. From the walls came a trickle of white lake water. It filled the vault to ankle-height among the floor lumps, with only a few crowns poking above, then stopped. The gold coin shimmered just at the surface.

Hilarión remembered the gold coin's inscription. *But fortune overflows the vault... When Vexing Heirloom's secret told.* How could he have missed it?

The vault was a terrain map of the ocean floor.

The mist dissipated. Ypriána pointed to the coin. "We'll find the treasure on that quay, one league off the northern coast, it looks." She turned to Lux. "Get boats."

Lux gasped, "Boats?"

"Squeamish already?" she said. "Find boats. We'll stop en route."

"En route where?" Hilarión said.

"Oriente, by safest route. A fresh start for us. For you... well, I've washed my hands."

"One chance at your loot," Lux said, "then eastbound with speed."

Necío studied the terrain map intensely. Hilarión glared at Bollísh and said, "What else haven't you told me?"

Bollísh said, "Better I hadn't. If you only knew..."

"Spare me the sermon. It was at your lying fingertips."

The Mambíses pulled them to their feet. The general whispered, "Just be ready."

"What—?"

"Let her find it!" Bollísh said aloud. "In her hands, it's useless, same as she is."

Ypriána stopped in place. Bollísh said, louder, "How crushing the emptiness had to be. Blaish and Ronto groomed for greatness, the little queen curling up with dogs..."

Hilarión said, "What are you doing?" Bollísh gave a subtle head-bob. In the pools, strings of bubbles were starting to form. A crack was snaking through the floor underwater. Same as the observatory, the vault was rigged to self-destruct.

"One mouth too many, Mellín, her father, would say," Bollísh said, louder still. "But one moonless night in M'Brae-dah, when the river is high—"

"Stop that," Ypriána said. Pain lay flush across her face.

"Yeah, that's enough," Hilaríon added.

"Just as her kin used to say," Bollísh said. "Enough... two boys are enough. An heir and a spare. No room, no need for a—"

"Shut up!" Ypriána's nostrils flared.

The streams of bubbles intensified, the water line receding. A faint creaking sound, like wooden beams straining, groaned in the waterlogged air. The floor was about to collapse.

Hilaríon pushed Necío towards the doorway. Ypriána took a step. Hilaríon raised his arm to stop her. Bollísh pushed his arm away. "On coattails since the day you were born," Bollísh said. "Bad enough not being the elect, but not even being the steel—"

"*Shut up!*" With a primal scream, she rushed.

Hilaríon lunged to stop her. "Don't!"

The ceiling cracked. The floor splintered. The Mambíses fell through the darkness below. Necío flung himself through the doors, grabbing Lux from the brink as he fell. Hilaríon hurled his body aside and clung to the threshold, above the abyss. Bollísh and Ypriána did the same. For an instant, above, the sequined sky glistened. Necío cried out, "Look!"

From the ceiling, a deluge of soil, flowers, and stones poured inside. On its heels gushed a cascade of milky lake water. Hilaríon took Necío's arms and clambered through the doorframe. The vault had turned a monstrous sinkhole. Ypriána and Bollísh pulled themselves standing, on the opposite side of the hole.

The cascade funneled into a pillar. The edges of the sinkhole flaked, save for a dwindling rim of stone. Hilaríon grabbed a driftwood branch. Across the hole, Bollísh and Ypriána grappled, as the rim beneath their feet crumbled away. "What are you waiting for?" Bollísh cried to Hilaríon. "Go!"

At the far left, the force of the cascade was weakest, the rim still firm enough to pass. "Go on!" Bollísh cried again. "Now!"

Stones from the walls of the crumbling shrine hurtled into the sinkhole, nibbling against the rim as they fell. Hilarión took a step from the doorframe. Lux grabbed him and said, "I need you."

He held the branch out to her. "Then hold tight," he said.

He stepped on the ledge with his back to the wall. He gripped the branch in his right, pulling himself along with his left. He inched his way forward, braced by Lux and she by Necío, wedged inside the doorframe. Stones crashed about his face. The flow where he stood was gaining speed. He could neither see through nor hear over it.

He thrust his hand inside the stream. The force of the water drove it down. He pushed back, crying, "Take my hand!"

Nothing.

The dark blotted all. He shouted, louder, "Take it!" There was but the roar of water. He took another step—

"Don't!" Lux held him.

The spout and sinkhole were relentless, like a malevolent, Biblical flood. In its veil, he could see Chay and Fenn drowning—old Wresh, too, bleeding out. He could see Ypriána's leering eyes as he clung to the cliff by his bare fingertips. But he'd left those vistas behind. A bolder world was his to mold. He let go of the branch he'd extended to Lux and reached for Ypriána. "Take my—"

"Many thanks," Ypriána said, clasping his wrist, emerging from the waters.

He pulled her from the flood. Her cheek and lips brushed past his own. He guided her along the wall, then led her hand to Lux's. The ledge flaked further. Bollísh was still in mortal danger. Lux said, "Leave the old man."

Hilarión pressed his back to the wall. The rock underfoot was all but gone. Ahead, the general strained for his hand. "Here!" Hilarión called, reaching. His fingers brushed against Bollísh's.

The spout belched. The sinkhole widened. Lux cried, "There's no time!"

Hilarión stretched to the edge of his sinew. He could see resignation in Bollísh's eyes. The sinkhole widened. Hilarión took the general's hand, hoisting him—

The ledge crumbled. Bollísh slipped from Hilaríon's grasp and disappeared into the roiling flood.

Lux pulled Hilaríon away. In a flash and blur of flesh and stone, the others stuffed him through the door and dragged him up the crumbling stairs. Above and behind him, the ceiling collapsed. All that remained of the shrine was mud and the odd, drifting petals of heliconias.

They clambered ashore. The Mambíses were waiting. The gurgles and slurps of the cascade slowed. The waterline leveled off. The underground chasm had guzzled its fill, taking Bollísh and his dreams with it. Hilaríon crawled to Necío's side. "I'm sorry about your father."

Necío stared into the distance. The pergola's spires, like old fish bones, jutted from the now-muddy lake. "He stopped being my father a long time ago. But for a moment, at least, he got to be yours."

The Mambíses trained rifle and shotgun upon them. Lux wrung silt from her hair. The thunder of gunfire off in the distance boomed above the rasping waters and chatter of M'Brae prisoners. "Filibuster's come," Ypriána said.

Lux said, "My men will be moving on Morón now. I'll need indemnity." She took a damp rag from one of her men and handed it to Ypriána. "If you please."

Ypriána knelt. "Hilaríon, you've done more than you'll know. I'll only be needing you once more. Until then..." She gently kissed him on the lips, then smothered the rag against his face.

The world spun fast, then swirled, then waned. Noxious vapors off the rag ripped him from his senses. He drifted off into the ether, same as in the woodland glade where she'd first laid him low. And as he swooned, he heard her voice say, "One treasure for another."

lix.

A salty whiff of ocean wind dispelled the noxious vapors. The drugs were wearing off. Hilarión slowly opened his eyes. He was slumped in the aft of a small wooden pram, rowed by Mambí oarsmen. Below them lay their shotgun and rifle. His wrists were bound with anchor rope. Necío hunched in the bow, staring aft. Ypriána and Lux flanked the oarsmen. "We should have seen it by now," Ypriána said.

Lux pointed. "Past the fog."

The horizons were obscured by mist. He'd lost all sense of direction. But behind the ashen wall of cloud, a gleam of sunlight belied high noon. He guessed he'd been asleep for hours.

He craned his neck. Fully thirty open boats, all of various shapes and sizes, trundled on the waves all around, each filled to its gunwales with M'Brae. He recognized some of Bollísh's men, beside his own, now freed from Morón. He could still see Bollísh's terrified eyes, and yet, he felt no guilt. He'd done everything he could. He remembered the vault's terrain-map and the coin that marked their elusive goal. "Dead-reckoning the open sea?" he said. "You might as well try threading a needle from a mile away in the dark."

Ypriána said nothing. She'd let him live while he was useful. Now, he was worth too much to kill. He said, "It'd be easier—"

"Then it wouldn't be treasure."

"Then empty your pockets, everyone. This galleon's about to get cramped."

Ypriána eyed where Hilarión sat and said, "I know where there's space."

"None of that," Lux said. "Oriente's not far."

"Then it's off to the Bronze Titan for me," he said.

Lux said, "The Bronze Titan's dead. Turns out, the Trocha has no exposed flank." She blessed herself with the sign of the cross. "Well, Cuba Libre, anyway. There are plenty of others who still prize your scalp."

Hilarión slouched down the spine of the pram. Why rage away his final days? The world he'd believed in was never to be. The Poet, the Bronze Titan, and his aunt were dead, their vision burned to ashes. This, instead, was a wasteland of intrigue, where strivers like the Butcher and Lux feathered their nests and demanded you thank them. "Cuba Libre," he echoed.

Lux said, "We've arrived."

The sea spread fast in all directions. Gulls and petrels wheeled overhead. There was no sign of dry land anywhere. Ypriána looked around and said, "This can't be right."

"Northeast from the coast, through the cluster of quays, then due north on the open sea," Necío said. "I studied the map and kept heed, too."

"Circling gulls and breakers," Hilarión said. "We're over a sandbar." The gray sky obscured the light. But he could swear there was something massive below, looming large out from the darkness.

The tendrils of fog spread, engulfing the boats. "Halt the others," Ypriána said.

"Like dancing fuck I will," Lux said. "We make for Oriente, now."

"Since when is that a fair exchange?"

"Since I left dry land."

A hint of panic twisted Ypriána's face. "I just need time."

"What you need is to come to your senses," Lux said. "There's nothing here. You've all been had." She nodded to the oarsmen. "Row."

The oarsmen pulled their oars. A tern hung motionless overhead, borne upon the warm updrafts. The choppy water shrunk to calm. The women, like she-wolves, glared at each other. The world seemed poised on a knife-edge—

Ypriána lunged at the weapons, grabbing only the shotgun. Lux raised the rifle at Ypriána. Ypriána raised the shotgun at Lux. "One treasure for another," Ypriána said. She spun around and leveled the rifle into Hilarión's face.

He stared down the barrel, nonplussed. He was a dead man by hers or some other's hand. Necío wheezed a sigh of ennui. They'd all grown accustomed to brushes with death.

Lux said, "Thirty open boats? You have no time. They'll find us."

"I came this far."

"You can come back."

"Take no chances." She charged the lever. "Grab whatever you can. Isn't that right, hilldevil?"

He pointed into the fog. "The others are drifting away."

Lux pushed the muzzle into the small of Ypriána's back. "Half a woman, living or dead. Whole's more useful. Stand down."

Ypriána heaved forlornly. "You're right," she said, "whole *is* more useful." She lowered the shotgun.

Lux said, "I knew you'd—"

Boom!

A crunch of snapping wood rang out. Ypriána had fired into the hull. She charged the handle and fired again. A hail of splinters filled the air. The pram split in two. Lux tumbled backwards. The oarsmen leapt into the water. The aft sped away. The bow bobbed like a dead fish's head. Ypriána dove below the waves.

Hilaríon sank into the brine. It flooded his mouth and nose. He thrashed with bound hands back to the surface. Beside him popped a barrage of bubbles. Necío was drowning.

Hilaríon railed at the oarsmen, "Help!"

They swam towards Necío. Lux said, "Save the traitor."

The oarsmen changed direction. Hilaríon flipped onto his back and kicked out of their grip. He dove beneath Necío and arched his back, pushing his friend above the waves.

Ypriána surfaced. "It's down there," she said in a euphoric voice, then dove seal-like back below.

Necío hacked the brine from his lungs. Hilaríon lurched along to the bow. Already the others had clung to its keel. Necío grabbed the gunwale. Hilaríon kicked to the serrated end. The wood was a jawline of jagged spikes. He hooked the rope binding his wrists on one of them.

Lux shouted for another boat. "Help!" she cried. "Come here!" But the boats were invisible through the fog.

Ypriána breached again. "I see it," she said, then sped back down.

Hilarión rasped his wrists down the spike. The old rope frayed. He broke his bindings, then untied Necío. Lux screamed, "*Over here!*" A boat loomed from the vapors.

Ypriána surfaced a third time. She said, "It's glorious," then just as quickly dove again.

The fog began to dissipate. Shafts of sunlight tinged the waves. Something was sprawled wide beneath them, underwater. Lux called to the boat, "Hurry up!"

Hilarión said, "We're not leaving her."

"Go to hell, capitán," Lux said. "Serves you right for growing a soul."

The boat drew closer, gathering speed. He didn't recognize its shape. "Just give me—"

"No." She motioned the oarsmen to seize him.

Ypriána surfaced. Hilarión let go of the bow and swam to where she treaded. She panted, "I can get it."

"I know you can," he said.

From the fog hissed a voice, "¡Allí están... *allí están!*"

Lux said to the oarsmen, "Whose voice is *that?*"

Ypriána said, "We came for this."

"But not *like* this," Hilarión said.

"Just one more try." She flipped. He grabbed her by her waist. Her strength was almost overpowering. But he would not yield her to the sea.

The call came again. "¡Allí están... *allí están!*"

The last wisps of the fog took flight. The sun shone overhead. To the north were the motley M'Brae skiffs, drifting aimlessly, disoriented. From the south, from the veil, a new craft emerged—then another, and then many more.

"¡Allí están... *allí están!*" This time, Hilarión recognized the voice.

Lux waved her arms. "Here! Over here! Over... here..."

Her voice dropped off. Her face turned stone. A single rifle-crack rang out. Her head snapped backwards. Her body sank. The sun, like warning signal-fires, glinted off Mauser barrels.

The boats were gun-scows. In command, saber drawn, was the demonic Gray Jaeger.

lx.

Mauser fire raked the sea. The two Mambí oarsmen crumpled, dead. Hilaríon lunged behind the bow and pulled Ypriána and Necío with him, then steered into enfilading gunfire.

Wave after hot, metallic wave of balls swept through the boats. The M'Brae cringed beneath the gunwales, adults pressing children low. Bullets crunching into wood thrummed a grisly drumline. The screams of the wounded wailed above the jaegers' ghoulish taunts.

"¡Tiburones hambrientos, es hora de comer!"

The Gray Jaeger raised his arm. His flagship wheeled a wide broadside and belched a rolling volley of gunfire. Ypriána cracked a shank of wood. Hilaríon grabbed her. "What are you doing?"

"Taking the serpent's head," she said. She clenched it in her teeth and arched to dive—

Another volley broke the air. Blood sprayed into Hilaríon's face. The force of the balls spilled the bow keel-up and leveled Ypriána. The shank dropped from her mouth. The water bled a menacing red. "Guamá?" she gasped, then withered.

He settled beside her in the bow. He pulled her face against his own and laid his cheek to hers. Life still flickered in her eyes, but fast exsanguinating.

Necío pushed both their heads low. Another salvo slammed the air. The screams around them intensified. The M'Brae skiffs were floundering, the jaegers' scows closing in. There was no place to flee to, or hide. There was no prayer of fighting back. The darkest of hours had fallen at last, at the hand of the Gray Jaeger.

Yet, amidst the pandemonium, a thought sprung to life in Hilaríon's mind, and fast began to grow. The disparate threads began to fuse. A tapestry took shape.

"A ruthless path through living earth
A Steeled Elect whose heart is true
A timeless hymn divined at last
Ere all is lost, a hope for you."

What all along Phellhe had scorned as myth, he'd saved his dying breath to reveal. And all of it had come to pass.

The journey had forged the M'Brae anew and brought them all together. No longer mewling, quivering quails, tomorrow was theirs for the taking. *A ruthless path through living earth.* Bollísh had been right.

The wan madrigal was more than a dirge. When bold M'Brae voices intertwined, there was truly magic in its chords, enough to draw wonders out of the sea. *A timeless hymn divined at last.* Necío had been right.

The Steeled Elect, and no one else, could bring about the treasure. That fate was unavoidable. *A Steeled Elect whose heart is true.* But Ypriána had been wrong. They'd all been very wrong.

It had ever been before him. It lay, resplendent, before him now. It had taken the heirloom's blistering crucible to make him see the truth.

Ere all is lost, a hope for you.

The people were the Steeled Elect. And just as Necío had said, only a wonder drawn from the sea could save them from the jaegers.

He clambered up the bow. The Gray Jaeger raised his fist in cease-fire. Hilarión held out empty hands. Weapons were useless here, like parasols in a tempest. He looked his people over. Their eyes bore in him the same confidence as ever they'd from the start.

The Jaeger glowered through him. Hilarión shouted, *"Cerca!"* He inhaled from the pit of his lungs and cried, "Our sires' yawning chasm spreads!"

The waves engulfed his weakened voice. Again, he tried, "Our sires' yawning chasm spreads!"

The jaegers in the scows held still. They watched with disbelief. Some pointed his way, as if he were mad. But not one spoke a word. He closed his eyes and cried aloud, *"Our sires' yawning chasm—"*

A lone Mauser cracked. He felt a nip. He opened his eyes as the nip turned a sting and then a searing pain. The Gray Jaeger stood alone, a smoking Mauser in his hands.

Blood ran down Hilaríon's leg. A red stain blossomed in his shirt. The cries of petrels overhead seemed a seraphs' choir, calling him to lands beyond. He steadied his legs and let go a wail, *"Our sires'—!"*

Another crack rang. A second bite of pain burst. It flared white-hot for an instant, then simmered into numbness. Hilaríon clutched his mangled flank, then stretched his body tall again. *"Our sires'... yawning... chasm..."*

A third shot cracked. His legs gave way. He withered to his knees. Strength drained from his arms. Sight fled from his eyes. This was far worse than Grijalva's bite, so long ago it seemed. Life was seeping from his breast. But there'd be no forsaking the M'Brae. They were his own people.

He shook his head and braced himself, then rose back to his feet. The sea's breeze wafted through his hair, dousing the heat of his blistering brow. The Gray Jaeger cocked his Mauser.

Hilaríon raised his arms aloft. He'd been born to die this way. *"Our sires' yawning chasm—"*

"Spreads!" The people sang,

> "...Parched our glories, myths untold
> Doubt devours my wasted heart
> Prayers unanswered, blood turned cold
> We'll be one in Ahr!"

The jaegers and their leader gaped. The M'Brae roared, a wall of sound,

> "Envoys of a better land
> In benthic depths, our sires' cry
> Leads me, weary wand'rer, on
> Roused my wonder, by and by
> We'll be one in Ahr!"

The M'Brae rose. Boat-mates took each other's hands. Hilarío n took Necío's, and cradled Ypriána's head. The chorus rolled across the swells, as if the sea had come to life,

> "My journey's end, my fathers' fount
> Oft-rememb'red, never known
> A flame rekindled 'midst the dark
> To hold, to have in grace alone
> We'll be one in Ahr!"

The chorus swelled to crescendo, then faded. Only the whispering waves dared speak as they lapped the edges of the boats.

The awe dropped from the jaegers' eyes. They broke into mutters of morbid glee and raised their gleaming weapons. Hilarío n called to the M'Brae, "Stand fast!" Beneath their flimsy wooden boats, the waves began to tremble.

The jaegers' scows sped closer. Hilarío n stood defiant. The sea below him rolled and pitched, tossing upright M'Brae down; wave upon briny, robust wave, until they could no longer stand. Still, the enemy hurtled near, gaining speed and closing. Necío covered his eyes. The mercurial ocean heaved once more. The jaegers cocked their rifles. Hilarío n said, "A miracle…"

The Gray Jaeger beamed with malevolent glee, looming tall above his gunmen, like a devil amidst imps. He looked at Hilarío n with transfixing eyes and raised a bony finger. "*Lejos!*" he cried, and swung his arm high, warning his men to ready to fire. He leered and screeched in his most vengeful voice, "¡*Abran fuego*—!"

A blue mass rose beneath the Jaeger's scow and shivered it to pieces. All about the M'Brae boats, leviathans breached the waves. Their bodies were like hulks of ships, their voices mighty trumpets. They raised their flukes and smashed the scows. The jaegers thrashed in roiling sea. Bellowing as demon bulls, the leviathans dragged them under. Between gratitude and disbelief, Hilarío n looked on. They were the stuff of myth made flesh, their brethren from a living lore, the miracle drawn from the sea.

The Ones Who Came Before.

The jaegers sank. The timbers of their scows tossed about. A tattered cloak adrift in foam was all that remained of the Gray Jaeger.

The leviathans sprayed and wheeled to the north. Hilaríon crumpled down the bow, beside Ypriána. Their blood mingled with the breath of the sea. "Follow them," he said.

Necío said, "To where?"

Hilaríon gulped a stunted breath, the last he'd ever taste, he felt sure. "To Ahr," he said. "The treasure is Ahr."

lxi.

Gaius pitched his spade through the sand, keeping time to the toss of the ocean. The mosquitoes whined about his face like small, bloodthirsty dragons. This land was wild and relentless, Flagler's railroad all the more. By day, the Rat's Mouth seemed like bliss. The Mooncussers, fortunately, kept to the shadows. By sunlight he was profitable: he could count on at least token safeguards. But nightfall never failed to remind him just how off the map he was. By dark, it was every man for himself.

A crisp wind wafted off the sea, rustling palmetto fronds. The seaside sparrows trilled their notes, like wandering musicians. For a moment life seemed filled with promise, a gift for unwrapping anew each day. He could settle here, expenses paid, work for the railroad then grow his own citrus. What tied him to the old world? Bluefield, West Virginia was a relic, just as he, in Bluefield, would ever be a relic. Here, he could be anyone. There were many reasons to make the leap, but still one big one not to.

"A golden world," he said aloud. He wished he'd truly meant it. He guided a clump of sand into a bag, then stacked it with the others.

In the mangrove, something stirred. A man was coming towards him. Now those fiends were walking in daylight? He curled his fingers around the spade. He'd be prey for no Mooncusser bushman—

"Gaius Hart!"

He sighed, then tipped his cap. It was the railroad's chief recruiter. "Morning, Mr. Mankins."

Mankins sidled beside him. His clothes were more suited to northern boardrooms. His pudgy jowls were flushed. "Still happy here in Eden, I trust," Mankins said. Gaius swatted a mosquito. The recruiter flourished his arm. "And this our life exempt from public haunt finds tongues in trees, books in the running brooks, sermons in stones and food in everything." He bowed.

"*Good* in everything," Gaius said, "and that's a far cry."

"Well, worse spots you could be," Mankins said. "World's a dangerous place. Whole island Cuba's up in flames, they say. You can see a faint glow off to the south at night. Be glad you aren't *there*." He tapped his palms together. "Made up your mind yet? I can't wait forever."

Gaius filled another sandbag. He didn't care for being rushed. Thirty-some years later, the phantom shackles of bondage still gnawed. "Me neither."

"We need men like you," Mankins said, "good men, with families. Roots for laying."

"They're back again, aren't they?" Gaius said. "Those Mooncussers."

"Who?"

"You know who. What are you going to do about them?"

Mankins scratched his head, donning an affected charm. "I sure wish I knew what—"

"I wish my wife wasn't so fond of Bluefield. Same goes for my daughters and son."

The ocean heaved a lusty groan. The surf crawled up the strand. The fiddler crabs, with gauntlets raised, scurried down their burrows. Gaius waited, then tipped his hat. "Nice day, then." He thrust the spade back through the sand.

"We're not sure," Mankins said, sheepishly. Gaius stopped digging. "We're not sure who they are. Seminoles, buccaneers... the lost tribes of Israel. They speak no language *I've* ever heard."

"They don't move by day or on clear nights," Gaius said, "only by cloud or crescent moons. At new moon they gather but always in silence. They watch the passing ships. At some of them, they point. And then they'll be gone for a month, and then—"

"Nine months, to be exact," Mankins said. "They're here three months until the new moon, and then you won't see them for nine."

Gaius' heart sank further. "You've known about them for a year? Before I got here, even?"

"We knew before *we* got here. Men who fished these waters told us. Wildlings in the bush, they said. Said to keep our distance. Stay off their favorite stretch of beach."

Gaius looked around. "What beach?"

Mankins stared at the sand. "Well, ahem… who could blame them? It *is* pleasant here at the Rat's Mouth, isn't it?"

Gaius said, "All this time, you knew?"

Mankins sneered through pearly teeth. "Seventh sons of seventh sons, swamp rats and reprobates, looking for handouts and attention. No reason to take them for serious."

"Ned might disagree," Gaius said. "And Caligula and—"

"Workers disappear off sites all the time. They find better work, or they just drift away. These bushmen have nothing to do with it. Don't let them spoil a great opportunity for you. Land we're standing on's the future of this country. Take my offer, make yourself rich, then look back years from this and laugh."

Mankins was working an angle, no doubt, but that didn't mean what he said wasn't true. "And that slab?" Gaius said. "The one with the carvings of the whales the bushmen seem so fond of?"

Mankins waved his hand dismissively. "Just some olden relics, there. We'll dig it out faster than you could wink. A homestead here is a treasure for life. And speaking of whales…" He pointed.

Gaius raised his head. In the distance, past the heaving swells, the emerald North Atlantic rolled, and like antediluvian gods, humpback whales gamboled in its veil. Their beaks like hilltops breached the waves, their snowy flukes, like flapping wings, flashed as stars against the blue. Their every move was playful grace, their every sound a song. Gaius' heart took flight. "They do that sometimes. It never gets old."

Mankins smirked. "Bet there's none like that in Bluefield."

Voices carried from the surf. Gaius squinted. "What on earth?" Among the whales were boats filled with people.

✲   ✲   ✲   ✲

Necío pointed to the shore, where two bewildered men were standing. A steamy mangrove rose behind them, its moss-draped branches filled with birds. The sand they were standing on was sugar-white. Generations of M'Brae had waited to glimpse this: Ahr, their treasure, at long last. Necío could hardly believe that his own eyes had been the first. "There!" he cried, pointing. "Over there!"

The warm seawater mixed with blood sloshed inside his little boat. Chropher hunched across the oars. By the grief writ on his face, he was regretting offering to help Necío row. Hilaríon and Ypriána huddled in the bow. Their flesh was ashen, eyes like a doll's. They couldn't lift their heads to speak. The leviathans surrounding them breached a final time, their blowholes puffing pungent mist, then slipped below the waves. "*Tehí daneph,*" Necío called to them, "thank you." Someday, he knew, he'd see them again.

The foamy breakers grabbed the boats and hurled them towards the shore. Necío braced the wounded ones. The rowboat slammed into the sand. Chropher and Necío jumped past the gunwales and dragged it from the surf. All the others did the same: clambering, hauling, then shouting for aid. They were sunburned, seasick, and riddled with balls. Their arms and faces dripped with blood.

Necío ran to the men. "*Táh yoyéa,*" he hollered, "*táh yoyéa!*" The men stared back, dumbfounded. It was not the welcome he expected. He tried the Vujoíe tongue, "Ayuda!" Their faces crinkled but they stood pat.

The M'Brae shrieks grew louder. Necío racked his brain. This land was what the Vujoíe called *Armorica*, wasn't it, where people spoke the Anglo tongue? He remembered the plays his mother had read to him. "Umm... *help?*"

The men rushed towards him. He pointed at the others. "Help *them!*"

The two men chattered frantically. They raced among the open boats and led the people to the shade. Then they pointed up the beach. Their babble reached a fever pitch, but Necío caught a single word.

Doctor.

He grabbed the heavy white man's arm. "Doctor?" The white man nodded.

Necío said to Aryei, "Keep them calm. Send someone for water. See if you can find fresh food." He turned back to the little boat. Hilaríon was fading fast, struggling for breath with purple lips. Necío pressed his brow to his friend's. "I'll be back with help."

The slender dark man led them on. They crashed through knotty overgrowth. The heavy white man fell behind. They sidestepped craggy coconut husks. The sounds of the M'Brae dwindled behind them, replaced by manly grunting.

The brush abruptly dropped away. A patchwork quilt of citrus groves spread in all directions, sliced in two by an earthen berm, upon which a railroad was taking shape. Dark-skinned workers cleared the trees and tended to the bountiful citrus. Tents and lean-to's dotted the groves. A bright clapboard building bore a sign:

Bocaratone

It felt, for a moment, like Cuba again, gazing westward over the Trocha. But this was a bold and virgin world. There'd be no bulwarks or prison-camps here. The white man shouted, "Stosh!"

A graying man stepped from a cluster of workers. He looked them over and said, "John Mankins and Gaius Hart, an unlikely pair if ever one was."

Gaius, the dark man, said, "Where's Doc?"

"Refugees at the inlet," Mankins, the white man, added.

The Anglo language was choppy and harsh, not silken like the M'Brae tongue or rhythmic like the Vujoíe. It was hard enough for Necío to catch the words, let alone gather their meaning.

"Refugees?" Stosh said.

"Off the ocean," Mankins said. "Young and able-bodied. Women, too." He shot a cockeyed grin towards Stosh.

"With gunshot wounds," Gaius said. "Bleeding."

Stosh returned the grin. "Just how able-bodied? And just how many women?"

Stosh rejoined the group of workers, all of them talking and pointing, then trudged back to Gaius and Mankins. "They tell me Doc never showed up this morning."

Necío's heart sank. Mankins said, "That's not like him."

"Anyone try his hut?" Gaius said.

Stosh sneered. "And how would you know about his hut?"

"Manners, Stosh, manners," Mankins said. "Gaius here is one of us. Said he's for the long haul. Going to purchase the southeast tract—"

"Begging thy pardon," Necío said. The railroad men chuckled. Necío remembered his mother had told him the Anglo plays she'd taught him were old, and no one spoke that way anymore. But it was the only idiom he knew. And with every wasted second, Hilaríon slipped a bit farther. "The doctor?"

Stosh led Necío and the other two men through a cluster of tents, arranged in orderly rows, like an army's. Ashes of campfires mixed with fish bones still smoldered from the morning's meal. A furry creature with a ringed tail and what looked like black spectacles chirped and chattered, raiding the refuse. Cuba was far behind, indeed. "If I had a half-eagle for every raccoon," Stosh grumbled.

Necío pictured birds hewn lengthwise. "What's *raccoon*?"

"You really *are* off the sea," Mankins said.

Past the tents was a circle of huts. Stosh led them to the farthest one. He knocked on the door and called for the doctor. Mankins peeked through a window. "Empty."

Stosh turned the doorknob. The door creaked wide. Inside was a musty, one-room cell. A metal cot stood against the far wall, a lone portrait pinned to its lower bedpost. A hat lined with mosquito netting hung in a wardrobe. A wash basin balanced on a rickety table, beside a stool and writing desk, dotted with bottles and flasks. One of the flasks had liquid inside. Necío uncorked it. It smelled just like the Lightleaf hide.

"Another absconder," Mankins said. "After what we paid him?"

Necío said, "Quit not, he hath."

"His clothes are gone, Shakespeare," Stosh said.

"But not his netting or medicine." Necío swished the elixir inside the flask, remembering Phellhe's sallow flesh, ravaged by swamp fever. "He'd need these."

"Unless he left the swamps altogether."

"And went where?" Gaius said. "Who else is paying?"

Necío stepped to the cot. The portrait was a daguerreotype, lovingly depicting woman and child. "He'd never forget *this*," he said. He hadn't realized how much he'd learned from Hilarío. His friend would be proud—if he survived.

"Reason to take those fiends serious now?" Gaius said.

Mankins rolled his eyes. "Stop that witchcraft drivel. I already told you, thugs and runaways—"

"Doc needs our help."

The railroad men dropped their eyes to the floor. The chattering of the spectacled beast outside grated against the prickly silence. Necío said, "Four's better than one."

"Now, wait," Mankins said, blocking the doorway. "We're the last people can help him now. And as for you... next closest doctor's south in Miami. *Eleanor Hitty* comes day after next—"

"I can't wait half that long."

"By boat's the only way," Mankins said, "and you'd be lucky even to find one that soon, what with the shipwreck south of here last night."

Gaius said, "Shipwreck?"

"*Lee* run aground on the shoals," Mankins said. "Crew lost and feared dead. The skippers are scared. *Hitty* comes twice a week, or you might just find a passing skiff."

"Time's wasting," Necío said, pushing past.

"Stop," Stosh said. He pointed towards the mangrove. "Look, going in there... it's just not a good idea. Gators, panthers, and water moccasins, and you'd be miles from anyone."

"Except for the *Mooncussers*," Gaius said. "Find them, we find Doc."

Necío shivered. Mooncussers. He remembered the tales his mother had told him. The word echoed like a long-lost refrain, a relic of a wilder age when raiders prowled the untamed seas.

"Hart, enough," Mankins said. "See, you've spooked our guest."

He turned to Necío. "Don't mind all that. Just think of how grand this land will be once it's connected by railroad. In the meantime, the sea waits for no man. Welcome to Florida." He pulled an orange from his pocket. "Try our citrus."

Necío looked at the colorful fruit. His stomach was roiling with hunger. But Hilaríon's life depended on him. And he'd faced worse than Mooncussers. "Thank thee," he said, and swiped the orange. "I track better when I'm full."

"Boy," Stosh said, "don't be a fool. You go in there, you go alone."

"No, he doesn't," Gaius said. "You talk about a golden world? If you're not coming, then help his kin at the inlet. If we're not back by sundown... Ah, you wouldn't do it anyway." He grabbed two machetes from under the bed and placed one in Necío's hand. "You track, I'll cover. Lead on."

They raced from the hut towards the edge of the mangrove. It rose above, a vast wall of green, daunting in its wildness. From the doorway, the railroad men yelled, trying to stop them, until their voices faded to chirrups beneath the swampland orchestra.

The air was leaden, the morning resplendent. The ground at the edge of the mangrove was trampled, the stems and stalks of the brush bent and torn. People had passed this way recently—and hurriedly. "Thou don't have to do this," Necío said.

"Tired of walking on my heels," Gaius said. "Tired of being expendable."

Necío sighed, "I know how that feels." He plunged into the mangrove.

lxii.

John Mankins could still hear his father's rebuke. *Don't ever recruit for a living. Even with iron nerves you'll meet the worms young.* His father had been living proof. The grind of finding butternut boys to trust cavaliers in a hopeless cause had indeed sent him to meet the worms in the loam of his beloved Old Dominion. John had held the words in his heart, until Mr. Flagler had promised him something he could hold even closer, inside his pocket. Filling his monthly quotas was torment, and that was in the best of times. But God, or nature, had answered his prayers. The three hundred-odd refugees at the inlet would pave his rise to stardom.

He led Lizzie Rickards along towards the beach. "I still don't understand why," she said.

"This calls for a woman's touch," he said. It called for a hard sell, actually, but the language barrier made that a stretch. The plantation's smiling matron would do.

They cleared the tree line at the inlet. The angry Florida sun beat down. The soft sand underfoot gave way. He stumbled in his saddle shoes, comprehending—not for the first time—why this was America's last great frontier. The refugees turned their blood-caked heads in their direction as they arrived. Lizzie said, "Why didn't you say?"

Mankins feigned a hangdog scowl. Some things just had to be shown, not told. "The grubbers and railway workers won't budge." He tugged his seersucker lapels. "What's a gentleman to do?"

Lizzie grabbed a coconut. She husked its husk, then cracked it. She handed him the fleshy halves. "Start with the children. Work your way up." She stepped back into the trees. "I won't be long."

"You're a saint," he said.

"You're right," she replied. She was on to his game, but he didn't care, and neither would the refugees.

Necío raced onwards. The mangrove was a virgin realm, untouched by man's cruel hand. The footprints were large and easy to track. Unlike Lux's meandering path in the hills, this trail was headed somewhere for sure. But the wild, untamed sloughs pulsed with peril. Hilaríon had taught him well. "Vain men," Necío remarked.

Gaius quickened. "What?"

"They didn't care if they were tracked, maybe even wanted to be."

"Men have been disappearing for months," Gaius said. "The railroad men won't say it, much less do anything. It's cheaper."

The M'Brae's journey had been fraught with death: they'd suffered in the hopes of finding a treasure. But what kind of treasure had they found? With men kidnapped, deemed not worth protecting, not to mention skulking rogues, just what redemption would they find in Ahr? "And Mooncussers?"

"They're behind all this, I know it. Caligula, Ned, Doc Chasbrook... a few other men and some horses."

"Why?"

"Ransom? A warning? Seems that doesn't matter now."

"It might help make sense of all this."

"They move about like gypsies. They watch the ships on moonless nights. No one's safe while they're here with us. If only I could prove it— *Wait!*"

The mangrove dropped to sawgrass prairie. It spread, a rolling sea of grass, its ripples set to the stylings of warblers, chattering in its leafy eaves. At the water's edge was a clump of rags, beside one-half of a man's shoe. The tatters of a wide-brimmed hat lay half a stone's throw into the reeds. Both were soaked in blood. Necío reached for the rags—

Gaius yanked him back. "Look." Log-like and motionless, a massive reptile lay just offshore. Only its golden eyes peeked out.

"*Cocodrilo*," Necío said. He could still hear Sunovín's screams.

"Here, it's *alligator*."

To Necío, it was all the same. He stretched out carefully and grabbed the rags. The beast's eyeballs followed his movements. He fingered the ribbons of fabric. "Woolen shirt," he said.

Gaius fondled the hat. "Poor old Ned." The pain in his eyes told everything.

"Your friend?"

"You might've said that, but we'll never know." He doffed his hat and bowed.

Necío knelt beside him. "I'm sorry."

"Beasts left him no chance," Gaius said. "He'd come here grubbing, just like me. But I heard tell that way back home, he'd been an electrician's apprentice… wires and light bulbs and such. He did some wiring work for the railroad. They'd pay him extra, here and there. What in hell was he doing out here?"

Something caught Necío's eye. Past the cattails, the ground was trampled. He crept on his knees. The beast kept vigil. Necío pushed the reeds aside. Carved in the mud was a groove, the telltale line of a rowboat's keel. "Wiring, you said?"

"That's right," Gaius said.

A story was taking shape. "And what did you say before? About the Mooncussers watching ships?"

"They move like gypsies, those Mooncussers. On moonless nights, they watch the ships."

Necío cleared his throat. Missing horses, doctor, and electrician. Land-based pirates, sprung from myth. The tale the trail told was becoming clear. What would Hilaríon have done? "The shipwreck last night," Necío said. "Where was it?"

"Three miles south, on the shoals. But why?"

Necío stood. Past the trampled mud was a stream, well-disguised amidst the sloughs and deep enough for a rowboat's draw. Its flow was south-southeast. "Alligators didn't eat your friend, or the doctor, or anyone," he said. He pictured his mother, grinning cynically. She'd always told him her stories and songs would make the difference between life and death. He was both indignant and glad she'd been right. "Know why they're called Mooncussers? It's because they curse the light of the moon."

He took off running down the bank. Gaius donned his hat and followed.

✻   ✻   ✻   ✻

Mankins swatted the air wildly. The newcomers watched with baffled eyes. What tribal dance was he doing? He was sure that was what they were all wondering. Proud and normally dignified, the hundredfold nibbles had bested his poise. The flies and mosquitoes were bad on good days. But the coconut juice caked thick on his hands had driven them into a frenzy. He'd drink double his quinine later. But if insects were his biggest concern, he'd count himself a lucky dog.

Mankins had even surprised himself. Bringing Lizzie had been a stroke of genius. The plantation wives had come when she'd called, leaving eggs ungathered and jams unjarred. For the newcomers, it was a Southern welcome. The wives had brought them food and water, led them to shelter and triaged their wounds. The wailing had stopped. Some, by Jove, were even laughing! Clean clothes and full bellies worked wonders. Mankins beamed. He'd have given his back a hearty patting, if only his arms could reach around. Now he could hear the clinking of coins. Maybe he'd buy one of those newfangled automobiles—

"Mister John," Lizzie said, "are there any more?"

There was only the fresh-mouthed scarecrow who'd run off into the mangrove with Gaius Hart. Those poor fools wouldn't be returning; prey for the gators or Mooncussers, for sure. And all that time pitching Hart gone to waste? He'd have to find another buyer. But now he had options. "No."

"Very well," she said. "Tom's waiting. The pullets are laying and tents being raised."

"Henry Flager thanks you."

She scoffed. "Not nearly enough."

Lizzie was short-sighted, stuck inside a wooden past. Tomorrow's world was built of steel. He waved his arm, encompassing the inlet in its arc. "In our lifetimes, you'll see, this land will rise. Railroads will carry the North to the South. New York bankers—presidents, even—will come here to play in the unshrinking sun. White sand beaches, lined with palms... high-rise hotels, painted pink... even—"

"A boy," she said.

"Well, naturally, children will be welcome—"

"No," she said. "There's another." Among the boats, a lone boy crouched. She walked towards him. Mankins followed.

The boy was spindly, all of twelve, hair bleached blonde and skin burnt red. In his fingers chimed a music box. The song was tinny, but captivating. Lizzie held out her hand for him. He pulled back and grabbed the nearest boat's gunwales.

Mankins gasped, recoiling. Inside the boat were two dead bodies, one young woman and one young man, half-submerged in bloody brine. Palm-leaves and driftwood littered their backs. The boy had tried to cover them. The elements had prevailed.

Lizzie hung her head. "These two must have been lovers," she said. "Look how he holds her, even in death."

Mankins snickered. Love was an ephemeral sylph. Bank notes were better. Bullion was best. He looked at the boy. "Your parents?" The boy gawked. Mankins tried again. "Mother and father?"

"*Hilarión,*" the boy said, pointing. "*Ypriána.*"

Mankins scratched his head. "What's an *Hilariónypriána*? No language I've heard tell."

"There's room in the settlers' plot," Lizzie said. "Unless it's been turned to a pink hotel."

Stuck in a wooden past, indeed. "Another time," he said. He reached to hoist the bodies. The man coughed weakly. The woman groaned. "No plot needed. These two are alive."

The spindly boy's eyes burst wide. He peeped a squeal of cathartic delight and snapped the lid of the music box closed. He ran off up the beach towards the others, shouting in a foreign tongue.

Mankins sighed, part smugness and part disbelief. Coming to Florida had been an adventure, bootstrapping its peculiar spell every day. He was happy he'd ignored his father. The golden world was his to build.

Fire flashed from the young woman's neck, a metallic burst of cobalt-blue like Mankins had never dreamed. He squinted in the afternoon sun. The flash burned motley streaks in his eyes. It was a silver medallion.

He cupped it in his fleshy hand. "I've seen this mark," he said.

It was the symbol from the slab on Gaius Hart's plot.

☆ ☆ ☆ ☆

Necío trained his eyes to the ground, cleaving to the path of the boat. Gaius cleared a swathe ahead. Plump snakes paddled in the stream, gaping wide with ashen mouths. They reminded Necío of the Gray Jaeger. Gaius said, "Water moccasin. One bite, Jesus welcomes you."

What kind of treasure *was* this place? Was this the Ancients' idea of a joke?

The stream emptied into a slough, surrounded on all sides by land. Covered with palm-fronds and yellowing ferns, a wooden punt lay in nearby brush. Three sets of prints led from the punt, two barefoot and the other one-shoed. The stride of the tracks was slow and deliberate. Whoever had left the trail hadn't rushed. Their destination had been near.

Necío raised his machete. He'd never lifted his hand to another, much less raised a weapon. But Hilaríon wouldn't be long for this world unless Necío found courage. "They're close," he said. "Be ready."

The trail wended among the trees, then disappeared into dried sawgrass. No tracks reemerged on the other side. Necío said. "Now what?"

A strange sound croaked from nearby treetops. Gaius said, "Do you hear?" Necío shrugged. "Carrion bird," Gaius said. "Something dead nearby."

Necío dropped to his elbows. He and Gaius slithered towards the sound. The undergrowth offered little quarter: roaches and millipedes danced on their forearms, midges like hummingbirds whined in their ears. Necío snickered in spite of himself: Cuba, perhaps, hadn't been so bad. He groused, "Some golden world."

Gaius said, "That depends on us."

The croak came again, just above them. A wisp of a voice answered, "*Shoo!*"

A stone's throw away, the woods dropped into scrub. A lone adult male, armed just with a club, leaned breezily against a tree. He was garbed in garish pantaloons, shirtless except for a bright yellow scarf. Kneeling beside him, a middle-aged man in khaki fatigues drew stitches through a woman's leg.

"Mooncussers," Gaius said. "Doc, too."

The doctor was tied to a tree by his ankle. Only one of his feet was shoed. The woman lay motionless on her back, dressed in pied, flamboyant silks. On the far side of the glade were horses, feedbags fixed onto their mouths, saddle-blankets on their backs. Fastened on each horse's flank was an electric lamp. Opposite them lay a man's dead body, caked with sand and bloated. Perched in the mangrove boughs above, a lanky vulture squawked with glee, anticipating its ghoulish meal. The man with the club, a guard, yelled, "*Shoo!*"

The glade was small but well-concealed. If not for the vulture's call they'd have missed it. "Well done," Necío said.

In the center were trunks, lids pried and empty. Each was stamped with the same words:

S.S. Gen. Robert E. Lee, C.S.A.

Necío made a hasty guess. In addition to the guard and woman, other Mooncussers had to be near. Whatever they'd plundered out of the trunks, it was likely they were stashing it. But they wouldn't have left the horses behind. They'd return, and soon. Time, assuredly, was not on his side. But the numbers were—for now.

The vulture croaked. The trees in which it perched were thick, a palisade of wood. It was the Trocha all over again. "We have a window," Necío said. "There's only one guard. Can you ride?"

Gaius said, "Thirty years in bluegrass country."

He guessed that meant *yes*. "That thicket's a blind spot. Any noise, that guard will move to see." He pointed. "Hide by the horses.

Get the doctor's attention. The moment the guard be outside your sight, cut the doctor loose and ride."

Gaius said, "And the woman?" Necío eyed the machete. Gaius nodded. "And you?"

"Just get the doctor back to the others. There's a man among them—Hilaríon. He gets priority, promise me." Gaius rose to his knees. Necío yanked him back. "Promise me."

"I'll see it done."

Necío shook his hand. "When this is all over, we'll find your friend Ned."

Gaius gave a kindly bow and slunk off towards the glade. Necío crept the opposite way. He ran his hand along his scar. Hilaríon's life was all that mattered. As long as he could buy Gaius time to escape with the doctor, what happened after made no difference.

He pulled off his shoes, slipped them onto his hands, and squelched a trail into the mud. The illusion would have to hold long enough. The Mooncusser guard slouched lazily. The horses munched away on feed. The mangrove's silence was hypnotic. With hard work and patience, Necío imagined, the wild land could in time be tamed and bear riches generations hence. But that all had to start with a foothold. And only Hilaríon could lead them in that. He rolled to his back, swiped a stone, and threw it at the vulture.

The bird cawed loudly, flapping away. The guard raised his head. Necío slunk to the base of a live oak a stone's throw from the thicket. Stuck in the nearby mud was a boulder. His mind, all at once, drifted back to M'Brae-dah. If the troglodytes could throw sounds, so could he. He whispered,

"Mooncusser, Mooncusser, show me your wares
What plunder of the winedark sea?"

The tune echoed. The guard snapped up. Necío said,

"Mooncusser, Mooncusser, bring me your light
The Devil waits upon you."

Gnath had sung him to sleep with that rhyme. Of course, she'd quizzed him mornings after.

The guard raised his club and stepped from the tree. He mumbled something to the woman, then shook his fist in the doctor's face. The horse closest to the wood line tensed. Gaius would be in place by now. A few more steps out into the open and the guard would be momentarily useless.

Necío scratched his blade on a stone. A metallic rasping bounced through the trees. The vulture swooped back into the glade and perched above the dead man. The guard took a tentative step his way, following the false tracks. Gaius peeked from behind a horse, making hand-signs to the doctor. Necío sprawled along the ground. As long as Gaius was silent and swift, there was nothing else for him to do.

The guard stepped into the thicket. He stalked, back and forth, head craned towards the canopy. Necío peered into the glade. The doctor had mounted a brindle mare. Gaius was clambering astride a young bay, unfastening the heavy lamps from its flanks. The woman lay still, likely drugged by the doctor. In just a few seconds—

"*Stop them!*" strange voices shouted, "*There!*" Gaius still wasn't fully mounted.

The guard wheeled around. Necío tackled him to the ground. The guard broke Necío's grip with a kick. Necío grabbed his leg and pulled himself atop him. The guard thrashed side-to-side. But Necío pinned him face-down by his arms.

Glass shattered in the glade, the sound of the electric lamps falling from the horses' flanks. The horses scattered helter-skelter, save for the bay and brindle mare. A gang of Mooncussers converged from the mangrove.

The guard bucked Necío off his back. Necío's head slammed against the boulder. The world, for a moment, swirled gauzily. Gaius goaded his two mounts on. The frightened horses wheeled about, snorting and rearing onto their hocks. The Mooncussers encircled the beasts on all sides, save for a dwindling perimeter gap.

The guard lunged to close the gap. Necío hurled his body against the guard's. The Mooncusser stumbled. Necío ran to the guard's far side, brandishing his blade. But all he needed to kill was time. He could never stab another.

The Mooncussers closed in. The horses screamed. The guard feinted right, then sprang to the left. Necío drove the butt of his blade at the guard's head. With a graceful feint the guard sidestepped, and punched the hollow of Necío's elbow. His arm went numb. The blade fell down. The guard caught the blade mid-fall and swung the butt into Necío's chest. It knocked the air from his lungs.

Necío, stunned, fell backwards. He kicked his leg at the guard's, in vain. The Mooncusser beamed a malevolent grin. He drew back the blade—

The flank of a horse flashed by. The Mooncusser tumbled, trampled down. The bay and mare loped away. "Hilaríon's first," Gaius cried, "I'll be sure!" The beasts disappeared past the mangrove.

Necío heaved an elated sigh. The Fool had done his part.

"You there."

He opened his eyes. Looming above him were five Mooncussers, dressed in gaudy pantaloons, sporting tricorn hats and earrings, like buccaneers of legend. They glowered with fiery eyes, as proper bloodthirsty pirates should. The sight was as terrifying as it was droll. He'd never have figured this for his end. He couldn't help but laugh aloud. What, now, did it matter?

One pulled out a rusty harquebus. He pressed it into Necío's brow. The metal bit cold between his eyes. But Necío's cause had already been won. Somewhere, Gnath and Bollish waited. Hilaríon would look after the others. Necío had no regrets.

He let his body go limp. He knew it would make no difference now—its magic had already been spent. But he'd always imagined the words from his lips: his own dirge, like the Hollow Man's. No one could tell him how not to die. He whispered,

"...Parched our glories, myths untold
Doubt devours my wasted heart..."

The gunman gasped. His grip went soft.

"...Prayers unanswered, blood turned cold—"

"*Loh'ohé ahr eph-Ahr,*" the man said. He sheathed the harquebus. From a pocket he pulled a golden doubloon. It glittered like a shard of sun. He held it to Necío's eyes. "*Loh'uj g'daev,*" he said.

The treasure is ours.

He bowed like a peacocking thespian, then vanished into the dappled dusk. All was sylvan silence again, save for the hungry vulture's croaks. The Mooncussers were gone. And they were M'Brae.

Necío wiped his face, rose to his feet, and took off running northwards.

lxiii.

The wildling lay in Morpheus' arms, her ashen flesh, once rich olive, made even more a mask of death in the lamplight of the tent. Hilaríon, dressed in only a gown, knelt at her bedside, elbows taut, as if his hands were clasped in prayer, imploring a merciful God. Some had insisted her arms be shackled, but he wouldn't hear of such foolishness. The journey's travails had tested them all. She'd done as best she could.

"Miles and miles of miles and miles," Necío said. "A new world. Golden days. And something that looks like an oversized rat with a striped tail, wearing spectacles."

Hilaríon laughed. The breath shanked his chest but the release was sweet. "And the Armoricans?"

"Elated we're here. They're looking for men to clear the brush, then settle down to farm. Grubbing, it's called. They couldn't have been more welcoming." Necío smiled. But his eyes belied fear.

"Is something wrong?" Hilaríon said.

"No, no. Overwhelmed is all."

But Necío was always overwhelmed. "Are you sure?"

"My mother... I wish she were here. How proud she'd be."

He couldn't help feeling proud himself. "A Steeled Elect," he mused.

"Outcasts and mosslings," Necío said. "The Guanahatabey who taught us to sing and the troglodytes who made us. The jaegers, even. All of them played a part in this. No one could have done it alone." He glanced at Ypriána. "That's where she was wrong."

Hilaríon stroked the rubbery keloids that sprawled across his gunshot wounds. It wasn't the art of troglodytes, but he had no complaints. The doctor had said he'd arrived just in time: a few more hours, and he'd have bled out. But he'd insisted the doctor treat

Ypriána first. There hadn't been time to argue. Now, all that mattered was her will to live—and the succor of others.

"Why torment yourself?" Necío said. He knelt beside him. "Would she have done it for you?"

Hilarión turned to her stony face, serene in repose, hiding a battle raging inside. He'd been a hilldevil with a death wish. She'd been under his rash knife, and yet, all along, she'd been the hunter. She'd have killed him before he struck. But, instead, she'd smiled. She'd seen past his ruse. The eyes had never let him forget. But she'd torn him down, then built him back, better. In her image and likeness, she'd birthed him anew. "But she did, Necío." He draped his arm across her chest. "More than she knows."

Necío rose. "Well, so much for the Vexing Heirloom. We can put that behind us, savor the fruits." He pushed the hospital tent-flap aside. The citrus groves, like casks of gold, rolled off towards the sunset.

"Don't be so sure," Hilarión said. "You remember what Bollísh told us? Somehow I think the story goes on. And, humbly, so do we." He laid his head in the crook of her neck.

Necío laughed warmly. "Good night, Hilarión. Don't wait so long you lose yourself."

A warm breeze whispered through the tent, carrying a promise of spring in its wings. Time peeled back. The world fell away. All at once, he was back at Cacarajícara, garbed smartly in his battle gear. Beside him stood two stalwart women: his aunt, a general; and Paola, all grown, now his lieutenant. The swarthy ranks of Castilian jaegers rushed uphill before them. At his back, his Mambí legions coiled, ready to strike on his command. Together, the warriors three drew swords. Then something caught his eye.

Away in the distance, far from the battle, a train of refugees cried out. Their threadbare rags masked bony frames, their sallow faces fraught with flies. Homeless, hopeless, they reached out. Their voices were as ghosts'.

The enemy closed, the Mambíses tensed. But Hilarión could not look away. His eyes were fixed on the refugees.

"Go," his aunt said.

"Go," Paola echoed.

He glanced back at the glorious battle-to-be, then sheathed his blade. His place was somewhere else—

Footfalls jarred him awake. He'd dozed off, still kneeling. The icy kiss of metal slithered slowly down his neck. "Feel familiar?" came Ypriána's voice.

His body tensed. "I waited for you," he said.

"You waited for *you.*"

A steel tent-rod lay under the bed. He reached for it, then stopped. "The story won't let you."

She tightened her grip. "You've grown."

"Towards you, but you'd gone. Which of us is Guamá now?"

"Before too long, they'll need Guamá."

Across the sea, in a shallow grave, Wresh's body rotted brown. Had they needed Guamá then? Who *was* this changeling, Ypriána? All he could muster was, "Why?"

"I'm thrall to no story, least of all yours. So there's *my* treasure found." She curled the blade high into his throat, then just as quickly pulled it away. "Relax, Hilaríon. You've earned a reprieve. How long depends on you." She draped the medallion over his neck and gently kissed the crown of his head.

"Wait," Hilaríon said. She stopped. He couldn't help but wonder. "Below the waves, what did you see?"

"Just what I came for," she replied. "Don't think I won't be watching you." With a flourish she was gone. The tent-flap rustled in her wake. Hilaríon was alone again. The night wind whispered eerily, foreboding stormy days ahead.

And then, through the grace of some nameless cause, Oriel's warning crossed his mind. It seemed so long ago, he'd almost forgotten. He'd thought it had already come to pass.

> "The Ancient sire who chased the dawn
> Before this fallen world departed
> A mighty treasure stowed away
> *And left a mightier dragon to guard it.*"

Ypriána was the dragon. Whatever hopes tomorrow brought, she'd ever lurk upon their heels.

His mind tormented, he lay awake, until the doctor's drams took him whole, and thrust him into frightening dreams.

✶   ✶   ✶   ✶

The first streaks of dawn dabbed the eastern horizon. Hilarión opened his eyes. The living earth's players were warming their pieces. Catbirds mewled their gripes in the oaks. Sandhill cranes trumpeted with élan. Life, and a brand new day, was calling. Ypriána, like the night, had fled. Neither held sway. Not yet.

And then he heard it.

The song was faint but unmistakable. Its charms had bound him to a race and called him from the face of death. He'd left the only home he'd known. He'd crossed a wide, uncertain sea. He could feel each word, like coming rains, in the deep core of his every bone. It was his song now, and he part of it.

> "Our sires' yawning chasm spreads
> Parched our glories, myths untold
> Doubt devours my wasted heart
> Prayers unanswered, blood turned cold
> We'll be one in Ahr..."

He rolled from the bed, climbed into his pants, and pulled his boots onto his feet. The medallion hung around his neck, just where she had left it. He pushed aside the canvas flap and stepped into the morning. Muskrats prattled in the marsh. Skinks like tiny gems scurried fro. The medallion's contours caught the light and threw it back into his face. He'd risked life and limb to capture it. But now he had eyes for something else.

> "Envoys of a better land
> In benthic depths, our sires' cry

Leads me, weary wand'rer, on
Roused my wonder, by and by
We'll be one in Ahr."

The song soared higher. His pace quickened. He passed the groves and railroad breaks, the chance-games of the lush frontier, where daring men had come to play, their yesterdays behind them now, the days ahead unknowable. And he was part of that brotherhood, too, pioneer in a green hinterland. The trail he'd blaze would shape the days of thousands, yet to come.

"My journey's end, my fathers' fount
Oft-rememb'red, never known
A flame rekindled 'midst the dark
To hold, to have in grace alone
We'll be one in Ahr."

The song broke into its crescendo. Hilaríon stepped out of the trees. Clothed anew, their flesh wounds dressed, their arms and voices intertwined, the M'Brae stood, now fused in song, a welded instrument. Between them lay a blue stone slab, shaped like the medallion. The people—*his people*—cheered as he passed. Carved in each face was a singular tale: Chropher, the rascal turned everyone's friend; Graciela, the mute turned siren; Maith, the widow made new mother; Necío, the runt made sage. All of their quests had come full-circle. And still, somehow, Hilaríon knew, the story had only just begun.

The new world pulsed with the din of life, an overture to destiny, beckoning to one and all. Gators bellowed throaty grunts, shaking boggy bottomlands, frightening lumbering manatees and putting ruddy flamingoes to flight. Raccoons, washing morning grub, chattered on like debutantes, in time with the folksy string-ensemble of damselflies and green frogs. Boars rooted with muffled grunts, lest they be meals for keen-eared cats, as goshawks screamed their warning cries astride the swirling thermals. Rock-ribbed men with boundless dreams drove picks and spades into the earth, forging what was wilderness into a stage for golden days. Their songs reverberated wide—and would, to the ends of the earth, for all of time.

But they were all of them drowned out by the din of three hundred voices raised in song, for the M'Brae had their treasure.

THE END

GLOSSARY

Almiqui: Cuban solenodon, an extremely rare and primitive mammal, resembling a large shrew

The "Bronze Titan": Lieutenant General Antonio Maceo Grajales, commanding general of the Cuban revolutionary army

The "Butcher": General Valeriano Weyler, Spanish military governor of Cuba from January, 1896 through October, 1897

Cacarajícara: battle between Cuban revolutionary army under Maceo's command and Spanish imperial forces under command of Julián Suárez Inclán, fought in the highlands west of Havana, Cuba in April, 1896

Cinchona: tree native to Central and South America, whose bark is used in the making of quinine, used to prevent and treat malaria

Guamá: Taíno chieftain who led a rebellion against Spanish colonial rule on Cuba in the 1530's; his name is used as an alias by Hilaríon

Heliconia: flowering plant native to the American tropics, with bright, colorful blossoms, resembling the bird-of-paradise flower

Hilldevils: bandits, often Mambí deserters but sometimes partisans or escaped slaves, targeting civilian refugees in the mountain passes of western Cuba

Hutia: medium-sized arboreal rodent, native to Caribbean islands, similar to a cavy or nutria

Jaegers: elite shock troops of the Spanish imperial army

La Habana: Havana; port city on the northern coast of western Cuba; also refers to the province in which that city is located

Mambíses: Cuban revolutionary army; the name refers to Juan Ethnnius Mamby ("Eutimio Mambí"), a Spanish officer turned revolutionary leader in the 1846 Dominican revolt against the Spanish, after which the Spanish army began referring to all colonial rebel fighters as "men of Mamby" or "Mambíses," which term was later reclaimed by those rebels with pride

Mantua: a small city located at the extreme western tip of Cuba, occupied by the Mambíses in January, 1896, which occupation was considered symbolic of the "national" nature of the rebellion, in that it had begun in the extreme eastern tip of the island and finally reached the western extreme

Mooncussers: land-based pirates who waylay and attack ships under cover of darkness, so named because they cannot operate on moonlit nights and therefore "curse" the moon

Occidente: western Cuba

Oriente: eastern Cuba

The "Poet": José Martí, the ideological father of the Cuban War of Independence, killed in battle in February, 1895

"Rat's Mouth" (Spanish: Boca de Ratones): moniker given to the rocky Atlantic coastal inlet of present-day Boca Raton, Florida, from which that city derives its name

M'BRAE TERMS AND PHRASES

Ahr [AHR]: legendary place where M'Brae and The Ones Who Came Before lived in harmony ages ago, and where souls of deceased M'Brae return to in death

Armorica [ahr-MOR-eh-kuh]: term mistakenly used by M'Brae to refer to "America"

Cacoch [kuh-KOSH]: M'Brae village that once stood in the hills of western Cuba near M'Brae-dah, but has since been abandoned

Esèh [ESS-eh]: "unnamed" or "unknown" people; the denizens of Ha-Yanrinol

G'daev [guh-DAY-ev]: "treasure" or "loot"

Golgaj [GOL-gash]: "west gate;" old, dilapidated fortress in the hills just west of M'Brae-dah, to which the M'Brae retreat in times of crisis

Ha-Yanrinol [HAH-YAN-ruh-nol]: "haunted wastes;" marshes along the southern coast of western Cuba, known today as Zapata Swamp

M'Brae-dah [em-BRAY-duh]: "place of M'Brae;" cluster of M'Brae villages in the hills of western Cuba, near modern-day Viñales

Oíc [HWIC]: "chief;" leader of the M'Brae

phéa-sjant [FAYA-sjant]: "crown soldiers;" Spanish imperial forces

Vujoíe [VOO-shway]: "outsider;" M'Brae term for Spanish Cubans

355

ABOUT THE AUTHOR

T. G. Monahan received his B.A. from Rutgers University and his J.D. from Albany Law School. He is a former Judge Advocate officer in the U.S. Marine Corps and a veteran of the Iraq War. A native of Hawthorne, New Jersey, he now resides in Albany, New York, with his son. *The Vexing Heirloom* is his first novel.

www.TGMonahan.com